Praise for The Aegis League Series

"Astonishingly imaginative and thoughtful..."

~ Samuel F. Pickering - Professor Emeritus of English, University of Connecticut & inspiration for the movie Dead Poets Society ~

"RECOMMENDED. A title like this is screaming for adaptation as a successful film..."

~ The US Review of Books ~

"THRILLING!...grips onto the reader and never lets go!"

~ Feathered Quill Book Reviews~

"FIVE STARS. Unique and compelling. Delivers on every level..."

~ Readers' Favorite Reviews ~

"What a blast! A roller coaster ride filled with heart-pounding action and a gripping plot that leaves the reader devouring every page right up to the last word."

~ John Kirk - As Seen on TV ~

"As a fantasy fiction writer I have to admit that I am a harsher critic when it comes to novels in this genre. Books in this class I feel should be able to captivate the imagination and place you in a different realm. AEGIS RISING accomplishes that and a whole lot more. It is truly a classic in the making!"

~ Michael Beas - Bestselling Author of 'Strump' ~

Publication Information

INKMAGINATION
Books That Engage, Entertain & Enlighten

AEGIS RISING by S.S.Segran

First Published by INKmagination, November 2013

Printed in the United States of America

Cover Design and Illustrations © 2013 by S.K.S.
'CERACCO' designed by Eric Newport..
Book Teaser and Trailer by: INKmagination.

S.S.Segran asserts the moral right to be identified as the author of this book.

ISBN: 978-0-9910813-0-1
eISBN: 978-0-9910813-2-5

Visit the author's website www.sssegran.com for behind the scenes extras, unpublished chapters and more.

AEGIS RISING

AN AEGIS LEAGUE NOVEL

S.S.SEGRAN

INKMAGINATION
Books That Engage, Entertain & Enlighten

To my Mom and Dad.
For your love and guidance.

"We can easily forgive a child who is afraid of the dark; the real tragedy of life is when men are afraid of the light."

~Plato 428-348 B.C.~

"The battle between the bearers of light and the forces of darkness is intensifying, and your role will always be to raise the torch and diffuse this light . . . and remember, it is essential that you always, always *do the right thing as prompted by your spirit—though doing the right thing may not always be the easiest."*

~Elder Nageau~

PROLOGUE

Somewhere off the coast of the Pacific Northwest,
circa 500 B.C.

The sleek, imposing vessel traversed the night, making hardly a sound as it sliced through the dark waters. The smooth, curved lines of its magnificent hull attested to the legendary workmanship of its builders. Its elongated prow, shaped like the talon of an eagle, reached ahead in the chilly air as if warding off shadows of misfortune. A soft glow spilled into the night from the living quarters above deck and rolled over the weathered railings, illuminating the ship with a ghostly sheen.

The exhausted commander on board the ancient vessel slouched against a mast, taking a sip of his elýrnì, a fermented beverage known only to his people. Grimly, he reflected that he would have to help his companions at the oars again in a little while.

He glanced up at the sky, noting the faint light the moon cast on the deck as it darted between large, shapeless clouds. The journey had been long, very long. Never again would the skipper want to go through that. They'd endured four moon cycles through rough seas and vicious storms. He shook his head and took another swig from his mug. *At least it will be coming to an end soon*, the captain thought in relief. *We will find tranquility and start anew in this vast land—that much I know.*

High up on the ship's mast, a man appearing to be in his late thirties scratched his shortly-trimmed beard and rested his elbows against the railing. A cousin of the captain, he wore a long black coat with a golden hood which he pulled up, throwing his face into the shadows. The captain had come up earlier, offering him a drink. He'd politely declined and sunk into his own world. The horrific images came back to haunt him, as they had so many times throughout this voyage. He remembered everything as though the horrors from four months back happened just yesterday.

It had been a very calm, bright day with azure skies. The sun was warm on the islanders' skin. Children were playing on beaches that hugged the island's coast while parents sat down nearby or drowsed. In an older part of the city, women were browsing the marketplace that was speckled with a myriad of colorful and aromatic stores. Located at the foot of a volcano in the middle of the island, the city boasted over fifteen thousand residents. It seemed like a perfect day.

Without warning, the ground started to rumble and shake violently. Jets of steam shot out from random spots around the city. The women in the marketplace screamed, dropped their purchases, and scattered. Moments into the earthquake, the long-dormant volcano erupted ferociously, lava flowing down its steep slopes and gathering momentum as it slid toward the city like a giant serpent.

"Mokun!" someone cried, and the lookout had spun around from where he stood gaping at the volcano. An older man with graying hair and a flowing white beard was limping toward him. "Mokun, help me retrieve the crystals from the temple!"

Mokun balked. "We cannot, Pèrzun! The temple is too close to the volcano!" He turned away and began to rush toward his home. "I have to get to my family!"

"The crystals, Mokun!" Pèrzun's tone rang with authority. "We need them, and you know I cannot get to the temple as quickly as you."

Mokun halted and shut his eyes, fighting with himself, then reluctantly gave in and both men hurried toward the grand temple. Mokun felt the heat from the steam around him, and cursed when he nearly slipped into a sinkhole. Beside him, the custodian of the temple was wide-eyed. He muttered to himself for a time and then, lifting his eyes to the sky with reverence, he murmured, "I will not let you down."

As the two rounded the city gates, they spotted the dome of the treasured sanctuary. The gigantic crown of the five-sided temple loomed, casting its shadow upon them. Columns carved with extreme dexterity and inlaid with gemstones spiraled toward elegant marble statues of slender human figures that held up the dome.

Mokun hastened into the temple with Pèrzun following as fast as his lame leg would allow him to. Inside, grand carvings of celestial constellations and beautiful paintings of the night sky decorated both sides of the massive entranceway. Around the two men though, the temple was already crumbling from the force of the earthquake and the rumbling of the volcano. The polished stone floor that ran the entire length of the hall still shone in places where the dust had not yet settled. At the far end of the temple hall, a shiny black goblet sat on an intricately carved marble post that was about four feet high; this goblet contained the crystals.

The tremors worsened and the whole temple shook more violently. The goblet teetered precariously on its stand. Rushing forward, Mokun grabbed the goblet just before it toppled to the ground. With the crystals safely in his hands, he urgently shoved the older man back toward the entrance. Outside, they saw the lava rolling down the volcano's slopes, frighteningly quick.

"You must find the Elders," Pèrzun ordered. "If at least three survive, then our culture may yet live on."

Mokun paused and stared at Pèrzun, then his eyes drifted past the older man. A woman and her daughter were rushing away from a house engulfed in flames. He shook his head and thrust the container to Pèrzun without replying and ran toward his home, feeling guilty for choosing to seek his family above the safety of the Elders.

Sprinting like a madman, he soon reached his house. Smoke and flames shot out from the roof as he barged through the main door. Fumes and ashes began to choke his lungs. He coughed as he called out to his family.

No answer.

Terrified, Mokun tore through his abode. His eyes teared up so terribly from the smoke that he could hardly see where he was going as the unbearable heat weighed down on him. His heart pounded as he struggled to breathe. He couldn't find his family anywhere. Then a thought struck him: *the cellar!* They may have panicked and sought safety below ground.

He ripped off the hem of his tunic and tied it around his nose and mouth. The smoke was so thick he was forced to feel rather than see his way to the cellar. He found the door to the cellar opened and tripped over the steps in his haste, falling to the ground. He pulled himself up and called out again to his loved ones. He got no response and stepped forward. His foot bumped against something and he jumped back. With growing dread, he knelt down in the darkness, squinting to make out three huddled shapes. He froze in horror, oblivious to the danger around him. His five-year-old daughters were huddled against their mother, and his wife had her arms wrapped around the twins. They didn't move.

Mokun snarled, rejecting the thought that his family was gone. He lifted his wife and balanced her over his shoulders, then hoisted his two daughters into his arms with inhuman strength and trudged out of the cellar. He laid their motionless bodies on the grass in the courtyard amidst the ash from the volcano and tried frantically to revive them. After a few minutes that seemed like a lifetime, he sat back and wept as the realization that he had lost them pierced into him like a knife through the heart.

Tears streamed down his dirt-stained face. He wrapped his arms around their cold bodies, cuddling them like a child as he sobbed for his dead family.

A hand touched his shoulder and he jumped. Twisting his head and looking up, he saw his youngest sister. She was small but feisty and looked squarely into his tear-filled eyes. Embedding in him the will to survive, she reached out and helped him up. In what felt like a gripping nightmare, Mokun looked back at his loved ones, and letting out a pained moan, allowed her to lead him away.

The volcano erupted again, this time with a force so tremendous that it threw the two of them onto the ground. A fissure appeared, splitting the earth and separating them. Mokun's sister pulled herself up and leapt over the growing rift toward her brother. She missed the ledge and nearly plummeted. Mokun let out a cry and threw himself towards the fissure. He managed to grab her hand just in time. Huffing in effort, he pulled her up beside him. Once they'd caught their breaths, she tugged at his arm and guided him with hurried steps toward the docks on the island's western shore where a boat was waiting. It had been all set to leave the island the very next day for trading, and had been stocked with crates of food and casks of fresh water, along with goods produced by the islanders.

That was the boat that Mokun and fifty other survivors journeyed in. Standing on the deck of the large trading ship as it sailed farther into the sea, the shocked survivors stared in disbelief at the fury and power of nature as the volcano erupted for the last time, the earth-shattering explosion obliterating what remained of the island. The island they called home for generations was no more. In its place was a forest of floating debris and hissing steam rising to the sky from the ocean.

A crashing wave yanked Mokun from his memories. He gasped, then realized his eyes were wet. Wiping them with the fold of his sleeve, he tilted his head back to look at the stars. The sky was calm, but the storm in his heart raged on. Ever since leaving the island, he'd been battling his emotions. His guilt for choosing to save the crystals instead of his family was beginning to morph into something darker, and he tried to shake the thoughts away, but they clung on like malevolent clouds over his head.

He took a deep breath to steady himself. Moments later, he was back on his job, narrowing his eyes and scanning for signs of land through the mist. At first, he didn't see it. When he ran his eyes just below the horizon again, he had to strain to make sure he wasn't just seeing things.

He shouted as he flipped himself over the railing of the crow's nest, grabbed onto the ladder attached to the mast and leapt down the last thirty feet onto the deck. The skipper, who had been leaning against the mast, whirled around, surprised. "What is it?"

"Land!" Mokun shouted.

The captain just stared, his mind clouded with fatigue.

"Land, Captain!"

"Are you sure?" the captain finally asked, excitement beginning to show on his face.

"Yes, sir! Straight ahead through the mist, sir! Not more than three hundred strokes of the oars!"

"Land ahead!" the skipper bellowed to the rowers below deck, slapping Mokun on the back. The rowers cheered and redoubled their efforts.

Two tribal youths patrolling their village on the coast had no idea what was coming. As they rounded a large boulder, they heard a strange sound. It was a series of muted, rhythmic splashes, like a pod of whales surfacing in unison. Frowning, they turned around and peered in the direction of the splashes. As their eyes adjusted, they stopped dead.

Appearing from the mist, a drifting phantom was heading directly toward them. Lit by the eerie dimness of the moonlight, the strange beast appeared to have slender wings on either side of a flared body. A long spike materialized from its tapered head.

The youths, brothers in their mid-teens, moved closer to each other. They whispered hastily, never taking their eyes off the thing. As it drew nearer, the youths caught a peculiar glow emanating from the beast, and that was the last straw. The older boy hoisted his hunting spear and darted from shelter to shelter, hissing warnings as his brother dropped to one knee and peeked from behind the boulder, his own spear readied. The hushed alarm rippled through the tribe. All around the camp, men rushed about quietly with weapons while the frightened women stayed inside with the children.

In an instant, the bustling ended and all the men were beside the two brothers. They had also seen the monster advancing in their direction. Bracing themselves, they crouched low to the ground and observed the beast through dark, flashing eyes.

At last the thing came to a stop, having beached itself on the rich, white sands of the shore. To the tribe's astonishment, men and women alike leapt off the creature with cat-like grace. These people were tall, slim, and though they appeared weary, held themselves with certain poise. Their skins were the shade of fine straw. And the hair! Ranging from black to brown, and all the colors of autumn leaves.

Suspicious of the strangers, the men decided to wait a little longer. When the outsiders began to laugh and dart about, the natives stiffened. As a man in a black cloak with a golden hood covering his face poked curiously at the leftover meat that was for the next day's meal, a few of the tribesmen let out annoyed growls. Then their lips curled back angrily when the man spotted the shelters at the edge of the tree line, called out to his companions, and started walking toward them.

The younger of the brothers charged at the man, letting his spear fly. The weapon sank into the man's arm, forcing a cry from his lips. Blood trickled from the wound. He dropped down and clutched his arm. His comrades spun around to face their attackers. Both the men and the women drew steel daggers with leather hilts from within their clothing. A few of them had darts which they pitched at the tribesmen. Some of the natives fell to the ground with howls as they were struck. The darts seemed to have a mysterious effect; the men who fell did not die, but they could not get back on their feet.

The tribesmen flung their spears at the strangers, loosing throaty barks. To the natives' bewilderment, the strangers neatly dodged their weapons, brows furrowed in concentration. Instead of launching a counter-attack, the strangers simply stood ready, sharp eyes flitting from one tribesman to another.

Furious, the tribesmen regrouped again and stuck close to each other. They dove forward as one, thrusting their weapons at the strangers. A seven-foot dart whistled through the air toward the outsiders, launched from an atlatl.

A lone figure that had silently stood on the top of the beast while the conflict raged suddenly leapt into the night, turning a somersault in the air as it did so, and grabbed the dart in mid-flight. The tribesmen stopped and stared, perplexed, at the form who'd whipped the weapon from its trajectory, but the darkness covered the stranger's face as he backed into the shadows.

The tribesmen shrank back in surprise, but one of the natives, undaunted, stepped forward and hurled his last spear with full force at the cluster of strangers. Instead of striking home, the spear slowed in midflight and came to a stop at the height of its arc. It hung in the air for a fleeting moment before flipping in the opposite direction and accelerating back at the native. The man yelped and just barely managed to jump out of the way in time. The spear struck the ground and buried itself deeply in the dirt. The tribesmen were astonished. What kind of sorcery was this?

A tall woman garbed in a black tunic torn off at the shoulders and leggings that covered three-quarters of her slender legs stepped forward from the group of strangers. She must have been around forty summers. Her hair was a glossy jet black, her eyes bright blue. She spoke to the tribesmen in a peculiar language. When she completed her short speech she waited for them to respond as she calmly surveyed them.

The native brothers glanced at each other and stepped forward, only to be pulled back by the others. A burly man with thick black hair—the tribe's chief—stepped forward. He spoke suspiciously to the woman. She cocked her head, appearing to not understand what the chief was saying.

The impatient brothers spat at the ground and snarled at her. Their chief tried to calm them down but the older one bellowed and propelled his weapon in the woman's direction with all his might. The woman stayed where she was and stared intensely at the spear hurtling her way. Her eyes caught the glint of the tip of the spear as it approached her. Ten inches from her face, the spear paused in mid-air, swung straight up toward the sky, then arced back toward the young man. With a startled cry, he tried to dodge out of the way but was a second too slow. The spear careened at him and pierced through his bearskin shirt to the flesh below his collarbone. He screamed in agony, a horrible, cursed sound to the ears of everyone there, before plummeting to the ground.

The tribesmen gasped and backed away from their fallen comrade and the frightening strangers. To their apprehension, the woman began walking toward them. Some dropped their weaponry and dashed into the familiar darkness of the forest, while others stood rooted, petrified. They watched with wide, alarmed eyes as the tall woman halted before the fallen youth and knelt down. It was so quiet that the only sound anyone heard was of the ragged breathing coming from the wounded youth. As the woman placed the palm of her hand on his cheek, the lad's brother leapt forward and shouted angrily at her. She looked up and raised a hand at him. He stopped immediately and with a sense of foreboding, backed away toward the line of remaining tribesmen.

Unsmiling, the woman lowered her hand back to the young man's cheek. His brown eyes were open and there was a hint of hysteria in them. Carefully, the woman grasped the shaft of the spear and, as gently as she could, drew it out. The youth groaned, saliva spattering out of his mouth. With a burst of energy, he reached up and clawed at the woman. She leapt back, covering her face.

Glaring, the youth rolled to his feet and staggered back to his tribe, blood dribbling out and leaving a scarlet trail behind him. His brother bounded toward him and lent him a shoulder to lean on. Hacking up clots of blood and crossing one arm upon his wound, the injured brother grabbed a spear from one of the native men and gripped it with a shaky hand, using it as a crutch to walk his way to a tree where he slumped down, his head lolling.

Suddenly, a deep, thunderous roar echoed through the forest like a gigantic avalanche tumbling down upon them. Both groups went still and glanced around. Children in the shelters began wailing and babies screamed in fright as mothers and older sisters tried hard to quiet them. From somewhere in the mass of people, one of the tribesmen shouted in horror. All eyes turned to him, then to the forest where his gaze was set. His tribe gasped in fear as they beheld five large silhouettes stalking through the trees with ferocious eyes gleaming out at them like black ice.

One of the strangers, a man with fire-colored hair plastered to his face, raised his long arms high above his head and bellowed an intense, wordless call.

There was a moment of silence. Then, like specters vanishing in the night, the mysterious silhouettes were gone. The tribesmen swiveled their heads and gawked at the lone man standing up.

"Tornrak!" cried out the injured youth sitting under the tree. His sibling and friends joined the cry. "Tornrak! Tornrak!" *Evil! Evil!*

The flame-haired stranger raised his hand. Quiet engulfed them once more. The woman in black walked over to him, and together the pair strode toward the wounded young man. As they reached him, the youth spat at them even though his dark eyes reflected fear. When the woman knelt in front of him and placed her hands on his forehead, the youth stiffened, scowling. She gently stroked his head, then let her fingers slide down to the gaping wound. He hissed in pain through his teeth and jerked away from her. Her gaze softening, the woman cupped the boy's face in her hands and murmured to him in tender tones. Hesitantly, the youth met the woman's eyes and allowed himself to be drawn in by the power of her chant. He shivered and his eyelids drooped suddenly.

The woman reached into a pouch at her waist and withdrew a pinch of silvery powder with her fingertips, then peppered the wound with the fine particles. A few moments later, the young tribe member felt a strange sensation around his wound. The blood that had been streaming out of him ceased its flow. He blinked in wonder, then looked up at the woman. As he felt the pain slowly beginning to subside, he gave her an uncertain smile. The woman smiled back. Amazement rustled through the tribe as they witnessed first-hand the miracle of healing brought about by the strangers.

A pitiful mewling sounded somewhere behind them. The strangers looked back. There, holding a small child in her arms was a woman short in stature, her long black hair braided in a single tress down her back. She had round, tired eyes. The baby let out a rasping, choking noise. Startled, every single one of the strangers fixed their eyes on the infant.

Her lips pursed, the tall woman rose up and with her cohort, walked toward the native and her child. The shorter woman didn't move but only raised her head to the approaching people. The chief tottered over to the woman, placing a protective arm around her, making sure the strangers would not harm either her or his son.

The man with fire-colored hair placed a hand on the baby's forehead. The child opened eyes dull with sickness, and parted his small lips as he beheld the strange people. The man cleared his throat and started muttering in a deep voice with his palm still upon the little one's brow. The baby's eyes slowly closed.

The stranger ended his incomprehensible phrases few moments later. He pulled a single leaf out of a leather pouch and held it to the baby's lips, squeezing the leaf until a single drop of liquid fell into the child's mouth. The stranger stepped back, ripping the now-dry leaf into little pieces and letting them fall to the ground. The chief and his mate peered anxiously at their son.

A minute later the baby stirred and opened his big eyes. His mother gasped. The child's eyes were brighter and filled with life, and there was more color in his skin. He smacked his lips, his small tongue darting in and out of his mouth as if tasting the air. A pleased exclamation emanated from the child's parents, and the woman caressed her son and rubbed noses with him. Holding the infant close to her chest, she dipped her head thankfully at the man who had healed her one and only child.

The tribesmen on the beach cheered and rushed to their leader's side, milling about the joyous parents, their fight much forgotten. The two strangers walked back to the beach and sat peacefully on the sand with their brethren.

The youth whom the female stranger had healed detached himself from his kin and strode with steady steps toward the assemblage of outsiders, challenging the fact that he'd ever been hurt. He halted in front of the woman and bowed. The woman smiled and nodded, acknowledging the young man. The tribe's chief then stepped up behind him. The youth exchanged glances with the older man and politely backed away.

Looking at every stranger, from man to woman, the chief solemnly extended a hand. He seemed less guarded now, and his posture was more open. The strangers reciprocated.

Gradually, the tribe and the strangers mingled. Though unable to understand each other in the beginning, the natives were astonished at how quickly a few of the outsiders were able to learn their language, and thus began a new friendship.

Years passed, with the tribe and the strangers coming together. The natives shared their land and traditions with the strangers. In like manner, the outsiders showed the tribe the secrets of their own way of life and their history. They taught them to open the gates of their minds to the incredible powers inherent in themselves and nature. As time wore on, the two different communities intertwined. Most of the strangers, whom by now the tribe knew as the Islanders, had intermarried and the people had truly become one, sharing not only their lives but also their rich cultures and most importantly, a powerful prophecy that was bequeathed from generation to generation.

PART ONE

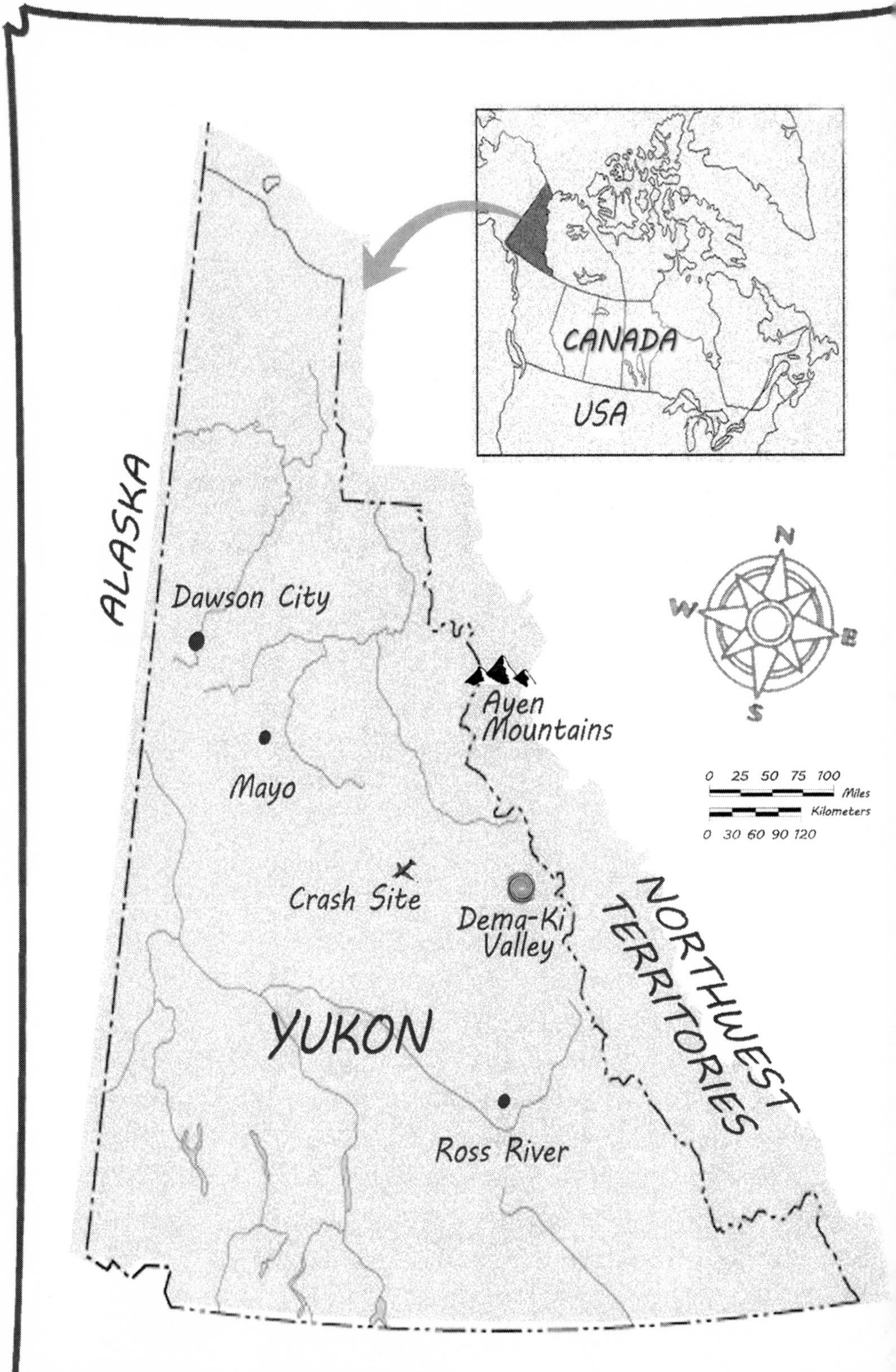
CANADA
USA
ALASKA
Dawson City
Mayo
Ayen Mountains
Crash Site
Dema-Ki Valley
YUKON
Ross River
NORTHWEST TERRITORIES
N
W
E
S
0 25 50 75 100
Miles
Kilometers
0 30 60 90 120

1

The small red plane shook violently as a flash of lightning streaked not more than two hundred feet from its nose. Muffled shrieks rose from inside. One voice rose above the others. "*Mr. Tyler!* We're gonna crash!"

A deep voice from the cockpit growled, "No we won't! Hang on!"

Tegan Ryder cast a terrified glance at her friends. The sixteen-year-old was scared out of her wits; this was without a doubt the most terrifying experience of her life. Beside her, Mariah Ashton drew in a sharp breath and clung to Tegan, her brown eyes wide and her body frozen. Although they were the same age, the fright that consumed Mariah made her appear like a horrified preschooler. Tegan only hoped that her friend was as strong on the inside as she normally was on the outside. She leaned back into her seat and screwed her eyes shut, attempting to will this horrible episode away.

Less than an hour ago, she had been enjoying a smooth flight on the Piper Comanche with her four closest friends. It wasn't a big plane, but it carried six people comfortably in three rows. Tegan was listening to her iPod and sketching a Siberian tiger on a notepad; it would be an addition to the large collection of wildlife drawings that she had accumulated over the years. She absently scratched her ear as she scrutinized her work, forgetting about her additional piercings, and winced when her finger caught on one. "Owww."

Seated next to Tegan, Mariah was completely engrossed in a five-hundred-page mystery novel which she'd nabbed from her basement full of books at home. She would only pause to push back her long copper-blonde hair and take occasional sips from a can of Dr Pepper, her favorite soda.

The girls were settled comfortably in the middle row of the plane. Jag Sanchez was seated in the back with Aari Barnes. The tallest one of the group with a golden-tan complexion thanks to his Brazilian-Italian ancestry, Jag was also the most athletic. He would occasionally participate in sports but, given the choice, would rather be honing his parkour skills or biking with friends.

Kody Tyler sat in the cockpit beside his father. He was proud of his short afro which he'd obtained from his father, and his striking green eyes that he acquired from his mother. Despite his skinny frame, he had an insatiable appetite for food, which astounded everyone around him. An aviation enthusiast like his father, he was on his way to attaining his Private Pilot's license as he'd been learning to fly from the age of twelve.

Slumping down in her seat, Tegan yawned and pushed some strands of her wavy ash-brown hair from her face. She looked out the window at the bright day and was just thinking how soft the clouds seemed when a yell of delight cut through the air.

"Dude, that's amazing!"

Tegan pulled her earphone away and turned around to glare at her friends. Mariah did the same.

At the back of the plane, Jag and Aari were staring in awe at something on Aari's portable gaming device. Jag gave Aari a congratulatory pat on the head but Aari ducked, not wanting his peaked, short-cut hair to be tampered with. "Oy! Don't touch!"

"Alright," Tegan sighed. "What gives?"

Aari elbowed Jag, eyes glued to the small screen. "You tell 'em."

Jag raised his eyes heavenward. In a voice that was husky for his age, he answered, "He's playing *Descending Tartarus*, the game that was recalled. Seems that el hacker here managed to sneak a download, and it's actually working." Then he added, amused, "Though I have no idea how he did it, and he won't tell anyone."

"Seriously?" Mariah peeked over her seat. "Can I check it out?"

Aari's reply was curt. "Nope. I went through a lot to get this download. You'll have to wait your turn. Come again in another year."

"You hog."

Aari didn't tear his gaze away from the device but his ice-blue eyes twinkled. His fingers quickly moved over the controls and it was easy to see that he was enraptured with the game.

"To think you guys didn't want to come with us to Dawson, just two weeks ago," said Tegan. "Poor Kody would have been all alone with Mariah and me during the trip."

Mariah nodded. "Imagine all the fun they'd have missed if we hadn't changed their minds."

Jag grinned. "Yeah. I wonder if we'll find a Sasquatch up at the lake-side cabin."

Tegan turned and reached over her seat to ruffle his hair. "With you around, who needs a Sasquatch?"

Jag pulled away and brushed his hair from his face, scowling at her. "Hey!"

Tegan snickered. Mariah prodded her with an elbow and chided, "Just because he's the tallest doesn't make him a Sasquatch."

Pretending to flex a muscle, Kody grinned and hollered from the cockpit, "He may be the tallest, but we all know who's the strongest!"

"Yeah, Sasquatch over here is," Tegan hollered right back to Kody's disappointment. It was true; the trouble-maker boy was strong. *If only he'd focus more on his studies and stay out of fights, he'd be a great student,* she thought to herself.

Kody sniffed. "Well, I'm the most charming, then."

"Yeah, *right.*" Aari looked up from his game. "Only in your dreams, you are. I've got more charm in my pinkie finger than you've got in your entire body."

Grinning, Jag leaned back against his seat with his hands behind his head, enjoying the jest and staying above it.

Tegan and Mariah looked at each other. "Charm?" Mariah croaked. "We'd probably run into a flying pig sooner than finding one person on this planet who has been charmed by either of you."

The two boys protested. "Come on," Kody complained, pointing at himself, "you girls know that this guy right here is the charmer of the bunch."

Aari raised an eyebrow. "Dream on, pal." He stuck his neck out to face Tegan and Mariah. "Look at me. You can't deny that my dark red hair is a chick-magnet. *And* you've both seen how I can charm—"

"Grannies!" Kody yelled, chuckling. "Yeah, you were really good at the seniors' bingo party at Sunset Home last week. Those wonderful elderly folks *adored* you, you 'cutie-pie' volunteer. But me, I charmed Jag's cousin. She's *gorgeous*."

"Hey, Kode-man," Jag said, the first sound he'd made in a while, "hate to break it to you, but Tess has a boyfriend now. Life has changed for her since she turned eighteen. Or so she says—I hardly ever get her teenage-girl ramblings."

"*What?*" Kody exclaimed.

Seeing another round of banter coming, Tegan promptly plugged in an earphone to shut it out and passed another to Mariah and looked out the window. She watched the scene that rolled out below the plane. It was a beautiful mountain range. Recalling the map they had studied before the trip, she guessed that these were the Mackenzie Mountains, the northern cousin of the famous Rockies. Then her sharp gray eyes caught something. "That's a really strange-looking ridgeline," she muttered.

Mariah leaned over. "Yeah." She blinked. "It's running east to west—the others stretch out from north to south. Wait . . . there's another one running adjacent to it."

The girls agreed that it was indeed unique, but as the plane advanced, the curious ridgelines fell out of sight and their interest drifted off elsewhere. The endless mountain range rippled beneath their gazes and before long the two had dozed off.

Now here they were an hour later; the plane was shaking like a leaf in the storm, terrifying the passengers inside. Tegan peered through her long eyelashes, now wet with tears. Although the Comanche was built tough, it wasn't designed for this kind of extreme pounding. The freak storm had come out of nowhere, taking Samuel Tyler and his passengers by surprise. The plane wobbled for a moment before its nose tilted downward. Like a roller coaster passing the tip of its ascent, the dive came suddenly. This time, there were no stifled shrieks; instead, deafening screams echoed throughout the cabin.

"Dad! Pull up! *Pull up!*" Kody wailed, his usual calm shattered.

Mariah screeched, rendering Tegan half deaf. Wincing, she leaned over and clasped her hand over Mariah's mouth. Mariah clammed up immediately. Tegan glanced back and caught the exchange of looks between Jag and Aari. She knew the boys were scared stiff as well.

"Great way to start off a vacation," Jag murmured to Aari, who had gone pale.

"Oh, God." The pilot's voice sounded distressed.

"Dad?"

"Mr. Tyler?"

"What is it?"

The lone adult in the plane looked back as he began to radio for help. His face was creased with stress and his eyes were troubled. "I think we just lost the left engine."

"What!"

Sure enough, the left side of the cabin went silent as the engine sputtered and came to a halt.

"Are we going to crash?" Aari asked, terrified.

The pilot's eyes narrowed. "No! The right engine is working fine—I just need to compensate with the rudder."

As Kody's father furiously fought with the flight controls, the friends held their breaths. In what felt like half a dozen lifetimes, the plane's nose slowly inched back toward the horizon.

"Okay," cheered the pilot. "We're back in business!"

Just as the friends started to breathe a sigh of relief, Mariah pointed up front and yowled. There, in the plane's path, another lightning bolt flashed. Tegan jolted in shock. They were not out of the storm yet. *At least we weren't there,* she comforted herself, and then spoke her thoughts out loud. "It's alright. Remember what they say: Lightning doesn't strike the same place twice."

She spoke too soon.

There was a blinding flash of light followed by an ear-splitting *crack* and the plane veered violently to the right. "Gaaah!"

"What's going on?" Aari barked.

"We got hit by lightning!" Kody bellowed. "It hit the *right* engine!"

Like puppets on a string, everyone turned their heads to look, and to their horror realized that Kody was correct. But worse, the only working engine they had left was on fire.

"We've lost all power!" Kody's father turned around. "We'll have to find a clearing and glide the plane in!"

Despite the situation, Kody raised an amused eyebrow. "A clearing, Dad? In this forest?"

"Just look for one!" his father snapped. "We're running out of altitude."

The friends quickly stretched their necks out as far as possible to look down.

A few frantic moments later, Tegan called out, tapping wildly at her window. "Hey! What about that clearing down there?"

"Are you crazy?" Mariah objected. "Look at the big rock smack in the middle of it! We can't land there!"

Aari looked up. "I think I found something!" He waved his hand in the direction of what looked like an opening on the forest floor. "Mr. T! Check out the clearing on your left by that creek!"

"That spot's too small for this plane!" Kody pointed out urgently.

Six pairs of eyes frantically scanned the surroundings below.

"Aw, *man!*" Jag exclaimed. "The fire's spreading in along the wing!"

That was followed by another shout from the cockpit. "We're losing airspeed! We have to land *immediat—*"

He was cut off by a loud blast. The right engine cowling burst apart. The plane was now trailing smoke and flame over the forest, no more than a thousand feet above the tree-tops. Like an injured dragon, the red Comanche bucked and twisted over alpine firs that punctuated the landscape.

Forced to choose between the clearings that Tegan and Aari had spotted, Kody's father decided to maneuver the plane toward the site by the creek. Although it was the smaller of the two, it appeared safer, with no jagged rocks to wreck their inevitable attempt to bring the plane down.

Mariah grabbed Tegan's arm with a look of mortal fear frozen on her face. Tegan grabbed back, wordless.

Kody was muttering under his breath. Aari sunk low in his place while clinging onto his gaming device. Jag, holding onto the crucifix on a chain around his neck, looked on ahead as though he was able to foresee the impending tragedy.

A blur of trees zoomed past the windows at a dizzying speed.

The plane rattled uncontrollably, jarring the passengers to the bone. A series of booms and screeches deafened them.

The last thing they heard before the crash was their pilot's words: "Hold on, kids! We're going in—"

Then it was all black.

2

The thunderous roar swept across the valley and echoed through the mountains. Many rushed out of their homes to gaze at the stormy sky, some stunned, some awed, and others curious. But only five of them were intent. They were the Elders. They stood in silence as the words of the prophecy echoed in their minds.

A bright red object was streaking across the sky. The long trails of flame and smoke from its wings resembled the fiery feathers of a bird legendary to the people of the tribe. There were gasps as blinding streaks of lightning reached for the creature. As they traced the object in the sky, it began to sputter. Within moments it went quiet.

The deafening roar was gone. In its place there was an eerie silence as the object started to spiral toward the ground, leaving a trail of smoke that drew circles in the sky. The inhabitants watched in muted shock as the object vanished behind a distant ridgeline.

The villagers turned to look at the Elders, confused and anxious. The Elders glanced at each other knowingly. One of them, a man with wispy white hair and bright blue eyes raised his hand. Understanding the signal, the other four followed him along a winding path to the edge of the village where they entered a five-sided shelter. Its walls were made of pine logs and its roof where the pointed peak met at the center of the pentagon was made of smoothened hides.

"So, what do you think?" the leading Elder asked the others once they'd sat down around a small fire that burned inside a shallow clay pit. He adjusted his black-and-silver cloak so it didn't crumple.

An elderly woman with lively green eyes nodded thoughtfully. "I believe that the time has come."

Another senior member of the village, this one with short, flame-colored hair, arched his thick eyebrows. "We cannot be sure," he muttered. "If it is, then the Guardians will show us a sign."

"True," agreed a tall female observer. She was the younger of the two women in the group. "I shall trust their judgment."

The last Elder ran his tanned hands through thick black locks and shrugged his muscular shoulders without a word. The others sensed his indecisiveness and let it go at that.

The leading Elder looked around at his companions. "Alright. We shall wait. Let us see what daybreak brings."

The five of them stared into the glowing embers in silence. In the stillness, the first lines of the prophecy recited itself in the deep recesses of their minds.

"From the flames of Cerraco five will arise,
Saplings of Aegis, the bearers of light . . ."

3

Jag found himself falling. He tried to yell for help but was unable to form the words. He felt the rush of wind whipping past his hair and stinging his eyes until they watered. He was still falling.

The sudden rush of cold water came as a shock; he had expected to crash on solid ground. Ahead, a huge wave rolled up and swelled over, submerging him. He tried to claw his way up to the surface for air. His vision was getting dimmer with every passing second . . .

Suddenly, he felt something come from underneath him and lift him up, out into breathable space. He gasped for air. As he recovered, he felt the heavy waves subside, and was surprised to find himself floating along with the now gentle current that was carrying him safely.

Jag's eyes eased open. Instantly the dream vanished. He let out a strangled gasp. His breathing was labored, and it was painful to take in the air for the atmosphere around him was cold.

He blinked. *What . . . where am I?*

Too confused, he allowed himself to shut his eyes. Exhaustion made his limbs and body uncomfortably heavy.

All at once, he realized that he was moving. But it wasn't him moving; something was moving *him*. The sobering knowledge sent a shudder through his spine. He noticed that he was lying facedown on something warm and . . . *furry?*

His arms were wrapped around something huge. Tightening his grip, he heard the rhythm of padded strides striking the ground beneath him and felt the rise and fall of calm breathing. He swallowed nervously, unsure what to do, but was soon distracted by an increasing awareness of a stinging pain on his left thigh. He lay still for a while, trying to ignore it. Then, jolted by a thought, he lifted his head. *The others! Where are they?*

The tremendous amount of energy it took to just raise his head left him weary. He gazed about, letting his eyes adjust to the night. The clouds had cleared and there was a crescent moon that threw a faint, shimmering light all around him.

What he saw made his heart jump into his throat. There were four humongous bears padding together in an arrowhead formation behind him, their fur outlined with slivers of white, and their dark eyes gleamed with curious light. He saw shapes set horizontally on their backs, and one by one, made out Aari, Tegan, Kody, and Mariah. His eyes grew wide.

Turning his head slowly, Jag looked at his own steed. Sure enough, it was a bear. He couldn't believe the size of it. He estimated that from its head to its back end, it must have been about twice his height, and it was stocky and muscle-bound. It was without a doubt the largest living creature he'd ever seen.

He grasped hesitantly onto the thick, furry neck of the bear and held on. He wasn't going to chance anything, including bounding off the beast; he wasn't sure how the animal would react, and he acknowledged that he was in no shape to do it anyway.

He managed to look up at the sky glistening with stars that seemed faintly lit. His grip on consciousness was slipping again. He tried to make sense of what was happening, but it all seemed like a dream once more.

The moments slid by as the lulling motion of the bear acted to numb his senses. His mind began to drift off again when suddenly the bear he was on stopped, wrenching him away from his hazy thoughts. It lifted its bulky head at a forty-five degree angle and made a low rumbling sound deep in its throat. Jag felt the vibration ripple through the bear's back and, for a moment, he felt like throwing up.

The other bears beside Jag's halted as well and stared expectantly at their leader. A moment later the large animals were on the move again. The question was, on the move to where?

A gust of wind lashed toward Jag, making him shiver. He buried his head in the hollow of his bear's right shoulder, shielding his face from the cold air. With his arms still enveloped around the animal's thick neck, he scrunched up into an awkward ball in an attempt to hide himself from the weather. He was astonished to find how much warmth the bear's long, dark fur provided. He half-smiled to himself, and with the rocking motion of the mighty beast, sunk back into his semi-conscious world.

4

Kody groaned and coughed up some spittle. He struggled to open his eyes—it felt as if his eyelids were made of lead. As he tried to take a breath, a sense of wariness came over him.

It took a couple of minutes for his vision to kick in completely. When it did, he found himself staring up at the inside of a smooth, pointed ceiling. He just barely lifted his eyebrows.

Feeling weak, he struggled in great pain to sit up, then looked around and quietly took in his surroundings. He was in what he supposed to be a hut. He turned his head to his left and saw two still forms lying beside him: Jag and Aari.

The energy from sitting had sapped too much of his strength. He collapsed back down and winced in pain as a dull pounding started up at the back of his head. His breaths came raggedly, as if he had just run five miles without stopping. He sluggishly turned over so he was belly-down on the ground. Faintly, he was aware of the comforting warmth that cloaked him. A ghost of a smile touched his lips. Opening one of his eyes a slit, he scanned downward and was surprised to see that he was in some sort of a sleeping bag. The outside of it looked a bit rough and patchy, but the inside felt warm and cozy and seemed to be lined with soft fur. He noticed that his friends were also in similar sleeping bags, and all three boys were resting on a wooden platform raised a foot off the ground. Kody was about to sink back into sleep when he heard the sound of a door opening as it scraped against the ground. He raised his head and glanced over his shoulder.

A tall form was silhouetted against the light from outside. Kody made out broad shoulders and assumed it to be a man. Seconds later, a distant-sounding voice called out from the outside in some unfamiliar language. The man turned his head and replied in the same language, his voice sounding slightly younger than an adult's.

Who're they? Kody mused tiredly, and closed his eyes. His ears were still open, though. He heard soft murmuring of two voices, one male and one female. Kody had no idea what they were talking about. His mind soon drifted elsewhere. *Where's Tegan? Mariah? And Dad! Where's Dad?*

Kody jerked up involuntarily, cringing as pain struck him once more, and the throbbing at the back of his head grew denser. He let out a pained growl. A cool hand placed itself on the back of his head and almost immediately, the soreness subsided.

He turned his head sideways and in the dim light found himself looking up at the source of the gentle touch. A girl with a striking appearance was kneeling beside him, her hand still resting upon his head. She looked to be around seventeen, and wore a buckskin tunic and a pair of knee-high moccasin boots. She gazed at him with warm, caring brown eyes. Her straight, raven hair tumbled over her slender shoulders, and her white teeth shone as she gave him a small smile that perfectly contrasted her light brown skin.

Kody's eyebrows shot up. He wanted to say something, but he lacked the energy and promptly fell back into his prone position. The girl stroked his head until he was wafted back into deep sleep.

Dad . . .

* * *

Mariah's eyes snapped open and she jolted upright. She blinked several times, her head bowed, trying to understand why she had awoken. Slowly looking around through a carpet of dark copper-blonde hair, she realized that she could barely make out a thing. She was able to tell that she was in some sort of a rustic shelter, wrapped in a sleeping bag. Faint light glowed somewhere. Some sense of relief washed over her as she spotted Tegan asleep beside her in her own sleeping bag. Taking in a deep breath, Mariah covered her face with her hands. She felt soft, rectangular patches plastered to her bruised cheeks. Drawing her hands away from her face, she observed long, ragged cuts on her forearms, although they appeared to have been cleaned. *How . . . ? Who . . . ?*

A murmur of odd words made her jump. She looked around, afraid. She thought that she'd been alone. In a far corner of the shelter sat a sweet-looking, raven-haired girl and a pleasant young man with regal features. They both looked to be older than her by a couple of years. The girl slowly got to her hands and knees and crawled over to Mariah. Mariah studied her warily but dared not move. She could see the girl was slim and graceful, and her eyes seemed kind and honest.

The girl halted beside Mariah and, from the ground next to her, picked up a mug and handed it to her. Mariah frowned at it and at the girl, obviously quite guarded. The girl sat back on her heels and held the mug in front of Mariah. Mariah glared at it. The girl moved the mug closer. Mariah pursed her lips and shook her head. Faint lines creased the girl's forehead, and she held the mug so close to Mariah that the younger girl nearly went cross-eyed. She pulled away and shook her head again, muttering hoarsely, "I don't know who you are, or why you're giving me this." She looked around. "Where are my other friends?"

The girl replied, or so Mariah assumed. She was not speaking English. The language sounded like nothing Mariah had ever heard before, but the girl's tone was so sympathetic and gentle that she decided to take the mug into her hands. She gazed down at it and her expression formed into one of repulsion. The liquid in the cup looked thick, and the color was a mix of green and brown.

The older girl pressed her fingertips against one of Mariah's hands and pushed the mug toward Mariah's nose. As Mariah breathed the scent in, she blinked in genuine surprise. The color may have looked disgusting, but it smelled of refreshing herbs. She couldn't resist the temptation to take a sip. As the warm liquid trickled down her throat, her pain began to fade. Soon, the remnants of her aches bowed in submission. Her eyelids drooped, and she smiled drowsily. Handing the mug back to the waiting girl, she mumbled her thanks and slid down into her sleeping bag. Exhausted, she nuzzled her hands like a kitten and slipped into restful sleep.

5

"Intriguing, isn't it?"

The words were spoken by the white-haired man with the black-and-silver cloak. He leaned forward, a strange gleam in his blue eyes.

"Yes," the woman beside him whispered. "Yes, Nageau, it certainly is." She wore a beautiful green ruffled blouse that matched her sparkling eyes. A small smile appeared on her lips and she clasped her hands together against her heart.

A slightly younger woman with a royal purple headband fiddled with the zircon bracelets that decorated her left arm and spoke. "The evidence is slowly building." She turned to the muscular Elder with black hair and ran her hand over his forearm. "Ashack? How do you feel about this now?"

Ashack exhaled quietly. "While it is true that the Guardians brought them here, Saiyu, more information is needed. As we all know, the prophecy is not to be taken lightly. There is a lot of responsibility resting on our shoulders as Elders of this community. If what we perceive to be true proves false, then we are accountable for the ills that befall the land."

His four equals nodded in silent agreement. Saiyu gazed into the embers at the center of the Elder's assembly shelter and continued to fiddle with her bracelets. "Perhaps now would be a good time to recollect the events of the last couple of days and ascertain if they unraveled as prophesied." She paused. "It began when that object appeared in the storm. It bore a resemblance distinctive to the Cerraco, even down to its flaming wings."

"From the flames of Cerraco five will arise," chipped in the Elder with fiery hair. He wore a white tunic with three thick, red stripes that stretched diagonally from his right shoulder to his waist. "And these five came from the bird itself, or so the Guardians indicated. Do we not believe them?"

The Elder in the green blouse nodded. "We do, Tayoka. The signals I received from the Guardians were unmistakable."

Nageau faced her, warmth radiating from his pleasant demeanor as he looked at his mate. "Tikina, could you please continue with the next line of the prophecy."

She smiled and recited, "'*Saplings of Aegis, the bearers of light*'."

"Agreed. They are young, mere saplings," Ashack said as he inspected the blue sash that was tied around his waist. "But after they have recovered, how do we determine if they are indeed the ones mentioned in the prophecy? How do we decide whether or not to provide them with the training that they would need if indeed they are the ones?"

Tayoka sat with his fingers interlocked and his gray eyes narrowed. "Exactly. Must we train the five first in order for them to fulfill the prophecy, or do they demonstrate their fulfillment of these verses prior to us taking them under our wings as apprentices?"

To ease the perplexity they faced, Nageau gently prodded his brethren. "Remember that our tradition calls for faith. Faith in not only what is apparent, but also in what is possible. It requires us to search our souls for an answer. The prophecy can only take us so far. It is but a guide."

They fell silent. Saiyu readjusted her headband before venturing, "Let us assume that the first line of the prophecy has come to pass and that the second line remains unanswered. Let us now reflect on the last two lines of the verse: '*Gaze upon them for portals that decipher, Shades of Earth, Sky, River, Mist, and Fire*'."

"I have always imagined that this somehow refers to our crystals," Tayoka said. "How does it apply here, though?"

The Elders contemplated the question. In the brief quiet, the only sound that prevailed was the crackling of the fire at the center of the assembly shelter. Around it were four low, wooden benches padded with soft hide that the Elders sat upon. On every wall was a long, polished pinewood shelf that held small Tiki-like statues and plants. Carvings of wild animals also rested atop the shelves.

At the far end of the shelter stood a marble table on which was placed a miniature representation of a beautiful island, encircled by golden sandy beaches and surrounded by a sparkling turquoise sea. A majestic mountain rose from the center of the island. Hundreds of small structures that looked like houses were placed around it. The details demonstrated the care with which the craftsmen who constructed the model must have poured into it.

Tikina lifted her gaze from the fire and stared up at the smooth, pointed ceiling. "I think the first step is to spend some time with our guests. We have not had an opportunity to speak with them since the Guardians brought them here. I would like to meet with them personally."

"Your tone suggests that there is something more," Saiyu remarked with a curious smile.

Tikina offered her friend a shrug of her slim shoulders. "I am not quite sure, but I do have a seedling of a thought. It is too soon to make anything of it for now. Perhaps we will figure it out in time."

They fell into silence again, their hopes of finding a meaning to the closing lines of the prophecy's first verse dormant for the time being. Ashack, who had been quiet, spoke up in his gruff manner. "This is sufficient for today. We have other matters to discuss regarding the village."

Nageau nodded. "When we bring this meeting to an end later, I suggest we retire to our abodes for meditation and reflection. We will meet here again tomorrow at sunrise. Hopefully, we will have fresh insights by then. Meanwhile, we shall let the children recover."

"Nageau," Tikina scolded. "Those five are not children. They are youths."

Nageau chuckled. "Ah, but at my age, these distinctions do get blurred."

6

Jag had been up for a while. He sat in his sleeping bag and stared at the wooden door of the rustic shelter, wondering what time of the day it was. He felt rested and was itching to discover where they were and how they ended up here. More importantly though, he wanted to find Mariah and Tegan and make sure they were alright as well.

He yawned, then made a face as he tasted his breath. Gently tracing the facial cuts on his natural golden-tan complexion, he winced when he touched a burning one. He darted a quick glance at Kody and Aari lying down on either side of him in their sleeping bags. He noticed Kody's eyes were open and staring upward.

Jag tapped Kody lightly. "Dude, you awake?"

"My eyes are open, so obviously, I'm awake."

Jag forced a small grin at his friend's dry response. On Jag's other side, Aari stirred and opened his eyes. Kody pulled himself upright and took in the shelter in full. "Anyone have a clue as to where we are?"

"None," Jag answered.

Kody looked around expectantly. "You guys see my dad anywhere?"

Jag shook his head. "He's not here."

"Then . . . where can he be?"

"Why don't we get out of here first then see if we can find him?" Aari suggested.

Jag nodded. "Yeah. We need to find Teegs and Mariah, too." He struggled out of the sleeping bag and found himself standing on wobbly legs. It felt odd using them; they didn't feel like his own. Tentatively, he placed his left foot forward, testing it. He looked down at his friends. "If you don't mind, maybe we can take it slow—real slow."

Aari bobbed his head eagerly as he too got out of his sleeping bag. "I'm with you. Zombie speed suits me just fine." With Jag's help, he managed to awkwardly stand up. They looked down at Kody. With an unspoken agreement, Jag took hold of Kody's left arm and Aari took his right one. Together, they got Kody up onto his feet.

Jag rolled his shoulders stiffly. "Ready?"

"I think so," Kody replied, leaning to one side from the aching in his right hip. "Aari?"

"Let's go." Although his voice sounded confident, it wasn't hard to tell that Aari was sore too.

Jag limped to the door, took a deep breath, and opened it. Twilight welcomed them. The three gazed up at the open heavens, agape.

"That's *beautiful*," Aari murmured in awe. "What is this place?"

His friends had no answer and they continued to stare upward. Stars were beginning to glitter brightly, and the shades of blue, purple, faint orange and pink melted with each other. It was nature showing off its work of art. For that moment, they forgot their pains.

And then—

A bark sounded. Jag, Aari, and Kody froze. The bark faded to a whimper after an almost inaudible, "Shh!"

Jag leaned closer to his friends and muttered, "We're gonna have to go on carefully. There are people here."

He took the lead again and the trio advanced cautiously, taking in the surroundings. It wasn't long before they heard the sound of flowing water. Jag pointed to a winding path between a few trees and they padded next to it, curious and alert, letting it lead the way. They noticed a gently rolling river alongside the entire length of the path. Jag frowned. He knew there wasn't much light and that the water would appear darker, but it seemed a peculiar color. Almost—green? Teal? He was mesmerized by the lively hue.

The boys half-limped along the path for the next few minutes in silence. Twilight was almost gone now, and the moon emerged to cast a glow in the darkening sky. Jag gazed up at it, remembering all of a sudden his ride on the massive bear. He recalled the mystical air around the creatures and their gleaming eyes. And their tremendous size! He still remembered the fierce yet protective sensation he got from his mount.

Wait. Was it all a dream? He stopped in his tracks, befuddled.

Aari bumped into him, and Kody bumped into Aari. They groaned as their aches flared.

"Did you have to stop like that?" Aari struggled to keep his voice quiet.

Ignoring Aari's comment, Jag turned around to face his friends. "Do you remember the bears we were on?"

Kody and Aari gave him looks as if demanding to know if he'd gone mad. "What bears?"

"The bears—you know, the huge ones that brought us here." Jag waved his arms around.

"I think the pain went to your head, pal," asserted Aari. "Are we really supposed to believe that we arrived here on *bears*? Get a grip."

"I saw them," Jag insisted in frustration. "I *know* I saw them, and I *know* I wasn't hallucinating."

Rolling his eyes, Kody muttered, "Yeah, you probably dreamt it, then."

Jag huffed, then relented and reluctantly agreed. "Probably . . . it was just so real, though."

They ambled on for a while more until Jag halted again, eyes trying to pierce the darkness ahead of him.

"What is it this time?" Aari grumbled. "A kangaroo doing ballet?

Jag raised a finger to his lips. "Shh. Did you hear that?"

Kody and Aari strained their ears. Suddenly, a large black shape leapt out in front of them, its thick tail flying. They heard a growl emanating from it, and the three stood rooted to the spot, petrified.

The creature advanced stiff-legged, hackles raised. They could make out a canine shape, but it was larger than any dog they'd ever seen.

The animal's yellow eyes gleamed and the teens saw a flash of sharp white teeth like daggers of ice.

Wolf!

Adrenaline kicked in. Jag's fear vanished almost instantly and together with it, his aches. He stood with his feet planted apart, ready to fight the animal should it attack them.

"Chayton!"

The wolf paused and looked back. A form was hurrying in their direction. Somewhat to the boys' relief, it was a human shape. As the person drew closer, Jag heard a quiet mutter of recognition from Kody.

The youth dropped down to one knee next to the wolf and slipped a rawhide collar around its neck, scolding it in an odd language. Jag, Aari, and Kody shared puzzled looks. The wolf lowered itself to the ground and whimpered roughly. The youth stopped his scolding and stroked the animal's head. He glanced up at the trio. The friends saw a smile playing on his features. He stood up, and holding the wolf by the collar, bowed slightly and said, "Akol."

Kody leaned toward Aari and whispered, "What?"

"How would I know?" Jag whispered back.

"Maybe it means 'sorry about that' in his language," Kody proposed carefully.

"Could be."

The youth, overhearing, shook his head and indicated to himself, repeating, "Akol."

Aari realized what he was trying to say, though he was a little startled that the youth had understood Kody since he appeared unable to speak their language. "It's his name!"

The youth turned to Aari, beaming. Jag raised his eyebrows and introduced himself and his friends. "I'm Jag. This is Aari, and that's Kody."

Akol said their names, seeming satisfied. He turned around, waving at them to follow him. After a moment's hesitation, the boys quickly limped after him. He led them in the direction they had been heading. The wolf looked over its shoulder at them and undecidedly wagged its tail. Its dark fur shimmered in the moonlight.

A couple of minutes later, the boys and the wolf turned in at a shelter almost like the one the trio had been in, but much bigger. The wolf wagged his tail eagerly and trotted through the open door. Akol and the younger teens followed him inside.

Inside, the shelter was warm and cozy. Although the material used to build the place appeared to be the same as the shelter the boys were in, the interior was very different as it was furnished much like a house. There was a kitchen, a living room, and a small dining area.

As the boys took stock of what was around them, Kody noticed the pretty girl who had been with Akol previously. She was standing in front of a shelf and arranging flowers in a marble vase. When she saw Chayton looking up at her with a canine smile on his face, she laughed and went over to a counter to grab a bone. She handed it to him, and the wolf accepted the treat in his jaws. Turning around, he padded out of the shelter and into the night.

The tall girl stared after him fondly and then turned to Akol and the three friends. She and Akol engaged in a dialogue, again in that foreign—but strangely melodious—language. After a few moments of talking, she turned and faced the trio. They shuffled uncomfortably under her amused, intense gaze. She said something and pointed to herself.

"Just a wild guess, but I think she's introducing herself," Aari whispered. Jag and Kody nodded their agreement.

"Huyani." Akol pointed at her as he looked at the friends.

"Her name is Huyani?" Kody asked. Both Akol and the girl smiled, appearing contented. Akol then jerked his chin at the boys and said to Huyani while specifying them in turn, "Jag, Aari, Kody."

"Jag, Aari, Kody," Huyani repeated. She gazed into the trio's eyes deeply, as if probing.

Akol, noting that the boys only wore thin-layered tops, went to one end of the five-sided cabin. He returned with pullovers similar to what he was wearing and distributed the woolen garments. The friends accepted them gratefully and slipped the pullovers over their heads. They grinned, thankful, then laughed at one another. Neither had seen the other wearing such clothes and it looked strange on them, although the multi-colored material looked good on Akol.

Huyani and Akol joined in the merriment, then Huyani walked over to what appeared to be an island counter in the kitchen. The wood was polished so well it shone. She handed the four boys a drink from the counter and helped herself to one as well.

"Wonder when was the last time I ate, because I'm *starving*." Kody clutched his rumbling abdomen in embarrassment when Akol, Huyani, Kody and Aari chortled at him, though not unkindly.

"That was loud," Jag grinned. He paused with his cup halfway to his lips when a pang of hunger tackled him. "Okay, now I'm hungry too. Thanks a bunch for mentioning it."

Akol chuckled and went to another side of the shelter. He brought back three strips of juicy meat. Huyani placed shallow wooden plates in front of the famished friends and proceeded to sprinkle some kind of a powdered spice onto the venison. She turned around to another counter flanking the first. This one had a glowing clay plate sitting on two rows of blue flames. As she proceeded to cook the meat on the hot plate, the mouth-watering aroma drifted from the sizzling strips of meat to the trio's noses, teasing them with its appetizing smell.

Akol pulled up three padded wooden stools for them to sit on as his companion served the grilled meat onto the shallow plates in front of the boys. Huyani turned around to grab something from a narrow counter behind her. When she turned back again, the boys saw she was holding some sort of cutlery with an astonishing resemblance to forks and knives. Handing the cutlery to them, she said something, though the boys couldn't make heads or tails of it.

Nor did they really care, what with the scrumptious food staring up at them invitingly. Huyani and Akol dipped their heads at the friends and exited the shelter.

As the boys dug into the delicious, expertly-seasoned meat, Aari asked, "Where in the world are we?" Chomping down into the food, he continued, "This place seems like some sort of getaway haven, but I'm getting the feeling that we're the only tourists here. Or is that just me?"

"That's one way to put it," Jag said. "We're definitely out of the way *somewhere*. I'm pretty sure this ain't Dawson Creek, although I'm getting that northern Canada feeling."

"I want to know where my dad is," Kody put in. "I'd feel better having him around."

"Don't forget the girls," added Jag, chewing his steak. "We need to find them too."

They finished their meal in silence after that. As they sat leaning with their backs against the counter and drank from their cups, Akol and Huyani came back in.

"Oh, joy," Kody muttered. "I'm hurting again. Not as badly as before, but still." He rubbed his temples and closed his eyes.

Huyani clucked her tongue and grabbed a bowl sitting on the far side of the counter. She dipped her hand into it. When she withdrew her hand, greenish-brown goop dripped from her fingers and she waved them at the boys. The trio leaned back with disgusted looks on their faces.

Behind them, Akol hooted with hilarity. Huyani's lips twitched as she tried to control her own amusement. Walking around the counter to Kody, she raised her messy fingers to his face. Kody eyed her and jumped off his stool, cringing as his aches started to throb again. Huyani raised an eyebrow and took a step toward him. Before Kody could move again, she reached out and dabbed the cuts on his face with the goop. Kody grimaced but stayed still as she applied the mud-like sludge, then ministered to the other two boys.

As the night rolled on, Akol stood up to stretch. He and Huyani were both enjoying their first proper interaction with the boys. He yawned and looked out the window, noting the setting moon.

Jag followed his gaze and realized it was time to leave. He was about to stand up as well when he saw that Aari and Kody were oblivious to the world and were being sweet around Huyani. He kicked their legs discreetly under the counter and the two were yanked back to reality.

Smiling, Akol led the friends out of Huyani's shelter and brought them back to their own. Thanking him, the trio ducked into the shelter and, though it hurt, flopped down on their sleeping bags, weary in both body and mind. They really wanted to find the girls but were too exhausted to remain awake any longer, and fell asleep within moments.

7

A soft blanket of mist lifted from the valley as dawn crept in to announce a new day. A glow of daylight gently rolled down the slopes of the mountains that bordered the snugly-nestled village. Birds began their early morning choir as they spread their wings and flew from branch to branch. Somewhere in the trees, a young fox barked excitedly as it spotted a shrew.

As the sun climbed over the snow-capped peaks that guarded the hidden valley, its rays shimmered on the surface of a slender river that meandered through the entire length of the village, neatly dividing it in two. Dotting the northern bank were an assortment of *neyra*, cabin-like shelters that were mostly five-sided and housed about seven hundred inhabitants of the valley.

Nageau rolled out of his bed and stretched easily. Entering the kitchen, he found his mate already catering their morning meal. She looked up and gave him a big smile. Warmly greeting him, Tikina said, "First-light meal is almost ready."

"Many thanks," Nageau replied, giving her a quick hug. "I will join you in a moment. Do not wait for me."

Tikina nodded and watched as he threw on his cloak and strode out of their *neyra*. Outside, Nageau paused and looked around. His people were already roused from their sleep, and as he passed them, they acknowledged him in equal measures of respect and friendliness.

A sheep trotted by, bleating, and nudged Nageau's leg. The Elder looked down with a smile and patted the animal's head fondly. Some of the barn animals often roamed freely around the southern side of the valley during the day, then instinctively returned to the barn at night.

As he scratched the sheep's fleece, his only offspring, a woman of thirty-eight summers, spotted him and walked swiftly over. She gave him a quick peck on the cheek as the sheep trotted off.

"Father, may I assist you in something?" she asked. Nageau beamed at her and ruffled her hair as he'd always done since she was a child.

"Actually, I heard that Huyani has done a wonderful job tending the injured ones," he said, adding, "I need to remind her that the Elders are expecting to hear from her about the five today."

"I will take care of that. When are you holding the meeting?"

"At quarter-morn."

"Then I must get to her right away." She embraced her father then twirled around and walked briskly to Huyani's *neyra*. Nageau watched as she poked her head in, then turned and retraced his steps. Back inside his home, he and Tikina had a warm meal of poached eggs, flax seed bread and goat's milk.

"Will Huyani come to the meeting to enlighten us on the five?" Tikina inquired.

Nageau nodded and continued chewing on the last portion of his breakfast. They drank down the milk and headed out along the winding path adjacent to the river. It led them to the western end of the village where the Elders' assembly shelter was located. They found Saiyu and Ashack already there. The couple looked up and Ashack's usually guarded features broke into the slightest of smiles. "It looks like Tayoka is the last to arrive . . . again."

"I am here, I am here!" The four turned to the source of the voice. A slim figure with a headful of bright red hair was running towards them, so fast he was almost a blur.

"Tayoka, how nice of you to join us." Nageau's face cracked into a grin at the approaching Elder.

Tayoka darted through the open door and pulled up beside Tikina, not at all out of breath. "Good morning, everyone." He gave the other Elders a sheepish look. "I apologize for being a little late. I am not as quick as I used to be."

Tikina warmly squeezed his shoulder and said, "Good morning to you too." She smiled. "You may have the speed of lightning, but age does eventually catch up with us. Or perhaps you are simply becoming lazy."

Tikina, Saiyu, Nageau and Ashack laughed at the youngest Elder's indignant expression. Saiyu had already started a small fire in the pit at the center of the room. They sat around it, relaxed and prepared to commence the meeting.

Nageau cleared his throat. "Have we come up with anything?"

Tayoka shook his head. "On my part, I am afraid not."

Saiyu peered at Nageau as she readjusted the bracelets on her arm. "What about you, Nageau?"

"I had many whirling thoughts, though none were concrete," Nageau replied glumly.

"I slept soundly," Ashack said. Not wanting to appear smug, he continued, "But Saiyu and I agreed with Tikina's proposal that we meet with our guests as soon as possible."

Tikina spoke up, keeping her gaze on the fire. "By meeting face-to-face with them, we may be able to unlock some of the mysteries of the prophecy."

Nageau nodded slowly. "Agreed. Huyani is coming to brief us on the progress the five are making health-wise. We can ask her about her encounters with them as we prepare to meet them."

Just as he spoke, the door opened and a beam of light flashed into the *neyra*. A second later, Huyani stepped in. She bowed to the Elders.

"Elder Nageau," she said formally. "Am I disrupting?"

Nageau smiled broadly. "No, not at all, Granddaughter." He patted the space between him and Tikina on the low wooden bench. "In fact, we are just about ready to hear what you have observed."

"There is a lot to share," Huyani said, taking her place between her grandparents.

Saiyu folded her arms on her lap. “We are most interested.”

“Well, if you are all comfortable, then I shall begin.”

The Elders nodded in unison, and Huyani began reciting her observations.

8

Tegan slowly came to and cracked open an eye. As she glanced about, the first thought on her mind was, *Where am I?* She saw Mariah lying on her back inside a sleeping bag and felt relieved that she wasn't alone.

She gently shook her friend. "Mariah." When she didn't stir, Tegan shook her harder. "Get up already!"

"Mmh . . ."

Tegan rolled her eyes. "Wake up or I'll let Kody at you."

Mariah bolted upright. "Don't you dare!" She looked around, her eyes settling lastly on Tegan. She was not amused. "Kody's not even here."

"Works every time," Tegan said with a tired smile. She pushed her hair back, letting the ash-brown layers cascade over her shoulders, then winced when she felt a sharp pain in her shoulder.

Mariah scratched her head. "Where are we?"

"I don't know. The guys aren't here, and it looks like we're inside some sort of cabin." Tegan peered into her sleeping bag, then at Mariah. "Who changed me out of my sweatpants and into a robe?!"

Surprised, Mariah pulled down her sleeping bag. "Um . . . I'm wearing one too."

"I'd like to know how."

"Let's get out and find the guys first."

"Good idea. Hopefully they know what's going on." As an afterthought, Tegan added quietly, "I hope they're okay." She got out of her sleeping bag, feeling stiff and uncomfortable. She took a few breaths, then headed toward the small cabin's door with Mariah right behind.

Tegan cautiously opened the door and they both instantly shrank from the harsh light that struck them.

Tegan shut her eyes firmly. Flashes of orange, yellow and black danced within her closed eyelids. Mariah was no better and muttered, "That was awful."

"I know, but we need to get out of here if we want to find the guys." Tegan turned back to the door and squinted. "Come on."

They took a few steps out and stared, open-mouthed. Surrounding them were majestic mountains adorned with snow-capped tips. As the sun bounced off the icy peaks, the light made a dazzling glow around the mountains, like a halo encircling them.

Midway down the mountain, pine trees filled the landscape, growing denser as they approached the turquoise river at the base. Woven between the tree line and dotting the banks of the river were many other shelters of various sizes.

As they scanned the structures cautiously, they spied one in between the trees not too far from where they stood. It looked identical to the shelter they'd been in. Exchanging inquisitive glances, Mariah asked, "Looks just like ours—you think . . . ?"

Tegan gave a hesitant nod, and they headed that way in anticipation.

A mound of bushes and shrubs rose in their path as they drew nearer. As they brushed past some ferns, Tegan's keen ears picked up a rustling sound. She stopped abruptly, swept a restraining hand in front of Mariah, and spun around.

Before she could hiss a warning, a golden-brown creature, about three times the size of a domestic house cat, sprang over them. It landed silently on its huge padded paws and turned to face the girls. Taken aback, it took the two a few moments to register that they were looking at a lynx. They eyed the wildcat in disbelief. It stared right back with something more than just feline intelligence. Was it . . . amusement? It had an almost human quality that sent shudders up the girls' spines. Sitting back on its haunches and blocking their path, it appeared that the lynx wasn't going to leave. It gazed at them, licking a claw, then leapt into the trees and disappeared.

A few heartbeats later, Mariah looked at Tegan with an air of incredulity and delayed fright. "Was that really a lynx?"

"Yeah." Tegan glanced back at where the cat had been to make sure the animal was no longer there. She didn't know what to make of that little incident. "That was really weird. Did you notice how it looked at us?"

Mariah shivered and nodded. Trying to push the encounter from their minds, they continued on. After weaving their way through a stand of fir, they came into full view of the shelter.

A mixture of anxiety and anticipation arose in the pit of their stomachs as they increased their pace. Questions were raging in their minds: *Are the guys inside? Are they injured? What do we do if they're not there?* They didn't dare wonder who might be inside if the boys weren't.

As they closed in on the shelter, they slowed down and lowered instinctively into a crouch. Not wishing to startle the occupants—whomever they were—the two treaded quietly over the uneven ground. To their chagrin, Mariah tripped over an exposed root and, with a muted cry, almost fell on her face. With quick reflexes, Tegan grabbed her friend's arm before the impact. At that exact moment, the door flew open and a tall figure stepped out from the shelter. The girls froze.

The figure turned back to the opened door, and with a husky voice the girls knew all too well, called out impatiently, "Hey, boneheads! Get your butts out of there—we gotta find the girls!"

Kody and Aari stepped out of the shelter, blinking sleep from their eyes. Tegan and Mariah looked at each other with joy. Shrieking, the two charged as fast as their robes allowed and flung themselves at their bewildered friends. Hollering in delight, Jag hugged them both fiercely, Aari and Kody following suit.

Minutes lapsed as the friends reunited with strangling bear hugs and cries of happiness. As they settled down, Aari stepped back and observed the robes the two girls were wearing with amusement. "Nice threads," he grinned. Mariah bowed at the praise, and was brushed into yet another bear hug from Kody. She grimaced good-naturedly.

Tegan laughed, then choked as Jag enveloped her in a playful headlock. "Hey, let go! You're gonna crack my head!"

Jag winked. "Yeah, right. Your skull's too thick for that."

"You'd better learn to sleep with your eyes open." Huffing with effort, Tegan scrambled out of her friend's strong grip only to be barged at by Aari. The five of them laughed, relishing the fact that they were back together.

"I feel almost whole now," Kody murmured as he sat down on a log. He combed his fingers through his short hair and stared at the ground.

The others glanced at one another, then quietly went to stand by his side. Jag rested a gentle hand on his shoulder. "We found each other. I'm sure it's only a matter of time before we find your dad.

Kody said nothing. The friends were silent for a while after that until Mariah tentatively asked, "Does anyone know where we are? Or how we got here?"

"Not a clue," Jag answered. "But there are people here. They don't speak English, but they found us and they've been keeping us alive, I guess."

"Speaking of that . . ." Mariah seized her stomach with her arms and moaned. "I am so hungry. I could really do with a burger and a can of Dr Pepper right about now."

Tegan patted her friend on the back. "I know how you feel." She looked around, squinting against the sun. "I wonder how long we've been in this place. A couple of days?"

"Actually, you have been recuperating here for nearly a week," a new voice cloaked in an unfamiliar accent surprised them.

The five looked at each other and turned around warily.

The youth, Akol, was standing behind them with his arms folded across his chest and a light grin on his face. Jag turned to Kody and Aari, then turned back to the newcomer. Startled, he asked, "Did . . . did you just say that?"

Akol dipped his head. "Yes."

The boys stared at each other, agape and baffled. Kody flicked a finger in Akol's direction and gave him a sideways, mystified look. "But, man, we were with you before . . . you only spoke in your language."

Tegan and Mariah shot Kody perplexed expressions, which he ignored.

Akol laughed, a little nervously, and rubbed one side of his face. "Let us just say that I am a quick learner."

Jag stared at Akol with deep suspicion. "That's pretty quick learning for anyone."

"Not really."

Tegan placed her hands on her hips and demanded, "Someone mind explaining what's going on here?"

Jag was still glaring distrustfully at Akol; her words fell on deaf ears. Akol, feeling the tension in the air, faced Tegan. "Let me introduce myself. I am Akol. I know your friends already, but what are your names?"

Jag rolled his eyes at the obvious dodge but remained quiet. Tegan and Mariah glanced at each other. "I'm Tegan, and this is Mariah."

"I am glad you are okay. I was a little worried when I could not find you in your *neyra*."

"What's a *neyra*?" Tegan asked curiously.

"They are the shelters you were recovering in." Akol smiled and was about to add something else when Tegan slapped her forehead. *What am I doing sharing small talk with this dude?*

Looking at the older teenager in the eye, she said, "Listen, we appreciate you being concerned for us, but where *are* we? What is this place?"

Akol realized he couldn't go on without giving some information and sighed. "Come. Let us go to Huyani's *neyra*. I am sure she will have some food prepared for us. We may speak afterward."

"Who's Huyani?" asked Mariah.

"It's the girl who was tending to us," Kody answered.

"Wait—is she tall with long black hair?"

"Yeah. You know her?"

Mariah nodded. "I saw her once. She gave me something to drink and it killed my pain."

Not wanting to expose the five to his people yet, Akol led the friends through an alternate route behind the tree line. As they trod along the winding trail, the five breathed in deeply. They liked the smell of the forest and the mountain air.

As they walked up an incline, the five saw an astounding sight through the pine needles that hung from the trees. On the opposite bank of the turquoise river stood an immense building about three-quarters the size of a football field. It had a pyramid-shaped roof and seemed alien in a remote village. It appeared to be clad in blue-green walls that were translucent, but the teenagers were too far away to make out what was inside. Next to that structure, smaller by comparison but quite big themselves, were buildings made of timber. They resembled a kind of stable or barn complete with a gambrel roof.

The friends kept the questions that were swirling in their minds to themselves, not wanting to be the first to break the silence that now hung over them. Akol also said nothing and walked steadily onward. They trudged along for a few minutes more until Akol turned around and grinned. "We are here."

Piloting the way out of the foliage and toward the shelter next to a grove of blue spruce trees, Akol opened the door to Huyani's *neyra* and ushered the friends in. When they entered the shelter, Tegan was startled to see a large black dog napping on the ground. As the six of them stepped inside, the dog opened its bright yellow eyes and raised its head, alert. Tegan gasped.

It was a wolf.

Beside her, Mariah's eyes nearly burst from their sockets. She grabbed Tegan's arm and dug her fingernails into her friend's skin. Wincing, Tegan jerked her arm away and studied the wolf with admiration. Fangs and claws gleamed like polished ivory when the wolf's lips pulled back into a wild canine smile as it raised itself off the floor and stretched. The muscular body, covered in thick midnight-black fur, rippled with power. Tegan noted how big its paws were, and how it moved with stealth as it drew near the friends. Driven by impulse, she dropped to her knees, her hands on the ground in front of her, and watched the wolf keenly as it watched her.

Akol's voice reached her ears. "Tegan, if I may, this is Chayton, one of the wolves who enjoys our company. We think he is about five years old, and he is a wonderful friend."

"He's your pet?"

"Goodness, no. These creatures are free. They come and go as they please, although Chayton seems to enjoy being around us more than the others."

"How many wolves visit you?"

"Four in total, though Chayton will probably be the one you will encounter the most. A number of other animals come by as well, notably a lone female lynx."

Twin cries erupted from Mariah and Tegan, startling the wolf and the boys. "A lynx? We had an encounter with one earlier!"

"Did she have a golden pelt with white stripes running down her shoulders?" Akol asked, an eager note in his voice. They nodded. "Then that was Tyse you met."

Tegan whistled. "This place is *amazing*."

"It is certainly quite incredible during the summer." Akol scratched his chin. "Then there is winter. It comes two ways, stunning and unforgiving."

"I don't doubt it. This is way up north, so it must be harsh." Tegan paused when Chayton was right in front of her, his black muzzle only a few inches from her nose. After a moment, he licked her cheek and playfully nibbled her hair. Tegan broke into a large smile and laughed, relieved.

Akol stared at her and the wolf, astounded. "He likes you the first time around. That is quite rare."

Kody rested an elbow on Tegan's head and hooted, "Akol m'man, you don't know this girl unless you've been around her long enough. She's got her ways with animals, wild or not."

Tegan grunted at the sharp elbow on her head and shook it off, then got up and shoved Kody. He tottered backwards and nearly tipped over, all the while snickering. Chayton slunk past and exited the shelter. No sooner was he gone than the door opened wide and a slender form stepped in. Seeing the six of them in her shelter, Huyani smiled and welcomed them warmly in her own language. Akol laughed.

"There is no need," he told Huyani. "We may speak to them in their tongue."

"Ah," she said with a gleam in her eyes. "So they know."

Akol looked sheepish.

Huyani shook her head with a smile. "Really now, brother."

The five gawked. *They're siblings!*

Turning to the boys, Huyani greeted them. "Nice to see you, Jag, Aari, Kody!" Her accented voice sounded like a nightingale's song; the friends felt lifted.

Mariah smiled. "Hi—I'm Mariah. I remember you."

Huyani nodded. "Hello, Mariah. My name is Huyani. It is lovely to see some color back in your cheeks now. And you are . . . ?" She fixed her dark brown eyes on Tegan.

"Tegan."

"Nice to meet you. How are all of you faring?"

"I feel almost good enough to do a backflip," Kody said. "That is, if I could do one in the first place, which I can't."

"We all feel that way," Aari confirmed as Huyani looked at the others with concern.

"That is good."

Kody looked around the cabin. "Where are we?"

"Hold on, Kody," Huyani said gently. "I must still examine each of you to check your condition for myself. Questions may come later." As Huyani lifted Jag's chin to see his facial cuts in the light, a rumbling noise sounded. She paused and shared puzzled looks with Jag. After a moment, Jag roared with laughter. Looking at Mariah, he called out, "That was you, wasn't it?"

Everyone stared at Mariah as she blushed, embarrassed. "Blame the hungry pet lion living in my stomach, people."

The shelter filled with howls of amusement. Huyani consoled Mariah. "I will make something for you."

"Thank you," Mariah said weakly. Huyani shepherded the friends toward another end of her *neyra* once she had checked on their condition. She gently pushed them down onto a padded divan made from moose-hide, and then went into the kitchen quarter with Akol.

"How did the meeting with the Elders go?" Akol asked quietly, out of the friends' earshot.

"I will tell you once we have the five settled down properly," his sister murmured back as she nodded in the direction of their visitors.

Tegan leaned back comfortably and gazed around, her gray eyes smartly picking up details. "I still want to know where we are," she muttered.

Aari patted her shoulder. "You and all of us."

A good fifteen minutes passed, or so Tegan estimated, when the delicious fragrance of grilled meat seasoned with herbs and spices tickled their noses.

Mariah sniffed the air and gushed. "That smells *good*."

Kody licked his lips. "If it's what the guys and I had before, then you two are in for a special treat."

Tegan eyed him. "I won't ask when you guys ate your meal, but I will say that your appetite never fails you. You're impossible to fill up *or* shut up."

"What I don't get is how you stay as slim as the rest of us," Mariah said.

"I work out," he boasted with mock pride.

"Sure, and my grandpa Joe was a merman," Aari retorted.

"Hey, I thought you said he was Bigfoot."

"Oh, good grief . . ."

Jag tried not to burst out with laughter. Tegan and Mariah both covered their mouths, struggling to not snigger at the pair's repartee. Kody and Aari's consistent banter was well-known at Great Falls High School in Montana, where the friends would be going into their third year the coming fall.

Huyani called from the kitchen. "Come! Your meal is ready!"

Mariah and Kody were off the couch in a flash and tearing toward their warm, waiting food. Jag, Aari, and Tegan followed. Mariah beamed at the grilled, seasoned meat on her dish and the accompanying mix of fresh greens.

"Awesome," she said hungrily as she and Kody attacked their steaks.

As Jag, Aari, and Tegan took their places and began digging into their servings, Huyani said, "Enjoy."

"Thank you!" the five chorused, their mouths full.

While the friends indulged in their meal, Huyani leaned against one of the kitchen counters. Akol joined her. "So how did the meeting go?" he asked softly, switching to his native tongue.

Huyani pushed a strand of her raven hair from her face, answering likewise. "Quite well. The Elders wanted to learn about the five's progress."

"So do they really think these are the ones? From the prophecy, I mean."

Huyani shrugged her slim shoulders. "I do not know, brother, but they were keenly interested." She paused. "Except for Elder Ashack. Always the skeptical one."

Akol laughed quietly. Huyani looked at him. "Akol, we must tell them something soon."

"You mean the five? Yes, I agree. I already told them we will talk after they have finished eating."

"Good. We cannot keep them in the dark forever. Question is: What do we tell them, and how much do we tell them?"

"W-ell . . ." Akol scratched his head. "Do we have permission to in the first place?"

Huyani's delicate features contorted into one of her rare scowls. "No. But I know that we cannot hide these things from them. We have to tell them something. They have the right to know. Do you not agree?"

"I do. How much can we reveal, though? I can tell they are a persistent bunch. If they are not satisfied, we will hear no end of their relentless questions."

They discussed back and forth until they reached a conclusion. Reverting into the friends' language again, Akol said casually, "Would you like something to drink? We have water and wild berry juices."

The five raised an eyebrow at each other. "I think we'll settle for water, thanks," Jag said. Huyani handed them their drinks.

"That was the best meal I've ever had in my entire life," Tegan announced delightedly. "Thank you so much."

Huyani seemed pleased. "You are most welcome. Would you like some sweets?"

Tegan's eyes widened. "You mean desserts? You have those?"

"I suppose that is the word you use. Yes."

"Nice—what do you have?"

"Well, we have a variety. We have lots of wild berries, sweet roots, potatoes and more."

Tegan was about to eagerly pick her dessert choices when Aari quietly clamped a hand over her mouth and looked at Akol and Huyani. "That sounds great, guys, and maybe we'll have some later. But first, we have to get at least some of our questions answered. It's been like a splinter in our minds, and we really need to get things straightened out."

Huyani gave Akol a confirming look, and they sat down opposite the friends. Akol began slowly. "I will try my best to tell you what I may, though be forewarned, some things will not be entirely clear to you . . . There are somewhat unmentionable actualities I must take out of this account." He took a gulp from his own cup and composed himself.

Unmentionable actualities? The five exchanged puzzled looks. *What on earth does that mean?*

"You were brought unconscious to us by some of the most amazing inhabitants of these forests. We refer to them as the Guardians. They are powerful and are very protective of the people. We have had great respect for them and their ancestors for many, many years. They must have heard the explosion. We believe they followed the flames in the sky and were led to you."

Jag pounded the counter with a fist, causing the others to jump. "Hold on a second, Akol. Are these 'Guardians' extremely huge bears by any chance?"

Akol coughed, surprised. "Yes, they are."

Jag hooted and pointed smugly at Kody and Aari. "I told you I wasn't hallucinating!"

Aari's jaw dropped in disbelief. Kody just stared blankly at Jag, who cracked his knuckles in contentment.

Akol took up his narrative again. "In any case, our people trust the Guardians with their lives. They are loyal, and have incredible tracking skills. When you were brought to us, our Elders instructed Huyani and I to care for you and keep you from falling into the void."

Aari interjected. "Who are your Elders?"

Akol took another sip from his drink. "They are our leaders. We revere and trust them. They are wise and caring people who guide us and teach us the ways of the tribe. We look up to them and love them dearly.

"This village, this tribe, has an amazing history. We are descendants of two groups of very different peoples. I will not go into details now, but suffice to say that the unification of the two groups brought about extraordinary capabilities in our tribe. We have developed abilities which may seem miraculous to outsiders. For example, you have experienced Huyani's healing skills. Also, as you have noticed, Huyani and I are gifted with unusual linguistic ability; I believe the word in your language for this skill is 'omni-linguism'. This is how we are able to communicate with you. Other people in our village have different abilities."

"But these are not miracles or magic," Huyani chipped in. "They are latent in each one of us."

Akol finished his drink. "This is as much as we can share with you for now. I am certain that the Elders will enlighten you further. They are looking forward to meeting all of you very soon."

"What?" Mariah tugged at her earlobe. "They're going to—we're going to meet them? When? Why?"

Akol appeared caught off guard by her queries. He looked intently at the five's faces and said, "It would be wise to stay patient for now. In time, things will become clearer, I promise you."

They nodded, uncertain. Tegan looked thoughtful for a moment, then ventured, "Really, who are you? And *where* are we?"

"My friends," Akol said as he stood up and stretched his arms, smiling, "welcome to Dema-Ki, the hidden valley."

9

The bright midday sun found the Elders outside their assembly *neyra*. Huyani had finished her briefing some while ago and left, and the Elders decided to step out to discuss what they had gathered from her observations.

"That was an interesting narrative from Huyani," Tayoka said, scratching his red beard.

Saiyu nodded. "It sounds like they are an amusing group. Bold, too, to step out into unfamiliar surroundings during the night."

Tikina shaded her green eyes from the sun's glare. "Huyani mentioned that one of the girls seemed rather guarded, the one with dark-golden hair."

"They have gone through a harrowing ordeal and being in a strange place is bound to be unsettling," Saiyu answered.

"The other girl, the taller one with brown hair . . . Huyani is yet to converse with her, so we have very little to assess her with," Ashack said in his deep voice.

Nageau started walking toward the riverbank. "Perhaps we should go see them. Huyani did say that she and Akol were planning to gather them at her shelter." He cast a look at Saiyu, who was walking silently now. "You seem distracted. What is on your mind?"

"It was something Huyani said . . . about their eyes," Saiyu muttered, then wandered back into deep thought.

Hearing her comment, Ashack paused. "That is strange. I felt that way too."

"Do you two ever have any differing thoughts?" Tayoka teased.

"When you finally pick a mate, you will know what it is like," Ashack shot back to the others' amusement.

"Yes, it is about time you found someone to share your life with, Tayoka," Saiyu remarked lightheartedly.

Tayoka snorted. "What? I am a happy man where I am, thank you very much. Do not try to drag me into the misery you call life-companionship."

That drew laughter from Nageau, who shook his head with a smile. Noting that his mate was silent, he turned and saw Tikina standing beside him, her eyes closed. He lightly touched her shoulder and before the others noticed, she snapped out of her brief meditative state with a mysterious smile.

"About their eyes—" she started.

Before she could finish, a young boy around ten years of age dashed by, crashing into Nageau. "Elder Nageau! Elder Nageau!" he gasped. "I am so glad I found you!"

Nageau steadied the boy. "What is it, Diyo?" he asked, alarmed.

"It is my father, he is sick!" The boy stopped for a breather. "Our neighbors have brought him back—"

"Where is he?" Saiyu demanded.

"This way!" The boy dashed downriver. The Elders followed him quickly. As they reached the shelter, Diyo veered off to find his mother.

A man in his late twenties sat hunched on a bed in a corner. His lips were chalk white, his face horribly pale. Two other men were tending to him. As the Elders approached, his body tensed and convulsed, and he vomited into a small bucket in front of him. He looked up at the newcomers with an agonized moan.

"Fiotez," Tikina murmured, as she sat beside him on his bed and wrapped a soothing arm around him.

"Elder Tikin—" he groaned. He tensed as if he were about to retch again, then his eyes rolled to the back of his head and he collapsed in her arms, unconscious. Tikina breathed in sharply.

Nageau glanced back to the open door as he heard hurried footsteps. Diyo burst into the shelter. He choked at the sight of his unconscious father. His mother ran in behind him and gasped.

Tayoka gently ushered them back out the door, saying kindly, "Keep Diyo away from his father for now." He added more quietly, "I am sorry. It is better for you to stay with your son. Let us take care of Fiotez."

He reluctantly shut the door on the dismayed mother and son, and sidled over to stand beside his fellow Elders.

"What do you think happened to him?" Nageau asked no one in particular.

His question was met with silence and apprehensive looks from the others. One of the men who had been tending to Fiotez before the Elders arrived stood up and turned to look at Nageau. He was stocky with short, wavy brown hair that bobbed as he dipped his head at the Elder. In a gruff but respectful voice, he said, "Elder Nageau, we are Fiotez's neighbors and are the ones responsible for bringing him back from our hunting trip."

"When did he start showing signs of illness?" Tikina queried, picking up some herbs from the household. She flattened the leaves on a pumice slab before rolling them into a pellet, which she gently inserted under Fiotez's tongue.

"When we were returning from our expedition to one of the mountains," said the stocky neighbor. "He seemed fine at first, but the symptoms became worse as we got closer to the village."

Tikina glanced up from scrutinizing her patient. "I think it is best if everyone vacates this shelter so we can have more air circulating. It will allow me to tend to him better."

The other Elders and Fiotez's neighbors headed outside silently, grabbing a quick look at Tikina as she continued to work on the sick man.

Outside, Ashack's voice commanded the other Elders' attention. "I pray that Fiotez's condition does not worsen. I have not seen such affliction before . . . Our people are usually strong."

Nageau didn't reply. He possessed a keen sense of smell and was disturbed by the strange odor he had gotten in Fiotez's shelter.

Tayoka nudged him, bringing him out of his reflection, then said, "I hope so too, but something tells me . . ." He looked at the two neighbors. "You said you were with Fiotez when he started becoming sick. Please describe everything that occurred during your trip."

"Well, it had been some time since the three of us have hunted together," the taller neighbor began, "so we were eagerly anticipating this trip. We had our mates pack our necessities. Also, Huyani asked us to collect some herbs she needed for her stock. Once she gave us a list of what was needed, we departed for Ekota."

"Ekota? That mountain is quite a long way," Tayoka noted.

"Yes, it is. It was supposed to have been a four-day trip. The weather held up rather nicely. We did not encounter any game until sundown on the second day, when some caribou were taking a drink from a small brook. We almost got one of the animals, but it was getting dark and we missed. The caribou escaped, leaving us to continue on our way. We camped by a lake and ate our food, then turned in for some rest. We departed early the following morning." He looked at Tayoka, who nodded and motioned for him to continue.

"We followed some game trails that led us to a dead deer near a stream. It was a strange sight as the animal was not brought down by any predator or by old age, and foam covered its muzzle.

"We turned and continued our hunt down one of the trails. Fiotez slipped on some lichen at one point and nearly tumbled into a crevasse. He must have passed on his clumsiness to us, because a few minutes later, we walked into some thorns." The man chuckled tiredly, rubbing his bruised arm. "Besides that, nothing else strange happened." He paused as his eyes followed a small insect in its erratic flight.

"Please, continue," Saiyu urged. "There must be something more."

His brows furrowed as he tried to recall. "Though our hunting expedition was rather unsuccessful, we managed to find the herbs that Huyani needed. As we were heading back, Fiotez insisted on trying to hunt game again. We reluctantly agreed, knowing what a passionate hunter Fiotez is. Late in the morning on our third day, he trekked to a nearby creek to refill his water pelt while we waited at the camp. We tried hunting for a little while after that, but fortune was not on our side. We got nothing and sought to come back, but Fiotez wanted to continue. We coaxed him to give it up and he reluctantly agreed; not so much because we outnumbered him two to one, but rather at this point it appeared that he was not feeling too well. So, that sundown we camped again around a good fire and made sure he was comfortably tucked in."

The man scratched his forehead and sighed, then continued. "The next day as we hiked back, he seemed to weaken. He complained that his legs were not steady, and at first we thought perhaps he was just sore from the grueling trek. But when he started getting dizzy and nearly passed out while descending a mountain, we knew something was wrong."

"We brought him back as quickly as we could, and it was then we called for help," the shorter man finished.

Nageau pressed his lips into a flat line. There was silence for a while. "What do you make of this?" he finally asked the other Elders.

Stroking his short beard, Tayoka said, "I do not know. Nothing appeared to be out of the ordinary except for the dead deer."

"It is hard to determine what this is right now, as we do not know the seriousness or the cause of Fiotez's condition," Ashack said, adding, "maybe we should give Tikina some more time to let her remedy take effect."

Saiyu glanced at Nageau. "It is past midday now. Perhaps we should adjourn. Let us have Huyani relieve her grandmother at sundown. That way, I will be able to take Huyani's place tonight. One of us must watch over Fiotez until dawn."

* * *

A tender hand shook Tikina's arm. The Elder opened her eyes blearily and gazed up at the youthful face of her granddaughter. Huyani knelt beside her and asked softly, "How is Fiotez doing?"

Tikina stretched and shook her head. "I have tried every combination I know of for healing him, but I see no effect whatsoever."

Huyani put a warm hand on hers and turned to look at the sleeping Fiotez on his bed. "I will see to him," she murmured. "You must go and rest."

Tikina gave her an appreciative smile. "Thank you. You must keep him hydrated. Squeeze the juices of these leaves"—she held up a fistful of jagged-edged leaves—"into his mouth every little while, and keep feeling for his temperature. At the slightest sign of spasm, call for me immediately."

Huyani signaled that she understood. They sat together for a little while, talking softly about Huyani and Akol's time with the five outsiders. "What did you do with them?" Tikina asked.

"We fed them some deer meat, which they consumed ardently. They said it was the best they had ever had. Afterward, Akol and I decided that we need to tell them a few things, as we felt it was not right to keep them in the dark for an extended time."

Tikina pursed her lips, and then nodded. "Tell me, though. What did you and your brother talk to them about, and how much did you reveal?"

Shrugging, Huyani responded, "We told them how we found them, and informed them about the Guardians. We did not say what they were, but Jag had been in and out of consciousness during the period in which the Guardians brought the five to us, and he figured it out. We told them about you, the Elders. We also told them about the skills we carry within ourselves. Akol and I only shared our abilities, as we did not want to overwhelm them. We said our skills are not impossible. Lastly, we told them where they were."

Tikina's eyebrows rose. "Oh? And how did they take to that?"

"They looked at each other in confusion," Huyani giggled. "It means nothing to them. They have no idea where this place is."

"Of course they would not know. As far as we are concerned, the outside world is not aware of us. I am pleased you did not give too much away."

"We told them that you would like to meet them soon."

Tikina smiled widely. "Could you perhaps arrange a time tomorrow where we may meet them?"

"I am sure I can."

"Very good. Is that all that happened?"

Huyani twirled a lock of her straight hair with her index finger. "There is one other thing. They seem to be getting impatient. They want to know when they will be able to leave."

Tikina sighed quietly. "It is only to be expected, I am afraid. As I have said before, I believe that these five are special."

"You think they are the ones?"

"I cannot say for sure, but I must admit that their arrival here is very intriguing."

A moment of silence followed, broken by a guttural cough from Fiotez. Huyani glanced at him and noticed he was still asleep. "Grandmother . . ."

"Yes?"

"Do you know anything about Kody's father?"

"Father?"

"Yes. He kept asking about his father, and when we told him we did not know what happened to him, he became forlorn. We tried to soothe him and take his mind off the uncertainty, and now it nags me. Did the Guardians indicate anything about his father?"

"Alas, they signaled absolutely nothing about this. If the boy's father had been with them and something ill-fated happened, we would have known about it from the Guardians." Tikina was quiet for a while, then added, "I will see what I can do to find out more about this."

Huyani nodded. After some time, Tikina bade her granddaughter good night and was about to exit when she turned around with a mischievous smile. "The two girls . . . one has gray eyes and the other has brown, am I correct?"

Startled, Huyani looked up at her. "How did you know?" She saw the playful look on Tikina's face and groaned, "Oh—the eyes of Tyse."

Tikina simply chuckled and left Fiotez's *neyra*, leaving Huyani in wonder.

10

"One word I have is *bizarre*," Kody muttered. He tapped a small bruise on his lower arm. "I mean, go figure this: Our plane crashed from a freak storm; we were picked up by giant *bears* and brought to this place in the middle of nowhere; we're healed by two people who say they learn languages quickly thanks to some skill they have, and there are others like them in this village. And now their . . . *Elders* . . . want to meet us? To top it all off, we don't know—*I* don't know—where my dad is, or how he is." His voice rose a notch in a combination of frustration and hopelessness.

It was late in the night, and the five were in the girls' shelter discussing the baffling events that had occurred.

Jag patted his friend's back, trying to console him. "Look, we were found—it only makes sense that your old man was found as well, right?"

"Then where is he?"

Jag had nothing to say to that, and they stared into space gloomily for a while until a voice from outside their *neyra* startled them. "Tegan? Mariah?"

Tegan called back, "Come on in Akol, we're all here."

Akol stepped in, grinning. "The boys were not in their shelter when we went looking for them, so we knew they either had to be wandering around again or were in here."

"We?"

"Yes, Huyani came with me." Akol stepped aside, allowing Huyani to enter.

Tegan and Mariah burst into coos when they spotted Tibut peeking at them from the safety of Huyani's arms. They rose to their feet. "Who's the little fella?" Mariah looked into the toddler's big brown eyes.

"This is our little brother Tibut," Huyani responded, affectionately kissing the child's head. "Would you like to hold him?"

"Are you sure he'll be okay with that?"

"Certainly."

Mariah raised the baby into her arms and tapped his nose playfully. Tibut squealed happily and burrowed further into her arms. The girls started cooing again. Even Jag, Aari, and Kody felt their lips pulling back into grins.

Tegan and Mariah took turns cuddling Tibut, who blissfully shared their warmth, while Huyani and Akol described the Elders' request. The five were unsure.

"You mean they want to meet us right now?" Kody asked.

"No, not now; in the morning," answered Huyani. "Besides, it is only proper for the hosts to meet with their guests, correct?"

Jag rubbed the back of his neck. "I suppose so. It's just . . . it's a little unnerving, you know?"

"There is nothing to worry about, my friend," Akol replied understandingly. "The Elders are wonderful people. They will be pleased to meet you all."

The seven of them chatted for a little while more before Huyani and Akol left, carrying Tibut. The five bade each other good night and the boys headed back toward their *neyra*. They were all wondering what the meeting with the Elders would bring even as they laid themselves down to sleep, yawning.

* * *

The next morning, a luscious breakfast was served inside Huyani's *neyra*. The siblings and the friends sat down, conversing noisily, Kody naturally being the one with the best tales.

The five were finishing off their meal when they were met by a voice outside calling out in Akol and Huyani's native tongue. The siblings chorused in like manner. The door to Huyani's *neyra* opened inward, letting in a blast of sunlight. A tall figure clad in a black-and-silver cloak stepped in, silhouetted against the glare with four other forms falling in gracefully behind him. The smell of pine needles and mountain air tickled the five's noses, and Tegan let out a quiet sneeze as they stared at the newcomers in awe. There was something regal about them; the fine facial features and the kindly demeanor radiated congeniality, while their intelligent eyes and stately posture commanded attention and respect.

One of the adults, a green-eyed woman with dark, wavy hair and light brown skin, turned to meet their gaze and flashed a disarming smile. In a melodiously accented voice, she murmured, "Do not fear, young ones." The friends were captivated—there was a magnetic air about the woman that drew them in.

Akol and Huyani stepped in between their guests and the newcomers. "Jag, Aari, Kody, Mariah, and Tegan," Akol said in a respectful tone, "these are the Tribe's Elders: Tikina, Nageau, Saiyu, Ashack, and Tayoka." In his own language, he introduced the friends to the five Elders.

Nageau took a step forward and gazed steadily into Jag's eyes. The lanky teenager was unsure what to do, so he dipped his head as gracefully as he could and mumbled, "Nice to meet you, sir."

His friends bit their lips in order to not smile at his self-consciousness. Nageau, on the other hand, lit up. He held Jag's shoulders and roared with laughter. "No need for that, Jag," he said. He spoke in English although, like Tikina, his voice had an accent to it. He looked at Jag and nodded approvingly, as if assessing the teenager's build, then turned to look at the others. "Would it be a fair assumption to say that you are all around fifteen or sixteen years in age?"

The five looked a little surprised. "Yes, sir," Jag affirmed.

Huyani giggled, and the friends gave her a questioning look. "You need not call the Elders *sir* or *madam*," she told them. "You may address them simply as Elder."

Elder Saiyu spoke aloud next. The friends had no idea what she was saying as she only spoke in her native tongue. Tikina stepped in, explaining that out of the Elders, only she herself and Nageau had the special gift of omnilinguism. She translated what Saiyu had said: "I am relieved that you are all recovering from your terrible accident. I trust Akol and Huyani have been treating you well?"

"Where to even begin?" Tegan said, a small smile appearing on her lips. "They've helped us so much. They looked after us, fed us, gave us warm clothing to wear, and they even explained a bit about the village to us. We couldn't have asked for better people to take care of us."

"We are delighted to hear those kind words." Tikina looked over at Tegan. The expression on the Elder's face was eerily familiar and it had an almost feline quality to it. *Where have I seen that look before?* Tegan wondered.

"Would you be more comfortable sitting?" offered Huyani politely, and when everyone nodded, led them into the living quarters of her *neyra*. The twelve of them, including Huyani and Akol, crammed into the smaller division. Once they'd settled in, Nageau asked the five, "How long have all of you known each other?"

Jag's eyes narrowed and he responded instead with, "What we'd really like to know is where we are and when we can go back home."

The Elders glanced at each other, not quite knowing what to say. Tayoka finally broke the odd silence by speaking in his language while pointing at the five, then turning to Ashack and adding something with a snort of mirth. The villagers all laughed as Huyani and Akol explained to the five. "Elder Tayoka says that we have never ever had visitors, and now that we have five . . . all they want to do is get away from here!"

Nageau, chuckling, added, "And he blames Ashack's stern looks for scaring you away." Noting the tentative expressions on the five's faces, he continued. "Worry not, though. Tayoka is always searching for someone to poke fun at."

Jag raised an eyebrow. "Reminds me of someone else I know." He, Aari, Tegan, and Mariah cast meaningful looks at Kody.

"I don't know what they're talking about," he protested to the others, prompting another round of laughter. This time, the teenagers joined in.

With the atmosphere now more relaxed, Nageau leaned back in his place and looked at the five. "We do not intend to let your questions go unanswered, but we will enlighten you in due course. There is a saying amongst our people: 'Only the patient bear catches the leaping salmon.' But even then, he has to be at the right place and at the right time." Nageau smiled. Catching his drift, the five nodded. "So, how long have you known each other?"

Jag drummed his fingers on his lap and said, "To put it plainly, forever would be the answer."

"That is a while."

"It is. We've actually known each other since we were really young."

"Where you come from, do you all spend much time with each other?"

Aari nodded. "Absolutely."

Tikina smiled, then turned to Kody. "Huyani has told me that you are a food enthusiast. Do—"

The friends burst into peals of laughter until they were gasping for air. Tegan exclaimed, "Enthusiast? You're being way too kind."

Kody gave her a resentful look and Aari had to hold him back from lunging at her as she laughed gaily.

Mariah jumped in. "Well, what Huyani told you is right. Back where we come from, pretty much everyone knows about his love for food. The real question is, where does he hide all those calories? I mean, get a load of this." She lifted one of Kody's arms. "Look at that. They're like chicken wings." Kody snatched his arm back, mumbling something unintelligible.

Tikina laughed, her eyes sparkling. Nageau translated for the other Elders, most of whom broke into guffaws. Tikina collected herself after a few moments. "Now, let Kody speak for himself on this one," she said. "So Kody, what are your other interests?"

Darting a glance at his friends, relieved that he finally had a say, he replied, "I'm into sports, like ice hockey—"

"What is that?" Akol asked inquisitively.

Kody proceeded to describe the sport enthusiastically. A bemused Akol nodded and commented, "It sounds like a fast-paced game. Do many people participate in this sport?"

Kody grinned. "You betcha. It's fairly popular where I come from. And you're right—it's one of the fastest team sports in the world."

"You need to clarify that you enjoy watching, brother," Jag said with a chuckle.

"Details, details…"

"What more do you enjoy?" Akol asked.

After a moment's thought, Kody said softly, "I love planes—I grew up around them."

"Oh?"

"Yeah." His voice grew even softer. "My dad's a pilot at the Air Force base near our home. He's been teaching me to fly one for a while."

His friends, sensing the swing in his mood, shifted a little closer to him. Tegan turned to the Elders. "Kody's one of those simple guys. Doesn't hold a grudge, doesn't take much to keep him happy."

Tikina, also seeming to know where the conversation would lead, nodded at Jag in a manner that seemed precautionary, as if she was attempting to avoid the subject that was his father. "And what about you? What do you like?"

Taken aback by the sudden query, he shrugged and responded dryly, "I love parkour. These four like watching, but Tegan's the one who's started getting into it."

"What is parkour?" Nageau asked the five curiously.

"It's a physical discipline," Jag answered, sitting up a little straighter. "It's a sport that requires you to overcome obstacles by running and climbing to quickly get from one point to another. My brother and I train together often."

"Ah!" Nageau raised his finger and wagged it. "Yes, we are familiar with this. You will be pleased to know that the youths of this village tend to do this routinely. However, we have not given it a name. But surely there is more in your scope of interest. Do tell."

Jag poked himself subconsciously on the cheek. "It's . . . I'm not very—"

"He's a really good football player," Tegan supplied. "He plays for our school team. Says that he enjoys the grueling training, which is odd. My honest opinion."

"You know what *I* find odd about this guy?" Kody asked. "The fact that he's pretty much obsessed with being faster than he already is."

Nageau raised an eyebrow. "Why would you want that, Jag?"

"It's not necessarily about wanting speed," Jag answered. "It's more about being sharp, being on the edge and pushing yourself as far as you can go both physically and mentally. Beating your own record, striving to be better, you know?"

"We can appreciate that," the Elder said, dipping his head agreeably, then nodded at Mariah, the question not needing to be spoken.

"Oh, my turn?" Mariah sat straight. "Well… I'm usually surrounded by books. All of us read, but I'm pretty sure Aari and I read the most. Horseback riding's my thing as well and Tegan's picking up the sport too. The guys are too afraid to give it a shot, though."

"Not true," Kody argued. "I was going to try it this summer, but then we had this trip planned before vacation started."

"Mmph—I'll let you get away with that excuse. For now." Returning her gaze to the Elders, Mariah said, "I love challenges, and I don't back down from one. Throw something at me, anything."

"Okay." Aari chucked a pebble at Mariah that he'd found while walking to Huyani's *neyra.* He grinned as it hit her smack on the side of her head.

"You loser," she growled. "You know I didn't mean it literally." She rubbed her head. "If I could, I would've flipped that thing around and made it hit you between the eyes."

Aari's grin widened. "Yeah, and that's called telekinesis, by the way. And if you had it, I think we can all agree that Kody would find himself headfirst in the nearest garbage disposal every time he goes off wise-mouthing." The friends laughed again.

The teenagers didn't catch the look of intrigue the Elders shared. The tribe members sat quietly for a while, observing the five intently as they spoke amongst themselves. Finding a brief pause in their conversation, Tikina turned to Aari. "And what of you, youngling?"

"Me?" Aari stretched out his toes. "Eh... People always say that I'm big on learning, which is true, I suppose. It's cool to know how things works. My parents say I'm pretty good with my hands—used to try and build stuff even when I was younger. That's what happens when you watch a lot of old-school cartoons and read Calvin and Hobbes, I guess." He grinned.

"He's a pretty tech-savvy guy too," Jag said. "Aren't you, Aari?"

"I'm a novice compared to everyone else in the field, really..."

"You gotta start somewhere. We all do. Compared to us you're a whiz."

"Oh, stop it. You're making me blush."

Jag snorted and raised his eyes heavenward.

A lull ensued, and Saiyu spoke up, Akol translating her words for the friends. "Elder Saiyu asks if you have any brothers or sisters."

Surprised by the switch in subjects, the five answered that all had siblings except for Mariah, and she was contented that way. "As long as I have either my family or my friends around," she said, "I'm good to go."

"What if we're not with you?" Tegan teased.

Mariah suddenly looked uncomfortable at the notion. "I can function, obviously," she said, though even to her friends her words lacked conviction.

The Elders had a few more questions for the friends and the five freely shared whatever they could, and the talk was sprinkled with funny stories and bantering. After a while, Tikina realized they'd left Tegan out during their earlier conversation and looked at the sixteen-year-old. "We have not forgotten about you, youngling. What do you like? What are your interests?"

Tegan made a funny face. "I thought I got a lucky break, but you got me. I don't really like talking about myself." She remained silent for a while, then shrugged. "I don't know . . . I like drawing,

I guess, but I really haven't been doing much of it lately. Most of the time, they're just sketches anyway. I love nature and animals, probably because my uncle used to run a small zoo and I'd help out a lot." She thought for a moment, then stretched her arms behind her friends' shoulders. "And I love my best friends. These four—I'd give my life to protect them in a heartbeat."

Jag and Aari, on either side of her, grinned warmly and Kody reached over to ruffle her hair. Growing up in a tight-knit neighborhood with their families as close friends, the group had naturally nurtured a strong bond.

Kody's cheery appearance gradually faded. His face grew sullen, his green eyes downcast. He slowly pulled back. His friends looked at him with concern. They missed their families as well, but not knowing where or what condition his father was in must have been harder on Kody than the others could have imagined. Mariah and Aari gently pulled him into a group hug with the others and they held him close.

Silence loomed around them until Jag stirred a little and looked up at the Elders. "Okay," he said quietly. "You've asked many questions and we've answered them." He hesitated, then continued. "I guess what I'm trying to say is, you promised you'd answer our questions."

Nageau smiled kindly at the five as he looked at each one of them. "You have all gone through a difficult ordeal. You need to rest and recover. Here in our village, you will be safe and cared for. We will answer your questions as promised, but for now, you must restore your energy. When you are revitalized, you will be ready to hear the answers to your questions. We will see each other soon, perhaps tomorrow."

Upon hearing that, the other Elders stood up and smiled at the five and made their way to the door. Nageau, the only one still sitting, got to his feet, unfolding his six-foot-five frame. He gave the friends a look of assurance and said his goodbye, then led the other four Elders out of the *neyra*.

Mariah squinted toward where the Elders had been just a few moments ago. After a moment of quiet, she said, "We practically got ripped off here. I'm kind of tempted to go after them and make them answer our questions."

Aari rested an elbow on her shoulder, a gesture he used to calm her down and keep her seated. Like Mariah, he was irked at the Elders. *But they're kind of right,* he thought discontentedly. *I still wish they'd answered our questions, though.* An odd silence engulfed the shelter.

Finally breaking the awkward feeling in the *neyra*, Jag stood up and stretched. "Man, I need a walk. Who's with me?"

Tegan got to her feet as well. "I am. I need some fresh air." She looked at Huyani and Akol. "May we?"

The siblings looked at each other for a few moments, then Huyani said, "You may, but please stick to the path behind the trees. Our valley is large, and the Elders have told us beforehand that we must keep you safe." It appeared that she was about to say something more, but she didn't continue. The five didn't think much about it and nodded in acceptance.

As Tegan and Mariah gently pulled Kody up, Jag said, "We'll just be hanging around our shelters, then."

Akol nodded. "Sure. We will bring your afternoon meal later. Or would you like to eat in here?"

"We'll have it out there, if you don't mind."

"Good as done, my friend."

"Thanks."

The friends said goodbye to the siblings and walked out of the *neyra,* then headed toward their shelters. They were silent the whole way, but at last Kody voiced what was on their minds.

"I want to go home."

11

That evening as the Elders were walking together toward their assembly *neyra,* Ashack became increasingly aware of a pair of mischievous gray eyes on him. He spun around and snapped, "What?"

Tayoka grinned. "What?"

"What?"

"What, what?"

Ashack was about ready to knock his head on the nearest tree. "Stop playing games with me, and tell me what!"

"What."

"Tayoka . . ." There was a hostile note in his voice.

Tayoka's grin widened. "Well, you told me to tell you 'What', so I did."

Saiyu and Tikina let out hushed laughs and Nageau smiled. Ashack glared at Tayoka, but the younger Elder only did a happy one-handed walkover followed by a handspring.

"Why are you so joyous?" Ashack growled, his curly black hair being blown every which way by the strong breeze. He tried in vain to push it back into place.

"I do not know exactly," Tayoka said, straightening, "but I feel glad to have met the five young ones and am exhilarated to have learned a few things about them." His festive expression gradually faded. "But it makes me feel a little guilty to be in such a mood when the five were rather unsettled as we left them earlier today."

Ashack voiced what had been on his mind. “While that may be true, my concern is for Fiotez’s health at the moment. Does anyone know his condition?”

Tikina nodded. “I checked on him after we parted at Huyani’s earlier today.” The other Elders stopped walking and looked at her keenly. She gazed along the pathway to their assembly *neyra*. Tall, elegant spruce trees bordered the sides of the path the Elders were walking on. Finally, she sighed. “It does not look as if he is faring any better, though it is hard for me to tell. With what I gathered from Huyani and Saiyu, he is rarely conscious and none of the herbs we are using seem to work. It is uncanny for this to happen. Our people have lived long and well in this valley; what could possibly be the reason for Fiotez’s condition?”

“Whatever the case, it is crucial that we find a remedy,” Tayoka said. “This *must* be solved quickly before others begin to fall ill.”

Nageau agreed. “We should also continue to keep Fiotez in isolation to protect everyone else.” He turned to Tikina and Saiyu. “But what of you? Are you and Huyani doing anything to protect yourself while tending to Fiotez?”

Tikina stood quietly for a moment. Her hand reached for the crystal pendant hanging down her neck and clasped it, then she looked at her mate and said gently, “We will be fine, Nageau. We have to take care of this. You know it well.”

Ashack shook his head and his stoic features softened as he put a muscular arm around Saiyu. “We do know it. But the situation is potentially unsafe. As Nageau said, you, your granddaughter, and Saiyu risk becoming ill.”

“It is a chance we must take,” Saiyu said firmly, turning to give him a quick hug. Then she looked at her cohorts. “Come. We have dallied long enough here.”

The Elders started to their assembly *neyra* again, never once spotting the shadow up in the trees about fifty yards behind them. Dark blue eyes had watched their every move and sharp ears had heard their every word. As the Elders walked, the lithe figure, clad in a sleeveless moose-hide jacket with white seams, leapt silently like a phantom onto a branch in the next tree. He kept in pace with the Elders until, on his last jump, a protruding sliver of bark pierced the skin on his right palm when he landed. He bit his lip and hissed in annoyance.

Nageau's head snapped up and he looked around at the trees. His companions turned to him curiously. "What is the matter?" Saiyu asked.

Nageau stood still as his eyes narrowed, and focused on a particular tree not too far behind the Elders. He said nothing for a moment, then slowly turned away from the tree and muttered, "I thought I heard something." With one last scan over the tree line, Nageau continued on, the other Elders falling in step.

The youth in the tree exhaled in relief. He was furious with himself for being that careless when he knew so well that Nageau had highly sharpened senses. A split-second decision to leap back to a tree away from Nageau's line of sight saved him from being caught.

Now, with the splinter removed and keeping well back, the shadow leapt quietly among the next few trees until the Elders entered their assembly *neyra*. He waited for a while, then, certain that the older villagers had settled inside, descended the tree swiftly, confident that he was a safe distance away from the shelter.

Like his brethren, this tribe member possessed inherent abilities. However, there was always the occasional person who was born with multiple powers and no one knew why it was so. This youth was one of those special ones. The people of the tribe would always wait to be bestowed by the Elders with a particular crystal meant for the individual. This youth had been extremely impatient and, in his selfishness, had broken one of the cardinal rules of the tribe. He had stolen some of the crystals from the temple to advance his abilities.

Lurking in the shadows of the subalpine trees, he calmed himself and entered a meditative-like state. Nageau had heightened senses; so did he. Focusing on the *neyra*, he strained to listen in on the Elders' discussion.

Tikina's voice became audible: "*. . . 'Shades of Earth, Sky, River, Mist and Fire', it says. We thought the prophecy was* *referring to the crystals, but I think we have to see it a little differently . . .*"

"Please explain," Tayoka prodded.

Tikina was animated. "Let us look at the prophecy again, my friends, especially the third line." Breathlessly, she said, "'*Gaze upon them for portals that decipher* . . ." She paused to study the expressions of her companions, wondering if any of them were able to foresee her line of thought. There was silence in the room as the other four Elders unconsciously lowered their heads and watched the fire burning in the fire pit, deep in thought.

Tikina tried a different angle. "Think about this: When you meet someone for the first time, where does your gaze fall?"

She watched them intently, waiting for some kind of reaction. She saw Saiyu's countenance light up with realization. "The eyes!" she exclaimed, then after a moment's thought, added, "What if the shades mentioned in the prophecy refers not to the colors of the crystals, but instead, to the color of the youths' eyes?"

There was dead silence.

A smile grew on Tikina's face. "Exactly."

"My goodness." Saiyu shook her head in disbelief. "And it does make sense, does it not? Eyes *are* portals. They are windows to the soul."

Nageau smiled admiringly at his mate. "The younglings' eyes are a perfect reflection of the shades mentioned in the prophecy. *Earth* is obviously brown, and *Sky*, blue. *Mist* is gray. *Fire* . . ."

"I suppose that would be amber," Saiyu answered.

Nageau turned to Tikina. "What about *River*? We have seen different shades of rivers."

Tikina smiled mysteriously. "True . . . however, what if it is referring to Esroh Lègna, the river in our valley?"

Nageau's eyebrows rose to his hairline at the notion. "Green . . . like the boy Kody's eyes, perhaps?"

Tikina nodded slowly. "And brown, like the girl Mariah's eyes."

Tayoka caught on. "Amber, like Jag's."

"And Tegan, her eyes are gray, like mist," Saiyu added.

Ashack, under the eager, hungry look in the other Elder' gazes, reluctantly finished, "And blue, like Aari's eyes."

They all leaned back in astonishment. "Amazing," Nageau murmured.

Tayoka grinned. "Tikina, you are brilliant."

Tikina shrugged modestly and smiled.

Ashack folded his arms and looked at his companions. "Does anyone else think this seems too easy?"

"Well, perhaps so," Tayoka said, "but Ashack, look: What are the chances of the events that have happened, happening?"

"I beg your pardon?"

"What I mean is, consider the chain of events that have unfolded lately. Remember the skycraft that took on the image of Cerraco as it soared overhead?"

Nageau nodded. "Just as foretold in our ancient narratives."

"Exactly. Also, what are the chances of having these five youths brought to us from Cerraco, by the Guardians themselves? It was not four, it was not six. It was exactly *five*, and they are not old—no, they are young, like 'saplings'." Tayoka looked around at his companions and saw them listening carefully. He continued. "Lastly, what are the chances of the shades mentioned in the prophecy matching the eyes of the outsiders? Could all of that be mere coincidence?"

That quieted Ashack. The black-haired man looked at the fire again and shook his head slowly. "I agree. There is too much here to be purely coincidental. But as I said earlier, it seems all too easy."

"Maybe so," Saiyu said. "But perhaps the miracle of the prophecy lies in its elegant simplicity."

Ashack nodded slightly. "But there is much more to the prophecy, and we all know how the other verses foreshadow future events. I just hope that deciphering those verses will be as effortless as this was."

"I hope so too, Ashack." Nageau stroked his chin, eyes half-closed. "The prophecy . . . It does paint a disconcerting picture of the future."

"My thoughts are with the five," Tikina said quietly, looking at her mate. "Will they—if indeed they are the ones—be able to stand together and carry the weight that we will place on their shoulders?"

Nageau wore an unsettled look. His mind traveled back to a time over three decades ago when he had been called upon to make one of the most difficult decisions as an Elder. Before he could walk further down that painful road, he was brought back to the present when Tikina rested a cool hand on his arm. He looked up at her, slightly startled, then quickly cleared his throat and responded. "Events are unfolding out in the world that will require their combined force," he said. "We are called upon to train and prepare them, and when they are ready, assign them their crystals."

"But they are so young," Saiyu murmured. "It seems unfair to expect so much out of them at such a tender age."

"If they are the ones, though, then destiny will guide them." Nageau attempted to assure the women, though Tikina couldn't help but notice a perturbed look in his eyes. "Moreover," he added quietly, "they will not be alone out there."

Everyone nodded, knowing full well what he meant.

The youth hiding behind the tree eased his eyes open. He had learned enough for now. He rose to his feet and sprinted through the trees like a spirit, away from the Elders' assembly *neyra*. He weaved his way until he spotted one of the three bridges that connected the north and south sides of the village, which were separated by the gentle flowing waters of Esroh Lègna.

He broke from the darkness of the trees and, ignoring the bridge, leapt thirty feet over the water to the other side in one smooth motion to throw off anyone who might possibly be following him. He landed softly, following through with a roll, then rose to his feet. He threw a glance over his shoulder at the river, immensely satisfied with his nimbleness and the fact that no one was tailing him. Slowing to a walk, he strode next to the river, following it downstream to the second bridge and crossing back to the south side of the village where his cohorts were waiting for him.

Along the winding path surrounded by trees, four buildings rose into sight; a massive teal-colored glass structure with timber frames, flanked on the right by a combined stable and barn. Next to it was a nondescript but hardy-looking wooden construction used for storage, and beside it was a uniquely-designed tool and workshop enclosure that exuded a certain charm. Together, these buildings made up the resource hub of the village.

Rounding the immense glass building, the youth walked through the doors of the stable. Inside was a group of villagers about his age, chatting and caring for the horses inside the structure.

One of the youths, sporting a brown mohawk, saw the lone one entering and nudged the others. They all looked up. The one with the mohawk grinned cockily. "How was your little sleuthing expedition, Hutar?"

Hutar leaned against a stall. The horse inside, a young, frisky stallion with a shiny black coat poked his head out curiously and Hutar fed it some hay. The horse's velvety lips tickled the palm of his hand. The girl inside who was grooming the horse paused and stepped out of the stall. A couple of other girls stepped out as well from where they were taking care of horses in other stalls. The boys—heavily outnumbering the girls—were sitting on bales of hay or standing around.

Hutar said nothing for a time, content to interact with the horse. His sharp, calculating blue eyes contrasted with his well-tanned skin. His black hair was shortly cropped at the sides and fuller on top.

"Well?" repeated the youth with the mohawk. "What happened?

Hutar snorted. Jabbing a finger at the mohawk, he said, "You are an impatient one, Relsuc." He paused for a few moments, then continued. "From what I have learned, the Elders have concluded the first verse of the prophecy, '*Shades of Earth, Sky, River, Mist and Fire*', corresponds with our unwanted guests' eyes."

Relsuc frowned. "You mean to say the shades mentioned in the prophecy refer to the shades of eyes? We always figured they were related to the crystals."

Shrugging, Hutar said, "Who knows what they really refer to."

"And the shades match *exactly* with five outsiders' eyes?" Relsuc asked incredulously. "That is unbelievable."

"Believable or not, that is what the Elders accept as true."

One of the boys milling around spoke up. "But we cannot forget that the Elders had met with the outsiders this morning. Do you think they would make a petty blunder on such a significant matter?"

"Who knows?" Hutar gave the boy a look that told him to shut up.

One of the girls wiped her brow and prodded, "Did they mention anything else?"

"Not that I caught. They will discuss more tomorrow, I assume." Hutar turned around and stroked the horse that he'd given the hay to. The young animal eyed him with a glint of mischief in its eyes and then grabbed Hutar's arm in its mouth. Hutar grunted in surprise.

Freeing himself, he turned to the others and said, "We must assume the Elders are in agreement on the idea of teaching those outsiders our ways and entrusting them with the crystals. It is not right; I myself have gone through the prophecy, and not anywhere did it mention that the ones to fulfill it will be from the outside world."

"Now wait a minute," protested an attractive, auburn-haired native. She placed one hand on her hip and held up two fingers. "Two things: One, while you do have a point, nowhere in the prophecy does it say people from this tribe would fulfill the prophecy, either. Two, we cannot assume that all the Elders are on board, because Ashack is naught but a grump and tends to be a skeptic. And remember, that was only the first verse. There is more."

"Matikè does have a point, Hutar," Relsuc said. "Until you get sufficient information and further decisions from the Elders, you cannot risk doing anything. And by you, I mean our whole group. Just like you, we are opposed to the idea of the outsiders being the fulfillment to our people's prophecy, but we need to tread cautiously here. You know we trust you as our leader, but we cannot afford to jump to conclusions. Also, I cannot begin to imagine the consequences that would arise from our defiance of the Elders if this comes out."

"No one will find out," Hutar said icily. "But I know, I just know, that somehow, these five are going to be trained by the Elders."

Relsuc shrugged apologetically. "Normally I would agree, considering how many times you have been correct when you make such suppositions, but at the moment, I am going to have to stop and wait and watch for a little while."

The group agreed quietly. Hutar, resenting it when the crowd went against him, kept a cool face. "Fine. We will each do our part to find out what we can before making a move. Meanwhile," he said with a cold glint in his eyes, "I suggest a few of us get friendly with the five. It would be better for those of us who are omnilingual to put that ability to good use."

"That leaves me out," Relsuc said thankfully. "But you, my friend, are fully capable. So is Aesròn." Aesròn, Relsuc's cousin with an aquiline nose and very light green eyes, grinned. Then his grin vanished as he said, "There is one little problem, though. How do we get close to them? I am sure they are under some kind of order preventing them from mingling with us."

A girl near one of the stalls leaned over the trough she was using to bathe a foal and yelled, "That is probably right! Huyani and Akol are seeing to that, are they not?"

Relsuc nodded. "I have spied on them shepherding the outsiders."

Hutar put a hand on one of Aesròn's wide shoulders and said with a flash of a malevolent grin, "Talking to Huyani would be no problem. There are ways to accomplish this."

"Do not underestimate her, though," one of the boys said, too quietly for anyone to pay attention to him.

"Her brother is rigid when it comes to following orders given by the Elders," Matikè countered. She had gone back inside the stall and was using a pick to clean the young horse's hooves.

"Not a problem. Between us, there has been talk going around that Akol is taking an interest in you."

The fair-skinned girl fumbled with the pick and blushed. "It is but a rumor. And besides, how would I be of help? I only speak in our native tongue."

"I did not say you would have to speak with the outsiders," Hutar replied smoothly.

Matikè finished picking the horse's hooves and stepped out of the stall again. "Listen, Hutar. As much as I am not pleased with these five in our valley, I refuse to manipulate Akol." Hutar was losing patience. "Now *you* listen. When we first overheard the Elders talking after the Guardians brought those five, there was an explosion of speculation. We decided then to pick sides. You stayed with us while your sibling ran away, afraid of what would happen if the Elders caught us. I repeat; you *stayed*. Now you must commit."

Matikè's eyes shot daggers at the group's tall leader. "Alright, fine, I will do it," she snapped. "But I will not be happy about it."

"No one said you had to be," Relsuc grinned.

Aesròn turned to Hutar. "Perhaps we should leave before sundown so we can join them for their evening meal."

"Good idea." Hutar smiled. "Matikè, you will be joining us."

Matikè swore vehemently under her breath and turned her back to the pair as she continued to care for the horse.

Back in their *neyra* after the Elders' meeting, Nageau sat at a table, gazing out the window silently. He hadn't spoken a word since he and Tikina entered the shelter, but his mate knew what was upsetting him. Holding up a mug, she brought a hot drink to Nageau and rested it on the table. He looked up, slightly surprised, then gave her a small smile in thanks. As he took a sip, Tikina sat down across from him. "Nageau," she said gently.

He glanced at her, then back out the window and sighed. "I am sorry, love. I should not bring such a discouraging atmosphere into a house of peace."

She took one of his hands and inspected his fingers quietly for a minute before murmuring, "Things of the past must remain in the past, Nageau."

He put the mug down and leaned back. His mouth moved as if he was trying to find the right words to speak, but no sound came out. Pulling his hand back from Tikina's soft ones, he buried his face in his palms. "I know it has been over twenty-five years, but it still weighs me down," he finally managed. "And now, with the arrival of the five, I cannot help but wonder if I did the right thing back then. What if there had been a better alternative? What if—"

"You did the right thing," she told him firmly. "We do not know for certain that the decision you made at the time has anything to do with the storm that is brewing in the world outside. In all my years that I have known you, beloved, you have never wavered even a hair's breadth from what is best for our people. You did the right thing."

He gazed at her and in his usually spirited eyes she could see him struggling to believe her. She looked down at the table for a moment, then reached for his hand again. He let her take it and tightly held her hand even as she did his. Not another word was shared as they sat together, staring out the window, taking in the strength of each other's company.

12

The five were lazing around outside the boys' *neyra*. They'd enjoyed a good lunch brought to them earlier by Akol and Huyani. Now, sitting out in the early-evening sun and feeling the cool breeze on their skin, the friends mulled over their situation.

Yawning, Mariah dropped her head to Tegan's shoulder and closed her eyes briefly. Kody's voice forced her eyes open again. "I don't know about you guys," he said, "but I personally am not eager to spend a few more days here. Sure, the food's good and Akol and Huyani are real nice, but I want out. I need to find my dad and find my way back to civilization." Jag muttered his agreement, and Tegan remained quiet.

Mariah and Aari glanced at each other, shifting uncomfortably. "Guys, look," Mariah said. "We're somewhere in northern Canada, in a forest, with the nearest possible town a long way from here. I'm talking maybe dozens or even hundreds of miles. I think we're better off staying put for now. Then those Elders can answer *our* questions, too. If we leave before they talk with us again, we could miss out on something really important. For all we know, once they speak with us, they could show us the way out or something. There might even be people out there looking for us."

Jag's head jerked up. "Right. The search and rescue teams should definitely be out looking for us."

Tegan shrugged. "They might have already done that."

"We've been here for at least a week now," Aari said. "Why haven't they found us yet?"

“It depends on how far from the crash site we are right now,” Jag answered. “I don’t know for sure how long we rode on those bears, but like Mariah said, we could be miles and miles from the crash site.”

“Yeah, but they’ve got helicopters and other aircraft. Surely they can spot a village from the sky.”

“But remember, the village is supposedly well-hidden. Isn’t that what the valley’s name means? Dema-Ki, the ‘Hidden Valley’? Akol mentioned it.”

Tegan pondered for a little while. “How long do these teams look for people before they call off a search?”

Jag snorted in response. “I don’t know. Shouldn’t you? Your dad’s a cop, after all.”

Tegan laughed sheepishly. “Yeah, but I never paid attention to those things. Okay. Let’s say they located the plane we were in. Kody’s dad could have been found”—Kody perked up—“but then they don’t find us. They would have started searching the area around the crash site. They may have also checked the towns nearby.”

Mariah lifted her head off of Tegan’s shoulder. “So if my guess is right, based on the discussion so far . . . the rescue teams have no clue where we are.” She added with an attempt at dry humor, “And we’re possibly on the news, with headlines screaming things like ‘TEENAGERS MISSING FROM CRASH SCENE’, ‘DAY WHATEVER OF MISSING KIDS’. Or quite possibly, ‘TEENAGERS ABDUCTED BY ALIENS!’”

Aari squinted at her. “You have the strangest mind.”

“Who, me? Nah, you’re looking at Exhibit F of weirdness. You want Exhibit A? Just turn your head and look at Kody.”

The five had to laugh. Laughing was always a thing with them, but given the situation they were in, the levity had a therapeutic effect.

“Well, I still want out,” Kody said, rubbing his eye.

Aari lay back on the grass with his hands laced behind his head and stared up at the clouds. “But heaven knows how we’ll even escape this place. We don’t have a map. Even if we did, we don’t have a compass to tell us which direction we're heading. Also, we've got to get past this wilderness first before reaching any village, town, or city." His analytical side had taken over. "Who knows what's out there? And you've got to take into account weather, food, water, emergency supplies, and shelter. And good clothing for this kind of environment, even though it's summertime."

"That's detailed."

"That's the truth, and it's no joke."

"I *know* it's no joke. And I'm not saying it's going to be a cakewalk, but I have a life and at the moment, it's not in my hands. I want it back in my hands. Who's with me?"

His friends kept silent and looked away, not meeting his gaze. Only Jag caught Kody's eye and gave him a quick, firm nod.

Content that he was not alone, Kody picked at a blade of grass. After a moment, he flicked it away and leaned back against the *neyra*. "It's not even nighttime and I'm feeling kind of drowsy."

"The meal was a little heavy," Tegan pointed out, eager to be on a different subject.

The five talked quietly about other things for a while before some of them slowly started to doze off until only Tegan and Jag remained awake. They gazed out at the river, both lost in their own thoughts and concerns.

Tegan shifted a little and stretched out her legs. "Jag?"

"Hm?"

"With all that we're going through right now . . . I want us to band together and not get pulled in different directions."

"We've always held together. What are you worried about?"

"We've held together through different situations before, sure. But this is *different*, Jag."

He turned and studied her closely, wondering where she was going with the conversation. She continued. "We just survived a plane crash. Kody has no clue where his dad is or what's happened to him, and we have no idea where we are. All these uncertainties . . ." She rubbed her forehead. "I guess what I'm trying to say is, I think there is a need here for us to stick together more than we've ever done before."

Jag's eyes narrowed as he began to read into her intention. "Go on," he said cautiously.

She turned now to look at him. "I think it's time that one of us steps up to lead the group."

Jag slowly crossed his arms. "We've never needed a leader, Tegan. We've been able to speak for ourselves and hold out on our own well enough."

Tegan noted his defensive posture and altered her tone. "Yeah, we can all speak for ourselves, but now it's time for us to speak in one voice. We need someone to keep this group together. I know we've never had someone formally leading us before, but you can't deny that we've looked towards you at times when we needed direction."

He held up a hand to stop her. "No. Don't even go there. I'm not cut out for this. Besides, we're friends. We're equals."

"Now don't you give *me* that. Sounds to me like an excuse for not stepping up to the plate." That earned her a sharp glare, but she pressed on. "We need you to take charge."

Jag looked away as a lump grew in his throat. The last time he'd taken responsibility for a group was nearly a year ago when he convinced a few friends to go rock climbing. His friends were new to the activity and he'd promised that he would take care of them. He could still clearly recall what had happened and flinched inwardly. The images were vivid, and as much as he tried to erase them, they stubbornly remained. Remembering the event was a gut-wrenching guilt trip.

Tegan gently nudged him and he looked back at her. She wore a concerned expression and, realizing what he had been thinking about, softened. "You can't keep blaming yourself for what happened to Roderick. It was an accident."

"An accident because *I* made a mistake up on the mountain—a mistake that paralyzed him from the waist down. Cade almost decked out, too. If it hadn't been for his safety harness . . . Roddy's wheelchair-bound because of me, Teegs. His life hasn't been the same since, and it never will be. And I'm responsible for that. I don't think I want to be accountable for anything else." His voice cracked, and he clamped his mouth shut.

She slid her arms around one of his. "You can't keep blaming yourself for this. It was an *accident*. No one could have known that cam was defective."

Jag shook his head, lowering his gaze. "I can't take the responsibility of heading our group." He ran his hands through his hair, digging his finger into the back of his head. "You guys are my second family. I don't trust myself to lead you. Why do you trust me?"

Letting out a sigh, Tegan rested her head on his shoulder. "Whether you realize it or not, you've been the one leading us throughout the years we've been together. It's only natural for you to take this up."

He didn't reply but rested his head against hers. The two leaned back, returning to their own thoughts. Tegan looked over at the other three as they slept and cracked a small smile. The group rarely ever napped; they didn't like wasting their day sleeping when there was the nighttime for that. Unbeknownst to them, the nights that were to follow would deprive them of more than a little sleep.

13

A knock sounded at the door.

Nageau rose to his feet from where he was sitting on a divan in the living quarter of his *neyra*. He opened the door and was astonished to find an elderly woman rapping at it with her knuckles. The lady paused with her fist halfway to the door when Nageau opened it.

"Mitska?" the Elder said worriedly. "What is the matter?"

Mitska had trouble speaking. Tikina appeared beside Nageau and gently ushered the older woman inside as her mate shut the door. Nageau got a cup of water and walked to the sofa where Tikina had settled their visitor. He passed Mitska the drink and let her catch her breath before asking, "Is something wrong?"

The elderly woman leaned against Tikina for support. "My mate has become ill. Normally the herbs I use work well, but this time, nothing is doing him good."

Tikina shot Nageau a wary look. "What are his symptoms?" she asked.

Mitska ventured to tell what had befallen her mate, describing some of the symptoms and his present condition. "Please, would you see to him?"

"Yes, of course."

Tikina got up and, leading the older woman outside by the hand, turned to Nageau, who had followed them. "Please warn the others, and then come. You know where the shelter is."

Nageau nodded and smiled reassuringly at Mitska, and the two Elders parted.

Tikina accompanied Mitska as they crossed the bridge to the north side of the village and entered a *neyra* nestled cozily among tall fir trees. The older woman opened the door and led Tikina to her bedroom. An old man lay on the bed, appearing deathly pale. He was conscious and, when he spotted the Elder, tried to sit up. Tikina gently stopped him from wasting precious energy and sat by his side, stroking his head. The man coughed and wheezed.

Without looking up, Tikina asked Mitska, "How long has he been like this?"

Mitska sighed. "He only became this ill last night, but it all began four or five days ago."

"And you are certain that you have tried all the herbs that are at our disposal?"

"Yes—and nothing seems to be helping. I considered calling Huyani to check on him, but I thought perhaps he may need the assistance of the Elders instead."

"That was a good choice." There was a rapping at the door and Tikina looked up. "That must be the others right now."

"I will let them in." The elderly woman bustled toward the door of her shelter and soon returned with the rest of the Elders.

Saiyu quickly walked over to Tikina. The two talked in hushed voices, then nodded at each other. Saiyu turned to the other Elders. "We should move him out."

The men understood and agreed.

"Did he have any contact with Fiotez?" Tikina asked Mitska, who shook her head.

"They rarely ever see each other, Elder Tikina. After all, Fiotez lives on the other side of the river. The only occasions when we meet would be during our community gatherings, and we have not had one for a while now."

"Then I do not think he contracted this sickness directly from Fiotez, though the symptoms appear to be similar . . . But we will not be able to tell for sure until we study further."

* * *

The Elders and Mitska gently brought Mitska's mate across the river to the convalescence shelter, careful to not attract too much attention. Huyani, who had been tending to Fiotez, was now checking on the old man. The Elders and Mitska walked out of the shelter, quietly closing the door behind them.

"What exactly has your mate been doing the past few days, Mitska?" Saiyu asked as they strode to the riverside. "We would like to know, to see if there is a link between what came over both Fiotez and him."

The old woman closed her eyes briefly and spoke. "A few days ago, before he became sick, he took our grandson on a trip to one of the lakes outside the valley. They both recounted that they had fun on this outing. However, during their return, my grandson told me that my mate was moving quite slowly as they drew closer to the village. Even though he is approaching seventy summers, he normally has much energy to spare."

Nageau frowned. "So something obviously happened during that time that caused your mate to fall ill. How is your grandson faring, Mitska?"

"From what I know, he is fine. Perhaps you would like to speak with him?"

The Elders glanced at one another and Nageau nodded.

"Come, then." Setting off at a surprisingly brisk pace, Mitska grabbed the folds of her long skirt and headed back to the north side of the river with the Elders in tow. When the elderly woman halted in front of a particularly large *neyra*, she knocked on the door. A young man opened it and when he saw Mitska, broke into a smile and gave her a warm hug. Mitska quickly told her son about his father's condition and the smile on his lips vanished. He looked past her to the Elders, nodded, and called for his son.

A bubbly young boy pranced to the door, munching on a fistful of roasted sweet potato. He had a cute smile plastered on his face that showed a gaping hole where he had lost a baby tooth. He gave his grandmother a tight hug and bowed at the Elders as his father invited them in.

As they settled down in the living room, Tikina asked the six-year-old to recount what had happened during his trip.

"Grandpa and I went hunting near that shallow lake outside the valley. We have been there a few times before." He stopped to munch on his potato.

"And what happened while you were there?" Nageau prompted.

"Grandpa showed me how to set a snare and we waited and waited but we did not catch anything so we went further into the forest. Grandpa made me my own bow and taught me how to shoot arrows—I nearly shot a squirrel out of a tree!" Clearly pleased with himself, the boy stopped talking and smiled.

"What else did you do out there?" Saiyu asked.

"I collected lots of berries, and Grandpa showed me what berries are good to eat and which ones were bad. He threw away a bunch of bright red ones that I had found and told me that they were poisonous. Then he showed me how to put up a tent." He paused thoughtfully. "Grandpa snored a lot at night. I heard something outside during the night but I think it heard Grandpa's snores and ran away." He had an innocent, sweet expression, but there was a cheeky glint in his eyes. The Elders had to try hard to not laugh.

"Tell us more," Tayoka prodded. "Did you do anything different from the last time you were there with your grandfather?"

The boy shook his head. "Nothing, really. It was a little hotter by the lake this time than the last trip and Grandpa ran out of water a couple of times. I was not as thirsty as he was," he said with a smile, "so I did not have to refill my water pelt, unlike Grandpa." He pouted then. "But Mama was not happy when she found out I did not drink much. She said that I should always drink enough water."

"And right she is," Saiyu said, smiling a little. "Continue."

The little boy tilted his head sideways, seeming to have not heard the prodding. "How is Grandpa? Father says he is ill. Why?"

"That is what we are trying to figure out. But do not worry," Nageau said kindly. "We will do our best to make him well again."

"Is there anything else that you can recall?" Tikina asked. "Perhaps when he showed signs of not being that well?"

The boy was silent for a while and then said, "We went for only two days . . . and on the second day—on our way back—he looked like he was having a little trouble walking. And his breathing was very noisy. He kept coughing, too. We stopped many times to rest when coming back home."

Tayoka was looking out a window, his mind appearing to be elsewhere. His gray eyes had an absent look to them. Then he stiffened. Quickly regaining his composure, he smiled at the little boy and jovially ruffled his hair. "Well, thank you," he said, a little too cheerily, and the other Elders caught it. "I think we have enough information for now. Keep praying for your grandfather and Fiotez."

The little boy nodded earnestly and padded off into a different quarter of the *neyra*. Tayoka walked out of the shelter, his companions following him closely after waving goodbye to Mitska and her son.

"Tayoka?" Saiyu asked worriedly as she caught up to him. "Is something the matter?"

Tayoka was rubbing his face. He paused for a moment and with a pained look in his eyes, said hoarsely, "The water. It is the source of the illness."

The Elders looked at each other. "The water?"

"Yes. When Fiotez became ill, it was after he drank the water from a stream. His friends did not drink the water, thus staying healthy. The boy's grandfather drank water from the lake, but the boy himself did not. And who winds up becoming sick?"

The Elders stared at Tayoka for some time, letting the words sink in. "The water is unsafe to drink?" Saiyu shuddered. "For ages our people have lived off the water from the rivers and lakes around our valley, and we have never had any problems. What has changed? What is causing this?"

They gazed at each other, thoughts swirling in their minds. *If* the water was unfit to drink . . . where did it leave the people of Dema-Ki?

Nageau broke the quiet. "Right now, this is only an assumption, albeit it has a strong foothold in the wall of reason. Still, we cannot announce it to our people just yet—"

"Why not?" Tayoka interjected. "They have a right to know. It concerns them greatly."

"You are right, they do. But we have the responsibility to be certain."

"How?"

"We need to test the water immediately, starting with Esroh Lègna."

14

Mariah woke with a start and found herself outside the boys' neyra. She lifted her head up and looked at her friends groggily. Jag was leaning against the outside of the shelter, fast asleep. Tegan's head rested on his shoulder and she too, was in slumber. Kody, who had dozed off next to Jag, had slumped down, giving the appearance of the famous hunchback of Notre Dame. Mariah cocked her head and giggled at the comical sight. Aari was at their feet, lying on his side on the cool grass and snoring softly.

She looked up at the sky as she stretched and was more than surprised to see the sun already slipping behind the mountains of the valley. Deciding that it was time for the group to get up, she tousled Tegan's hair with one hand and Jag's with the other. As the two started out of their nap, she went over to Kody on her hands and knees and tickled him until he woke up laughing hysterically. The laughter roused Aari, who, when he saw the sight, had to grin.

When the laughter died, Aari took a good look around. "We fell asleep!" he exclaimed.

Jag yawned. "It's not like we have anything better to do, anyway."

"I'm feeling a little ripe," Kody said. "And my head itches a tad. I need a shower, pronto."

"While we're on the subject, have you noticed that they have hot water piped to the shelters?" Aari, being the ever observant one, asked. "Like in Huyani's place. How do they do that? And the stove fire in Huyani's kitchen—it lights right up when she strikes a flint. How's that possible out here in the middle of nowhere?"

His friends were not entirely surprised by his astute observations. They simply hadn't paid attention to it, although it did intrigue them a little.

They were so deeply engaged in their chatter that they did not notice Akol sneaking up on them. Without so much as a warning, he pounced and grabbed Mariah by the shoulders from behind, hollering, "*Mariah!*"

Mariah shrieked and jumped to her feet. She whirled around and saw Akol grinning like a Cheshire cat. "Why you . . . !" With what was left of her dignity, she swatted him on the head and he accepted his punishment.

Rubbing his crown and still grinning, Akol bowed to her. "My sincere apologies, Mariah. I could not resist the temptation."

"Yeah, right." Mariah had to purse her lips in order to not burst out in amusement and threw her arms up. "Guys are the same everywhere."

Jag gave Akol a thumbs-up. "Kudos, bro. Way to keep that girl on her toes."

Mariah gave him a look. "Do you want to get hit on the head as well, Jag?"

"Uh, no. Sorry. I'll shut up."

"Please and thank you."

Akol smiled at the friends. "Huyani and I have a few interesting table games that we can play before the evening meal."

"Table games? Like board games or something?" Tegan asked with a tilt of her head.

"Something like that. My sister and I sense you are feeling a little bored, so we thought perhaps you would enjoy some entertainment."

"Could you dance like a monkey and tell some really funny jokes?"

Akol stared at Tegan, chagrined. "I cannot promise you the jokes, but the monkey thing, I can try."

The five laughed as they stood and followed Akol to Huyani's *neyra.*

* * *

Aari watched his four friends sit on either side of a wooden board. To him, it resembled a chess game except it was twice the size. The square quadrants were over a beautiful painting that showed an aerial view of a forest. There were game pieces representing wild animals and the elements, all artistically carved and vividly colored.

Akol was guiding Jag, Kody, Tegan, and Mariah as they played the game. Aari quietly stood up and walked over to stand beside Huyani, who was preparing their meal. He passed by a shelf that held a few rolled up parchments. Jag had spotted them earlier and asked what they were. Akol explained them to be maps that outlined the valley and the surrounding areas, and that Huyani used them to mark spots where she could gather certain herbs. Aari vaguely remembered the glint in Jag's eyes as he listened intently to Akol's words.

Huyani glanced at Aari and gave him one of her charming smiles. "Are you here to help me cook?" she teased.

"Sorry, that would be Kody's department. I'm a lousy cook." Aari leaned against one of the two counters. "Actually, I'm curious about something."

"Oh? And what might that be?"

"How do you get hot water running in here?" he asked.

Huyani's smile widened. "I did not think anyone would be interested. The answer is simple: We have pipes leading from our hot springs to almost every building in this valley."

"Hot springs?"

"Yes. Perhaps we will show you where they are located sometime."

"That would be great. But out here in the middle of nowhere, where do you get your pipes from?"

"Well, we make them."

"Make them—here?"

Huyani chuckled. "We may be isolated . . ." She paused, trying to think of the right words. ". . . but what you call utilities are not lost on us."

"What do you mean?"

"Mm, nothing," she backpedaled.

"I hate being kept in the dark."

"I apologize, I do not mean to. If it helps to allay your curiosity, the pipes are made of clay that is glazed."

"Glazed clay! Hey, that would be like the terra-cotta pipes people in ancient times used."

"Yes. My ancestors used clay to make pipes as well as other things. A lot of the workings that you see in Dema-Ki exist thanks to their insights and the handing over of that knowledge from one generation to another."

"That explains the hot water, but I've got other questions too." Aari pointed at the stove. "How do you start the fire up so easily like that? It seems to work like the gas stove I've got back home. And I've noticed glass being used in windows. Also, that humongous building across the river appears to be made entirely out of glass. How's that possible? How do you get glass here? Don't you need some kind of a machine to make it?"

Huyani smiled again. "My, you are a curious one, are you not?"

Impervious to the comment, Aari raised an eyebrow and prompted, "Well?"

Huyani put down her spatula and turned to him with a gentle look. "When the time is right, I am sure you will be shown how things work around here."

Aari rolled his eyes. "Here's that expression again: 'When the time is right.'"

She didn't respond to Aari's remark. Instead, she gave his arm a comforting rub and turned back to her cooking. "Please call the others. Let them know that the evening meal will be served shortly."

* * *

They were enjoying their meal when there was a knock outside Huyani's *neyra*. Huyani, curious, left her meal and opened the door. The handsome faces of her fellow villagers Hutar and Aesròn grinned at her. Her eyebrows rose in astonishment and she smiled sweetly at them. In her native tongue, she said, "Ah, what a surprise. What are you both doing here?"

"Actually, Matikè is here with us as well." The boys stepped apart, revealing the slender girl behind them. Matikè cracked a smile. "Hello, Huyani." The two girls hugged each other. As they let go, Hutar and Aesròn stepped between them, hiding Matikè from Huyani's view once again.

Huyani clasped her hands in front of her. "What are you doing here?" she repeated.

Hutar said smoothly, "The whole valley knows of our visitors. We thought it might be nice of us to acquaint ourselves with them."

Akol suddenly appeared beside his sister and leaned against the doorframe. "Hutar, Aesròn," he greeted. "What brings you here? Should you not be having your evening meal?"

"We were wondering if we could join you here and associate with the five guests," Hutar replied.

Akol raised his chin a little higher. "Why the sudden interest?" he asked, trying to keep suspicion out of his voice. He'd never really liked Hutar. There was something about the eighteen-year-old youth that just didn't click.

"It is not sudden, Akol. We have all been wondering. You know as well as we do that we have never had visitors in our quiet little valley. We would like to get acquainted with them. You could say we are intrigued."

Akol shook his head. "That is very considerate of you both, but the Elders have told us that the visitors are not to be exposed to the people just yet."

"Oh, it is not just the two of us, Akol," Aesròn said as he and Hutar stepped aside, revealing Matikè.

The girl offered Akol a faint smile. "Hello, Akol. How are you?"

Akol's eyes widened a little and he fumbled with his words. "Uh, just fine, thank you. I did not realize you were here with these two."

Matikè nodded. "We would like to get to know the visitors. Do you mind if we join you for the evening meal? It smells like you have prepared something scrumptious."

Akol looked to Huyani for an answer just as his sister caught a quick exchange of glances between Hutar and Matikè. Matikè bowed her head slightly and stared up at Akol with saddened eyes. "Well, alright then. I suppose we shall take your silence as a refusal."

Just as she turned to leave with Hutar and Aesròn, Akol blurted, "No! It is quite alright. You may join us, but please do not disquiet our guests. They are still recovering from their ordeal."

As the three youths took off their shoes before entering, Huyani pulled Akol aside. "What is the matter with you?" she hissed. "The Elders will not be pleased if they learn we allowed our people to make contact with these five."

Akol shrugged defensively. "I am sorry—I did not know how to turn them away."

"It was more like you did not know how to turn Matikè away. Listen to me, brother. You cannot, absolutely *cannot* allow her to curry favors with you like she did just now. I feel she was using your emotions for her to get inside with the other two."

Akol huffed. "Impossible. No one knows my feelings for her except you, and I know you would not tell a soul unless I agreed."

"No, I would not. But I have heard talk going around. This is not good, Akol."

"I promise it will not happen again." Akol led the way into the dining quarter of Huyani's *neyra*.

The friends looked up from their meal in surprise at the newcomers. Mariah and Tegan gave each other glances when they spotted the two male youths. *Dang*, Mariah thought. *What's this? The Village of the Gorgeous Genes?*

One of the newcomers, a youth with close-cropped black hair and dark blue eyes set above high cheekbones, took stock of the five even as they studied him. He looked to be around the same age as Akol and was built much like him, with well-toned arms and a tall, athletic body. He wore a brown hide jacket with white seams and his skin was tanned like Akol's, though Mariah sensed the three arrivals were not relatives of the siblings.

She turned her gaze to a second boy who had uniquely light-colored eyes and dark brown hair. He had fair skin and an aquiline nose. A predator's large incisor was strung around his neck. There were faded brown stains on the fang that she guessed were blood. Like the other two boys in the *neyra*, he was lean, broad-shouldered, and exuded a calm bearing.

Lastly, Mariah took stock of the girl following the two boys. In a sense, she was similar to Huyani with her slim, attractive figure and fluid motions, but the likeness ended there. Matikè's eyes were more rounded and were light green with what appeared to be gold flecks in them. She wore her brown hair in a long ponytail, and her skin was the shade of mocha. While she appeared delicate and was slightly shorter than Jag, something about the way she moved made Mariah believe she could give the sixteen-year-old a run for his money in parkour.

Akol introduced the newcomers to the five. "My friends, I would like you to meet a few of our fellow Dema-Ki youths: Hutar, Aesròn, and Matikè."

The two boys and Matikè smiled at the five.

"Aesròn and I can understand your language and speak interactively with you, but dear Matikè does not have our ability," Hutar said to the five. Then he extended a hand. "It is a pleasure to finally meet our very first visitors."

The friends each shook his hand as Huyani served the three, and Akol brought out more seats. Hutar took a spot beside Mariah and Aesròn sat beside Hutar. Matikè joined Huyani across from Aesròn. Akol sat back down beside Jag.

Hutar, taking the first bite from his meal, complimented Huyani on her cooking and she smiled at him gratefully. He then looked at the five and studied them in quiet for a while. Having chewed on a spoonful of wild rice, he finally asked, "How are you all feeling? Surely the way you have been injured is not to be taken lightly."

At the five's surprised looks, he added, "You are not a secret to those of us living in this valley. Though most of us have not seen or met you, we have heard talk. That is why my companions and I came by; we wanted to get to know you and wash away the rumors that have arisen, especially amongst the younger people of the village." Hutar leaned forward. "We would like to know more about you."

The friends shared looks, and then Kody spoke up. "We're doing fine, thanks. Huyani and Akol have been just great to us, so we're getting stronger every day. And I love the food here."

Jag elbowed him sharply in the ribs. "Will you for once get your mind off of food?" Turning to Hutar and his two friends with a shake of his head, he said, "We've all known each other since we were little, so after listening to this guy ramble about his hunger attacks for a while, it gets really exasperating."

Aesròn chuckled. "Ah, he is still growing. I remember constantly needing to eat when I was a few years younger." He fiddled with the fang on the black string around his neck.

Aari seemed intrigued by it. "What animal is that from?"

Aesròn and Hutar looked at each other briefly and Aesròn smiled. Leaning forward on his elbows, he took his necklace off and passed it to Aari. "I stalked a cougar for this gem. Killing it was not much of a guilt thing and no one disapproved me of taking the life of another hunter of the forest, because it had been rabid and needed to be dealt with. I, along with one of my cousins, tracked the creature for a few days into another valley not far from here and . . . and I need not go into details. Whatever you need to know lies with what you are holding in your hands."

The five took turns examining the tooth on its black string before Aari passed it back to Aesròn. "Cool," he said admiringly.

"How do you feel about Dema-Ki?" Hutar asked.

Kody leaned back in his chair. "We actually haven't seen much; we've just moved about between our shelters and this one."

"Really?" Hutar and Aesròn looked at each other again. Hutar rested his chin in his hand and said with a growing grin, "Perhaps my friends and I could show you around."

"Uh, Hutar," Huyani cut in, reaching over and putting a hand on his arm to stop him. "That is very kind of you, but we have orders from the Elders. They will meet the others and get to know the village in due time, but not just yet. Is that not correct, Akol?"

Akol nodded. "Yes. But once again, that was very nice of you to offer." Akol and Hutar's eyes met for a couple of moments and the look in the other youth's eyes chilled Akol a little.

Hutar kept a pleasant face. As though suddenly remembering Matikè, he turned to her and translated. Matikè raised her slim eyebrows at Akol but continued eating silently. Akol's face flushed, but out of what emotion he did not know.

Kody tilted his head toward Jag and muttered under his breath, "Jeez! We can't be seen outside. What are we, celebrities?"

Jag grimaced. "I guess in a weird way, we are. I mean, apparently they haven't had visitors here, ever. Who can blame them?"

"Jag." Jag turned to look at Hutar. "Akol and Huyani say the Elders told them you cannot be seen by anyone else. So we have an idea. We could give you a tour without our brethren laying eyes on the five of you." Hutar winked at the friends. "What do you say?"

As Huyani interjected and engaged Hutar with her objections once more, Akol whispered to Jag. "Jag, say no."

Just as quietly, Jag mumbled, "Why?"

"Just say no. I do not trust him as much as I would like to. Besides, the Elders would be extremely disappointed if they found out Huyani and I defied their orders."

Jag said nothing. His friends glanced at him and gave him questioning looks.

He found it odd that the seemingly peaceful people of the valley would not be at ease with one another. He thought Hutar seemed pretty genuine, and from the expressions of his friends, they thought so too. But he trusted Akol more. He looked at Hutar. "Thanks, but no. Sorry."

Hutar and Aesròn's faces dropped. Recovering quickly, they shrugged at each other. "No matter." Aesròn grinned. "Perhaps some other time when we get acquainted more."

Huyani coughed. "I am afraid there will be no 'some other time' unless the Elders say so," she said firmly. "We cannot disobey orders. As it is, you are not supposed to be in contact with our guests."

Hutar causally slouched in his seat. "That is too bad."

"It is," Aesròn agreed, gazing at the five. "We could have become close associates." He pushed back his empty plate. "Huyani, Akol, thank you very much for letting us eat with you. It was delicious."

Hutar stood up and said, "I believe it is time for us to leave." Switching to his first language, he spoke to Matikè, and the girl got up. She smiled and fluttered her fingers at the five. Akol led them out. He returned moments later and slumped down in his seat with a sigh.

Jag fiddled with his cutlery, then glanced at Akol. "Spill, Akol. Why didn't you want those guys to show us around?"

Akol took a sip from his drink. "As Huyani and I have mentioned several times previously, we have orders from the Elders."

"But if the Elders had given permission for us to tour, would you have let Hutar and his friends show us around?"

"Regrettably, no. I know you think we are tranquil people, Jag, and for the most part we are. But we do have the odd *uncertainties*. It is just the way life is. Hutar—he is not quite right."

"Why? What's wrong with him?" Tegan asked.

Akol grinned at her warmly. "Just be cautious if you come across him again."

"Or any of his friends, for that matter," Huyani said. "Now, who would like some dessert?"

Six hands shot up. Huyani smiled and served them some yam pudding.

As they ate, Akol watched the five, his mind churning. They were getting restless, he knew. They felt caged and needed to move. Without the friends noticing, he tugged at his sister's arm and Huyani understood.

"Excuse us for a moment," she said charmingly. Taking the lead, she and Akol walked out of the shelter and she turned to him as she closed the door behind them. "What is the matter, Akol?"

"This is not good. We knew it would come to this at some point."

"What are you talking about?"

"Did you not notice what happened in there when Hutar and Aesròn offered to show the five around? They were enticed to take the bait, and they would have, too, if we were not there to pull them back. They cannot be confined like this; it will cause all of us much angst."

"What do you suggest doing, then? The Elders told us not to expose them to the village."

Akol scratched his ear, feeling exasperated. "I do not know!" He stopped then, a furtive look on his face. "Actually, I take that back."

Huyani eyed him. "Oh, someone help us. What do you have in mind?"

Akol crossed his arms with a grin. "The Elders said not to let the five be seen by eyes other than ours. It does not mean that they have to be limited to just our shelter and theirs."

"Continue."

"I could show a couple of them around, but in secret. No one would be the wiser."

"This is exactly why I am grateful that I am around when your unpredictable ideas pop up—to tell you that it is risky and not right. Besides, how can you pull it off when we have over seven hundred of our brethren living in this valley?"

"Come now, you underestimate your brother's wiliness."

"No, you overestimate your ability."

"Will you unwind? The five are feeling confined and they need this. Even you cannot argue with that. And in any case, you *know* I am not good when in comes to these kinds of situations."

Huyani looked at Akol, her arms folded. She cocked her head sideways and gave him a long stare. Akol gazed heavenward for a minute then looked back at his sister. "And . . . if we do get caught and the Elders find out, I will say it was my idea. I would not be lying."

"Alright, I am convinced. Now we should get back inside. The five are probably wondering what we are up to. I must leave shortly to check up on the two patients in the convalescence shelter, so I will leave it to you to unfold your plan."

Akol smiled and together with Huyani, entered the *neyra*.

15

The moon crept to its zenith in the sky, rain clouds building up around it. An owl hooted somewhere from the trees and launched itself into a glide, the wind rustling through its brown, speckled feathers. Aari and Tegan ducked as it swooped over their heads. Turning around and watching after the creature, they smiled at each other with the same thought: *Amazing.*

The two were just returning from the tour. When Akol offered the friends a secretive expedition, only Aari and Tegan had been keenly interested and jumped at the opportunity. Jag had turned down the invite and convinced Kody to do the same. Exchanging whispers, Jag and Kody managed to persuade Mariah to stay behind and then the three had walked back to the boys' *neyra*.

Now, with the tour wrapped up and Akol advising them to catch some sleep, Aari and Tegan entered the boys' *neyra*. Mariah leapt from where she was sitting and tackled the two. "What took you so long?" she demanded.

"It's a pretty big valley, 'Riah," Aari reminded her.

Mariah flushed. "Well, yes, but—"

"What happened? Why are you so edgy?"

She pointed at Jag and Kody who were sitting on the ground, leaning against a wall and grinning. "Those two . . . they've planned an escape."

"Escape?" Aari and Tegan echoed, looking at the two boys.

Kody's grin widened. "Well, most of us want out, right?"

Mariah's eyes narrowed. "Keyword being 'most'!"

"Whoa, whoa, and whoa." Aari put a hand up. "Calm down." He turned to face Kody and Jag. "Guys—escaping. Are you serious?"

Kody nodded. "Jag and I were talking about it. Don't you want to go home? See your baby sister? Your mom? Your dad? Sleep in a *real* bed?"

Aari just stared at him, still trying to process what Jag and Kody had agreed upon. "Escape?" he repeated again. "No wonder you insisted on not coming with us on the tour . . ."

Kody rolled his eyes. "Aari, listen—"

"No, don't listen," Mariah grumbled. "You know what? We'll talk about this in a while. I'm so tired of listening to these two lunatics. I'd rather hear about how your tour went."

Aari and Tegan looked at each other, somewhat confused, then shrugged. Aari sat down with Tegan beside him and started, "Well, it was . . . incredible. You would not *believe* the stuff these people have come up with to survive here and at the same time remain hidden from the outside world." He scratched his head, looking overwhelmed. "Man, there's so much we've learned from this tour that I don't even know where to start."

Tegan patted his shoulder. "I'll help." Facing the other three, she said, "One of the things that caught my attention is that the valley's divided into two by that river. The north side, where we are right now, is more residential by design. In other words, this is where you'll find most of the shelters."

Aari chipped in. "Speaking of shelters, have you guys noticed the spiral patterns stained on the roofs? The locals got them done to match the surrounding foliage when viewed from above. Akol boosted us up outside Huyani's shelter to have a look at what they've done, and all I've got to say is that these guys are amazing. I swear, if I'd been looking from high above, I wouldn't be able to tell that this was a man-made structure. It's ingenious."

"Most of the shelters are grouped in circles between shrubs and trees," Tegan added, "and they're spread throughout the valley in groups of five."

"It's kind of weird," Mariah said. "I mean, the shelters themselves are five-sided, and now you say they're clustered in groups of five."

"Now that you mention it," Tegan said, blinking in surprise, "the number of Elders they have is also five."

They shared questioning looks. "Weird," Kody said finally as he pointed at each one of the friends, counting them. "One, two three, four"—he tapped his nose—"five."

Aari, excited to share the other discoveries he and Tegan made, continued with the story. "Anyway, the south side of the valley hosts the industrial activities of the village."

Jag raised an eyebrow. "What do you mean by industrial?"

Aari replied with a question. "Where do you think all this comes from?" He waved his arms around vaguely. "The shelters, the food, the plumbing, the heat, the camouflage?"

"I have no clue, but I've got a feeling you're gonna tell us."

Aari leaned forward with a sparkle in his blue eyes. "You bet, but it'll take a little while." With great enthusiasm, he took his time to share what he and Tegan had learned.

It was a half hour later when Mariah, Jag, and Kody leaned back, mesmerized by Aari's account. A part of them now wished they'd gone on the tour as well. It would have been interesting to have seen the wonders of the village for themselves.

After a pause, Tegan sighed and looked at Mariah. "Alright, let's go back to what you guys have been up to. What was it that you were annoyed about?"

Mariah exhaled noisily and glared at Jag and Kody. "They've been cackling and devising plans and escape routes and whatnot ever since we got here a couple hours ago. Fifteen minutes into the discussion and I wanted to run out of here screaming like a maniac. They were talking like every one of us was going to agree on leaving this place." She looked expectantly at Aari and Tegan, as if waiting for them to support her.

Aari and Tegan looked at each other, then Tegan got up to walk over to the two boys and sit in between them. The boys' grins grew as she spoke. "I find this place really interesting and the people not half bad. But if I continue to stay here, I'm going to go crazy, and then *I'll* be the one who's running around and screaming like a maniac."

Mariah stared at her friend in disbelief, and then turned to Aari. "What about you? You feel the same way?"

Aari shook his head. "I'm not leaving this place for two reasons: One, this village has lots of cool stuff and I want to learn how they make things work around here. Two, and I think this obviously overrides my first reason, is that it's *safer* here. Out there . . . hey, didn't we already have this discussion before?"

"Huh, we did." Tegan looked at Jag and Kody, amused.

"And like I said then," Aari continued, "there are all sorts of dangers out there, and as far as I know, we don't have enough experience to go wandering around and hope that good fortune will smile down at us and bring us to safety."

Kody sighed. "I don't want a recap of the conversation earlier, so I'm gonna lay out the two choices; either stay put, or leave. Take your side."

"I just did, dimwit."

Kody's face twisted into a grimace. "Okay, whatever. This is what I really mean: Jag and I are going to leave this place. I think Tegan's coming too?" He looked at her and continued when she nodded. "So are you two just going to stay put here or leave with us?"

Aari let out a laugh, though it sounded more harsh than humored. "Are you serious, Kode-man? Listen to yourself. You three wouldn't leave Mariah and me here alone and wander off."

Mariah agreed. "He's right. We've been through too much over the years for you to actually leave a part of the group behind."

"That plays two ways," Jag said finally. "If Teegs, Kody and I left, you guys would hate being all by yourself, stuck here."

They stared at each other, confused, hesitant, and helpless. Tegan groaned. "Come on, guys. We need to decide this now, so think about it. What do we gain from remaining here?"

"Oh, gee, I don't know," Aari replied sarcastically. "Maybe staying alive?"

"Okay, that's debatable," Tegan admitted. "But . . . you two, come on. What could we accomplish by avoiding making a decision? I don't want to waste any more time here. I want to go back to Great Falls and be with my family."

Aari said nothing but gave his friend an understanding smile. The *neyra* was silent and for a while, the only sound to be heard was of the rain falling outside. At last Aari said quietly, "Okay, what plans have you guys made?"

Mariah, beside him, groaned and gave a solid punch to his shoulder. "You're a loser, you know that? I was *counting on you* to hold your ground against this madness."

Aari seemed regretful but also determined. "I know, Mariah, I know," he answered softly. "But if you think about it, what *are* our options, really?"

"What about these people? They've been sheltering us, caring for us, feeding us . . . For crying out loud Aari, if it weren't for them, we'd be dead."

"I'm not suggesting they're bad people," protested Aari. "I like them. We all do. We can't continue to live here is all I'm saying."

"And I don't know about you guys," Kody added, "but even though I've kind of grown fond of them, I feel imprisoned. Surely you would have noticed by now how they've curbed our movements. And they don't want anyone else to meet us. Kind of disturbing, if you ask me."

"But they *are* nice people," Tegan supplied quickly.

Jag shook his head. "Nice, yes. But there's secrecy about them that I don't get, and it's making me feel uncomfortable. Kody made a really good point. The restrictions they've put on us makes me feel like I'm a captive or something." He glanced at Mariah. "You can't tell me you haven't felt that."

Mariah sighed. "I never said that. Look, the main thing I'm concerned about is our safety. That's all."

"Believe me," Jag said, staring at his hands, "we're all a bit worried about that."

Tegan looked up at him. "Looks like we're all on the same page now. Well, more or less." She cast a nonchalant glance at Aari and Mariah. "I think it's about time you laid out your plan, Jag."

Jag looked at Kody and nodded once in confirmation. Kody reached under his sleeping bag and pulled out a rolled-up parchment. Tegan sat straight and peered at it inquisitively. "What's that?"

"A map from Huyani's *neyra*," Kody said slyly. "One of the dozen or so she's got."

Aari and Mariah leaned closer. "You stole it?" Aari asked incredulously.

"Hey, talk to the man who told me to swipe it," he shot back, jerking his thumb at Jag. Tegan, Aari, and Mariah looked at Jag, who shrugged and said, "I'd like to think of it as borrowing."

Mariah crossed her arms. "Without the intention of returning it."

Jag cleared his throat. "Not true. I do intend to . . . somehow. Plus, we need something to rely on when we're out there."

They watched as Kody picked gingerly at a knotted string holding the parchment in its tube form. The fiber fell away, and slowly the map unfolded by itself. The five crowded around it, hungry eyes picking up every detail. It was definitely an old map but whatever ink the maker had used to sketch it was still very much visible. Rubbing their fingers over the material, they realized the map was fabricated from animal hide and was cool to the touch.

As the rest watched, Jag and Kody carefully outlined the plot for the group, working out some details and taking in suggestions. The main idea was to leave Dema-Ki from its western end and enter an adjacent valley marked with a pinecone on the map. They were to keep heading in the direction of the route the bears may have taken when they brought the teenagers to the village.

Jag was hoping that by following that course through the 'pinecone' valley, it would somehow lead them to the crash site. He traced a fine line on the map through the adjacent valley that may have been an actual path. To his recollection, the mountain range with its valleys had been to the east prior to the crash; to him, it seemed logical to trek westward. Once at the crash site, they would search for the plane's radio and call for help. If the radio was broken, they would have no choice but to head to the closest town. As they recalled from the map they'd studied before the trip, it would be either Ross River or Mayo. Or so they hoped. Even then, as Aari pointed out, it would take a good number of days before they reached either place.

As the thrill grew between the friends, more time was spent discussing the escape. The night wore on with the rain pouring steadily outside. The five decided to break away only after they poked their heads outside when the rain ceased, surprised to be greeted by the first light of dawn.

Although sleep was the furthest thing from their minds, they knew they would require all the rest they could get. Besides, there was a fair amount of preparation to be done. They bid each other a wry good night as the girls headed back to their neyra.

They didn't notice a figure crouched high on a branch of a tree in the shadows, not far from the boys' shelter. The figure watched silently as the girls trudged toward their *neyra*. He waited patiently as they disappeared from sight, then leapt off the branch and half-swooped toward the ground, landing quietly on his feet. He looked around cautiously, then slunk through the trees, head down. A hint of a sinister smile grew on his lips as he weaved his way toward his shelter, and his fierce blue eyes glinted with malice.

16

The soft yet steady footsteps alerted the squirrel that a visitor was nearby. Squeaking, it dropped its nut and scrambled up a tree with its bushy tail waving.

Pulled away from his foreboding thoughts, Tayoka glanced up at the creature that was chattering irately at him and smiled. He paused at the foot of the tree, bent down to retrieve the nut, and looked up at the squirrel. "Sorry, old friend. I did not mean to scare you out of your business. I believe this is yours." He held open his palm with the nut resting atop. The animal gazed at it for a few moments then clambered down onto Tayoka's hand. Grabbing the nut, the squirrel whizzed right back up the tree and hid itself in the safety of the leaves.

Refreshing, mused the Elder as he continued walking. *The little things in life that can make a man's day so much brighter.* He hefted the glass jar in his hand and pursed his lips. He was heading to a lake to gather a sample of the water to see if it was contaminated. He and six other men were venturing outside of Dema-Ki. After a quick briefing earlier in the morning instructing the men not to drink from the waters they were testing, Tayoka had sent his brethren off in different directions to collect the water samples from varying sources.

The lake the Elder was heading to was the same one where Mitska's mate had camped with their grandson before falling ill. *What in the world would have seeped through these waters?* Tayoka wondered. *They've been safe for generations.*

He grabbed a water pelt from his daypack and took a quick drink, then glanced up at the sky through the trees and wiped his brow with the sleeve of his shirt. It was midday, which meant he'd been walking for a few hours already. He figured that at this pace, he would reach the lake shortly.

The forest had the fresh yet damp scent after a good rainfall that Tayoka very much enjoyed. He spotted several birds pecking at the ground, attempting to capture a delectable meal in their beaks. Not wanting to bother them, he walked around the creatures and continued on for the next half hour in silence.

Maneuvering around a large boulder, he halted in surprise, for not ten feet in front of him was a dead mountain lion. *Goodness, what happened to the poor fellow?* The Elder put his jar and pack on the ground beside the boulder and carefully made his way over to the animal's carcass. He grabbed a broken branch and prodded the body. As he flipped its head over, he snarled and leapt back. The stench emanating from the creature's open jaws was beyond repulsive. Yellow foam encrusted its mouth and dried blood soaked the animal's fur. Upon closer observation, the Elder found that the source of the blood was the creature's maw. It had bled internally. Disturbed, he walked in circles around the mountain lion. It could have been rabies that the animal had contracted, but there was a tugging in his gut that told him it was something far more serious that stole the life of this once-magnificent creature.

Retrieving his belongings, he gave the carcass a wide berth as he strode past. The image of the dead animal still bothered him as he reached the lake. Walking down the pebble beach, he rubbed his head and squinted against the sun, spotting an unusually large poplar tree with massive overhanging branches. He walked toward it and placed his hand on its bark. Then, in a catlike manner, he leapt onto one of the branches and found a comfortable spot to sit on. He shrugged off his daypack and fished through it, bringing out a caribou jerky. He took a big bite from it and smiled. Leave it to Saiyu and Tikina to pack him off with something he loved most. He made a mental note to thank them both once he returned.

Scanning the lake from his vantage point, he munched down the last of his jerky and grabbed another quick gulp of water from his water pelt. He placed the pack on his back and leapt fifteen feet down from the branch, landing in a fluid motion with his knees flexed.

He padded down to the shore, then uncapped his jar and filled it with lake water, making sure his fingers did not come in contact with the water. Deciding to walk further down the shore, he reached the midpoint of the beach. Here he removed another jar from his daypack to collect a fresh sample from this location.

As he bent over to fill the jar, the wind picked up and with it he became aware of an awful smell. It was the stench of something rotting. Scrunching his nose, he recapped the jar and walked until he came upon a sight of dead fish scattered at the edge of the water. He crouched by the fish, forehead creased with worry. He thought their bodies were still preserved until he peered at one and found it partially eaten. *Oh, no.* Tayoka looked away from the fish toward the shore and pinched his bottom lip. Confirming his fears, a raven lay dead on the ground about thirty paces from the waterline, its blood-encrusted beak open and its feathers dry and brittle. *The animals that eat the contaminated creatures are also dying.*

Tayoka's apprehension heightened. Making a quick decision, he took out the wrapper in which the caribou jerky had been packed in, flipped it over and wrapped one of the fish in it and carefully placed it in his now-empty pack.

The Elder stood up and stared across the beautiful blue-gray water with ominous thoughts swirling in his mind. As he watched, he noticed dark storm clouds forming over the far side of the lake. He figured it would be best to start trekking to the village in haste. As he turned and began walking back, still thinking about the dead animals, he wondered: *If the contaminant in the water is so lethal, how long do the infected ones in the village have before they succumb to it as well?*

17

"If we get caught, I am ditching you guys. I'll tell them I was trying to stop you," Aari hissed as he glanced back and realized that they had covered a fair bit of ground since leaving their shelters. It was the dead of the night and the valley was eerily silent, as if all the inhabitants were quietly watching the friends leave the valley.

Jag chuckled. "I'd like to see you try that, especially with Tegan here."

Aari glanced at Tegan, who was smirking at him, and rolled his eyes. The gray-eyed girl did not take kindly to those who turned their backs on a team.

Jag looked at Aari with a puzzled grin. "It's odd, though. I thought you agreed on us leaving this place a couple nights ago. You even suggested some ideas while we planned this escape."

"Yeah, but . . . I'm still wary about the whole thing. It's my nature to be skeptical."

"I thought it was in your nature to advance, what with your partial German heritage."

"Hey, what's that supposed to mean?"

Jag's only response was another grin as he walked past Aari and weaved in between Tegan and Mariah. Putting an arm around each and drawing them closer, he murmured quietly, "Huyani's shelter is coming right up. Since you are both more nimble and . . . eh, lighter on your feet, it's probably a good idea if one of you went ahead to scout it out, just to be safe."

Tegan nodded, slid the pack she was carrying off her shoulders, and quietly padded ahead. Jag, Mariah, Kody, and Aari silently watched after her. Kody muttered, "Someone should've told her to watch out for that wolf—what's his name?"

"Chayton," Mariah answered. "But I don't think we really need to worry about him. Plus, he's often in and out of the village. And he's made good friends with us." The friends remained quiet after that, looking over their shoulders once in a while to make sure no one else was around.

It was the second night since the five agreed to leave the valley. The day after the decision was made, the friends wandered around parts of the village where they were permitted, casually strolling and deftly swiping supplies they figured they would need for their journey.

They'd managed to cajole Akol into giving back their original clothing, which had been mended by some of the women in the village. The boys happily slid their hoodies on and the girls were more than pleased to have their jackets back. As they'd changed into their clothes, the five noted that the women had also added a thin but incredibly warm layer of hide inside their clothing for insulation.

The food and the packs had been the hardest of all to obtain, but with Tegan's craftiness and Kody's humoristic charm, they persuaded Huyani to give the five some "extra food to munch on throughout the day and a bit more for Kody's large appetite." Huyani had thoughtfully put the provisions in a medium-sized pack, which Kody took while giving Tegan a discreet wink. With one bag already in their hands, Jag and Aari seized four more from shelters that hadn't been occupied during that time. There'd been some commotion afterward, but Akol told the friends that the villagers figured some mischievous children had decided to pull a prank and would fess up in due time.

Though the five were relieved to hear no one suspected them, the thieving didn't make them feel exactly merry. They kept a low profile for the rest of that day and the next, resting as much as they could in preparation for the escape.

Now, in the middle of the night, wearing their comfortably extra-padded clothes, the five waited for Tegan to return. Mariah turned to Jag. "I still don't know why you insisted on going through this way," she whispered. "There was an exit on the east side of the valley closer to where our shelters were. We could have taken that route."

Jag cocked his head at her. "We've been over this. I've pointed this out on the map before. I'm convinced the bears we were on brought us through the Pinecone valley, which is west of Dema-Ki, so logically the wreckage would be in this direction."

"You better not be wrong, Jag. I'd hate to find a few hours from now that we're on the wrong track."

He smirked. "Thanks for the vote of confidence."

Tegan returned and nodded reassuringly. Picking up her pack, which contained the garments the friends had been wearing for the last couple of weeks, she waited for someone to direct them on. Jag took the lead and guided them past Huyani's *neyra*. Carefully weaving through trees and bushes, they kept a steady pace.

Having stealthily slipped past several clusters of *neyra*, they reached an incline at the western edge of the valley and mounted the grassy slope. When they reached the top, they halted and their mouths rounded with amazement as they gazed at the sight about thirty paces in front of them.

"What is that thing?" Kody murmured, pointing to the shiny spherical structure ahead. It appeared to be about two stories high. The entire surface of the sphere seemed to give off a faint glow. At its base, two cylindrical assemblies protruded for a good length before submerging into the ground.

Kody walked up to the sphere and pressed his fingers against a foot-long metallic strip attached to a grove on the structure. With a muted yelp he drew back his hand. "That thing is *hot!*" Behind him, he heard Aari laughing out loud, followed by a "Shh!" from Jag and the girls.

Kody whipped around and glared at Aari, shaking his burning fingers. "What are you laughing at?" he growled.

Aari waved at the sphere. "That . . . is probably the villagers' hot water reservoir, you moron."

"Well *excuse* me for not being aware because hot water tanks are normally not huge globe-like structures. And besides, how do you know? Did Akol show you?"

Aari shook his head. "Nope. We didn't get this far during the tour. I just figured it." He tapped his temple with a smug little grin.

"How?"

"Pipes leading into the tank from the ground. Pipes going back into the ground for distribution, and—your scalded fingers. Duh."

Now the girls were trying to suppress their laughter. Kody hissed at them and pressed his hand to the dew-covered grass to cool it. "Not even out of the valley yet and I got my first injury," he muttered. Looking back at the sphere, he ventured, "Why then is it so shiny?"

"It's made of glazed clay," Aari explained. "Huyani told me that her people use it a lot around here. The pipes are made of it as well. It's a great way to channel water and the clay is extremely heat resistant. The strip that you touched is probably some kind of gauge the villagers use to monitor the heat inside the tank."

"Smart people," Tegan commented. "So I guess it's from this reservoir that the folks get their hot water and heat piped in."

"That's my guess," Aari replied.

"But wait." Mariah paced around the sphere and tried to look underneath it. "I don't see a fire or any source of heat that would boil the water. So how . . . ?"

Aari narrowed his eyes and walked around it as well, then snapped his fingers as he suddenly recalled something. "Huyani told me about this. They must have built it over a hot spring."

"A hot spring?" Jag sounded surprised. "Up here, this far north?"

"Oh, dude, hot springs are everywhere on the planet regardless of climate or geography. It comes from inside the earth. I think they use the sphere to capture the steam and carry it through a series of pipes to the entire village."

"Ingenious," Mariah said approvingly. "And isn't the sphere the most efficient shape for pressurized content anyhow?"

Aari nodded slowly. "Yep."

"Guys, look over there." Tegan was standing beside Kody a few yards off, close to the river. She was pointing over the water at something the two were staring in awe at. The others walked up to them and couldn't muffle the stunned gasps that escaped their throats.

On the far side of the river, the land was sloped as well. It was nearly a mirror image of the side the friends were standing on. There was one dramatic difference though: An astounding five-sided structure rested on a beautifully landscaped terrace carved out of the hill. Five large columns built from logs rose to a height of about thirty feet. What appeared to be statues of human figures stood at the top of each column, holding the domed roof in place.

What was more amazing was a dazzling, multicolored flame that streamed from a cauldron at the center of the foyer of the building. Now Aari was baffled. "How does that work? How can it continue jetting fire like that?"

Since no one had an answer, they stood together and enjoyed watching the colorful flames flare against the dark of the night. Mesmerized as they were by the sight, it took them several moments to shake off their trance and continue on with their journey.

They had walked on for a good ten minutes when Jag noticed a massive shadow looming up ahead. He frowned, his dread growing as they drew closer. They stopped and stared up at what appeared to be a dead end. In reality, it was a near-vertical incline along the line that, according to the map, separated Dema-Ki from the Pinecone valley.

Kody scanned it from bottom to top, wearing an aggravated look. "No way am I climbing *that*."

"Oh, it's not that bad," Mariah said hopefully. "It can't be more than a hundred feet . . ."

"Do you hear yourself?" Jag demanded. "You put one hand or foot in the wrong place and you'll drop like a rock. And we're carrying packs too."

"The bears couldn't have climbed over that, especially not with us on their backs," Aari said quietly. "Jag, we'll have to go back to the other side of the valley to get out."

Jag's face fell. "No, wait. Maybe there's a way around this. We'll comb through this area for a passage or something, and if we can't find anything . . . then we'll double back to the eastern end."

"Time's a-tickin', guys," Tegan said anxiously.

"Fan out," Jag ordered, spreading his arms.

They spread out, rapidly covering the base of the incline. Aari climbed onto a ledge and turned around. The clouds had parted, allowing light from the full moon to bathe the valley. The turquoise river shimmered in the light and could be seen winding through the center of the valley. The tops of the villagers' shelters were barely distinguishable from the vegetation. To a casual observer, the village was nonexistent.

As he looked across the valley, the realization of what they were about to do hit him. They were parting from security and launching themselves against the power of the northern forests. They were truly putting themselves at the mercy of nature.

The clouds regrouped and obscured the moon, throwing the valley into the shadows once again. Jag walked toward the ledge and looked up at Aari, giving the other teenager a half-hearted grin. "Come on, Aari. We need to keep things moving."

Aari nodded. As he jumped down, a happy exclamation caught the boys' attention. "Found it! Think I found a way out!" Mariah waved at them from the north end of the wall.

The four looked at each other. "I figured we'd probably be stuck here for a while trying to find it," Kody grinned. "I guess Lady Luck loves us."

"Well," Tegan said as she walked up to where Mariah was standing, "let's hope this little romance lasts."

The boys sauntered over to the girls and gazed in the direction they were looking. A path was barely visible, tunneled into the rock wall. The five peered into the looming darkness ahead.

"Should we use that portable oil lamp we took from Huyani's?" Kody whispered nervously.

"We've only got a limited supply of oil in that thing," Tegan murmured back. "We should try to not use it unless it's absolutely necessary."

The four looked at Tegan, peered into the dark tunnel, and looked at Tegan again. Kody clucked his tongue. "Methinks that right now, it *is* absolutely necessary."

Tegan gazed into the tunnel and reluctantly agreed. Opening her pack, she took out the clay torch. Flicking a slim lever with her thumb, a small flame erupted to life and blinked. A crystal globe encircled the light. "Who wants to go in first?" she asked. The five looked at each other, no one volunteering.

Finally, Aari took a tentative step forward into the tunnel and put the hood of his jacket up. Tegan passed him the torch and his friends slowly followed him in. Jag took up position at the rear of the group and looked at the ground, noting in the flickering light how well-trodden it was. It gave him some comfort that the tunnel was obviously used by the villagers.

The five trekked on in silence for a couple of minutes, then Kody piped up. "Are we there yet?"

"No, Kode-man," Aari replied.

Silence again.

Then: "Are we there yet?"

"No, Kode-man."

More quiet ensued.

Finally: "Are we there yet?

"*Oy!* Shut up!"

Kody remained silent the rest of the way. Jag chuckled quietly, then looked around the tunnel. There was barely a clearance over the five's heads, and the passageway was about six feet wide. *The bears must walk through here in single file,* he mused. In the small dancing light he observed the patches of moss that clung to the sides and water droplets falling from the ceiling. No one spoke for a length of time. The sound of dripping water seemed magnified in the stillness of the tunnel.

"I think I can see the end," Aari reported after a few minutes, his voice low. Relief swept over the group. "I'm gonna turn off the torch to conserve the oil." Before long, the five exited the tunnel.

As they stepped into open air again, Jag looked around. "So this must be the Pinecone valley."

Aari handed the torch back to Tegan, who carefully put it back into her pack. "Yep. It feels more open out here."

"Definitely matches the drawing on the map," Jag agreed. "Less vegetation here compared to Dema-Ki."

They'd taken a few steps forward when Tegan halted abruptly, causing Kody to bump into her. "Hey," he said. "What gives?"

She smiled at them. "Just smell the fresh mountain air. Isn't it nice?"

Her friends breathed in deeply, and as they exhaled, felt a pleasant sensation from the tops of their heads to the tips of their toes.

"Kind of reminds me of the scenic drives we used to take to the national park back home," Aari noted.

Mariah agreed. "And it's just as pretty here. I'd love to see this place when it snows."

"Can we stop to grab a bite?" Kody pleaded.

"We should walk for a while more, and then we'll put up for the rest of the night," Jag said. "We need to put as much distance as we can between us and the village."

The five kept trekking for two hours more until Kody muttered another complaint about his hunger. Jag, Tegan, Aari, and Mariah glanced at each other and nodded. They came across an area of soft grass nestled in a grove of tall firs. Kody, apparently satisfied with the spot, sat down and opened the pack he was carrying. "Grab whatever y'all want."

As the five ate a quick snack and took a few gulps of water from the water pelts they'd taken, they sat back against the trees and talked quietly for a bit. The girls unpacked the group's sleeping bags and laid them side-by-side. The friends crawled into them and listened to the sounds of the night.

Just as they started to nod off, they heard a branch snap. Bolting upright, the five instinctively held their breaths. They waited a couple of minutes, then hesitantly lowered themselves back into their sleeping bags, but not before Kody whipped up a sturdy stick for safekeeping. "My insurance," he explained.

"It was probably just some small animal," Tegan said as she closed her eyes. "Good night, guys."

"Night," the others murmured. Within moments, the group was lulled to sleep with the quiet sounds of the forest.

Barely an hour into their slumber, a loud, spine-chilling roar reverberated through the forest. The five awoke in fright. Not even an ice-cold bucket of water could have jolted them out of their sleep that quickly. They sat up and froze in place.

A ferocious snarl echoed through the trees, forcing the five to scramble to the center of the sleeping site where they huddled together. A clash of roaring and snarling exploded again. Blood drained from the friends' faces as they listened to the horrifying sounds.

There was an eerie pause, and as the five tentatively let out the breaths they had been holding, an unnerving animal scream rang in the darkness. They clung on to one another, wide-eyed.

The noises cut off abruptly. Apprehensive, they waited as time ticked by. Once they were certain the noises would not return, they broke off from each other and collapsed in heaps.

"What was *that?*" Tegan asked, looking around.

"Some kind of beast, that's all I know." Aari's breaths were ragged. "Man, I can feel the blood pounding in my head."

Jag held his head in his hands. "Yeah, me too." He looked up after a couple of minutes. "You guys alright?"

They nodded. Kody was up on his feet and already packing up his sleeping bag. "I'm alright, but I'm outta here. I can't sleep after that. Let's get moving."

The group hastily agreed and folded their sleeping bags up, putting them into the packs. They continued trekking for the next hour at a heightened pace, quickly consuming their water supply. Flicking his water pelt and listening to the slosh of water inside,

Kody observed, “We’re going to need to refill these things from the next river or stream we come across.”

“Is it safe to drink straight from them?” Tegan asked.

Aari grinned. “Are you kidding? Mountain water is fresh and pure. Nothing’s wrong with it—it’s perfectly safe.”

Their brisk pace slowed and soon they were just traipsing along, swerving around large rocks and fallen trees. After a while, Kody yawned loudly. “I need to rest.”

“Thought you were worried about the animal that freaked us out,” Mariah said.

“Right now I could care less. I’m tired. How long do you think we’ve been walking? Aari? Got a clue?”

Aari pulled his hood further over his head. “I’m thinking . . . in total . . . probably four, maybe five hours.”

Kody was shocked. “That’s it? Then why am I so tired?”

“I think it’s because we’re still recovering from the crash. And we haven’t really gotten much exercise. Our bodies are probably kinda stiff.” Aari tugged at his earlobe. “I don’t think we should push ourselves too hard right off the bat. Hey, Jag—we should stop and rest up real soon.”

Jag halted in his tracks. He stared up at the sky and blinked several times. Maybe his eyes were fooling him, but in the darkness he thought he saw a light from an aircraft some ways off. He stared at the spot in the sky and tried to trace the light source but it had vanished. He scanned the heavens again then reluctantly said, “Nah. Let’s gain some more distance before we take a break.”

Kody puffed out his cheeks in discontent. Reaching into his pack, he tried to sneak some food but dropped it right back when Mariah slapped his hand. “No food for you, Mr. Eat-everything-till-there-is-nothing-left-for-us.”

“Actually, I’m Mr. Eat-everything-before-anyone-else-gets-the-food. I’m a go-for-it type of guy.”

“I’m sure you are, Kody, I’m sure you are.”

Jag looked up at the sky a while later as they walked, hoping to spot an aircraft again. Instead, he saw the dark sky now beginning to get speckled with light. "Sunrise in a while," he said. A hush fell over the group as they hiked onward.

A peculiar sound reached the five's ears; they paused in their tracks at the same time and cocked their heads to listen.

"You guys hear that?" Aari murmured. "Some sort of—rumbling?"

"A storm approaching?" Kody wondered aloud.

Jag shook his head slowly. "No. I know I've heard the sound before, when . . ." His eyes began to lit up. ". . . when the bears were bringing us to Dema-Ki."

"When we get closer to the mountains in Great Falls back home—remember that sound?" Tegan asked.

Kody tilted his head. "You don't suppose . . ."

"A waterfall?" Mariah finished.

"Only one way to find out." Tegan loped toward the sound. Her friends followed her eagerly, at times calling for her to slow down. She would pause and wait impatiently until they caught up before trotting off again. The sound grew steadily louder the closer they got to the source.

The sky was beginning to lighten. As they cleared a large group of trees, the five found themselves staring at a stunning sight of water cascading over a ledge; it came down with thunderous intensity from two hundred feet up. The pool that was created at the foot of the waterfall was large but calm toward its edges. The tree line made a crescent shape around the pool, welcoming the friends and appearing to embrace them with protection. Jag was the last of the five to clear the trees. He passed one with darker bark than the others. He brushed his fingertips against the trunk and scrutinized it quizzically, then continued on.

A cold blast of air hit their faces as they stepped closer to the waterfall. It refreshed them, slowly releasing the tensed feeling knotting in their stomachs.

"Woo!" Kody ran to the pool and immediately filled up his water pelt. Jag, Aari, Tegan and Mariah did the same. Glancing up at the waterfall, Jag silently admired the grand showcase nature offered them. Setting down his pack, he laid back-first on the ground and propped himself on his elbows. A fine spray of mist coated him and he smiled, enjoying the revitalizing sensation the droplets provided. His friends joined him not long after.

Tegan stared at the white-blue water rushing down from above, astounded. "It's gorgeous."

"I'll say." Mariah pointed a finger skyward. "It's still not fully daylight yet, but the color of the water is already so beautiful. Kind of makes me want to take a dip."

Jag half-closed his eyes and lazily watched the scenery. The hypnotic rhythm of the waterfall had nearly lulled him to sleep when he saw movement and spotted Tegan and Mariah walking close to the falls. As the two stood beside it, he watched them curiously, wondering why they were looking so intently at the rushing water. He called their names but they didn't hear him over the roar of the water. He continued watching, noticing their movements becoming more and more animated as they pointed at the water.

"Wonder what they found?" Kody murmured as the girls waved the boys over. Curious, they picked up their packs and walked over. There, the spray of water on their faces was more intense.

"Guys, you won't believe this," Mariah yelled over the pounding water. Indicating the waterfall, she instructed, "Take our spot and tell us what you see."

She and Tegan stepped back and allowed the mystified boys to take their place. They clung to the rock wall beside where the water was rushing down, peering intently but could not see anything. Nonplussed, they looked back at the girls. "Don't see anything!"

"Look harder," Tegan directed. "*Look harder.*"

"It might help if you squint a little," added Mariah.

Three pairs of eyes raked over the entire side of the waterfall. Aari shook his head. "I don't see anything at all—whoa!" He spun around. "There's a cave behind this waterfall!"

"I see it now!" Kody confirmed excitedly. "You see it, Jag?"

"No—wait! Yeah, yeah, I see it." Jag stepped away from the waterfall and wiped his water-sprinkled face with the sleeve of his baggy black-and-silver hoodie.

Mariah was eager. "I want to check it out. Anybody wanna come along?"

Her friends grinned. Jag tossed the girls their packs and they slung them over their shoulders. "Be careful, Teegs," he warned as she took the lead.

Tegan hugged the slippery wall and inched her way closer to the waterfall along a narrow ledge. Saying a quick prayer, she slid behind the water and tumbled into the cave.

Mariah followed her in the exact same way, as did the rest. They got up, trying to wipe some of the water off themselves, and looked around. "Epic!" Kody walked around in backward circles, attempting to take in every detail of the cave. It was large and spacious, and to their surprise, it wasn't cold. The surface was mostly sandy and the friends could hear the particles crunch under their shoes as they walked around. The cave seemed to be lit, but the five could find no possible source of light.

Jag tapped the cave wall with his knuckles. "Why is it kind of bright in here?"

"Refraction," Tegan answered. "I think it's the angle the water falls over the cave's entrance that's giving it this appearance." Aari nodded in agreement.

"It doesn't seem to be a typical cold and damp cave that nobody would want to stay in," Mariah remarked. "It's kind of cozy in an odd way, too. I wouldn't mind resting here for a while." She chuckled at the thought.

"Well, why don't we?" Kody asked.

After a pause, Aari said, "That's actually not a bad idea."

Mariah tugged at her sleeve uneasily. "Do you think an animal might come in here?"

"I'm not too worried," Tegan answered. "I get a stale smell but it seems pretty faint. Whoever or whatever used this place hasn't been in here for a long while. Let's get out the sleeping bags."

Once everyone was contentedly settled in after having a snack and drinking some water, they snuggled into their sleeping bags and fell asleep immediately, exhausted.

18

A few hours later, with the land already basking in the sun's golden light, the five reached the end of the Pinecone valley and stood shoulder to shoulder on a ledge, looking at the descending slope that led to a flat expanse. The massive basin was moderately forested except on the banks of a long river that coiled in a north-south direction in the middle of the plain.

The five had been walking with renewed energy since their rest in the cave. Nothing had bothered them in there. They'd napped peacefully and woken up refreshed.

Without a word, Mariah began a nimble jog down the slope. Tegan and Kody raced each other and Aari and Jag followed slowly. Together, the five looked up at where they'd come from.

"How far do you think we've come since last night?" Mariah asked.

"Hard to say with all the obstacles that we had to skirt around. Maybe fifteen, twenty miles," responded Aari.

"Is that good?"

"I have no clue. I hope so." He squinted up at the sky. "I *think* it's almost midday. I'm sure the villagers will have realized we're gone by now."

"Not necessarily true," Tegan disagreed. "They sometimes leave us alone until noon. We still may have a good lead here."

Kody, bored with the conversation, loped to the river and began refilling his water pelt, smiling with satisfaction. He took a big swig and smacked his lips, feeling re-energized.

"You finished your water *already?*" Aari asked incredulously as he crouched by the river to dip a hand and test the water's temperature. Kody just nodded, contentedly taking gulps.

Jag stared at the river. "So I did remember right. The bears did cross a river after all."

"You can't be too sure it's this particular river, Jag," Mariah said half-absently as she watched Aari step back from the river. "Whoa—whoa! Aari, watch out!"

Too late, Aari's foot slammed a couple of feet down into an abandoned rabbit hole. He fell backward with his foot still stuck and landed with a thud on his back.

Jag, Kody, Tegan, and Mariah rushed to him and helped him up. The girls fussed over him. "Are you okay? Is your back hurting? How about your leg?"

"I'm fine, you two," Aari answered, smiling gratefully at them. "And my leg doesn't hurt that much. I did lose my shoe though." Kneeling by the hole, he rummaged for his missing sneaker. "Got it." Withdrawing his hand, he put his shoe back on. Casting a random glance back down the warren, he stopped and immediately plunged his hand down the hole again.

"Hey, Jag," he said, holding up his hand in amazement. "I think this is yours." Hanging from his fingers was a chain with a dog-tag pendant and a silver crucifix. Jag took it carefully, astonished. "My chains! I thought I lost them in the crash! How did this end up here? The plane is nowhere in sight . . ." He looked around, mystified.

"Wait." Tegan stared at the hole where Jag's necklace had been. "Jag." He was gazing in fascination at his chains. "Jag."

"Yeah?"

"Was your chain around your neck when we crashed?"

Jag thought for a few moments then shook his head. "No. I took them off and held onto them when the first engine blew." He paused, thinking about what he'd said. "Which means it would have been thrown out when the plane crashed." He turned to Tegan, eyes wide. "The plane's got to be around here somewhere." He gazed across the river as he pulled his chains over his head to let them hang down from his neck, exhilaration entering his husky voice. "We need to cross that river. I think the plane is on the other side."

Kody went over and stood beside Jag. "Yeah? And how do you suggest we do that?"

Jag beamed shrewdly. "Who's up for a swim?"

"Over my dead body, bro," Kody retorted.

"Hold on, guys," Aari interjected. "There could be another reason why Jag's chains ended up here. Some animals and birds are really attracted to shiny things and will carry them around for a while before dropping them off somewhere. For all we know, the place where the animal may have gotten these could be days from here, maybe not even on the other side of the river at all."

Mariah was getting frustrated. "We can't keep halting and second-guessing our first thoughts. Stick to one and just go with it."

"What if the initial ideas are completely off?" Aari demanded.

"Doesn't matter! If we keep up this pattern we'll make no progress and the villagers will catch up to us. This is their home turf after all."

"Mariah's got a point," Kody agreed. "Sooo . . . Are we going to cross the river?"

"Everyone needs to agree first." Tegan looked at Aari, waiting.

Aari heaved a long sigh. "Let's do it."

Jag watched a drifting branch being carried rapidly with the river's current. While the water was fast-moving, the river itself didn't seem too deep. "There has got to be a way across."

"Maybe we should split into two groups to look for a crossing," Kody suggested. "One goes that way, and the other goes the other way." He stretched his arms and pointed in opposite directions along the length of the river.

"Sure. Mariah and I'll go that way." Tegan began heading upriver, Mariah following. The boys looked at each other, a seed of concern growing in their minds. Neither wanted to call the girls back and tell them not to go alone. Tegan and Mariah despised it when people thought they were too delicate and needed constant protection.

As the boys hesitantly began walking in the opposite direction, Jag hollered, "Call if you find anything! And don't cross the river alone!"

Tegan, without turning back, raised her hand, indicating she heard him.

The boys followed the river's current. "Most rivers are crossable at some point," Aari mumbled to no one in particular. "Hopefully this one's no different." He jogged ahead, scanning the place for a natural bridge. "There has got to be one here somewhere."

They passed a few rocks that seemed ideal, but when they saw the water splash over and completely cover them from sight, they walked right past.

"I don't hear anything from Mariah or Teegs," Kody said, a little worriedly. "You think they're okay?"

"I think they're fine," Jag answered, although he sounded a little anxious himself. "They just haven't found anything worth yelling out for."

"Here," Aari called. He was a couple of dozen feet down from where the two boys were standing. He pointed to a line of large rocks in the river that extended toward the other side. "What do you think?" he asked when Jag and Kody reached him.

Jag and Kody observed the rocks and looked at each other. "Well?" Kody asked.

Jag shrugged. "Seems fine."

Kody dipped his head and then yelled at the top of his lungs for the girls to come back. They didn't have to wait long, and soon Mariah and Tegan were standing beside them, praising Aari for his find. "Who'll go first?" Mariah asked.

"I'm game," Kody announced and bounced forward one rock at a time, carefully balancing himself. Once he crossed, he looked at his friends and yelled, "It's about forty feet across! Be careful! Some of the rocks are kind of slippery!"

"I'll go next." Tegan warily made her way across. Kody offered her a hand. She grabbed it and he helped her to the other side. Mariah was next, then Jag, then Aari. Kody looked proudly at what they'd accomplished. A word formed in his throat but it vanished when he saw a couple of packets resting on the ground on the opposite bank. "Whoops, I think some food dropped out of my bag."

Tegan walked behind Kody and closed the pack on his back securely. "Smarty," she smiled. "Fetch?"

"You bet." Using the stepping stones again, Kody quickly hopped back to the other side, picked up the food, carefully placed them in his pack then closed it tightly. He turned around, gave the rest of the group a thumb's up and sprang onto the first stone. Some water splashed onto the rock but didn't bother him. He bounded confidently to a couple of more rocks. More water splashed and drenched his right shoe. Momentarily distracted with the uncomfortable slopping and squishing, he put his left foot on the next rock. His foot glided over some wet moss that had grown on the big stone and, with a startled yell, he lost his footing and fell over backward into the river. His friends on shore cried out in alarm.

Kody's head went under the swift-flowing water. Forcing his arms and legs to move, he propelled himself back to the surface. He gasped for air and spewed out swallowed water as he tried to grab at a rock. He was a second too late as the current swept him downstream. Panic shut down his mind and he only moved automatically to keep his head above the water. He didn't even notice his food pack being tugged from his shoulders by the rapid-moving waters.

Jag began sprinting along the bank to keep up with Kody. His long strides were still no match for the increasing speed of the current but he didn't stop. He kept an eye on Kody, seeing the other teenager's head constantly bobbing above and then under the rolling water. *Hang in there, bud.* Jag's eyes flicked up and ahead for an instant and he saw that on the side closest to him there were rocks that extended halfway to the middle of the river. He bellowed at the top of his lungs, "Kody! Move to the rocks!"

Kody didn't hear, and as Jag watched, his friend's struggles began to diminish as he started losing energy. Desperate, he roared again, "*Move toward the rocks, Kody!*"

Jag's voice must have reached Kody's ears at the last moment. The fallen boy strained his body toward the rocks. He slammed into the granite and groaned out loud. He hung on, the cold water splattering his back.

Jag finally reached the rocks. He rushed over them as far as he dared go and stretched out his hand. Kody reached up and was about to grab it when he lost his grip on the rock and the current swept him away once again.

Horrified that he was so close to saving his friend and the chance had literally slipped through his fingers, Jag quickly backed up to the bank and continued running. Kody was several seconds ahead of him. Intent on reaching his friend, Jag didn't notice the fallen tree resting on two huge rocks over the river about fifty yards away until moments later. An idea formed in his mind. He gathered his energy and forced himself into a full sprint. Passing Kody, he reached the fallen tree. He climbed on, panting, then trod to the center and lay down. The tree itself was a few feet above the water; no way could Kody grab onto it.

As Kody drew nearer, Jag stretched out his hand. Kody tried to reach for it but the current was too fast. Not willing to lose his friend for a second time, Jag flipped over at lightning speed to the opposite side of the trunk and made a wild grab at Kody's shirt as the other teenager passed underneath the tree. For a moment, Jag thought he'd failed again but realized the collar of Kody's shirt was crumpled in his clenched fist. He tried to haul Kody out of the water but wasn't strong enough. *More strength and more speed, that's what I need!* Jag thought to himself, his teeth gritted from the effort of holding onto his friend.

"Jag!" Mariah's voice rang out. He cast a quick look over his shoulder and saw the other three racing over to the tree and clambering on.

"I've got him! Help me pull him up!" Jag shouted over the noise of the current. With some effort, the four managed to pull their sodden and dripping friend out of the water and onto the fallen tree. From there, they guided him back to shore where Kody collapsed, shivering uncontrollably. After a few minutes his shuddering subsided just enough for him to thank Jag, Aari, Tegan, and Mariah, who were rubbing his arms and back vigorously to warm him up. He stared at the river, shivering. "I c-could have been swept away t-to who knows w-where . . ." He trembled again, both from the cold and the thought.

"Are you alright?" Jag asked worriedly. Waving the question aside, Kody curled into a ball to conserve the little warmth his body had. His friends watched him silently for a minute more while rubbing his back until he'd warmed up a little. He stretched out and struggled to his feet, trying to wring out his clothes. "You'd think," he complained, still shivering, "that with all the cool inventions those villagers came up with, waterproof insulation would be among them. But nooo . . ."

Jag felt himself grin. "Yeah, you're definitely alright." A breeze picked up and blew toward the group. Kody shivered again and muttered something in annoyance. The other four smiled sympathetically. Mariah passed her pack to Kody and ordered him to change out of his soaked clothes.

"Where am I gonna change?" Kody protested, stiff with cold. Mariah pointed to the trees and reluctantly, Kody obliged, walking quickly into the forest and soon being out of sight. Several minutes later he walked back out, looking more relieved. His shivers were settling down. He passed the pack to Mariah, then the girls wrapped him in a hug to help him warm up faster.

Kody looked at his friends ruefully. "I'm so sorry. The food's gone."

"Better the food than you," Tegan said gently. Kody smiled a little in response but it was clear he was unhappy with himself.

"It wasn't your fault," Aari consoled him. "Accidents happen."

Kody sighed. "Still. I feel like an idiot. Now we've got no food at all."

The friends glanced at each other. Truth was, they *were* concerned that the pack was gone. It contained the food they all depended on.

Mariah looked up. "We should get going."

"Yeah. Come on." Jag turned and walked northward, keeping close to the tree line. His eyes astutely picked up details as they continued on for the next fifteen minutes. He frowned as he looked at the trees further ahead. A number of them appeared to have burn marks on their bark, and some of their trunks were scarred badly. The trees gave the surroundings an ominous feeling. The only thing that lightened the atmosphere was the small creek that snaked from the main river and disappeared beyond the trees.

"This is kind of creepy," Tegan quietly remarked as she walked beside Jag, looking at the blackened trees. He nodded silently and scanned the foliage as they continued to walk. Then, without warning, Tegan tumbled head-over-heels, rolling several yards down a small slope. Caught off guard, Jag and Mariah scrambled down to her and helped her to her feet. "What happened?" Jag asked, bewildered.

Tegan was wide-eyed. "I have no idea. I think my foot hit something."

The friends looked back and saw Aari and Kody standing at the top of the slope where Tegan had tripped. The two boys bent down, brushed away some dirt and pulled off a few broken branches. Jag and the girls made their way up to the pair, who were now crouched and staring blankly at something on the ground in front of them. The sunlight that filtered through the trees reflected and bounced off a shiny red object.

Kody pulled it out from the ground and held it up for the group to see clearly. "From the plane."

Realization dawned on the five. Jag switched his gaze from the red object to the lacerated trees around them and spoke softly. "The plane's got to be here somewhere." He looked over his shoulder, deeper into the forest where the marred trees beckoned. His movements brisk, he headed further in, following the stream. The rest caught up and warily stayed close. The forest got darker the farther in they went. Climbing over and down a large fallen tree in their path, they halted and stared, aghast.

Thirty feet away, through some tall coniferous trees, was the partly charred wreckage of the Piper Comanche.

19

The Elders were pacing back and forth in front of their assembly *neyra* when Akol ran back to them, breathing hard. Chayton was at his heels, whimpering anxiously. "I have looked everywhere, and there was not a single trace of them," he said, puffing. "They must have left during the night."

"Why would they foolishly stray from our protection?" Saiyu demanded. "They were safe with us. Against the power of the forest, they are mere fledglings!"

"They may have been protected, but I believe they were a little less than happy to stay in our village," Tayoka said. "Do you not recall? When we had our first talk with them, they wanted to know when they could leave."

"But to wander out there alone! My goodness!" Saiyu faced Tikina. "We must find them."

Tikina nodded and stepped away. As she closed her eyes and prepared to enter her meditative state, a bloodcurdling scream ripped across the valley. Snapping her eyes open, Tikina exchanged stunned looks with the other Elders and Akol. They heard footsteps rapidly approaching and Huyani burst through the trees, panting for breath, her brown eyes wide with fear.

Akol stepped beside his sister and held her as she tried to form coherent words. "Fiotez . . . I do not know what happened . . . he is—he is . . ." She leaned against Akol to steady herself, pressing her palms to her face, and tried to regain her composure. Chayton nuzzled her knee, looking concerned, his ears folded back.

"Where is Fiotez right now?" Nageau asked.

Huyani pointed straight ahead. "He was in between the convalescence shelter and the school."

"You mean he is out of his bed?" Tikina asked, alarmed. Huyani nodded.

The Elders turned and rushed westward, leaving the siblings and the wolf behind them. They crossed a path and ran over it into the trees until they reached a second path, parallel to the first, and found themselves near the convalescence shelter and the school building where the younger children were. What they saw shocked them to the core.

Fiotez was half-stumbling, half-racing around the school, screeching as if he were a dying animal. Blood was streaming from his nose and ears. When he opened his mouth to bellow, crimson splattered out. His eyes were reddened, and he heaved a long, metal object high above his head.

"An ancient sword!" Saiyu gasped. "He took one of the ancient swords from the temple!"

Fiotez swung the blade at a young child who was screaming and running away in terror. As Fiotez lunged at the boy, the Elders realized that it was the madman's own son.

Diyo tripped and fell as he tried to dodge his father. He looked up to see wide, crazed eyes, and foam dripping from his father's mouth as Fiotez stood over him with the sword raised. The boy screamed again, tears running down his face.

As the Elders raced forward, Fiotez's manic eyes registered recognition as he stared at his son. For a brief moment, a look of utter pain and remorse flitted across his face. Then, without warning, the sword fell from his clenched, claw-like fingers and he dropped to the ground, writhing.

Saiyu bounded ahead of the others. She lifted Diyo to his feet and hurriedly ushered him back toward her companions. By this time Huyani and Akol had caught up with the Elders, and Saiyu left Diyo in their hands. Chayton weaved between the young boy and the siblings, fretful.

Nageau approached Fiotez carefully and stopped when he was several feet away from the fallen villager. Fiotez's thrashing was settling down but he was still twitching uncontrollably. Foam had encrusted his mouth and his bloodshot eyes slowly glazed over until he stopped moving altogether.

Nageau watched with a stony expression and cautiously moved closer to examine Fiotez. A minute passed before he turned around, his blue eyes saddened with grief, and told the others somberly, "He has passed on."

He walked up to Diyo and knelt in front of the young boy. As he gazed into Diyo's light brown eyes, he knew that the damage had been done. Diyo would never—could never—forget this day when his father attempted to end his life. He would never be consolable. For such a young soul to have experienced such a traumatic, disturbing occurrence—the poor lad would be scarred for life.

Nageau stood and gently kissed the child's head. Diyo burst into tears once more and wrapped his arms around the Elder's waist, his heavy sobs being the only sound anyone heard for a while until Tayoka and Ashack began warding away onlookers who came to investigate the noises they'd heard.

"We should strap Mitska's mate down," Saiyu said. "Else we shall witness this scene repeat."

"I agree. It perturbs me that we must go to this length to take care of our ill, but now the concern lies with the safety of the community." Tikina lifted Diyo into her arms and looked at the Elders and her grandchildren. "I will take care of Diyo. You just go ahead and strap our remaining patient down."

With that she walked straight past the school and convalescence shelter toward Esroh Lègna and quickly crossed a bridge to the west side of the valley.

* * *

"Are you sure he is properly restrained?" Akol asked nervously, looking over his sister's shoulder at Mitska's mate. The old man lay on the bed with fiber bands wrapping his chest, abdomen and legs. He was asleep, appearing very ill and chalk-white.

"Trust me, Akol, he is." Huyani checked the straps just in case and stood beside her brother, unhappiness enfolding her. "This feels immoral, to fasten one of our kinfolk to the point where he can hardly move."

Akol squeezed her shoulder. "I know, but it has to be done."

The sound of footsteps outside the convalescence shelter alerted the two and they looked over their shoulders in time to see the Elders entering. They walked over and took a long look at Mitska's mate. Nageau shook his head. "This disquiets me. For many generations we have been safe . . ." He let the sentence hang in the air.

The Elders, Akol, and Huyani simply stood in silence for a while until Huyani asked timidly, "What has become of Fiotez's body?"

"We have made arrangements for him to be buried this evening," Saiyu answered.

"And how is Diyo?"

Tikina, who had entered the shelter with the other Elders, replied with a sigh. "I brought him to his mother and informed her of what just occurred . . . The poor boy fell asleep whilst crying in my arms before we reached his family's shelter."

The door to the convalescence shelter burst open and one of the youths popped in. Her eyes were wide and she looked frightened. "Oh, thank goodness you are all here . . . Elder Nageau, Elder Saiyu! My brother's health has deteriorated—he can hardly move!"

"No, no, no . . ." Ashack muttered. "Did this just happen?"

Before the girl could answer, another youth's head appeared beside hers, wearing the same expression of fear and panic. "Elder Tikina! My mother is extremely ill! She needs help—she is muttering things that do not make sense. Please, you must see to her!" The newcomer's voice cracked as he tried to control his dread.

Nageau spun around and faced his companions. "Tikina, Tayoka! See to this young man's mother, please, and bring her here. Saiyu and Ashack, please look after this girl's brother." He turned to Huyani and Akol. "And I would appreciate it if you both could prepare a few more beds and bring out more straps."

"Um, Grandfather?" Akol raised his hand as if in a classroom environment. "There is the urgent matter of searching for our five missing guests . . ."

Nageau nodded quickly, then turned to Huyani. "Are you alright preparing the beds by yourself? I do not like to leave you to handle this alone—perhaps you could enlist a couple of helpful hands."

"Rest easy, Grandfather. I will cope." She left with everyone else, leaving Akol and Nageau alone inside the convalescence shelter with Mitska's mate.

"Akol, I need you to take charge in gathering people to search for the five. I will leave it to you to decide how it should be done." Nageau rested a strong hand on his grandson's equally strong shoulder. "Are you able to handle it?"

Akol nodded sharply. "Good then," Nageau said. "If there is anything you need to see me about, I shall be with Magèo."

* * *

Nageau walked hurriedly from the convalescence shelter toward the edifice beside the greenhouse building. Unlike the other structures, trees surrounded it from all sides. A trodden dirt path snaked between groves toward the door of the building. Constructed from logs, the large structure was quite rustic, but Nageau knew that inside those four walls, amazing inventions and creative ideas were brought to life.

The Elder knocked on the large, wooden door. A voice yelled, "Who is it!"

"It is Nageau." Moments later, he watched as the door opened, revealing a tall, chubby man in his seventies with sparse white hair on his balding head and a white beard hanging down to his stomach. He had brown skin and two different-colored eyes stretched wide. There were deep wrinkles on his forehead and laugh lines around his mouth. When he saw Nageau, he bellowed a hearty welcome and bear-hugged the Elder.

"Nageau, my old friend! How nice to see you." He turned around and said crisply, "Come inside, come inside. If you do not mind, please shut that door. It is not my favorite weather that greets us this late morning."

"I find it curious that you are the only one in this village who does not enjoy the sun." Nageau carefully closed the door behind him and followed Magèo.

"Well, you should not. We have known each other long enough for you to realize how much I despise that sweltering ball of heat. Makes me feel as though I am cooking inside this old body of mine. Ah, here is a stool you may rest on. Give me a moment and I shall join you quickly."

Nageau sat on the stool and watched as the elderly man walked up to one of the walls and pulled down a large lever. Blinds lifted from twenty windows set high in the walls. Light entered the building, illuminating its inside.

The building was a laboratory and design house, complete with long wooden benches and clay water-basins. Shelves that held different types and sizes of glass containers lined the walls, as did tall jars of brightly-colored liquids. The workshop was a chemist's dream come true, which was precisely the reason why this laboratory was made for Magèo; he was Dema-Ki's inventor and scientist, and admittedly a somewhat eccentric one at that.

Magèo glared up at the windows and muttered, "Perhaps I should design a device that would enable me to see perfectly without sunlight."

"Perhaps," Nageau said, adding firmly, "but there are more pressing matters to resolve first."

"What? Oh, yes, yes, I know." Magèo hurried to one of the sinks in his laboratory to wash his hands. He then walked over to a bench lined with glass tubes in racks, all of which were carefully labeled. He pointed to Nageau and said, "This is where I am labeling the source of the water samples, but I am not conducting my experiments here." He became quiet and stared up at the high windows, looking distant.

"Magèo?" Nageau asked, trying to bring the man back. He knew Magèo's mind worked much differently than many others'. "You were mentioning something about your experiments?"

"Ah, yes, yes." He reached over to grab two tubes filled with clear liquid. "Tell me if you can observe any difference between these, Nageau."

The Elder cautiously sniffed both tubes twice, then narrowed his eyes to study the contents closely. "I detect no difference."

"Well, allow me to tell you first that your suspicion about the water being contaminated is correct."

"Oh?"

"Yes. Also, one of these two tubes holds the contaminated water."

Nageau was dubious. "What?"

"See? If *you* with your heightened senses are unable to pick it up, then surely our regular ones will not be able to. However, I have set up an experiment to prove that the contaminant is indeed water-borne. Walk with me." Magèo led the way to the back of the room at a brusque pace. There, on a long table, were six large beakers, each with a small fish inside. Nageau bent over to get a better look at them and noticed that only two out of the six fishes were moving. The rest were all floating belly-up, dead.

"What in the world is this?" he asked, perplexed.

Magèo wore a big—though grim—smile. "I have labeled all these beakers with the names of the water sources. That day when you sent Tayoka and some men out to collect water samples from various sources, they came back to me with their glass jars and I immediately got to work. As you can see, I have labeled each beaker with the names of the places where the water was taken. I had a young lad bring me these six small, healthy fish, then I placed one in every beaker and watched them. These two that are alive and well were happy in their water." He motioned to the other beakers. "The others were normal at first, but I spent an hour constantly observing their behavior and over that time they became quite agitated, those four. Some even attempted to leap out of their beakers! They swam aggressively and splashed water everywhere. Within the next one to two hours, they died."

Nageau's eyebrows met in a frown. "Have you heard of what happened a little while earlier?"

"No. Why?"

"Fiotez went wild and attacked his son with one of the ancient swords. Blood and foam was dripping from his mouth, and his eyes had a frenzied look. He then fell to the ground and . . . *died* in front of our eyes."

Magèo's jaw dropped in disbelief. "That is uncanny! What a terrible loss! A fine fellow, he was. Bless his mate and child—they will need much support to carry on." He stroked his beard thoughtfully. "He reacted as the fish did, only the fish became hysterical much more quickly because they have smaller immune systems than humans."

"As you can imagine, I came to tell you to please hasten with your research. We have two more people who have fallen into the clutches of this disease, and who knows how many others will succumb to it as well." Nageau laced his fingers together in front of his face and walked up and down the width of the room for some minutes, lost in his thoughts. "So you have labeled the beakers, therefore you know from which areas the water is contaminated," he murmured. "Have you tried to trace the source?"

"I beg your pardon?"

"Have you at all attempted to figure out where the contamination is from? With the labels that you have, we could pinpoint it. There must be some sort of pattern."

"Actually, no I have not. I have solely been trying to find what the contaminant is, not where it came from."

Nageau rubbed his chin. "Do you perchance have a map we could use?"

Magèo scuttled to a cupboard on the wall opposite from the one they were facing. He came back with an old, rolled-up parchment and set it on the table. He slowly rolled it out until it covered the entire tabletop. Nageau leaned over it, eyes scanning the map. It showed Dema-Ki as the central point and displayed a three-hundred mile radius around the valley, portraying the topography of the entire area. It revealed that the early Dema-Ki settlers had very thoroughly explored the landscape, as the map depicted every detail from mountains to clearings to waterfalls to creeks, and more.

Magèo and Nageau gazed at the map for several moments, then looked at the labeled beakers of water with fish, eyes narrowed. Magèo tapped two areas on the map. "So the two water samples where the fish are alive came from the river in our valley and the river on our sister valley's western doorstep."

"The creek to the east of us was where Fiotez refilled his water pelt before falling ill on his hunting trip. It gets its water from this river which forks out—Mayet."

Magèo nodded. "Indeed." He peered down at the map once more, then back up at the beakers, then back down at the map again. "The lake where Mitska's mate camped at is also to the east of our valley, and is fed by this river." He traced his finger along a river in the direction he knew it flowed. Nageau traced the Mayet River in the same manner. Their fingers moved toward the right side of the map where they eventually met as the two waterways merged. They kept following until they reached the source of the water: a cluster of mountains miles to the north of Dema-Ki.

Nageau and Magèo slowly looked at each other as they leaned over the old map. "The Ayen mountain range," Nageau whispered. After a couple of moments, he looked at the other man, an idea forming in his mind. "Magèo, how quickly could you design a method to test the water? It should be small enough to be carried in a pouch and when submerged in water, will tell us if it is contaminated or not."

Magèo scratched his nose and started pacing to and fro, muttering to himself. "Well, it depends. First, I need to find out what type of contaminant we are dealing with. If I cannot identify the specific contaminant, I should be able to at least ascertain a group of contaminants that will react to my test methods. Give me a few sunrises."

"We may not have a few sunrises."

Magèo continued pacing and muttering. Without looking up at Nageau, he said, "In that case, begone with you. I have work to do." He retrieved a pair of thin gloves and scooted to the far corner of the building.

As Nageau nodded and turned to leave, the door of the laboratory opened and Akol took a step into the building, grasping a long metal spear. "Grandfather, we are about to leave."

"Where are your manners?" Magèo barked from the other end of the room. "Have your parents never taught you to knock and wait for permission to enter?"

If Akol had a tail, it would have been tucked firmly between his legs. He seemed to have missed the twinkle of humor in the chemist's eyes. "I am terribly sorry, Magèo. I had no intention to be rude or—"

"Quiet your mouth, boy. I am busy, and therefore I simply *cannot* engage in any conversation." Magèo returned his full attention to his project and paid no more heed to the others in the building. Nageau grinned at his grandson, and Akol finally caught on that Magèo was not actually annoyed with him.

Nageau ushered Akol out of the building quietly. Before the Elder closed the door, he called out, "I shall see you later, old friend."

"What? Oh, yes, yes. Close that door."

Outside, Akol listed off the names of youths he had got together and split into two search teams. "One of the groups will head out to the eastern opening of the valley, and the group I am heading will take the western route through the adjacent valley. We will take a few horses with us, and have packed everything we need."

Nageau smiled warmly at Akol. "Wonderful." He gazed into his grandson's eyes. "You are growing up to be a fine young man, Akol. I am very proud of you."

Akol smiled back and the two shared a brief hug. As he turned and began walking away to find his group, Akol stopped. He looked over his shoulder and said quietly, "I had intended to ask Hutar to join us, considering his skills, but I do not think I trust him enough to work confidently with him."

Nageau tilted his head slightly, then nodded after a moment. "This is your decision to make, and I trust *you* to choose wisely."

Akol allowed himself a small grin.

"Have you asked Tikina for assistance?"

"Yes," Akol replied. "She said not to worry and that she will be with us, just so long as we keep looking out for her."

"That should not be hard. She will be using either of her favorites, Akira or Tyse."

Akol waved to Nageau and jogged away to rejoin the group he would be leading to search for the missing five.

20

Kody stared at the wrecked plane, dread knotting his insides. With his heart pounding, he raced toward it, quickly gaining speed until he was sprinting. "Dad! *Dad!*" His yells rang across the small clearing.

His friends reached the mangled plane shortly after he did and eyed the aircraft. They shuddered at the thought that they had been inside when it crashed and somehow survived. The first thing they noticed was that the plane was upside down on the forest floor with its right wing charred. The second thing that caught their attention was that the Piper's left wing was nowhere to be found; not even a quick eye-sweep could help the group locate it. As they ran their eyes over the aircraft, they also noted that the tail had been torn clear off and was buried under two large broken branches.

Immediately Kody headed for the cockpit and the other four cautiously followed him. He knelt down by the pilot's side of the cockpit. "It's dark inside. I'm gonna go in and see if"—Kody took a breath—"see if he's there."

His friends nodded and watched him get down on his hands and knees and wriggle through the broken windshield. They waited quietly for a few tense moments before Kody crawled back out. The look in his eyes told the others that there was no sign of his father in the cockpit.

"Hey, you know, he could have been thrown out of the plane," Mariah suggested softly. "Tegan, let's go. We'll look around. You guys just see what we can salvage from here, and find the radio too."

"Hold on, Mariah," Kody said. "He's my dad. I'll go with you to look for him."

Mariah and Tegan exchanged glances and blocked him as he tried to skirt around them. "Let us do the searching," Tegan said.

"If you find him, I want to be there."

"Then we'll call you over if we find him"

"Don't try to talk me out of this, Teegs. I'm going." He tried to maneuver around the girls but again they held him back.

"Kody, listen," Mariah insisted; neither she nor Tegan wanted Kody to be around if they found his father and he wasn't alive. "Just stay here with the guys, and leave the scouting to us. Okay?"

Kody looked from Mariah to Tegan, noting the firm look they both wore. He didn't feel like arguing with them, but threw them a glare and turned to slowly walk up to Jag and Aari, who each clasped his shoulder. The girls wandered away from the plane into the surrounding trees. The boys stood back and observed the aircraft.

"Tell you what," Aari said gently. "Let's clear off the rubble from the plane and then you two can go inside and see what you can find."

Jag nodded. "Right."

It took them a few minutes to clear away enough debris that Jag and Kody could get into the plane safely. Inside the remains of the plane, Jag and Kody surveyed the scene. The cabin appeared to be mostly preserved, although it was a little hard to tell with the ceiling inverted. Jag, on his hands and knees, began shoving away debris from inside the plane. He looked up at the seats to make sure he wouldn't bump his head and saw some brown fabric hanging down. He stretched an arm under one of the seats and yanked at the fabric. When it wouldn't come free, he used both hands to wrench the item out and it fell on him. He held it up and saw that it was a knapsack. Without thinking, he rummaged through the bag's contents and looked up at Kody with a mildly amused expression. "'Riah's. It's got her, er . . . stuff in it."

"Oh. We should take it, then." Kody poked his head out of a broken window and was somewhat surprised to come face-to-face with an ankle. "Um, hello?" He tapped the jeans-clad leg wearily. "Who might this be?"

"It's me, genius." Mariah crouched down. "I've switched with Aari. He's with Tegan now."

"Haven't found my dad yet?"

"Not yet, Kody." Her tone was sympathetic. "You guys find anything?"

"Your knapsack."

Mariah's eyebrows rose. "It didn't get burned or damaged?"

Jag good-humoredly nudged Kody aside to stick his head out the window. "Not really. It was hooked under the seat, so it probably got luckier than any of our other things." He pulled his head back and stuck the bag out. Mariah took it thankfully. "If you guys find other things, just call out and I'll grab them."

"Sure thing." Kody turned around and continued searching inside the plane.

"Kody, where's the plane's radio?" Jag asked.

Kody scoffed. "In the cockpit, where else?" He crawled into the cockpit, finding it odd that he was kneeling on the ceiling of the plane, and looked up at the pilot's seat. A quick glance into the chair was enough to see dark red stains splattered across it. The display sickened him but he continued searching for the radio.

Meanwhile, Jag had found a can of clam chowder and passed it to Mariah. She looked alarmed. "Don't tell me this is all that you found."

"Relax, there are still a few cans here. If you ask me, though, it seems like some of the animals beat us to most of the provisions." He withdrew, then returned a few moments later and stuck his hands out. "Here are two cans of tuna, and more cans of other stuff."

Mariah took them and stuck her tongue out in distaste. "I love fish, but not tuna. Better than nothing, of course," she said quickly. She placed it down, then looked back at him with a hopeful glint in her eyes. "Are there any cans of Dr Pepper in there?"

He shook his head. "You Peppers and your obsession. No, there's none."

She sighed. "So that's it?"

"Yep. I'm gonna go check on Kode-man." Jag turned in time to see Kody crawling out.

"Found the radio," Kody informed him. "But it's not working."

"Needs batteries?"

"Wouldn't help. The thing's broken. The crash busted it."

Jag sat back with a groan. "We're up the creek, then."

"Pretty much."

They sat for a while until Jag started to crawl out of the plane. "Let's head out. It's too stuffy in here."

Once outside, they waited until Tegan and Aari came back. Kody looked at them with tentative hope but the unsmiling faces of his friends told him they hadn't found his father.

Aari was sullen. "I'm sorry, Kody. No sign of him anywhere."

Kody ground his teeth, holding back the tears he wanted no one to see.

"Maybe the search and rescue folks found him and took him to an ER somewhere," Tegan suggested.

Kody shook his head and sat beside the plane's fuselage. With a sigh, he leaned back and said, "No. If they found the plane, there'd be signs of investigations to figure out what might have caused the crash, like taking away the propellers or parts of the engines. They'd also leave emergency supplies here in case any survivor returned to the plane. No one's visited this place. No one knows where we are."

"Well, what about the radio? Is it working?"

"It's broken."

Tegan covered her face in exhaustion. "Okay, fine. So two choices, then."

Jag scratched his head. "Let's hear them."

"We stay here and build a land-to-sky SOS signal like a smoke fire or something of the sort, or we keep walking toward what would hopefully be a town."

"I'd go with whatever the brighter option is," Mariah muttered. "But by the looks of it, neither one is great. Why should we stay if the plane's been here for two weeks or so and no one's found it? Then again, why should we keep walking? Who said there'd be a town around here? Who said we might be heading in the right direction *to* a town?"

There was an accusatory pause as the others turned to look at Jag. Jag threw his hands up. "Oh, come on! We talked about this in the village. Some support would be appreciated. And besides, we may still be heading in the right direction. We found the plane, didn't we?"

Kody rose to his feet and turned around to stare at the dirt-covered aircraft. Swiping one finger over it, he said, "We could write a message on here, in case people find the plane."

"So you don't intend to stay here?" Aari asked.

"No. Mariah's got a point. Staying put here probably won't do us much good. And we can't forget about Akol and Huyani and their village. If they catch up to us, do you honestly think they'd let us stay here?"

"Oh, Scarecrow, you do have a brain," Tegan said with teasing affection. Kody gave her a look but then cracked a smile.

"Alright, Kode-man and I will write a message. You three . . ." Jag stopped short. "What's that over there?"

"Huh?" Aari looked around. "What are you talking about?"

"That thing under there, where the plane's tail used to be."

Aari, bemused, looked around again until he spotted what Jag saw and went to retrieve it. He came back rummaging through a medium-sized canvas bag. "Some rotten little critter's already been through it," he grumbled, showing several small holes at the bottom of the bag. "If there was food in there, then we have nothing." He dug around some more. "We've got a couple of flashlights here, but I think one's broken. Got some fire starters, a box of matches, a portable first-aid kit . . . Ah, this must be the emergency bag. And—hey, look. A flare gun." He pulled out the pistol with a grin.

Jag took it from him and smiled. "I remember using this last year. Dad showed me how to load one up and fire it."

Aari looked into the bag again. "I see only two flares."

"Here, hand it over. I'll carry it." Kody reached out for the bag. Aari passed it to him once Jag handed the gun back.

Mariah looked at Jag. "You gonna write the message?"

Jag blinked. "What? Oh, right. Yeah." He found a pair of serrated rocks and passed one to Kody. "Better use these than just writing on the dirt." The boys began scrawling letters onto the plane and when they finished, stood back to gaze at their message.

"Good enough?" Jag asked the others.

Mariah read it out loud. "'Left to find a town. Samuel Tyler is not with us. Please send help. Signed Aari, Jag, Tegan, Kody, and Mariah.'"

"Not great, but it will have to do." Tegan walked up to the plane, took Kody's rock and added an arrow. "So they know the general direction of where we're headed." She picked up Mariah's knapsack and tossed it to the other girl, who caught it and slung it over her shoulders. "We should get moving."

The rest picked up their packs and the five continued trekking northward, resisting the urge to look back at the Piper Comanche as it slowly disappeared from sight.

21

The sun was beginning to set over the mountains ahead of the group as they walked. Tegan gazed up. "Can we call it a day?" she asked quietly. The other four nodded wearily. Aari, who'd been heading the group, stepped back and allowed Jag to lead the friends.

Tegan slowed down to fall back beside Mariah and Kody, whom she noticed to be uncharacteristically quiet. Kody looked at the girls, his face expressionless, lost in his own world. No doubt a world far away from here, Tegan thought. She rested a hand on Kody's forearm. "Hey," she whispered.

He responded with a quiet grunt.

Trying to make light of the situation, she joked, "What, suddenly you're a caveman now?"

He sighed. She elbowed him. "You're not going to poke fun back at me?"

Kody glanced away, neck muscles tight. "Look, I'm not always going to come back with some joke or sarcastic comment or what have you."

Tegan wanted to retreat into a shell. "Sorry. I didn't mean—"

"I'll crack the jokes when I'm around you guys—whatever. It helps to forget about this whole situation with… with Dad. But it just seems weak, distracting myself by trying to make you guys laugh."

Mariah, on his other side, hugged her arms around one of his briefly. "That's you being strong, Kody, not weak. You can put a smile on people's faces in hard times. You know what my mom says about you, ever since we were really little?"

Kody's expression became one of surprise and curiosity. "What?"

"That the world needs more people like you—people who can laugh at themselves and at anything, not hold grudges, and bring light into a dark situation, no matter how dreary everything seems."

Kody stared at her for a long while as he soaked in her words. With a slightly softened countenance, he patted her hand and she let go of him.

The group continued walking for the next several minutes in complete silence as they took in their surroundings. A raven swooped down and landed on the ground in front of them, peering at them suspiciously, then took off again.

The group halted when Jag stopped and looked up. They were staring at a rock face that was about thirty feet high and stretched for dozens of feet. Jag eyed it quietly for a moment then glanced to his left where something caught his attention. He moved toward what appeared to be a crevice in the granite wall, but was actually an opening just wide enough for him to squeeze through. He slid in, then motioned for the others to follow.

When the five reached the other side, they found themselves inside a large enclosure. The rock wall curved around, making a circular shape like the Roman coliseum, lacking only columns and seats for spectators. Creepers and vines hung down ornamentally from the top of the wall. To the right of where the five stood was a fair-sized pond. The sun lit the surface of the water, rendering it a deep, vibrant shade of blue.

"This is amazing," Tegan murmured as she gazed around.

"It's like it was meant for us," Mariah said. "Our own haven."

"I wanna check this place out." Aari trotted toward the pond and placed his pack down a few yards away from its edge. The others followed him and soon the five were all over the enclosure, calling out to each other animatedly as they discovered interesting spots.

"Look at these huge boulders around the base of the wall," Kody commented. He scaled one quickly and assumed the King of The World position. His friends smiled, glad that his mind was currently occupied on something other than the fact that his father was still missing.

Tegan was gazing up at a grove of black spruce and lodgepole pine trees to the left of the pond. Jag couldn't help himself and clambered up one of them. The trees were tall, seeming to reach for the sky.

Mariah was exploring the opposite end from where the group entered and shouted out so the others could hear. "There's another entrance from this side!"

"How wide is it?" Jag yelled back from where he was up in the tree.

"A touch wider than the one we walked through!"

Tegan paid no heed to their conversation and sauntered off to join Kody up on the boulders. Aari was looking around, gazing at the almost circular rock wall, noting how it varied in height. He guessed the lowest point to be ten feet and the highest point to be perhaps forty feet. As he observed the enclosure, he heard both Tegan and Kody announce that they were hungry as they jumped down from the boulders. The group started heading back to where they'd left their packs.

"We have two cans of tuna, three cans of chicken soup, one can of clam chowder . . . and one can of Malaysian satay sauce?" Mariah looked at Kody who'd helped pack the food for the trip to Dawson City. He shrugged sheepishly. Mariah rolled her eyes and said, "We're going to have to ration the food in case we don't find a town soon."

Kody was aghast. He looked over his shoulder at the pond. "Maybe there's fish in there," he suggested hopefully. He, Tegan, and Aari peered in, but even with the sun hitting the water they realized the pond was too dark a blue to see anything under the surface.

"Let's get a fire started first, then we'll come back to the food," Aari said. The five spread out to look for firewood and met back a few minutes later. Tegan had already cleared a spot near their packs for the fire and had collected some kindling. Aari and Mariah hauled some rocks over, and Jag heaved several large logs. As he dumped the last log, he looked around. "Where's Kody?"

His answer came trotting toward them, carrying a few broken branches that were long and sharp. The four stared at him. Jag scratched the back of his neck. "Um, Kody? You know those things burn up pretty quick, right?"

Kody looked at him as if he were crazy. "Who said anything about these going into the fire? They're my insurance, the same way they were last night. Remember when we tried to sleep out in the open and heard the roaring and all that?"

The friends exchanged a look and decided to let it go. "I think we should make a bonfire," Aari said, tapping one of the rocks with his shoe. "We've already made a pretty big pit for it, and the stones will make a good barricade. What do you guys think?"

Kody raised his hands. "You know what, man, I don't care. I just want the dang food."

As they placed the stones in a wide circle, Mariah looked up and stared at something with wide eyes. The others saw her and turned to look. At the opening in the rock wall where they'd entered stood a honey-colored lynx, its white-silver stripes appearing to glow in the light of the setting sun. Its familiar golden-green eyes bore into the five's and it turned around in frantic circles, hissing urgently.

"What's the matter with it?" Mariah murmured warily.

Tegan shook her head in wonderment. "No clue. It's not attacking us."

"Well, something's bothering it. You think we're settling down in its territory?"

"I'm pretty sure we've trekked into different territories over the past hours, and we haven't had an incident. The lynx would either attack us or leave us alone."

"Then what is it *doing?*"

"That's wicked," Aari grinned. "I've never seen a lynx in the wild before." He studied it closely. "Hey, that looks like the lynx Akol described. Remember? Ticks, Tikes, Toes . . ."

"Tyse!" Mariah exclaimed softly. "He's right. Tegan, we saw her before, when we first went looking for the guys."

Tegan's eyes registered recognition. "It's her alright. Is she following us?"

The lynx was still acting anxious, sitting on her hind legs and clapping her paws in the air. The friends looked at each other, mystified. In a seemingly desperate attempt, the cat leapt into the air and made odd sounds in her throat. The friends were still confused by the feline's odd display.

The lynx growled, obviously upset at the group, then craned her neck and stared right up at the sky. She didn't look down, so the five looked up into the heavens to see what had caught her attention. In the darkening sky, a golden eagle soared overhead, gliding in large circles around the site. When the group looked back down at the cat, all they saw was her tail as she sprinted away.

"That was strange," Kody remarked.

The eagle that had been gliding above suddenly swooped down. It flew around the perimeter of the enclosure, screeching the whole way. The friends watched, agape, as the eagle hovered not ten feet in front of them, flapping its wings and creating a great gust of wind in the five's direction as if telling them to leave. It cawed restlessly and after a few moments soared right over their heads, did a turn, and flew back over to a tree at the top of the rock wall, settling onto a branch.

Not knowing what to make of these occurrences, the five continued to place the logs to start the fire. They lit the kindling with a couple of matches from the emergency bag from the plane.

Once they had a good fire going, the girls unpacked the sleeping bags and spread them in a semi-circle under a large tree not far from the flames.

Mariah took off her jacket and threw it onto her sleeping bag. "This is a decent fire."

"Food," Kody grumbled. "Let's crack open the tuna cans. They can be eaten straight out."

The group washed dirt off their hands by dipping them in the pond. Jag and Kody then pulled back the tabs and passed the tuna cans around as they all sat on their sleeping bags.

After they'd finished eating, they leaned back under the tree where the girls had spread the sleeping bags. They were disappointed that they didn't have more food to spare, but were grateful for the little they had.

Kody was silently berating himself for not having the food pack. It had been well-filled. "Ninety-nine bags of burgers on the wall, ninety-nine bags of burgers," he sighed.

"Take one down, pass it around, ninety-eight bags of burgers on the wall," Tegan continued. Soon they were all singing, counting down to seventy-eight when they decided to stop and crawl into their sleeping bags. They lay down with their feet facing the fire and watched as some sparks flew from it. One by one they nodded off until they were all in deep sleep.

22

The night was quiet. The fire crackled by the five's feet; it had gotten a tad smaller but still burned brightly. There was no wind, and it seemed like nothing stirred inside the enclosure or around it.

Jag slowly opened his eyes. He didn't move and kept his chin slightly tucked in under his sleeping bag. He could hear the fire and looked around without moving his head. He saw Tegan's dark hair on his left and Mariah's lighter tresses beside hers. He knew Kody was on his right and Aari was on Mariah's other side. By their breathing he could tell they were all asleep.

So why then had he woken up?

He sat up quietly and squinted at the fire, then looked down at the other four as they slept. His eyes returned to the large, warm flames and he licked his lips uneasily. Something didn't feel right.

He reached into his sleeping bag, pulled out his hoodie and shrugged it on before zipping it up. He sat for a little while, not sure what to do, then glanced up when he saw something out of the corner of his eye. The eagle that had perched on the tree high up on the rock wall was still there, its wings spread as the wind picked up a little. All Jag could see of it was its silhouette, and for some reason it made him more than a little nervous.

The large bird launched itself into the air and swooped around the enclosure like it had earlier, keeping close to the rock wall. Jag watched it warily. It soared back around for the second time and flew right past the group, creating a sudden gust of wind, and screeched sharply. Jag flinched and covered his ears.

Mariah, Tegan, and Aari jolted awake and looked around in terror, then caught sight of the eagle up in the sky. "What's that crazy thing doing?" Aari complained groggily.

Jag kicked out of his sleeping bag and muttered, "We need to get out of here."

Mariah looked over at him, puzzled. "What's the matter? It's just an eagle."

"No, I'm serious. Something's wrong. We need to get out of here *now*."

His friends couldn't ignore the alarm in his usually calm tone and wriggled out of their sleeping bags. Jag looked over and saw Kody still in a deep sleep with a cluster of long sticks at his side. Jag grabbed his shoulder and shook him. The other boy half-opened his eyes and glared up.

"We're moving out, Kody. Get up."

Roused by the uncharacteristic tenseness in Jag's voice, Kody quickly wormed out of his sleeping bag into the cold air. Jag moved to the base of his own sleeping bag to roll it up and pack it away. Beside him, Tegan was doing the same. He glanced about to check if the eagle was still flying around but didn't see it and finished rolling. He shifted uncomfortably; the fire was hot against his back.

As he was putting his sleeping bag away, he felt the hairs on the back of his neck stand up. Slowly, he looked toward the opening the five had squeezed through earlier in the evening. Two glowing red embers hovered in the darkness, a few inches apart. Jag strained to see what they were, but the firelight didn't reach far enough.

Unsettled, he leaned closer to Tegan and whispered, "Look."

Tegan looked up. She saw the red orbs against the dark background and breathed in sharply, then bent her head closer to Jag's. "What is it?" she asked softly.

"I don't know."

The others noticed nothing as they continued packing. Jag and Tegan kept their heads bent together and stared at the red lights.

Suddenly two more pairs, exact replicas, appeared on either side of the first one.

They heard a gasp behind them and heard Aari and Mariah talking quickly in quiet tones. Tegan and Jag looked over their shoulders past the fire. At the other entrance in the rock wall were three more glowing pairs of red orbs. Kody looked over to see what they were muttering about and started.

"What are those?" Aari rasped.

"More on this side," Tegan murmured. The others turned to look and their eyes widened. Jag looked into the fire and saw a log the length of his arm, one end of it aflame. He grabbed it and hurled it as far as he could toward the first entrance.

The burning log landed several feet from the entrance and the five froze. The fire glinted off three separate sets of large, sharp teeth and cast ominous shadows onto the rock wall. The middle pair of orbs drew closer toward the burning log.

In the firelight the five saw the face of a scarred, angry timber wolf. Only the front of its body was visible, but it was easy to tell that it was frighteningly large. From its paws to its chest it was nearly three feet tall. The dark gray fur on its face was matted with dried blood and clumps of fur were missing on its muzzle. One ear was torn, the other heavily scratched. Foam was lathered around its jaws and dripped to the ground at its massive paws. The flames reflected in its eyes, making the wolf appear to glare out at the friends.

The animal turned its head slightly toward where the other half of its pack was closing in from the opposite entrance, circling the pond toward the five. The friends rose to their feet to stand back to back beside the tree they were under. Kody passed a pair of his improvised spears to Aari and Jag and held onto one himself.

"What do we do?" Tegan whispered. No one knew what to say as they watched the wolves close in from both directions.

Jag's mind was racing as his eyes darted from side to side. "Get around the pond to the other entrance," he said quietly.

Mariah looked at him. "What?"

"Go around the other side away from the wolves, and head for the exit." Jag didn't take his eyes off the animals as he roared, *"Run!"*

Mariah spun and raced around the pond, Aari hot on her heels. One of the wolves that had come in from the second entrance saw her and charged back to intercept. Mariah halted and turned around, nearly colliding into Aari. She tore past him towards a cluster of boulders. There was a small gap between them and Mariah headed right for it, chancing it even though she didn't know if she could fit in. The wolf that had tried to intercept her rocketed after her, ignoring Aari.

Mariah dove head-first between the boulders and quickly pulled her legs into the tight space, breathing heavily. *Stupid brute—*

She screamed as the wolf that had chased her suddenly forced its jaws into the gap in the boulders, its sharp teeth snapping. Foam sprayed everywhere. Mariah whimpered in fright. She lifted up one foot and aimed a kick at the wolf's face. Her foot smashed against the animal's nose and it withdrew, letting out a series of short barks. But instead of deterring it, she had only enraged it. The wolf shoved its muzzle into the gap again, lips pulled back into a snarl as it furiously tried to reach her. Mariah bum-scooted as far away from the wolf as she possibly could in the narrow space.

Suddenly she heard a low growl from behind and froze. Slowly turning her head, she came face-to-face with the snapping jaws of another wolf. She shrieked, attempting to move to the center of the small refuge, and tried to pull her knees closer to her chest.

Aari saw the coordinated attack by the two animals and wanted to help Mariah, but was surprised by a wolf charging at him from his right flank. He yelped and sprinted toward the exit. He knew he wouldn't be fast enough to escape and instead scrambled up a tree near the second entrance. The wolf tried to propel itself up after the boy, digging its claws into the bark, but slid back down. It circled the tree and whined in frustration, red eyes glaring up at Aari. Aari stared back from the safety of a branch, wondering what would cause an animal to have such maddened eyes that even its pupils were reddened.

The wolf again attempted to climb the tree and Aari kicked it down, being careful not to get bitten as he saw foam spraying from its mouth. Jeez, they're rabid! No wonder they're flying off the handle. It leapt, digging its claws deep into the tree, and pulled itself up. Aari goggled and scampered further up the tree onto another branch.

Seeing little chance of reaching the exit, Kody had jumped into the pond. He was a good swimmer despite having been overcome by the fast and furious rapids the day before, and thought he would have the edge against the wolves. He front crawled toward the middle of the pond where he stopped and straightened, kicking his feet underwater to keep himself afloat. He gazed out to the shore where a wolf was racing around the pond, hopping up and down and whimpering in frustration as it looked at him. Kody couldn't help but laugh at the helplessness of the animal.

"Loser!" he shouted as he treaded water. He waved his index finger around his head, motioning to the pond around him. "You want to mess with all this? Well good luck, pal!"

The wolf stared at him for a moment, silhouetted by the fire behind it, then careened into the water and dog-paddled madly after him. Kody squawked and swam from the wolf as fast as he could.

Tegan had been following Aari and Mariah as they ran toward the second opening and had witnessed the oncoming wolves, so instead she'd raced straight for the rock wall where boulders were piled on one another like the steps of a giant staircase. She vaulted onto the first boulder and clambered up on top of the second one. When she landed on the third, she turned back to look down and panicked when she saw a wolf already up on the first boulder. She turned and gazed up at the next boulder above her. Its surface was at least six feet above her. She retraced her steps until she was at the edge of the boulder she was standing on and glanced back down.

When she saw the wolf clawing its way up onto the rock below her, she turned and ran, launching herself at the edge of the boulder above. She grabbed on and hung there for a moment, trying to get at least one leg up onto the boulder, but found herself unable to. Instead, she army-crawled up, giving no thought to scraped elbows and knees. Once she made it, she rolled onto her side and looked down again. The black wolf was now on the second boulder, staring up at her. It was smaller than the others but equally aggressive. It snapped its jaws in her direction and tried to scrabble its way to the third level. Tegan didn't wait for the wolf to reach it. She whirled around and quickly mounted the next boulder.

Standing by the fire next to the pond, Jag faced the giant wolf that had been the first to enter their refuge. He'd lit his spear on fire and kept the burning end at the wolf's eye level. The wolf tried to lunge at him but swerved away when Jag brought the burning tip around. He never took his eyes off the animal, knowing that if he did, it would surely go for his throat. He found the wolf's eyes unnerving, more so with the flames reflected in them. From the creature's confident stance he guessed that this was the alpha male.

Leading with the flaming stick in his hand, Jag tried to gain ground by advancing. The wolf backed away, its tail high, before trying to lunge at him once more. Jag jumped back and thrust the stick at the wolf. The wolf swayed from side to side, trying to get past Jag's defense, then leapt to Jag's left. The boy whipped the stick in the animal's direction and it backed up, growling.

Jag suddenly remembered something: the flare gun. He needed to reach it, but it was in the emergency bag. That was thirty feet away under the tree with their packs. He dared a rapid glance behind and saw the tree. He quickly looked back at the wolf and sidestepped as it attempted once more to attack him. *Come on, Jag,* he thought desperately. *You're a traceur. This is what you've been practicing back home. Parkour. Use your environment. Just do it!*

He counted silently to five before jabbing the stick at the creature, letting it fly in the process, then turned and tore toward the tree. As expected the wolf sprinted after him. Using his momentum, he kicked a leg up onto the trunk and ran a couple of steps up the tree. Arms outstretched, he gripped a branch with both hands and swung himself up in an arc onto the branch. He stared down and let out his breath. *Made it.*

The wolf was staring up at him, and it looked furious that it had been outwitted. Jag quickly climbed up over another branch so he was hidden from the creature's view by the thicker foliage. From his perch, he stared through to the ground below. His eyes landed on the emergency bag. He knew he would have to be very careful, because he would have to take his eyes off the wolf to get the pistol out once he was back on the ground.

He took a few deep breaths, then launched off the tree and hit the ground rolling. He threw himself at the emergency bag and struggled with it until he found the flare gun.

The wolf snarled and ran around the tree the instant it heard Jag land. It bunched its muscles and leapt. Jag knew it was coming. He loaded the flare cartridge into the pistol and rolled out of the way. The wolf landed, missing Jag by a couple of feet, then turned and lunged at the sixteen-year-old again. Quick as lightning, Jag cocked the gun, pointing the barrel at the oncoming animal, and fired. Bright orange and red blinded him but he rolled out of the way before the wolf could land on him. He turned to look at the creature. From its chest, the dark gray fur was on fire. It dropped to the ground and rolled on the moist grass, yelping as the fire singed its fur and scorched its skin and burned up to its face, blinding it. It bounced up to its paws and galloped in loops before dropping to the grass again, twisting and turning. Intent on putting the fire out, the wolf paid no attention to where it was headed as it stumbled and rolled toward the bonfire. Jag stared on with a mix of awe and horror as the beast tripped over the rocks surrounding the fire pit and tumbled into the blaze. The licking flames surrounded the creature, swallowing it into the depths of the inferno.

Watching as the wolf's agonized writhing slowly dissipated, Jag sat down on the damp grass, legs shaking slightly. Within moments the animal's movements ceased altogether and the creature was consumed by the bonfire which enveloped it completely in its burning embrace. Jag quietly ran his hands through his hair and shut his eyes tight.

All this time, Kody had been swimming in circles around the pond as the wolf after him paddled feverishly to catch up. Kody could tell it was tiring, but it would not quit. He was desperate. He needed to get away from the wolf before he too was exhausted. Glancing quickly over at his pursuer, he took a breath and dove down, hoping he could shake the wolf off his track. It worked. When Kody disappeared, the wolf faltered, ears twitching. It swam around in agitated circles, whining, but couldn't find the boy.

Submerged, Kody was unable to see a thing. The water was too dark. He stayed down though, and kicked away from where he had been. Being a good swimmer, he'd spent a lot of time learning to hold his breath for extended periods, so he was under for over a minute before he had to pop up for some air.

He shot to the surface and took a gulp of air. He didn't see the wolf and exhaled gratefully. But as he turned around, color drained from his face. The wolf was right there, not three feet away, staring at him. He choked, splashing the water. The wolf shoved its face at Kody's, fangs gnashing. Kody turned and swam for his life. *"God save me!"* he screamed before getting a mouthful of water.

Jag heard Kody's yell and looked up. The light from the bonfire illuminated the water and he could see Kody swimming wildly away from an enraged wolf. He jumped to his feet and ejected the used cartridge from the pistol and put in the second one, the last one. He hollered, "Kody, duck!"

Kody heard Jag and paused in the water, looking around as he tried to stay afloat. Jag yelled again. "Keep swimming, you idiot! And *duck!*"

Kody saw his friend on shore with the flare gun. A spray of fiery colors emanated from the barrel of the pistol. He shot underwater just in time. He could see a bright flash above him but didn't dare surface yet. Instead, he kicked away for several yards, then came up to look for the wolf. It wasn't hard to find. The flare had lodged itself into the creature's mouth and was burning furiously. Kody watched the scene in disbelief. Flames reflected on the water around the animal. The wolf thrashed in agony as fire shot out of its jaws, burning its face. It swam in dizzying circles, a ghastly animal scream torn from its throat as it choked and tried to put out the fire.

Over by the rock wall, Tegan was about to scale a sixth boulder when she heard the wolf in the pond screaming in agony. She looked over and saw the unbelievable sight, but didn't allow her astonishment to distract her.

She was about to look down at her own pursuer but flinched when she heard the sound of claws scraping against granite. She quickly went for the topmost boulder. When she finally reached the summit, she blew out a pent-up breath and gazed down, squinting to see better because the fire's light didn't reach this far. The wolf was just two boulders below her. She looked around frantically. She needed somewhere to go, else she'd have to jump off to save herself from the wolf. She turned and, for the first time, clearly saw where she was. She was on a flat-topped boulder a few yards from the top of the enclosure wall, about twenty-five feet up from the ground. A fallen tree had created a perfect bridge for her, linking the boulder and ledge. Tegan didn't even think but bolted to it and started to cross. She didn't have a problem with heights, but she was feeling as though the wolf was breathing down her neck.

Behind her, she could hear the beast scrabbling to reach the last boulder, the one she was on. Though every single one of her senses screamed at her to keep moving forward, she couldn't resist looking over. As she reached the middle of the log, she saw the wolf's head popping over the last boulder, eyes glowing eerily red even in the faint light. It was trying to dig its claws into the rock and haul itself up. When it saw Tegan staring at it, it pulled its lips back in a terrifying snarl.

Tegan whimpered and faced the front, making her way over to the top of the rock wall. At one point her foot slipped and she nearly fell. From there on, she crawled over to the ledge.

The wolf was already about to cross the log bridge, but it seemed cautious of the drop.

When Tegan made it to the other side, she turned and saw the wolf was almost halfway across. Fear made her actions frantic and she started kicking at the log, hoping to push it off the ledge. It was heavy. She cursed as she attacked the log. She heaved it with all her might and suddenly felt it budge. Shouting out in triumph, she continued heaving. The wolf realized what she was doing. As it prepared to lunge off the bridge, Tegan gave one last push with both feet and the log rolled free. The wolf yelped and tried to claw at anything to keep from falling, but in vain. It plummeted, thrashing all the way down.

Tegan knelt and looked down. The wolf lay motionless on the ground below, between the stack of boulders and the rock wall. She gazed at it for a while, then sat back and hugged her knees close to her chest, groaning in relief. Once she caught her breath, she looked around. How do I get down?

Jammed into the small gap between the boulders, Mariah was terrified for her life. She was trapped by two brutal, feverish wolves hell-bent on ripping her apart. She yelled for help, then nearly jumped out of her skin for the hundredth time as the wolf in the front of the gap tried to force its head in.

Suddenly she heard a spine-tingling screech. The wolf's jaws disappeared from the entrance of the tiny gap. Mariah was too frightened to leave her refuge to see what had happened.

From his vantage point in the tree, Aari had watched helplessly as two wolves tried to force their way into the narrow space between the boulders where Mariah had retreated. Now he watched in astonishment as the eagle that had earlier wakened the group battled the large black wolf. It screeched and sunk its talons into the back of the animal's neck, clawing toward the scalp. The wolf whimpered, backing away from the winged warrior, its fur matted with dark red streaks, but was not about to surrender. It jumped into the air and tackled the huge bird, trying to drag it to the ground, but the eagle would not give and instead shifted its grip to the back of the wolf's head. The wolf let go and reared up, crying out in misery.

Aari had never seen such a thing in his life and was completely awestruck by both the fighting and the absolute fearlessness of the eagle. Although the eagle had a wingspan of about eight feet, the wolf was far more massive.

Aari's eyes went back to the boulders where Mariah was hiding and saw the second wolf still attempting to get its jaws into her hideout. He was trying to figure out ways that he could help her and didn't notice his own relentless stalker clawing its way up the tree with sheer brute strength. It was almost a third of the way up when Aari looked down and saw its muzzle three feet below. Startled, he flailed his feet and managed to kick the creature under the jaw. The force of the impact was enough to send the wolf skidding back down the tree trunk. It leapt free at the last second and snarled up at Aari. Aari sucked in his breath. I think I just blew my chance of being best buddies with him, he thought as he climbed onto a higher branch.

Still treading water in the pond, Kody was still staring at his flaming pursuer when he heard his name called. He turned around and saw that he was close to the shore where Jag was. He splashed over and Jag grabbed his arm as he got out. "This is the second time in two days I've had to pull you out of water," Jag commented idly. "I'm not in favor of this habit, bro."

"Well, if you heard my yell right, I asked for God to save me. You're not Him," Kody retorted. He shivered with cold as he looked around. "Where's everyone else?"

Almost at once, they heard Tegan shouting for them. They looked around until they found her silhouette on the ledge of the enclosure, her arms waving above her head frantically. They ran over to her and she yelled down, "How the heck do I get off this thing?"

"How did you get up there in the first place?" Kody yelled back, bewildered.

She stomped her foot impatiently. "That can wait, Kody! Help me down!"

"Okay, okay. . ." Kody gazed around. "Here, there's a vine to the left. Move over there, like three paces." Tegan moved to the right. "Not your left, *my* left!"

"And I was supposed to know that, how?" she replied sarcastically.

"You know, I think it's better to leave you up there for the moment. You're cranky right now." His joking tone sounded flat as he looked behind him, worried that a wolf might attack at any moment.

"Well I'm so sorry if I just nearly avoided being ripped open by a fanatical canine."

"You and me both, sis." He turned back to look up at her. "Alright, so move to my left."

Tegan did and peered down. "I can't really see anything. You sure there's a vine?"

"Trust me." Kody squinted. "Yeah, there's a vine. Just bend down and feel around until you get a grip on it."

She carefully reached down. "Found it."

The chorus of snarls that echoed around the enclosure suddenly picked up. The three froze for a moment, then Tegan started to quickly scramble down the vine. In her haste to reach her friends safely, she nearly lost her grip.

"Be careful!" Jag called out. He and Kody moved closer to act as a safety net in case their friend fell. They saw the log and the wolf's body and stepped around them, sharing worried looks. The boys helped Tegan down as soon as she was within their reach.

"Where are Mariah and Aari?" she asked.

Jag looked at the group of boulders and felt a jolt when he saw a wolf viciously attacking a small opening. "Mariah's in there, but I'm not sure where Aari is."

"He's probably up in the tree that wolf is trying to climb," Kody said. Sure enough, through the tree's needles they saw the familiar color of Aari's light gray jacket.

Tegan stepped over the wolf's carcass and the boys followed her. Jag quickly loped to the bonfire and then ran back once he'd grabbed a handful of burning brands from the fire. He passed one each to Kody and Tegan and they approached the boulders where Mariah was trapped.

They halted when they saw the eagle fighting with the wolf, blown away by the ferocious engagement. The wolf bounded skyward and the eagle hovered just out of reach. When the wolf landed back on the ground, the eagle screeched and dove at it, talons outstretched, clawing at the wolf's eyes. The wolf yelped and shook its head. Blinded in one eye, it turned tail and fled the scene. The eagle followed it and chased it out of the enclosure.

Though captivated by the battle, Kody, Jag and Tegan had more urgent matters to deal with. They approached the second wolf attacking the boulders Mariah had taken refuge in and jabbed the flaming sticks at it. It backed away hesitantly, its tail twitching from side to side. Just as the three thought the wolf would flee like its comrade had, it hopped forward, muscles bunched, and launched itself at them, jaws wide open to reveal sharp, stained fangs.

Her instincts heightened, Tegan saw this coming. She held her ground and in the split second the wolf was airborne she shoved her flaming stick into its jaws and right down its throat. The wolf landed short of its targets, choking. Tegan pulled the stick right back out and the wolf fell to its paws as blood clotted its scorched throat. It tried to howl but was unable to. With its tail tucked firmly between its legs, the wolf turned and stumbled out of the enclosure as if intoxicated.

Kody and Jag, on either side of Tegan, stared at her with a mixture of respect and shock. Tegan just shrugged as if it was all in a day's work, but an instant later realized her knees were shaking and quickly tried to steady herself.

From up in the tree, Aari yelled, "Hey, Tegan! That was great! Now could you pull the same stunt on my friend over here?" He pointed at the hysterical wolf trying to climb his tree.

In response, Tegan waved her flameless stick. The boys were coaxing Mariah into the open and helped her make her way out. Jag put an arm around her and she limped along beside him. Tegan ran up to them and gave Mariah a quick hug. "Got a bum leg?" she asked.

Mariah nodded. "Think it's sprained. Probably happened when I kicked the wolf in its face."

"What am I, chopped liver?" Aari hollered from the tree. "This little four-legged nuisance is still trying to rip my legs off, just to let you know."

The four looked at each other. Although they were extremely tired from fighting for their lives, they felt more assured. Kody smiled blearily. "One more. Shouldn't be too hard."

They pulled themselves together and advanced toward the last wolf. As they drew closer to the creature, a howl echoed from the second entrance, the sound amplified as it bounced off the walls of the enclosure. The friends froze. They scanned around, feeling as if the wind had been knocked out of them. Their eyes caught sight of six pairs of red eyes on six shadows. Hackles raised, a second pack of wolves stalked toward them.

Tegan, Kody and Jag let go of their sticks, worn out. The friends didn't have the strength to face six new predators. The sight of the menacing creatures depleted their newly-won confidence from the last battle.

Tiredly, they watched with heavy hearts and drained emotions as the creatures of death approached them.

23

The wolves moved toward Mariah, Tegan, Jag, and Kody, keeping low to the ground. The friends were frozen in place. Worn and exhausted, they came to the painful realization that, barring a miracle, their chances of survival were next to none.

From the shadows of the night, a figure flipped high over the friends' heads and landed a few feet in front of the group. Two more figures somersaulted over the four's heads and landed on either side of the first. One landed in a crouch, a fist on the ground. The other figure landed straight as an arrow. All had their backs facing the friends.

Hidden from view up in the tree, Aari was dumbfounded by the unexpected entrance. He peered closely at the newcomers but the bonfire's light was against their backs. Even then, he was almost certain that the arrivals were—

He felt a sudden rush of wind past his face. He looked to the left and would have yelled if a hand hadn't covered his mouth. He came face-to-face with Akol. Once Aari had regained his wits, Akol removed his hand and smiled.

"Akol," Aari whispered, gawking. "Akol! Man, am I glad to see you!"

Akol chuckled. "And I you, my friend. Now stay here."

"What—"

"Stay here and do not move. My kin and I will take it from here." Akol's eyes twinkled the same way his grandfather's would.

"You five managed to hold your ground quite well against the first pack."

With that, Akol did a backflip out of the tree, well over the wolves' heads, and landed facing the creatures. He spun around to flash a smile at the four stunned friends on the ground and then turned back to face the beasts.

The animals were as surprised as the friends were. They kept their eyes on the humans as Akol and his three companions spread themselves out in a line, preventing the wolves from reaching Tegan, Mariah, Jag, and Kody. From their garments, they pulled out slim, cylindrical objects made of polished wood. They slid their thumbs over a something on the device and suddenly both ends of the cylinders produced extensions, one end of which was a spear and the other a blade. The youths spun their weapons over their heads and to their sides. The collective sounds made a "whoomp-whoomp-whoomp" like a helicopter's rotor. The blades were a spinning blur.

The wolves lowered themselves further to the ground. One of the wolves growled deep in its throat and took the smallest of steps forward. A teenager with short brown hair and dark skin reacted instantly and rushed at the wolf as it leapt toward the humans. The youth roared and pierced the wolf through the ribs as it lunged at him. Using the wolf's momentum, he hoisted his staff and the creature over his head. He followed through the wolf's trajectory with a backflip, gripping his weapon firmly, and was in mid-air when the wolf landed on its back with the weapon speared right through its body. The youth completed the backflip, pulling out the spear at the same time, and ended with a perfect landing.

The friends stared, completely mesmerized. The whole motion had been fluid and had taken only seconds to complete. The wolf lay on the ground, lifeless. Its pack snarled uneasily, their tails slowly swinging back and forth.

Without missing a beat, two other youths put away their staffs and quickly pulled bows that were slung across their backs, each nocking an arrow. Drawing back on the strings, they let their projectiles rocket toward the wolves. They both nocked another arrow and let those fly a mere second after their first volley. The youths' arrows struck their intended targets. The creatures dropped in their tracks.

Akol faced off with the three remaining wolves. Two of them lunged at him. Not having room to use his staff, he ducked and sprang into a handstand before kicking out with his legs. One wolf was struck full in the muzzle and fell to the ground, rolling away. The other was hit under the snout and tumbled backward.

Arching his body to the ground, Akol straightened up and spun his staff as he approached the creatures. The wolves backed away reluctantly. One of them crouched and prepared to leap. Akol, with his staff still whirling, knocked the beast on the side of the head. The force of the impact threw the wolf's head sideways. Before it could react, Akol pierced it through the chest and pulled his staff back out as the wolf went limp.

The youths took a few advancing steps forward. The two remaining wolves hesitated for a few moments before bolting out of the enclosure.

The friends were at a loss for words. Akol looked up at the tree and called out, "You can come down, Aari."

Aari descended the tree cautiously, making sure no other wolves were lurking about, then joined his friends in staring at the villagers with a thousand questions buzzing in their minds.

"Akol," Tegan said, sounding out of breath, "what . . . how did you . . . ?"

Akol held up a hand. "I understand you will have many questions, but first things first. Are any of you injured?"

The five checked themselves and each other, then Jag said, "Only Mariah. It looks as if she may have sprained her ankle."

Akol looked over at his fellow villagers and said something to one of them in their language. The youth with short brown hair slung his bow back over his shoulder and carefully picked Mariah up. Mariah wanted to squeak in embarrassment but kept her mouth shut as color bloomed in her cheeks. Even having gone through their ordeal, her friends managed teasing looks in her direction.

The friends watched as Akol grabbed one of the dead wolves' carcasses. He pulled a face at the sight and smell of the creature up close. "The horses will be pulling this one," he muttered. He motioned with his head for everyone else to follow and exited the enclosure.

Outside, they found two horses grazing calmly. With some help, Mariah mounted one of the horses because the youths refused to let her walk all the way back. Akol and his comrades quickly fashioned a stretcher from thick vines and branches. They rested the carcass on top of it, then tied one end of the stretcher to the second horse. Instantly the equine whinnied and tried to pull away, ears pinned back; the smell was terrible to its nose. The youths quickly jumped in to settle the horse. Akol secured the wolf's body, then looped a rope around the horse's neck. He went around to the front of the horse and stroked its forehead, saying a few soft words in his language. The animal calmed down almost immediately.

The five were still bursting with questions but Akol stopped them. "I shall provide you with answers later, but for now, we will head back to Dema-Ki where you will be safe."

The friends nodded, too tired to argue. Having witnessed the amazing feats of the youths who had come to their rescue, they were rather eager to head back to the village. As Akol took the lead, the five were all thinking the same thing: *Maybe it wouldn't hurt to be with these people for a little while longer.*

PART TWO

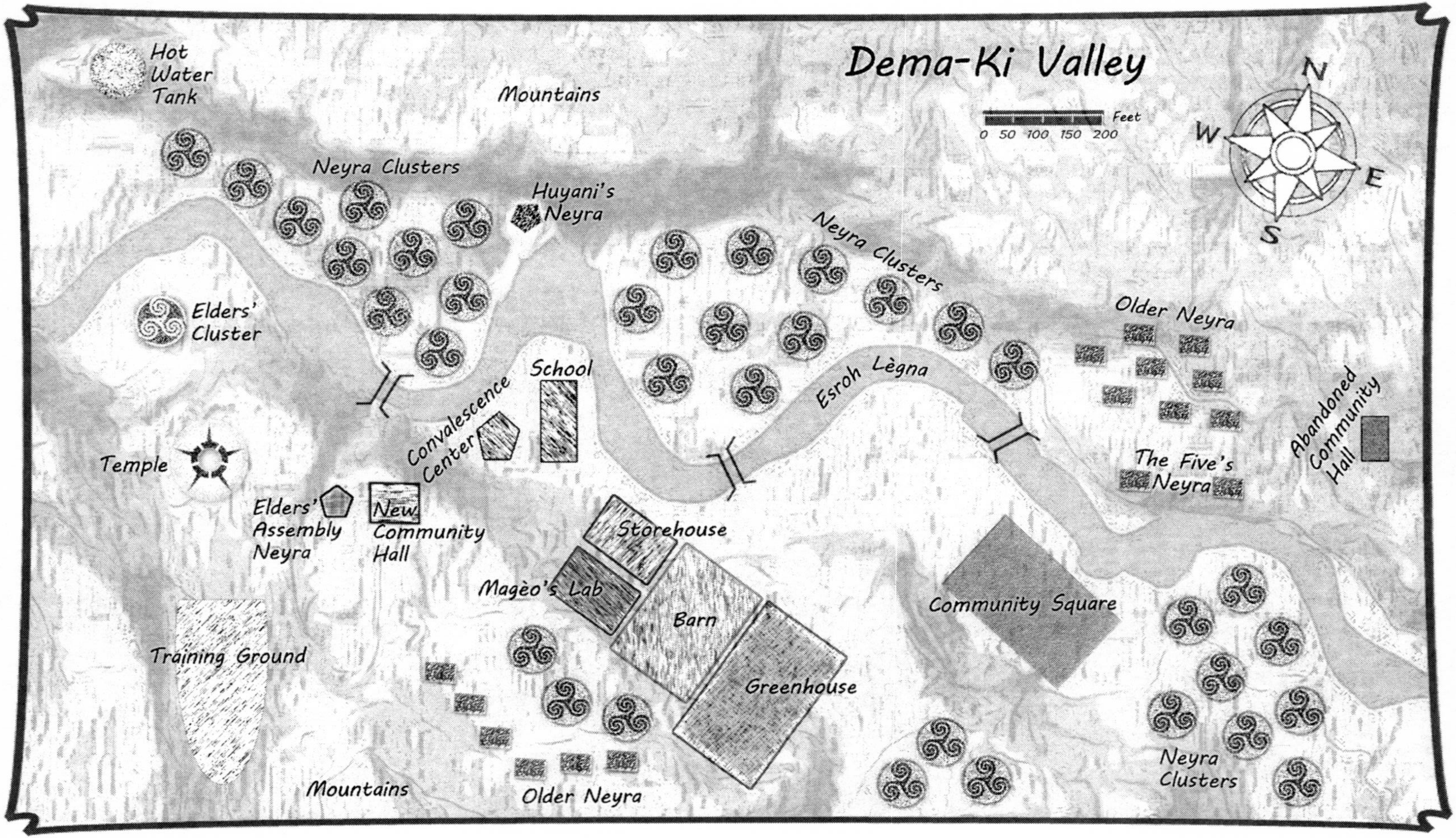
Dema-Ki Valley
Hot Water Tank
Mountains
Feet
0 50 100 150 200
N
W
E
S
Neyra Clusters
Huyani's Neyra
Neyra Clusters
Elders' Cluster
Older Neyra
School
Esroh Lègna
Convalescence Center
Abandoned Community Hall
Temple
The Five's Neyra
Elders' Assembly Neyra
New Community Hall
Storehouse
Magèo's Lab
Community Square
Barn
Training Ground
Greenhouse
Neyra Clusters
Mountains
Older Neyra

24

Nageau and Akol were walking side-by-side along the river that snaked through Dema-Ki. It was just after noon, and Akol was reporting the details of what had occurred during and after the rescue of the five.

Nageau listened quietly, asking short questions only on occasion. Once Akol was finished, the Elder couldn't help but smile. "You always make us proud, Akol. Without fail."

Akol dipped his head, grateful for the compliment. "Grandmother was a great help to us," he said modestly. "I am thankful that she was able to help out the five long enough until we got there."

Nageau nodded and continued walking for a moment before turning serious. "Are you sure none of the five were hurt by the wolves?"

"We checked them immediately after we killed the animals. They were scratched and bruised, and Mariah has a sprained ankle, but they were not bitten. When we brought them back, Huyani took a good look at them and said they were alright. Mariah is already faring much better thanks to her."

"I saw that you also brought back one of the wolves' carcasses."

"Yes. I gave it to Magèo to study."

Nageau nodded once more and clasped his hands behind his back. "How did the five react when you mentioned they would be brought back here?"

Akol squinted as he recalled. "They did not resist. I think they now truly understand that they are in danger if they are alone out there."

"Do you suppose they would be willing to stay?"

Akol shrugged. "Unfortunately, I am unable to answer that. You would have to ask them yourself."

Nageau raised his head. "Then we shall see them. Once they have rested and are feeling better, please inform us. We would like to speak with them."

Akol bowed and headed toward his sister's *neyra* where the five were being treated.

Nageau stood by the water's edge and watched him go, then closed his eyes and breathed in deeply. He remained still for the next several minutes, clearing his mind of all thought, then opened his eyes and walked upriver to cross a bridge to the south side of the valley.

He found his comrades outside the Elders' assembly *neyra* and together they headed inside. When they'd all sat in their respective places around a small fire that Tikina made, Saiyu asked, "What is the news with the five guests, Nageau?"

Nageau smiled. "They are safe and mostly uninjured, with the exception of Mariah who sprained her ankle."

"At least that is something to be thankful for," Saiyu sighed. "Now I only hope that they will not attempt to run off again."

"After what they have been through, I doubt they will," Nageau replied. The Elders hadn't slept well during the night; the mixture of worry about the five and the illness in the village had caused them some stress. At least with the five now safe and sound, a portion of their concerns were eased.

Ashack, being the skeptic that he was, spoke in his deep, dulcet tone. "We seem to be facing a problem. On one hand, there is the task to decide whether these five youths are the ones foretold in the prophecy, and if they are, we have a responsibility to train them. Yet on the other hand, our village seems to be falling into turmoil. We have now had up to four cases of illness, and one of them has passed on in the most horrific manner. It is of extreme importance that we discover what is causing this sickness and how to protect ourselves from it."

"We do not have to make a choice between our responsibilities to the prophecy and the responsibilities to our people," Tikina said. "We should be able to do both."

Ashack rubbed his temples and then slid his hands back into his dark hair. "Perhaps I am not constructing my thoughts properly . . ."

The voices of his companions faded in Nageau's mind. He stared fixedly into the fire, then raised a finger. The Elders went quiet and looked at him. He was in deep thought and, after a few moments, said softly, "Everything that is unfolding before our eyes . . . are these things not mentioned in the prophecy?"

The others fell into thoughtful silence. Saiyu rose from where she was seated and went to a table in the far corner of the *neyra*. She picked up a parchment and returned to the others, carefully unfolding the paper and revealing runes printed neatly and with utmost care. Saiyu ran her finger across the parchment, then softly murmured the verses of the prophecy.

When she finished reciting, the Elders looked at each other but no one spoke. Then Tikina quietly said, "I suppose the decision to train the five must be made based on our own judgments, given the conflicting challenges we are facing right now."

Tayoka held his hands close to the fire and gazed at his fingers. "And to help us make that judgment, I think we should give them the image assessment." His companions cocked their heads interestedly. He continued. "That way, we will be almost certain that they must undergo the training. After all, only our people have the innate ability to complete that assessment. If these five are the ones, then they should have no trouble passing this test, even if they are from the outside world."

"That sounds reasonable," Tikina said slowly.

"Saiyu, Ashack?" Nageau turned to the couple. "What do you think?"

The pair exchanged glances, and then Saiyu dipped her head. "I believe we are both in agreement to this. In addition—upon them passing the image assessment—within the first few days of the initial stage of their training, we should know if we are indeed on the right path."

"So then, since we are all in agreement, I expect all that is left to do is convince the five to stay and train with us," Tikina said. "This should be interesting."

"What if they do not want to stay?" Ashack demanded. "What would we do then? Certainly we would not hold them against their will."

"No, we would not," Nageau said sharply. "We must carefully think through the manner in which we will approach this subject."

"After the nightmare they have been through, perhaps convincing them that we really do care and being frank with our proposal would be the best course of action," Saiyu said.

The Elders conferred further on the topic before deciding how exactly the subject would be broken to the five. It took them a while to reach an agreement.

Clasping her fingers high over her head and stretching her spine, Tikina asked, "Have you arranged a time to meet with the youths?"

"Akol will call on us. I expect the meeting would occur after their dinner."

Saiyu smiled. "Speaking of Akol, he is a truly remarkable young man, Nageau. You and Tikina must be incredibly proud of him. He conducted the entire rescue operation in an exemplary manner."

Nageau and Tikina beamed proudly and Nageau nodded. "Thank you, Saiyu. Something tells me that he will be doing much greater things as he matures into full adulthood."

"Tikina did well, too," Tayoka said. The other Elders agreed.

Tikina smiled coyly. "I simply held the fort until Akol and his companions came along. Poor Akira has some injuries, but she will be fine in no time."

"That eagle's tenacity and willingness to work with you is incredible," Saiyu commented.

Tikina's smile widened. "The Guardians were not far behind Akol and his friends, though. They would have intervened if our youths were unable to handle the wolves."

"Were they patrolling the southern corridor?" Saiyu asked.

"Yes . . . our most vulnerable side to outsiders."

Nageau held his mate's hand. "We have been well protected for centuries. It will not change. Now, I would like to know if anyone has anything to report about the ailing patients in the convalescence shelter, or of any other happenings."

The others shook their heads.

"So far, everything is peaceful," Tikina said.

"How are the patients?"

"They are all quiet and cooperative." Tikina grimaced. "I will admit, though, that it is difficult to see them strapped down to the beds."

"Pray that there will be no more incidents," Tayoka grunted. "Perhaps the universe will grant us that blessing."

* * *

The friends were sitting on the couches in Huyani's living area, waiting for the Elders to arrive. Chayton, who had greeted them each with a friendly, slobbery lick to the face, was now curled near the entrance of the *neyra*, dozing. The five envied his calmness; they were worried about what the Elders might say or do because of their attempted escape.

Huyani walked in and smiled graciously at them. "Relax," she advised. "The Elders are not coming to chastise you or yell at you."

Kody fidgeted. "Yeah, but I'm pretty sure we caused an inconvenience for you guys."

"Nay. In fact, I do believe that your little expedition broke a few of our people from their habitual routines. Gave them a little more excitement than usual, if you will." Huyani patted his cheek before withdrawing to the kitchen quarter of her shelter.

Kody smiled comically. Tegan and Mariah gave him a look. He shrugged. "What? Being mollycoddled gives me a nice feeling."

"She wasn't mollycoddling you, Kody," Tegan said. "It was just a light pat. Mollycoddle means she was pampering you."

"Call it what you will."

The group quieted down when they heard the unmistakable tone of adult voices. A moment later, Huyani and Akol guided the Elders into the living quarter where they sat on the couches and a couple of chairs that Akol had pulled in.

Once everyone had settled comfortably, Nageau focused on the five. "I must say, my young friends, you are a bold and daring group." His smile was so winning that the five didn't know if they should say thank you or be ashamed.

Nageau leaned back. "There is nothing to feel chagrined about. The only thing here that needs to be said—and I am sure Akol has already told you this—is that we are glad you are safe. It is dangerous outside this valley. The untouched wilderness does not take lightly to people with no credible navigational experience or survival skills."

Aari rubbed his forehead. "So we found out," he said, then looked up at the Elders anxiously. "Are we in trouble?"

Tikina was pleasant. "No, you are not." She shared a look with the other Elders. "We do have a *proposal* for you, though."

The five frowned at each other. "What kind of proposal?" Jag asked.

Nageau came out directly. "That you stay with us, and that we train you to be as skilled as our people."

The friends were stunned into silence. This was most definitely not what they expected. One question surfaced in their minds—"Why?" Jag asked.

"My companions and I feel that there is something very special within each one of you," Tikina answered, "and we would like to help you uncover your skills."

"But *why?*"

Tikina pressed her lips together, then said, "There is something you must know, younglings. The people of Dema-Ki are half-bloods. We are part native, but our other ancestors were from an island long gone."

The five raised their eyebrows slightly, wondering where this was heading. "What's this got to do with us?" Kody asked.

Nageau leaned forward, elbows resting on his knees. "There is a very old prophecy of ours. It tells of a darkening time throughout the earth. A world in turmoil." He paused, clucking his tongue as he searched for words. "Preceding this darkness, five younglings would descend from the sky, and we would train them as part of our duty." He met the eyes of each of the friends.

"We didn't descend from—oh, wait, yes we did." Kody's eyes widened in realization and he waved his arms in front of his chest. "Whoa, there," he said. "I think I know where this is going, and I'm just going to say straight up—"

"We are not the people from your prophecy," Jag stated firmly.

"Come now," Tikina cajoled. "All we are saying is that we would like to extend our hand and teach you some valuable skills."

Mariah folded her arms. "What exactly would we be getting ourselves into if we did agree to this idea?"

Nageau answered her. "We will help you unleash the latent powers of your minds. Once you learn how to control your mind over your body, you will be able to increase your physical capabilities by leaps and bounds."

The five stared at him blankly. "Pardon?" Kody said, looking slightly dazed.

Nageau beamed. "It means we would help you increase your prowess, with the end results being, among other things, increased speed, agility and strength, learning how to move objects with one's mind, how to handle physical adversity, how to survive in harsh environments and so forth."

The five looked at him a little guardedly, but their eyes shone with newfound interest. Aari pondered for a moment. "We would all get those talents?"

"It depends on your core skills."

"What honestly makes you believe we are the ones, though?" Kody asked.

"The prophecy states five younglings would rise from the flames of a fiery bird. Your aircraft, as it was struck by lightning, caught on fire and resembled our legendary fire bird, the Cerraco. You indeed did arise from it. Also, the colors of each of your eyes match the shades stated in the prophecy's first verse."

Tegan shook her head. "I'm sorry, but that isn't enough proof for me to want to stay and train with you. Coincidental occurrences, sure, but I just don't find it to be proof."

Akol and Huyani were rapidly interpreting the conversation for the other Elders, who were beginning to look a little nervous. Then Tayoka spoke up and Akol translated. "Elder Tayoka says that he understands how you might mistake us for crazed people living in the middle of a forest, raving about divinations. However, as we have revealed before, we are descendants of an advanced civilization. They were the ones who passed down their knowledge and helped us survive and grow as a people. This prophecy came from them and we have never once doubted their wisdom and ability to predict the future."

"Quick question," Aari asked. "How exactly do you know what skills we have that need sharpening?"

Nageau smiled. "We do not, but if you do agree to stay—and not flee again—then we shall take you through an assessment, followed by the first stage of your training. Within three days of training, we will know if you are indeed the ones. By then, we would have identified the hidden faculties we must help you uncover."

The five looked at each other, unsure what to say. They were tempted to become as skilled as the villagers, especially after the manner in which they had been rescued, but the thought was still outlandish. Tikina said softly, "You need not give us an answer right away. Perhaps we will hear your response tomorrow after you have had a chance to speak with each other?"

Jag nodded in relief. "Please and thank you."

The Elders rose to their feet with warm looks. They said goodbye to the seven teenagers in the *neyra* and left. Akol plunked down on the couch the Elders had been sitting on and ran a hand through his short-cropped black hair.

"Akol?" Jag said. Akol looked up and nodded for him to continue. "What do you think about the whole thing?"

Akol leaned back and stretched his long legs. "Could you specify?"

"The whole bit about the prophecy. And the training . . ." Jag pulled at a thread on his hoodie absentmindedly. "What's your take on all of this?"

Akol crossed his arms and thought for a moment. "Let me begin by saying that the Elders mean well. They are not ones to deceive people, in case that happens to be on your mind. About their understanding of the prophecy . . . The Elders are incredibly wise, as were all the Elders before them. Prophecies are serious matters with us because they *are* real. If they truly believe you could be the ones, it would be prudent to heed their words. You will not be forced if you do not wish to be a part of this, but . . ." Akol was not sure how to finish. ". . . But it may cause a disturbance in the order of things."

The five looked at each other, concerned. Akol quickly added, "I am sure it will not be something drastic. In the end though, the decision is yours to make."

"So you don't have a doubt about the validity of this prophecy?" Aari asked.

"None."

"Therefore you think we should do the training."

Akol was slightly amused. "My opinion should be of no matter to you, my friends."

"Yeah, sure, but we've kind of grown to trust your judgment."

"I feel privileged that you think that way." Akol paused for a minute and chose his words carefully. "In our view, the training is beneficial groundwork for every human being. All of us here go through it at one point or another before reaching adulthood. The training that you will go through—if you indeed are the ones, which the Elders do seem to believe—will follow through the basics to enhance your skills. The Elders will then take it a step further; whatever that is, I am afraid I cannot tell you because I have no idea. But even if you are not the ones, you would have experienced a little bit of training, and that is very valuable. So yes, I would say that it is best to do the training."

The five let his words sink in. Jag looked at his friends and said, "We still have some time before we give the final decision . . . we'll talk later."

The friends stood and stretched, then said goodbye to Huyani and Akol before heading out to their own *neyra*.

25

"Blasted idiot!"

Hutar stabbed his knife into the wooden table angrily. His comrades shared nervous looks. He rested his hands on the table on either side of the blade and leaned forward, his shoulder up to his ears. "That pest. He ruined it. He and his little companions *had* to interfere."

"I suppose in hindsight, we should have seen it coming," a girl said, and flinched when Hutar whirled around to glare at her. If looks could kill, the girl would have been burnt to ashes.

"It was a fantastic plan," Relsuc interrupted, idly brushing back his mohawk. "It was incredible how you steered the wolves into the enclosure, Hutar."

Hutar held up his hand and clenched and unclenched his fingers. "I know," he muttered. "It was all going so well. The five would have been taken care of if it were not for Akol and his friends." He yanked his ten-inch knife out of the table. "Even when he does not realize what we are doing, he thwarts it. He is a thorn in our side. He needs to be gotten rid of."

"We can talk about Akol later, no?" Relsuc asked hesitantly.

Hutar took a deep breath and nodded. "Right." He sat on a chair and crossed his arms.

The group was in a small abandoned *neyra* on the north side of the valley. The shelter they were in had been built many decades before and was never used. There were a few of these types of shelters scattered around the valley and no one ever gave them a second glance; it was a perfect place for the group to meet and speak without disturbances.

"What did they talk about this time?" Aesròn asked Hutar, knowing that the other youth had eavesdropped on the Elders again. He held up his necklace with the predator's incisor to his light green eyes, observing it in the dim light.

"They have proposed an image assessment prior to training the outsiders."

A collection of moans and angry comments flew. Hutar allowed them to complain for a few moments, then held up his hand for silence. The *neyra* quieted down immediately. Hutar looked at each one of them. "Let us prepare ourselves should the five agree to this proposal and pass the assessment," he said slowly.

"We will make their life here miserable," one boy growled.

"That goes without saying."

"We need to scare them," Matikè said. "Make them fear the training."

Relsuc was nodding. "Yes. Feed them horrific stories of pain and a death or two resulting from the training."

"No, no." Hutar rubbed the back of his neck. "Those are flimsy suggestions. If we had more time I might agree, but this is a pressing matter. A more radical method is what we need."

"Like?" Aesròn asked impatiently. "We have already attempted to eradicate them with the wolves. The only way we could get more radical is if we get rid of them with our own hands."

Hutar didn't respond. He rested his head back against the chair, eyes closed, and after a few moments asked, "Any ideas?"

One of the boys in the *neyra* shrugged. "I could sneak into their shelters tonight and deal with them personally." He pulled a knife akin to a switchblade out of his pocket and rubbed his thumb over the hilt.

Relsuc groaned. "Are you not thinking? That would be too noticeable. The entire village would go berserk. Everyone would suspect everyone else."

The boy with the knife went onto the defensive. "Perhaps that is what we need—fear and suspicion to go with this strange sickness. It would be good for us because we would not be the only ones suspected, it would be the whole community."

"That is too much trouble," Hutar said as he opened his eyes. "Remember, all we want is to get rid of these five nuisances. We are not out to sabotage our entire village." He paused. "Speaking of this strange sickness, I want you all to avoid the waters outside of the valley."

Aesròn looked up. "Is that where the illness is coming from?"

"The Elders and Magèo suspect so. I want you to stay clear of those waters, understood? Good." Hutar stretched his legs out in front of him and became silent.

"Let us break off for today, and gather here again tomorrow afternoon?" Relsuc suggested quietly, as if he was afraid that if he spoke loudly Hutar might lash out; Hutar was an unpredictable figure, making him all the more dangerous.

Hutar spoke not a word, his gaze cold. The group sat still for a minute, until two of the youths quietly got up and walked out of the *neyra*. The others followed, all of them tentative and wary. Soon, the shelter was empty, leaving Hutar alone to contemplate.

26

At the crack of dawn the next day, the Elders met at their assembly *neyra*. The weather was slightly chillier than usual but the villagers were not bothered. As Saiyu, Tikina, and Ashack chatted, Nageau asked Tayoka, "Have you had the men gather everything they will need for the expedition?"

"Yes," Tayoka replied. "But we can always double-check when we meet with them."

Nageau nodded. A couple of hours before dawn, Magèo had raced across the village to inform Nageau that he had spent the last thirty-six hours devising and creating a technique to verify if a water source was contaminated, just as the Elder had wished. The village scientist had not slept at all since he had last spoken with Nageau.

Nageau called for the Elders to begin heading to the temple. There they would be meeting four men who had volunteered to head out and follow the tainted rivers to their possible source, the Ayen Range.

As they walked westward, the trees cleared and an incline at the western edge of the valley rose into view. The magnificent temple welcomed the Elders. Four men were already there, waiting in front of the temple for the arrival of the Elders. They bowed respectfully. The Elders smiled and Nageau spoke. "Good morning, my friends."

One of the four tall villagers, a man with black hair and mocha-colored skin, smiled in return. "Good morning, Elder Nageau."

"Have you all gotten your necessities for the trip?" Nageau asked.

"We generally understand our task ahead, but we would appreciate it if we could have it explained in greater detail."

"Most certainly. You will divide into pairs. One team shall follow the Mayet River, and the other will be tracing the river that is at the bottom of the valley, on the eastern end."

"And we follow it up toward the Ayen Range?"

"Yes. It will be about a three-day trip each way, so we will be expecting you back in the village in about six to seven days. Now, just to be clear on what you will be doing: as you trek beside the rivers, you will stop at timed intervals to check on the contaminant. You will know if the contaminant is there by filling a jar with water and dropping the crystalline gels that Magèo has created into it. If the gel turns a vibrant color, then you know the water is infected. If there is no color, then that means the contaminant is not present."

"How are we to know the intervals?" the man with black hair asked.

Nageau blinked in surprise. "Did Magèo not explain it when you went to retrieve the devices from him?"

The men shook their heads and the Elders sighed. Ashack muttered, "Leave it to that boffin to exclude the important details."

"He has many things on his mind, Ashack," Tikina chided.

"In any case, you did retrieve all the gadgets you will need, did you not?" Nageau asked.

One of the other trekkers replied. "Yes we did. We have all our food and water packed—we will not be refilling them from any of the streams or lakes or rivers. We have the jars and the crystalline gels, and this object Magèo gave each of us . . ." He pulled out an article that looked like a small metal sphere.

Nageau took it. "Ah, this is exactly it. You asked how you would know when the intervals would be. This is the way. You will hold this sphere and when it vibrates, that signals the interval. It will vibrate for a few moments, then it will stop and pick up again at the next interval."

The man, indicating that he understood, took the device back and put it in his large fin-shaped pack. "One more thing, Elder Nageau. What do we do if we find the source?"

"Return in haste and inform us."

"Alright."

Nageau gazed at the four men, all of them in their late thirties. He briefly made eye-contact with one of them and smiled a little; it was his daughter's mate. "One last thing: A messenger falcon will be flying with you, alternating between your two groups. We shall use the message beads attached to its talons to keep track of your position. Any final questions?"

The men looked at each other and showed that they were satisfied. "Good," Nageau said.

The Elders led the men into the grand temple's stunning foyer. The flames erupting in the middle of the floor took on the shape of a torch as it flared brilliantly in its cauldron. The Elders motioned for the men to stand in a semi-circle around the fire.

Once they were positioned, Nageau held his palms up on either side of the flames and brought them together until they met in the fire. Cupping his hands, he raised them out of the fire and turned back around to face the men; his skin was perfectly unharmed. On his palms sat a small flame. He moved to the first man. The man clapped his hands over the flame and Nageau stepped back. When the villager opened his palms, the flame came to life. He passed on the flame in the manner that it had been given to him and the next man accepted it, as did the other two. Once the last man held the flame, he closed his hands. When he opened them again, the flame was extinguished.

The Elders stood in a line in front of the men. "Go now," Nageau said. "And take our blessings with you."

The trekkers straightened their fin-shaped backpacks. With a short nod to the Elders, they strode out of the foyer and back into the village to head out in search of the source of the sickness that had befallen their people.

27

Mariah shifted impatiently from side to side as she ran a hand through her hair, trimmed the night before, then flipped her side bangs out of her eye. Jag looked over at her, grinning wryly. "What's the matter with you?"

"You know what the matter is," she growled. "We talked about it last night."

"You're still unhappy that we've decided to take up the Elders' offer?"

Mariah stopped shifting. "Look, I'm sorry, but it just doesn't feel right. I don't know how to explain it."

"But I thought you felt safer staying with these people," Jag said.

"I *do*. But being part of a prophecy and training with them? Isn't it a wee bit odd?"

"You sound just like Tegan."

Tegan came out of the girls' *neyra*, catching Jag's words. "Don't talk trash about skeptics, pal," she muttered.

"I wasn't talking trash."

"Your tone implied it."

Jag groaned. "All I'm saying is, we had this discussion last night and the talk ended with us all agreeing to stay. Also, I find it strange that you're being skeptical, because you're not usually like that."

Tegan raised her hands in surrender. "Fine, whatever. Maybe I'm just out of whack. Maybe it's just that I'm a little homesick and don't want to stay here."

Jag put an arm around her shoulders. "It'd be incredible if one of us wasn't homesick."

The five were quiet for a few moments as their thoughts drifted back toward their homes, wondering what their parents would be doing right about now. It made their hearts heavy to think about the sadness and distress their families were going through. They were also worried about Kody's father; there had been no news about him and Kody was as distraught as ever.

Unable to stand the silence, Aari said, "We should start heading toward Huyani's place."

The others nodded and together they began making their way across the valley. They hadn't gone far when they ran into Akol, who was walking toward their shelters to meet with them. "Hello," he said cheerily.

Mariah and Tegan shared suppressed grins; both found Akol rather adorable. "Hey," Tegan replied. "We were just heading over."

"Perfect." Akol slid into the group as the friends continued walking. He looked them over. "Hmm . . . I see Huyani has been scissor-happy. Some of you got a haircut?"

"Well, the old 'fro needed to be trimmed," Kody said as he patted his head.

Tegan snickered. "What 'fro? You're almost bald."

Kody gasped. "Untrue! I've got the Will Smith type of short hair. That is most definitely not bald."

They walked into Huyani's *neyra* ten minutes later and took their shoes off. Huyani hugged them all warmly and pointed at the meal she'd set on one of her two island counters in the kitchen. The five took their places and dug in after thanking her. As she and her brother leaned back on a counter against the wall, Kody looked up and asked, "Aren't you guys gonna join us?"

"We have already eaten, Kody," Huyani replied. "Just go ahead and enjoy your meal."

"When are the Elders going to come and see us for our answer?" Jag asked.

Akol smiled. "They should be here fairly soon."

* * *

"We have decided to accept your offer."

The Elders broke into large, jubilant smiles at Jag's words. "Wonderful," Tikina purred. "We shall begin now."

The five were caught off guard. "Now?" Kody repeated.

"When did you suppose we would begin?"

"Uh, not *now.*"

"It is the beginning of a beautiful day. We did not want to tarry any longer if your answer was yes."

"So . . . what do we do?" Aari asked curiously.

The Elders stood and motioned for the five to follow them out of Huyani's *neyra*. It was mid-morning and there wasn't a cloud in the bright blue sky. The Elders led the group over a bridge to the other side of the village and up toward the temple. Akol and Huyani followed quietly. As they mounted the slope, the five stopped in their tracks and stared at the magnificent building. The Elders turned to look at the five and smiled. "Come along, younglings," Tikina said. "There is plenty of time for exploring later."

The five nodded and followed the Elders past the temple but still found it hard to tear their eyes away from the sight. The Elders walked at a brisk pace, obviously not wanting to waste any time. They came upon a stone wall, similar to the one the five had encountered as they were attempting to get out of the valley a few nights before. This wall, however, had a large wooden gate. It stretched for a good twenty-five feet across and its height extended up to fifteen feet.

With ease that the five thought would not be possible for men their age, Nageau and Ashack pulled the heavy gate open and walked through. Tikina and Saiyu ushered the friends in, then followed them inside. Tayoka, Akol and Huyani closed the gate behind them.

When the gate was shut, the five stood by the entrance, dumbfounded. What they had mistaken for a full wall of stone was actually the barrier of an immense enclosure. It was hard to tell for sure how big it was because groves of tall trees were everywhere.

Without looking at them, Nageau said, "The first thing we need to do is to carry out what we call an image assessment. The path to passing this assessment is through deliberate contemplation in a calm state."

Aari frowned. "As in meditation?"

"You could call it that. Now, in order for this to work properly, you must be clear of distractions—that means you will be separated and placed in different areas of the training ground." The Elders had the friends sit down on the grass and passed them each a transparent crystal the size of a thumb. "With this," Nageau explained, "we will learn what we are supposed to teach each one of you. You must focus on naught else but the crystal. Clear your minds of any thoughts in this world, for they are now insignificant. If an image appears in the crystal, do not forget it. I cannot stress how important this is. When we come back at the end of the day to take you out of the grounds, you must tell us what you have seen."

The five cried out in dismay. *An entire day?*

The Elders chuckled and Nageau explained that the reason was because focus was something many people, especially younger ones, needed to work on. "But when we say end of the day, rest assured, we do not mean when the sun sets. It should be of no matter to you, however, because you should be focusing on the crystal alone and attempting to gain absolute silence in your minds. Good luck, younglings."

Once the instructions were given, the Elders led each individual of the group to separate areas in the training grounds, then left them alone for the day.

Kody was having trouble concentrating on the crystal and attaining "absolute silence." It wasn't so much that he had a short attention span; he simply found it boring. He knew his friends could endure boredom better than he, and the thought frustrated him.

What's the use of this exercise if someone can't hold their focus long enough to complete the stinkin' process? he grumbled.

He lay stomach-down on the grass and held the crystal in front of his face, hoping that something would appear in it so he could get it over with. Nothing happened. After a few minutes, he put the crystal on the ground and rolled onto his back to gaze up at the sky through the trees. It truly was a nice, bright day. Kody smiled a bit as he gazed up, feeling a little less agitated than when he'd first received the crystal.

He watched the sky for a little while, breathing in deeply. He wasn't sure how much time had passed. It could have been twenty minutes or it could have been two hours. When he figured he was calm enough, he sat up. He picked up the crystal and stared intently at it, but the image that was shown was only that of his reflection. He squinted at it for a while, noticing the stark contrast of his emerald-green eyes against his darker skin. He wasn't *dark*, per se, but it was easy to see the African heritage. He chuckled to himself. His father's genes must be quite dominant, because even his two younger brothers had the same shade of skin as he, although only he had inherited his mother's eyes.

As he rolled the small crystal between his fingers, he allowed himself to think back of home a little bit, though he knew the Elders would not be pleased. His mother was never the cook in the house, his father was. His two younger brothers, one age nine and the other five, were constantly getting in his hair—not that he didn't like it; he just sometimes wished that he could have a little more time to himself.

Kody sighed and focused again on the crystal. Still nothing. It was going to be a long day.

Tegan grumbled to herself. Depending on her mood, she either wanted to sit and relax, or be up and about doing something that would give her a workout. She was keenly interested in doing the latter at the moment. Unfortunately, she was stuck sitting and staring at a crystal that was currently revealing nothing to her.

She hadn't been entirely sure what she expected the assessment to be like, but this was certainly not it. She never meditated, finding it to be precious time that could be used for something more productive.

Keeping the crystal in her hand, she got to her feet and decided to explore her surroundings. There wasn't much of course, seeing as the Elders had chosen spots with the least amount of distractions for the five to use. Tall trees were around her and the grass was a healthy green. Other than a few rocks here and there, the place was as boring for her as the activity was.

She rubbed her eyes. What in the world had they gotten themselves into, she wondered. Training because they were part of some foreigners' prophecy. She sighed. Was it really worth it to stick around when they could have easily been on their way out of the valley and back home by now?

I guess we'll have to just wait and see.

28

The four men whom the Elders had sent out early that morning had split themselves into two groups and were following the two different rivers upstream. Akol's father, Rikèq, and Hutar's only uncle, Aydar were following a river to the east of the valley toward the Ayen mountain range. There was a mysterious mountain in the range often mentioned in several of the villagers' folktales. Known as the Ayen'et mountain, its peak towered above all the others in the range.

As instructed, the men stopped and scooped water samples into a jar at every interval as determined by the timing device. They had dropped the crystalline gels into the samples and, so far, the gels had changed color every time, indicating that the water was contaminated.

As they walked, the men spoke of many things, most of little importance. There was a pause in their chatter for several minutes and Aydar lost himself in his thoughts. Wistfully, he said, "I wish Hutar was more like your son."

Rikèq glanced at the other man. Aydar continued. "Ever since he lost his father in that accident, he has grown solitary."

"I have seen him with a few of the youths in the village, though."

"Yes, but he does not consider them friends." Aydar rubbed his face. "He did not want me going on this trip, you know. He does not want to somehow lose me like he lost his father."

"That is understandable especially since, after all, you are the only family member he has."

Aydar shook his head. "As he grows older, I see something in his eyes. I cannot quite put my finger on it, but he seems distant . . . cold, even."

Rikèq glanced again at Aydar. "I have noticed that his demeanor has changed, too. What do you suppose is spurring this?"

"That is what I have been trying to understand. It is frustrating because I do not know what is causing him to be this way." He paused, trying to work it out in his mind. "He never knew his mother and growing up with only his father must have been hard."

"Have you ever tried speaking about your concern?" Rikèq asked.

"I have, but he seems to sense the impending question and retreats before I even get the chance." Aydar sighed. "For goodness sake, he is my nephew and I try to reach out to him but he dodges my hand. He knows I love him, and I know he cares for me, but it truly does not appear as if he wants any sort of help."

Rikèq readjusted his pack. "Perhaps he would like to figure this out on his own. Some youths tend to prefer solving their dilemmas by themselves."

"Be that as it may, it troubles me." Aydar stepped over a tree root, startling a shrew that was on the other side. "Tell me, Rikèq. How do you and Akol deal with the challenges of the growing years?"

Rikèq chuckled. "Akol used to get into some mischief when he was younger, but growing up, he has shown some restraint and has become more responsible. Mind you, he has his sister to talk things over with, so he is not alone in that regard."

"I have seen him and Huyani. They certainly have an incredible bond."

"Indeed. They rarely come to us with their problems. They seem to be quite capable of sorting matters out on their own."

Aydar nodded, silently wishing that his nephew would one day demonstrate those qualities.

For the next few hours, the men trekked northward along the river, stopping only to test the water. The river was contaminated at every checkpoint and they were beginning to get impatient. "How much longer will we have to walk?" Rikèq grumbled. "The one night my mate makes her appetizing fish tart stuffed with delicious herbs, I have to be out."

Aydar snickered. "Hush now, my friend. You would not want the Elders hearing you complain."

Rikèq laughed out loud. "As Nageau and Tikina's son-in-law, I will be easily pardoned."

"You wish," Aydar retorted with a grin. "If anything, you would be reprimanded even more harshly."

"I know. In all seriousness, though, they are such wonderful people. I am blessed to be related to them."

"That is quite an honor, to—" Aydar was cut off by a loud, peculiar noise.

Startled into silence, the men looked at each other. They decided to investigate, intrigued.

They strayed away from the river and into the forest. Following their ears, they hiked for several minutes through the trees and around rocks and bushes. The sound slowly grew louder and more terrifying. Rikèq came to a sudden stop behind a bush and crouched, Aydar almost tripping over him. Rikèq pulled the other man down beside him just as the noise erupted again, fierce and wild. Aydar balanced himself, keeping one hand on the ground, and peered from around the bush. His eyes widened.

In a clearing twenty feet in front of the men, four mountain lions were entangled in a gruesome battle. The largest of the four, a male with his entire muzzle slashed and bloodied, lunged at the smallest—a female—and dug his foam-covered jaws into the back of her neck. The female screamed in pain and tried to twist out of the other cat's grip. The screaming stopped as the male violently shook his head from side to side, severing the female's spinal cord. The other two cats were entangled in their own fight and the female's anguished cry didn't faze them. It was a disturbing scene, with the two males ripping at each other in savagery. Their claws pieced the other's pelt and grazed down. Their muzzles were stained and revealed large, chipped incisors when they opened their jaws to let loose a roar.

Rikèq and Aydar looked on in horror as one of the males clamped its jaws down on the other's muzzle and tore the skin away. They knew instantly that these predatory cats had been affected by the sickness. They glanced at each other and then, as one, rose to their feet. They slowly and carefully backed away, keeping their eyes on the cats.

As they retreated, Rikèq's heel struck a root. He tripped and fell backward. The three male mountain lions looked up and spotted the men through the bushes. Their lips curled back into snarls, revealing stained teeth. Rikèq cursed himself vehemently as he sprang to his feet and started at a sprint, Aydar following closely.

The large male dropped the female he'd killed and advanced toward the men at frightening speed. The men looked around frantically for an escape as they ran. They could hear the large male chasing after them. Neither Rikèq nor Aydar had great stamina, but they could sprint for short bursts.

The cat leading the chase leapt and tackled both men. Aydar managed to quickly wriggle out but Rikèq was pinned. The mountain lion hissed, foam dripping from its jaws. As it opened its maw to bite down, a thunderous roar boomed over them. The cats froze, only the tips of their tails twitching. Rikèq attempted to crawl out from under the big male's grip but the cat hissed again. As it was about to clamp his jaws around Rikèq's neck, another roar sounded and a huge mass of darkness bowled over the big male. The cats yowled and the one trapped under the surprise attacker screamed.

Aydar quickly helped Rikèq to his feet and the men dodged behind a tree and looked from around it. They gasped. A gargantuan bear was holding off the three cats, evidently defending the men. The two smaller males jumped onto the bear's back and dug their claws into its thick fur, trying to grab hold. The bear, weighing nearly three thousand pounds, shook the cats off effortlessly.

The large male sprinted at the bear head-on, spraying foam everywhere, and lunged at the massive creature. The bear reared on its hind legs and now stood taller than two men. The cat tried to halt when it saw the bear rise but couldn't stop its momentum. The bear came crashing down onto the smaller animal, crushing its body. The mountain lion hadn't even had time to make a single sound before its swift and merciless death.

The bear turned to look at the other two deranged cats and roared again. The men behind the tree winced and covered their ears. If there had been any creatures around that hadn't already vacated the area, they would have been completely debilitated just from the shock of that sound.

The cats yowled again and fled; though the sickness that had pervaded their bodies drove them to kill, they feared the gigantic death instrument on paws and did not want to be trampled.

The bear stared after them for a few moments, making sure they had left the vicinity, then turned and lumbered over to the men. The men stepped out from behind the tree as the bear drew to a halt in front of them. Rikèq and Aydar gazed up at it with reverence and rightful fear, knowing that this was one of the five Guardians. They murmured a few words of gratitude. The Guardian snorted, almost as if amused. With a shine in its dark eyes that seemed to tell the men to stay safe, the bear brushed past them and disappeared into the trees.

* * *

Breyas and Keno, the other two men who were tracking the source of the illness, had heard the roar. They exchanged glances and kept walking along the Mayet River. Only the Guardians could produce such a resounding sound. Whatever problem that had arisen must have been dealt with by now if a Guardian was around.

Breyas had volunteered for this outing because of his father, who had come down with the illness; he wanted to do *something* to stop the progression of the malady, and he figured this would be as close as he would get. Likewise, Keno, who was Fiotez's brother, wanted to help stop the spread of the disease and prevent more horrific deaths. He hadn't been around to witness the demise of his brother but he'd heard the stories and was shaken. The funeral the village had held for Fiotez two nights before was a somber one. The villagers were in deep shock, as they'd never had such a violent death occur to one of them. Many started to truly fear the illness and, although the Elders attempted to insert a calm reassurance, many were still apprehensive.

As Breyas stooped down to retrieve a sample of the water, Keno said, "Why do I have a strange feeling that in order to find the source, we will have to hike all the way to the Ayen'et mountain?"

Breyas emitted a sound of dismay. "Oh, please do not say that. I would rather not have to walk the entire length of this river only to find out that the source is actually in that accursed mountain." He dropped the crystalline gel into the jar and the men regarded it closely. They watched as the translucent crystal gave way to color. "Still contaminated," Breyas muttered. He tilted the jar and let the water sample drain back into the river, along with the crystalline gel.

Keno shook his head. "I am telling you, we should just pass along this entire river and head straight up to the mountain."

Breyas grunted but otherwise said nothing. He was not keen to get too close to the Ayen'et. As a child, he had never had any good memories while visiting the mountain. He looked up at the sky and said, "Let us walk for another two intervals, and then we should put up for the night."

Keno agreed. The hours passed quickly enough, and the source of the contaminant remained unfound. The men set up their tents and built a fire, then sat around it whilst eating their packed food. They talked of unimportant things, trying to forget the strange sickness that kept attacking their people, before turning in for the night and silently praying that they would soon find the origin of the terrible disease.

29

Aari and the others were sitting outside on the grassy hill beside the boys' *neyra* that overlooked Esroh Lègna, the beautiful emerald river that rolled through the valley. The friends were relaxing after their dinner, discussing their day in the training area with their crystals. They were stupefied by the fact that they had all been successful in finding an image in their crystal; all except Kody, that is. Aari and the others listened to Kody as he grumbled about his problem.

When the Elders had come much later in the day to retrieve them, they'd asked the five if they had seen anything and were jubilant when told that they had. Jag's image was that of a lone paw print of a wildcat; Mariah's was a full moon over a crest of wave; Tegan's had been an image of the eye of an eagle; and Aari's had been a silhouette of half a dragonfly. Kody had stood there, unable to provide an answer. He'd briefly contemplated making up an image, but cleared that thought. The Elders had complete trust in the five—he could not forsake that simply because he felt left out and embarrassed.

Tegan scooted over so she could sit behind Kody and rested her chin on his shoulder. "Hey, remember that little song your mom made up when we were all sleeping over at your place when we were kids?"

"Which one? She made up many."

"The one about the little sea lion who felt left out because he was unable to fish as well as the other little sea lions."

"Oh, sheesh, please don't go there."

Jag grinned and started to hum the tune. Aari joined in, then Tegan started to sing along with Mariah. After the first sentence Kody was rolling away, covering his ears. "Spare me!" he yelped. "Please!"

"We're not going to stop singing until you give us the moral of the song," Tegan threatened.

"What? No way. Scram. Get outta here."

His friends sang louder and repeated the song as if they were a broken record. Kody, sure that his ears would begin to bleed any second, finally gave in. "Alright! Alright! I get it! Don't give up, and don't give in to self-pity because others achieved something you didn't. I got that. Now just *stop!*"

His friends beamed victoriously. From his jeans' pocket Kody pulled out the small crystal the Elders had lent him until morning in hopes that perhaps he would get his image yet. He bounced it in his palm and then held it up to the sky to gaze at it. "How on earth did you guys manage to get your images, anyway?" he asked.

The other four looked at each other for a few moments, hesitating. Mariah shrugged. "For me, it kind of just . . . happened. I can't explain it."

"Same here," Tegan agreed.

Kody looked a little discouraged. "What kind of thoughts did you have before you saw your image? Did you go all Zen? What did you guys do?"

"I really don't know, Kody. All we did was focus, just like we were told to," Aari answered. "Initially, there was a lot of noise, a lot of distracting thoughts, but it eventually got easier with practice. At a certain point, there would be total silence. It was brief, but that's when we saw our images."

Kody got up and paced back and forth, holding the little crystal in front of his face and staring at it in disgust. "Who knew that some of the anguishes in my life would come from an inanimate object that isn't even the size of my thumb?" He snorted and stood in silence for a couple of minutes, then said, "Think I'll turn in early."

Though the sun had only just set, the friends didn't protest. After wishing them good night, Kody walked into the boys' *neyra*. Aari leaned back on the grass, propping himself up with his elbows. "Poor kid," he commented. "I wonder why the rest of us got our images and he didn't?"

"You know how he is," Jag said. "Boring stuff doesn't suit him well."

"We all found it boring," Aari replied. "But I do get what you mean. The guy has less focus than we do . . . But still. Even Tegan managed to get an image, and you know her—Miss Ants-in-her-pants. She can't sit in one spot for too long."

Tegan smiled slightly. "I feel like I should be offended, but I can't because I have no argument there."

* * *

It was the middle of the night when Kody bolted upright in his sleeping bag. "Got it!" he whispered triumphantly. He held the small crystal that he'd been gazing at under the lamp up over his head.

When he'd entered the shelter to sleep almost six hours ago, he'd fallen into his sleeping bag and slumbered off. Something had woken him not long after, though he did not know what. Blinking sleep away in the darkness, he could just barely make out Aari on his right and Jag on his left, and could hear them snoring softly. Unable to fall back asleep, Kody had lit the lamp a couple of feet away from his head and turned over to lie on his stomach. Facing the light, he'd pulled the small crystal from his pocket. He wasn't sure how long he'd been staring at it, but the image suddenly flashed in the crystal: a five-pointed star woven from twigs.

He now sat in his sleeping bag, too excited to sleep. He didn't know if he should leave to find Huyani and Akol and tell them, or wait until morning. He shifted impatiently but decided to wait until daybreak. He grinned at the crystal and muttered, "And you thought you could evade me, you deceptive piece of *rock*."

Aari cracked open an eye but quickly squeezed it shut when the light's glare hit him. After a few seconds, he eased both his eyes open and raised his head. He saw Kody. Trying to get his vocal chords to work, he mumbled, "Kodng . . ."

Kody looked over at him, quizzical.

Aari tried again. ". . . Kody."

"Yes?"

"What are you doing?"

Kody grinned and showed the crystal. "I found the image," he replied, keeping his voice low so as not to wake Jag up.

Aari laid his head back down and closed his eyes. "Congrats," he snuffled tiredly. "Do you mind turning that bloody light off now?"

"You're so grumpy when you're groggy, you know that?" Kody said as he reached over to turn off the lamp.

But Aari was already fast asleep. Kody rubbed his eyes, feeling suddenly tired. He snuggled back down into his sleeping bag and fell asleep with the small crystal clutched in his hand.

30

The next morning, the five stood with Akol and Huyani outside the large wooden gate of the training grounds, anxiously looking at each other, waiting for the Elders to emerge from the temple. They were curious and keen to find out what stage one held for them. The Elders had briefly given them a general idea: Basic physical and mental training.

The Elders had been overjoyed when Kody told them earlier what image he'd seen the night before. In fact, they seemed *more* pleased than Kody felt, which slightly puzzled the five.

Huyani and Akol smiled at the friends now, urging them to calm down. "You will have your mentors soon enough," Huyani said.

"Will they be people we haven't yet met?" Mariah asked.

Akol shook his head. "The Elders themselves will be teaching you. Each one of you will be assigned to one of the Elders. The training ground is more or less divided into five sections, each fitted for the development of your individual skill, and there you shall practice alone with your mentor."

The five sighed impatiently. It was another ten long minutes before they spotted the Elders walking up the grassy knoll toward them. When they reached the teenagers, Nageau greeted them and said, "Aari. Ashack will be your teacher throughout your training. Akol and Huyani will rotate translating his instructions for you." Aari nodded.

"Jag, you shall train under Tayoka. As with Aari, either Akol or Huyani will be translating his words for you." Jag glanced at the red-haired Elder and nodded.

"Tegan, Tikina shall be guiding you."

Tegan smiled; of all the Elders, she was happy to have either Nageau or Tikina train her.

"Mariah." Mariah looked up as Nageau addressed her. "Saiyu will be working alongside you to hone your skills."

Nageau then turned to face Kody. Kody grinned. "Guess I know who my mentor is," he said.

Nageau smiled. He looked over at everyone else and nodded. "Once you walk through this door, younglings, stage one formally begins." He clapped his hands once. "Let us begin."

The Elders opened the wooden gate. The five glanced at each other, nervous and eager, and stepped forward. They were still unclear what to expect, but they had a growing feeling that it would be incredibly beneficial to them. They all wanted to excel in life but had never been sure how or where to begin. This could be a groundbreaking start.

The Elders and Akol and Huyani walked in after them and shut the gate firmly. At once, each Elder walked away from one another. The five stared after them, unsure what to do. The quick glances Akol and Huyani lent them were enough to give them direction and the friends jogged off in pursuit of their individual mentors.

31

Keno and Breyas had trekked for three days along the Mayet River, hoping to come upon the source of the illness. So far they'd had no such luck. It was now nearly midday, though the sky was dark and overcast.

"I wonder how the other two are faring," Keno sighed.

Breyas took a small sip from his water pelt, then wiped aside the shaggy hair that was matted to his forehead. "Knowing Aydar and Rikèq, they must be plowing along just as we are."

A few birds were flying back to their nests, cawing. The men looked up warily, wondering if any one of the creatures had ingested the poison. With a desperate need to pin the blame of his father's illness on something, Breyas muttered, "I really do hope we will not have to travel up that mountain. It has been a curse to our community."

"Breyas!" his companion reproached. "Nature is our friend. No misfortune shall taint that relationship."

Breyas grunted in response. Although Keno attempted to persuade him that nature was what they made of it, he was still convinced that the Ayen'et mountain was the demon's spawn of bad luck in the forest.

By the end of the hour, the two men had reached the point where the river branched off from the one Rikèq and Aydar were tracking. They tested the water there and found it to also be contaminated. Disappointed, the men sat down on a couple of boulders and pulled out their lunches. They were only a few bites into their meals when they heard their names being called out. Rikèq and Aydar were making their way over to them, waving their hands above their heads. As soon as the four men reunited in a friendly greeting, Rikèq and Aydar sat on the boulders to eat with their friends.

"Any luck finding the source of the contamination?" Keno asked.

Rikèq shook his head. "None. It looks as if we will have to cross this river." He pointed at the waters that flowed swiftly ahead of them.

"Splendid," Breyas responded sarcastically through a mouthful of food. He looked at the mountain up ahead. Its peak was hidden by gray overhanging clouds. Slowly, he asked, "Do you remember the stories about the Ayen'et that we were told as children?"

Aydar chuckled. "You mean the tales of the mountain being alive and that at the top of its peak where it is often shrouded by clouds, an 'all-seeing' eye would spot disobeying youngsters and carry them away into the night to feed on them?"

"Yes."

"Tsk. Those are tall tales to encourage children not to stay awake past their bedtime. I tried telling the stories to my nephew when he was younger." With an amused snort, Aydar added, "Hutar did not believe them, though."

"Of course they are tales. But I remember how my father used to describe the mountain to me when I was a young lad." Breyas shuddered. "I suppose old feelings do not fade easily."

"Did you find anything out of the norm as you followed the river you were tracking?" Keno asked the other two, wanting to change the subject.

Aydar and Rikèq shared looks, and Aydar smiled slightly. "Nothing much on the contamination." He leaned forward. "But we *do* have a story for you." He related their encounter with the mountain lions to a startled Breyas and Keno. He ended his tale with how a sole Guardian had gone out of its way to save them.

"Incredible," Keno murmured.

"What of you?" Rikèq asked. "What did you come across?"

"More carcasses. Birds and fish were strewn here and there." Breyas wrinkled his nose. "The stench of rotting flesh was awful."

"We saw a doe and her calf, too," Keno added. "Both were dead, unfortunately, and were being fed on by some birds. They were farther away from the river, but Breyas ran at the carcasses and scattered the birds. He claims that he was just trying to keep them from falling ill, but I saw the childlike streak as he dashed at them."

Breyas grinned. "I was simply gathering a little bit of joy for myself. My mother always told me that we should come to the aid of others with a happy heart."

The quartet chuckled and finished off the rest of their meals, then did a quick check of their supplies to see if they all had enough food and water. Once they were satisfied that everything was set to go, they walked over to where the two rivers became one. "The currents are strong here," Rikèq noted, frowning. "We are going to need our boats."

The men shook off their journey packs. The specially treated, fin-shaped moose-hide was designed to be used as a kayak once unfolded, or a one-person tent when completely extended. Sturdy, retractable wooden frames were anchored to one side of the pack and could latch on to the other side once folded out. It was an ingenious device designed by Magèo many decades ago when he still had a liking for the outdoors.

Once the men were ready, they carried their kayaks to the edge of the water. "Be careful," Rikèq warned. "We do not know if the poisoning occurs solely through consumption, or if it is also through contact. We should avoid the water at all cost."

The others nodded. Pushing their kayaks halfway into the water, they carefully climbed in and used their paddles to push off from the shore. Almost immediately the current tried to drag them downstream, but the men were strong and paddled forward, fighting the flow furiously.

"We are almost there!" Rikèq shouted.

The bank on the other side was just a few yards away. Aydar brought up the rear of their little line and paddled after the other three. Suddenly, a trough opened under his boat and tilted him violently to one side, nearly causing him to capsize. He frantically shifted his weight and, after what felt like an eternity, managed to balance out his kayak. He gripped his paddle until his knuckles turned white, relieved that he had not fallen into the water. Once he'd relaxed enough, he paddled to the shore where his friends helped him out.

"Are you alright?" Rikèq asked, being careful to not touch the wet parts of the moose-hide as he pulled Aydar's kayak onto land to dry with the others.

"I am alright." Aydar sat down on the grass with Breyas and Keno and rubbed his face. The men only had to wait a couple of minutes for their kayaks to dry before folding them back up into their journey packs; the hide was treated and waxed so that moisture never clung onto it for long.

Breyas crouched by the water and tested it for contamination. Keno peeked over. "Well?" he asked.

Shaking his head, Breyas stood up. "It is still contaminated." He looked apprehensively up toward the mountain. "It appears we will have to continue trekking toward the Ayen Range."

"That should take around half a day." Aydar took a few sips from his water pelt. "Shall we get moving?"

The men quickly followed the river, noting a couple of birds on the ground. Though they were now relatively used to the sight of dead creatures, it still unnerved them to think that there was something in the water stealing away the very life force of living, breathing beings.

The group conversed amongst themselves, sharing stories and laughing, attempting to ignore the mountain range as it steadily grew larger in their field of view. One peak stood out ominously from the rest. While it appeared to be part of the chain, it was actually a solitary mountain that stood a mile in front of the range. It was the Ayen'et mountain, for which the range was named.

During a lull in the conversation, Breyas said in a low, fretful voice, "With any luck, we will find the source soon." He pointed at the towering peak. "It seems like the closer we are to the mountain, the gloomier the forest gets."

Rikèq glanced around them. "That did not occur to me until you brought it up."

"I have never been so close to the Ayen'et," Keno murmured, eyes stretched wide.

Suddenly, Breyas' ears picked up a distant, deep reverberating sound that carried on for several seconds. He halted as the noise died away. "Did you hear that?" he muttered.

"Hear what?" Rikèq asked.

"That sound . . . like distant thunder."

The men stood still, waiting to hear the noise again, but it did not return and they continued walking, in utter silence this time. They took note of how accurate Breyas' observations were: The forest did seem gloomier the closer they got to the mountains.

A raven shot out from a tree and swooped overhead, cawing, making the men twitch. Not long after, the rumbling noise returned. The men halted again. As the sound died away once more, Keno looked at Breyas. "We most definitely heard that."

"What do you suppose that noise is?" Aydar asked quietly.

Breyas fidgeted. "It does not sound like any animal I am familiar with."

The quartet continued walking for the next hour. As they were preparing to do another test of the waters, the rumbling noise returned, louder now. The men slowly looked up at the mountain.

"It sounds like the noise is coming from there," Rikèq whispered. The men stood still, less than eager to continue their trek, but they knew it had to be done. Aydar took the lead, and the group reached the base of the mountain as the sun was beginning its descent beyond the low-hanging clouds, out of the men's sight. The rumbling noise had been continuing on and off since the last time they'd heard it, and as they neared the foot of the mountain, it got loud enough that the four men almost felt it as much as they heard it.

The group followed the river until they saw a cave where the water emerged a quarter of the way up the mountain. After a half-hour hike they reached the mouth of the cavern and peered inside. Aydar quickly took out a portable lamp and lit it, then led the way in. Inside the dark, wet cave were two narrow banks on either side of the river. In here, whenever the noise came back, the men could clearly feel vibrations all around them.

"Something is happening here," Keno murmured. "Breyas, could you check the water, please?"

Breyas crouched by the rapidly-flowing river and carefully retrieved a sample. After a few moments, he announced, "Still contaminated."

The rumbling and vibrations came back, nearly causing Breyas to lose his balance and tip over into the water. He held on to a rock embedded in the dirt and waited until the vibrations and sound faded, then got to his feet and quickly moved away from the river.

Aydar shone his lamp ahead. "The cave turns here, my friends." He looked back at the others. "Shall we continue on?"

Although it was obvious that he was not eager to continue this quest, Rikèq was firm. "Turning back now is not an option."

Aydar nodded and turned the corner, disappearing from sight. Rikèq and Keno trailed after him. Breyas looked over his shoulder at the mouth of the cave. He caught sight of the last bit of light outside, then turned to follow the others and allowed the darkness to envelop them.

PART THREE

QUEST MINING SITE

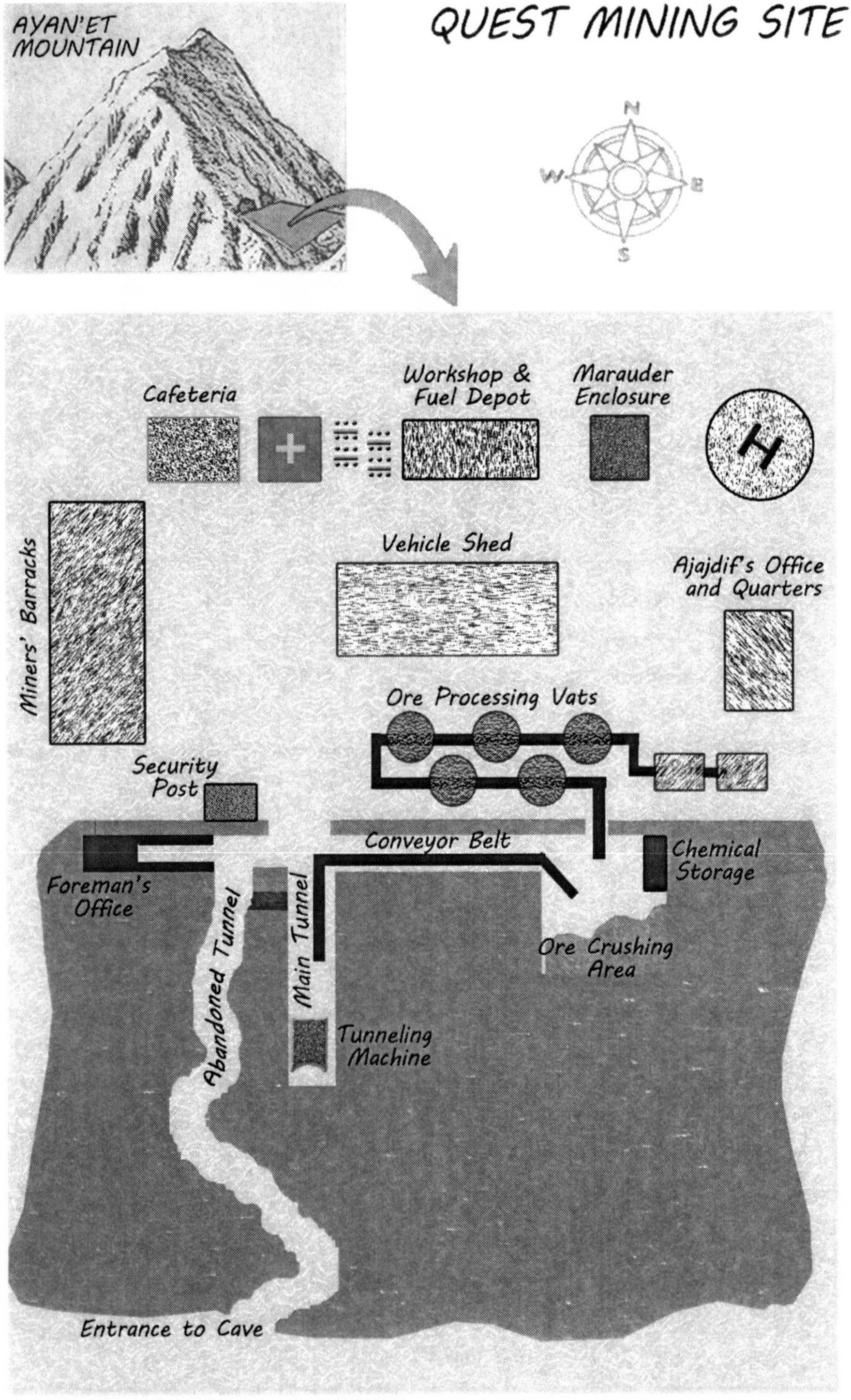
AYAN'ET MOUNTAIN
N
W
E
S
Cafeteria
Workshop & Fuel Depot
Marauder Enclosure
H
Miners' Barracks
Vehicle Shed
Ajajdif's Office and Quarters
Ore Processing Vats
Security Post
Conveyor Belt
Chemical Storage
Foreman's Office
Abandoned Tunnel
Main Tunnel
Ore Crushing Area
Tunneling Machine
Entrance to Cave

32

The view from the large, frameless glass window where Adrian Black stood was astounding. The beautiful blue waters of the bay were dotted with countless sailing boats catching the breeze on this picture-perfect morning. To the west, on the iconic Golden Gate Bridge, traffic was busy as usual for a weekday morning. Parts of the waterfront belonging to the small artsy city of Sausalito peeked out at Black. Not a man of the arts, he turned his head away from the city, uninterested. Toward the north, the bay's waves were breaking onto Alcatraz Island where tourists armed with cameras eagerly explored the site that once held many infamous prisoners.

Black turned away from the window to look back into the boardroom. Captivating as the view outside was, his mind was burdened with an urgent business matter that, if left unresolved, might cost him more than his job.

The boardroom was on the highest floor of a nondescript forty-story building, owned by a well-funded establishment with a global reach called Phoenix Corporation The gray-colored tower blended in with the other high-rise buildings in downtown San Francisco. Fondly referred to as "Tower 51" by its inhabitants—a joke spun from the military base in Nevada due to the secrets that lurked in the corporate corridors—it served as the company's head office, and its unremarkable appearance deceived many about what lay within.

Black scanned the empty chairs in the boardroom, waiting impatiently for his associates to arrive even though he arrived early by choice. The boardroom was extravagantly fitted out. A deep-red oval mahogany table surrounded by twelve luxurious black leather chairs served as an impressive centerpiece. At the end of the table farthest from the windows, a chair was missing. In its place was a large silver screen mounted onto a curved wall. Though visually impressive, what escaped the eye was even more remarkable. Cleverly designed and neatly tucked into the structures of the room was a plethora of high-tech devices, including a satellite-linked communication system that connected the company's entire global operations; a multi-projector holographic conferencing platform, and state-of-the-art touchscreen computers concealed inside the polished conference table for each person seated. Behind the curved wall was a well-appointed lounge with an exquisite and fully serviced bar where the executives could unwind after a hard day's work.

As the chief executive of Phoenix Corporation, Black was responsible for running a diverse corporation with subsidiaries engaged in industries such as mining, armaments, biotech, and construction across the globe. Discreetly, the company also made substantial contributions to selected social organizations, media groups and politicians. The broad scope of the business kept him on his toes and he enjoyed the challenge. He was, however, beginning to feel the stress from one crucial project where things were not moving at the pace that was expected of him.

He was deep in thought and did not hear the footsteps on the plush carpet as one of his colleagues walked into the boardroom. Jerry Li, a short, tubby man who always wore a bowtie with his suits was the chief financial officer for the corporation. His black hair was gelled back and his Asian eyes, gleaming with mischief, were framed by large, thick-rimmed glasses. He tiptoed over to Black and startled the six-foot-two CEO with his high-pitched, "*Good morning!*"

Black spun around. "Li! Are you trying to give me a heart attack?"

Li grinned. "I try, but it never seems to work."

Black shook his head and readjusted his tie. "Still trying to grab my job?" he jested. "I've never met a senior executive, especially a financial wizard, who is so doggone cheerful all the time."

"What's that supposed to mean? The higher up the ladder I am, the more of a stick in the mud I have to be?"

"It means," a raspy voice cut in, "that you are quite a unique fellow."

The two men turned to look at the newcomer. Dr. Albert Bertram, the chief science officer of Phoenix Corporation, came strolling into the boardroom with a thermos of hot coffee in his hand. He was a rather plump man in his early sixties, though it was apparent that in his younger days he had been quite handsome. With a full head of silver hair and bright blue eyes, he could have passed for Santa Claus if only he had the red hat and suit to put on.

Li smiled. "Why thank you, Al."

Dr. Bertram returned the smile and looked at Black. "Good morning to you, Adrian." His voice had a trace of a German accent.

"Mmph. It would have been nice if you all arrived on time."

"We are on time. *You* chose to come early, my friend."

"Where are the other two? We need to begin."

Just as he spoke, the executives of two subsidiary companies walked into the boardroom, greeting the others as they took their places around the table. Dr. John Tabrizi was the head of Quest Chemicals, the chemical research and manufacturing arm of Phoenix Corporation, and Luigi Dattalo headed the armaments division known as Quest Defense; he'd just flown in from Nevada for this meeting.

The three men by the window went to take their respective seats. Black tapped something on his touchscreen computer. "Linda, do we have Vlad on conference yet?"

A woman's voice replied over the intercom. "We're trying to establish the satellite connection, Mr. Black. It might take a little while. We're not getting through for some reason."

"Keep at it, Linda. This is important."

"Yes, of course, Mr. Black."

The men conversed quietly for the next few minutes until the voice came back over the intercom. “We have Mr. Ajajdif on line three, Mr. Black.”

“Thanks, Linda.” Black tapped his computer again. “Vlad, you there?”

There was some static for a couple of moments, but then a deep voice, tinted with a heavy Russian accent, came on the intercom. “I am here, Adrian.” Vladimir Ajajdif was to be the sixth person in the meeting. He was the head of Quest Mining, one of Phoenix Corporation’s subsidiaries, currently on assignment at a distant location with his team.

“Alright, good. Jerry, Dr. Bartram, Dr. Tabrizi and Luigi are here with me.” Black looked at his watch. “It’s nine-thirty. Let’s get started. Vlad, give us a status update.”

“I’m assuming you received my weekly report?”

“Yes, I have. But we need to know what the latest situation is.”

“Well, as you are aware, we have run into several challenges over the last few weeks. We’ve been having problems with the equipment and getting the parts. The weather has been unpredictable and the visibility has been horrible some days, so much so that we can barely see past our noses up in this altitude. It’s hard to get a chopper flying out to us from Mayo.”

Li jumped in. “But we are willing to pay the premium to get the flights out to you. Why can’t you convince them to bring it in?”

“Out here in this godforsaken land, not everything is about money. This place is shrouded in thick clouds most days. We’ve tried talking to different companies, but it’s hard to find a pilot who will fly in.”

Black rubbed his forehead. “We can’t just sit on our hands and wait for something to happen. We are running far behind schedule as it is . . . and you know the boss doesn’t take these things lightly.”

There was a moment of icy silence. Finally, Ajajdif sighed. “Trust me, it’s not like I haven’t been trying. We are in the middle of this remote place and our options are limited. Which reminds me, Dr. Tabrizi? We are running out of the leaching compounds at the mining site. Without those chemicals, the mineral extraction comes to a standstill."

Dr. Tabrizi was stunned. "I sent two hundred barrels of the chemicals and you've *already* run out of them? How much do you need to extract the darn fenixium?"

"We have used up most of it and there is about fifty barrels sitting in Mayo that the pilots won't fly out to us, but even those will not suffice. The soil here soaks it up like a sponge and we're getting very low yield of that mineral."

"I thought you said this place was supposed to be saturated with fenixium, Vlad," Black said sharply. "And you and your team were supposed to be in and out of there within a hundred-and-twenty days. Ninety days have gone by and you've only extracted six kilos. At this point you should be at nine kilos."

"I only report what my geologist tells me. And yes, we were planning to complete the mining operation within four months, but I need one month's extension, just to be safe. Listen, I've got a great team of mining engineers and crew who are willing to put in their blood, sweat and tears to get back on schedule—and believe me some of them literally have—but . . ." Static crackled over the intercom, cutting him off.

Black sat up straight. "Vlad? Are you there?" He was answered by more static. "Vlad?"

"Did we lose the connection?" Dattalo asked.

A few seconds later, their colleague's voice came back on the intercom, agitation and a bit of anger in his tone. "You just need to get me the tools I need and I'll get the job done."

Black leaned back in his seat. He rapped the table with his knuckles, fighting to get his anger under control. "Alright, I'll give you another month. But that's that. No more extensions."

"Thank you."

Dattalo cut in. "Vlad, Luigi here. Look, I know you and your team are putting in your best effort, and I know this mineral is extremely difficult to extract, but I need you to understand that at the Defense division, we are invested heavily in making sure our research and production moves along as scheduled. Without the mineral, we simply cannot proceed."

"*Da*, no pressure there," Ajajdif responded coldly.

Trying to deflect the tension, Black asked, "What about the supplies for your crew? I know it's tough running a group of eighty-five people on a mountain in the middle of nowhere. Is there enough food and supplies for them? And how's their morale?"

"Yes, and they're fine," he answered curtly.

"Speaking of being out there," Dr. Bertram cut in eagerly, "Dr. Deol at Biotech wants to know what you thought about the hybrids that she sent."

"God, those beasts are unbelievable." Ajajdif's voice picked up for the first time during the meeting. "Thank the good doctor for me, will you, Al? And let her know that all five of her babies are just fine. The Marauders have been a great benefit here at the site. Just the other night, a grizzly wandered into the camp and two of them brought it down within minutes. Neither one of them got a scratch. I got one of my guys to cut the grizzly up, and you can trust that the Marauders fed like kings." He chuckled. "There's enough meat from the kill to feed them for the next couple of days."

As the two conversed, Black leaned over to Li. "Do you know if our two Ospreys are back from their assignment in Asia?" he asked quietly.

Li nodded. "One of them arrived this morning, actually. I spoke with the pilot and they're not scheduled for any activity for the next week."

"Good. If those bush pilots out in Mayo won't do the job, we'll do it ourselves. I want those birds heading to the mining site ASAP. They'll be delivering the chemicals and spare parts."

Li nodded again and turned to his computer to confirm the request. The V-22 Osprey, built by Bell and Boeing for the United States military, was capable of vertical takeoff and landing. They had been recently made available for the commercial market and Phoenix Corporation seized the opportunity to purchase two units. At sixty feet in length, and with a cargo capacity of twenty thousand pounds, the non-military version of the aircraft was an obvious choice for Phoenix Corporation's operations in remote locations.

Black looked back up and interrupted Ajajdif's and Dr. Bertram's conversation. "Vlad, I'm arranging to send one of our planes out to you with all the supplies. They will also do a loop to Mayo to get the remaining compounds."

"Sounds good. How many more barrels will I get?"

All heads turned to Dr. Tabrizi. "I'll have another hundred prepared before our plane takes off from here," he assured them.

"Thanks. So when can I expect the—" A distant boom sounded over the conference system, bringing the meeting to an abrupt halt. Someone could be heard calling out to Ajajdif urgently in the background. When Ajajdif's voice came back on, he sounded rushed. "I think we've had an accident over here. I have to go. Just send everything as soon as you can." There was a click, and then silence on the other end.

The men sat there, stunned at the unexpected end to the call. Li finally spoke up. "Should we try dialing back?

The chief executive ran a hand through his dark hair. "No," he said wearily. "Let him deal with the situation there. I will call him later. In the meantime, let's get things in motion over here."

"You got it, chief." Dr. Bertram stood up, followed by the others, leaving Black to sit alone in the boardroom as the men quickly filed out. Black waited a moment before calling out to Dattalo as soon as the others were out of sight. Dattalo came walking back in, curious. "Yes?"

"I got a call from the boss yesterday."

Dattalo stared at Black and noticed beads of sweat appearing on the other man's forehead. "What happened?" he whispered, as if he were afraid someone was listening in.

Black rested his head in a hand and closed his eyes. "I was told in unmistakable terms that we need to get this whole thing back on schedule right away. I need to know if you have everything under control at Quest Defense."

Dattalo patted Black's shoulder. "I can assure you that everything is set to go on my side," he replied. "We just need to ensure that the mineral gets here on time. The amount we've received from the mining operation so far has been barely sufficient for research purposes alone. To move into testing and production, we're going to need a whole lot more."

Black nodded. "Let's get it done, then."

33

As soon as Ajajdif hung up the phone, he grabbed his black trench coat and hastily threw it on as he rushed out of his office to investigate the boom he'd heard. He headed for the tunnel where a group of workers in orange and yellow coveralls with hardhats stood peering into the entrance of the shaft.

"What's going on?" Ajajdif barked, coming up behind his employees.

"There was an explosion!" one of the workers called out.

"What?" Ajajdif shoved his way past the gaggle and into the tunnel, grabbing a couple of workers to go with him. The workers turned on the mining lights attached to their hardhats and hurriedly walked along the steel tracks that the tunneling machine used. Thick dust and smoke hung in the air. About two hundred feet into the tunnel, they found that the machine had been thrown off its track.

The large diesel-driven engine with massive rotating drills was designed to dig through the toughest material. Painted bright red, it had all the capabilities of a standard tunnel-boring machine, only it was smaller, about the size of a Greyhound bus; it was meant to be mobile and used in remote areas.

Coughing from the smoke, Ajajdif instructed the workers to inspect the damage. After a few moments, one of them called out. "Sir! The machine operator's assistant is here. He's got burns and he's unconscious."

Ajajdif hurriedly made his way around the machine. The two workers were crouched beside a man who lay motionless. He knelt on one knee next to them and carefully removed the unconscious worker's dust-covered safety goggles and singed respirator mask. He gently patted the man's cheeks. "Can you hear me?" he asked loudly.

The worker didn't move. He tilted the man's head back to open the breathing passageway and placed his ear close to the man's mouth, watching for the rise and fall of his chest. "He's breathing," he confirmed. He turned to one of the men with him. "Get a stretcher and get him to the medic right away." The worker nodded and rushed out of the tunnel, the sound of his hard-toed boots echoing into the distance. Ajajdif gestured to the other worker. "I want you to find the operator."

Ajajdif stayed with the unconscious man while waiting for the stretcher. A few minutes later, he heard the worker call out. "I found the operator, sir, but I think he's unconscious too."

Ajajdif hastened to join the worker on the support platform at the back of the drill. As he looked around, he found the operator slumped over a railing. When the worker removed the operator's safety goggles and hardhat, they saw blood matted over his entire face. Ajajdif gingerly checked for the man's pulse. He felt nothing. He felt for the man's pulse a few more times but still nothing. Ajajdif was livid. He could not believe that one of his employees was dead. "How did this happen?" he spat.

The worker, pale with the realization that his colleague had been killed, looked around shakily. "There was an explosion," he stammered. "Don't know what caused it, sir."

Ajajdif stayed silent. As he scanned around the dark tunnel and gazed through the lingering smoke, he began to suspect what might have been the cause and felt a pang of guilt.

Judging from the damage, he guessed that there had been a gas explosion. His chief geologist had warned him of methane buildup from carbonaceous rocks and insisted that the miners check for this danger regularly. Ajajdif had provided his men with two handheld gas detectors but both were broken. He had requested replacements but was yet to receive them.

He turned to look at the dead man and vehemently bad-mouthed the company, although he knew he was to blame for pushing his workers to keep going in hazardous conditions. After a few moments, he snapped, "Take care of everything here." He stormed out of the tunnel. "Someone get the equipment engineer over here, *now!*"

The workers scrambled to find the engineer, and when they did, they shoved him at Ajajdif, almost as if to say, '*Here, take him and spare us.*'

The equipment engineer peered down at his shorter boss. "Yes?"

"I want that machine brought out of the tunnel and repaired. We only have that one, and it's crucial that we get it fixed as soon as we can."

"Sir, I just took a quick look. The machine is quite far into the tunnel, and it's off its track. We'll need to devise a way to put it back on its tracks first before it can be pulled out. That is going to be tough with the limited equipment we have."

Ajajdif glared at the engineer. "It needs to be fixed. I don't care how you do it. Just get it done. We are way behind schedule and if we don't clear this mess up, things will go to hell in a hand-basket very quickly."

Taken aback, the engineer assessed his options. "Well . . . we have winches and cables. Throw in a couple of blocks with tackles and with sheer manpower we might make it work."

"Then get to it already."

"Yes, sir."

As Ajajdif spun on his heel and headed toward his office, he shouted over his shoulder, "And tell the workers to keep at it! They can use shovels to load the ore onto the conveyor belt if they have to."

The moment he entered his office, Ajajdif told his assistant to page his geologist and chief mining engineer. "Tell them to come to my office immediately." She obliged and hurriedly went to put the call out. He hung his coat up and stood by his desk, running his hands over his face into his short, wavy auburn hair and muttering to himself. He took a sip of his coffee, now cold after the call with Adrian Black. He sat down in his chair and stared into his mug, silently cursing in his mother tongue all the bad luck that has been thrown his way lately.

He paused, acknowledging to himself that while he spoke Russian fluently, he'd never learned his father's language. Actually, he never did remember meeting his father. He had departed before Ajajdif was born to move back to the city in Algeria where he'd been raised. Ajajdif's mother was left to rear their son on her own in a small, poor Russian town while bouncing around from job to job. Ajajdif spent the first seventeen years of his life in his place of birth, roaming the streets with gangs after dropping out of school at an early age. Sometime after his eighteenth birthday, his mother had pleaded with him to move to America so he could start his life anew and prosper. She gave him the money that she'd been saving and, after some arguing, Ajajdif reluctantly agreed.

When his plane touched down in the new land, Ajajdif found himself on the streets of San Francisco, doing odd jobs just to survive. With his keen mind, he learned English quickly enough to improve his condition but old habits die hard and he soon got caught up in the life of petty crime again. It was at the point of turning from minor to more serious criminal activities that he'd been rescued by the most unlikely person—whom he later found out to be Phoenix Corporation's founder and boss—who'd seen his innate talent for leadership and organization. It had been a long journey, but he had been well taken care of by the company and owed his allegiance above everyone else to the boss.

"Sir?"

Ajajdif looked up. His assistant was standing at his door with two other people. He thanked her and then addressed the other two. "Sit," he told them brusquely.

They took their seats on two chairs in front of Ajajdif's desk. Arianna Abdul, the geologist, exchanged worried glances with the mining engineer, Francis LeChamps.

Ajajdif went straight to the point. "The head office isn't happy with our pace. We are way behind schedule and they are accepting no more excuses from us."

"We are doing our best with what we have," LeChamps answered tentatively. He turned on his iPad and looked at it. "The conveyor belt has broken down three times in the past week alone. The bearings need to be replaced, as do two of the motors, but we are out of spares and the makeshift repairs we've done to patch it up won't hold for much longer." His eyes scanned as he scrolled down his notes on the touchscreen. "Of our Bobcats, only two are currently working. We need parts to fix the others, and we don't have those parts." He looked up at the head of Quest Mining to assess his reaction before continuing. "We placed an order three weeks ago but we still haven't received them. Also, we are running drastically low on the leaching compounds."

Ajajdif rubbed his face again, weary. "I talked to Adrian about an hour ago and explained our predicament to him. He managed to track down one of the Ospreys and is sending the plane out to us with the parts and chemicals."

"When?"

"He said as soon as he could. What else do I need to know?"

LeChamps scratched the top of his head. "Well, nothing else at this point, except for our extreme disappointment with the yield that we're getting from all our effort."

"What do you mean?" Ajajdif asked.

"You know. The quantity of the ore that we've been able to extract is nowhere near what we were promised by the geological reports."

Ajajdif turned to Abdul and raised an eyebrow as anger flitted across his face. The geologist knew what was coming and shrank in her seat. "You and your team searched all over the world and, having spent millions of dollars, came to the conclusion that the mineral was in abundance here, in this very mountain." His voice rose an octave as he tried to control his temper. "Explain to me." His eyes pierced her. "Explain to me why we are not seeing the yield that we were promised?"

Abdul, though fearful, defended her position. "This is not perfect science. We did our best. We tested, we studied, and we sampled. This still remains the best place on the planet to extract the fenixium."

"You tell that to the boss," Ajajdif snapped. "We were supposed to be in and out of here in four months, and we've already spent two—*nyet,* three months here now. In case you've forgotten, speed is essential because we're not licensed to mine, only to explore. If the Canadian government gets wind of this, it's game over. So much is riding on this ore, you have no idea. It would cost us more than you can imagine if we don't get the required amount."

The other two sat quietly for a minute, and then Abdul, twirling her red curls nervously, said, "I . . . I can understand your frustration. I'm sorry that we aren't finding as much as we should. All our tests were conclusive. This mine is the only site that is capable of producing the ore in the quantity we need. It may be slow getting to it, but rest assured, it *is* there." She waited a while before cautiously adding, "There is something else that I have been very concerned about—it's the indiscriminate use of the leaching compound outside of the standard process. It's supposed to be used only inside the vats so that it can be properly contained and disposed of."

"Using it in the tunnel cuts the processing time, so we can get to the ore a little faster."

"But if the compound finds a water source, it would have devastating effects on the environment! This is cyanide we are dealing with, sir, not a benign chemical."

"It doesn't matter, Arianna. We need the mineral, and we need it fast. Besides, we are a million miles from anything."

She turned to protest, but Ajajdif slammed his fist on the table, eyes narrowed. "We will get it, whatever the cost."

With that, he dismissed them.

34

The Elders gathered inside the assembly *neyra* for the meeting that Nageau had called. Tayoka was the last to arrive once again. He apologized and gave the best excuse he could: "I am getting old!"

The Elders laughed. "So are we, Tayoka," Saiyu replied.

They took their usual seats and Nageau looked at his companions. "I called for this meeting today because I think we need to reconvene on what is happening. Tikina, what is the condition of our ill in the convalescence shelter?"

Tikina looked up, troubled. "The four patients in the convalescence center remain in critical condition." Concerned murmurs rose from the others. "Rest assured, Huyani, Saiyu and I are taking good care of them, but the need to identify and contain this malady is now paramount."

"Let us hope that the men we have sent out will return quickly with the source uncovered," Saiyu murmured.

"We should call for a community gathering," Ashack said gruffly. "The village needs to be informed of what is happening. We must prevent the rest of our kin from falling ill."

Nageau nodded. "The same thought crossed my mind," he said. "We have not had a village meeting in a long while. It is time."

"I could not agree more." Tayoka turned to the other Elders. "I have been meaning to ask—how fare your apprentices?"

Saiyu smiled. "My time with Mariah has been very rewarding. I have noticed, though, that she is a lot more, how do you say—

audacious?—when she is in the company of her friends. Alone, she appears to be a somewhat withdrawn. However her training is progressing quite well, and I see a lot of potential in her strong-spirited ways. How about yours, Nageau?"

Nageau chuckled. "Kody is very energetic, that is certain—I already have my hands full with him. He has some trouble focusing, but when he does, his enthusiasm about the learning process amazes me. I feel compelled to make note, though, that his humor is at times a bit much. I wonder if it is perhaps a self-defense mechanism of sorts—maybe a way to cope with the situation surrounding his father?"

"Utilizing humor as a means of deflection and safeguard is not uncommon," Tikina said thoughtfully. "It is certainly preferable to other coping methods."

"True..." Nageau stroked his chin, then addressed Ashack. "What about Aari?"

"Aari is keen on learning as well." Though Ashack's voice remained gruff, he couldn't keep a little bit of pride out of it. "He is a bright young man, he is. Learns quickly. He constantly questions everything. That attitude of learning transcends just practical and physical things; he strives to learn the truth in all matters. That will be a great asset for him in unfolding his eventual abilities."

"Wonderful." Nageau gestured at his mate. "What of Tegan?"

"She was tentative at the beginning, and certainly still is, but she has opened up a bit and is actually eager now that she is aware of the gifts of the mind that she is blessed with."

Nageau smiled, then turned to Tayoka. "And Jag?"

Tayoka wore a cheeky grin. "I do believe it will take some time for him to get used to my unique quirks."

"Your eccentric quirks, you mean," Tikina sighed.

"Mmh, I suppose."

Nageau patted the other man's shoulder. "Go easy on the lad. He comes across as a type who would excel under a serious tutelage."

"I am preparing him," Tayoka said.

"For what?"

"To lighten up and learn to laugh at himself. Life has a way of throwing the unexpected at us. He will not always have the luxury of working in secure conditions, and there will be distractions. He is strong physically but he has a tendency to be too rigid in his mind. It will be essential that he learns the value of being open to new ideas, to look at things from a different perspective."

"And you intend to make the most out of your wiliness to give him a whole range of perspectives," Saiyu guessed.

"Oh, most definitely."

The Elders looked at one another. They appeared pleased with each other's reports, and it gave them a reason to smile amidst the stress bearing down on their shoulders.

Saiyu tucked a loose strand of hair back under her headband. "It has been half a moon cycle since our visitors were brought to us by the Guardians. There are already lots of rumors around. We need to bring clarity to the village in regards to the five and the prophecy."

Tayoka stroked his thick beard. "The question is, how much do we tell?"

"I think it is time we introduced our guests to the community and reveal what has transpired since their arrival." All eyes turned to Nageau. He explained. "The five have proven themselves with the crystal assessment, and having trained and observed them during the last three days, we have made the determination that they *are* the ones. The people have a right to meet the five and become acquainted with those who are destined to fulfill the prophecy."

The Elders nodded to each other. "I will invite them to be at the gathering tonight," Tikina volunteered.

"Perfect. Now, is there anything to report on the four we have sent out on the expedition?"

"They are due back in about two days," Tikina answered. "Through the message beads on the courier falcon, we have learned that the two separate groups have met and are heading toward the Ayen Range."

"So they have not yet found the source?"

"No."

"Hm . . . They still have a couple more days. Let us pray for the protection and wellbeing of these four brave men. They are in uncharted territory as far as safety is concerned. Our village has never been challenged in this manner since our forefathers established this settlement." Nageau closed his eyes to hold sacred space in meditation and prayer for the four men. The other Elders joined in.

After the span of silence, Tikina quietly voiced a thought that was at the back of all their minds. "I have been wondering, my friends. We all have a hint as to how powerful the dark forces are. We know that the storm which is gathering is global in nature." She stared at the floor, pursing her lips. "The challenges that the younglings will be faced with from beyond the boundaries and the safety of our village . . . Will they be able to handle this? I know we have discussed this briefly before, but the feeling of foreboding in my heart remains."

"I understand your apprehension." Saiyu reached for Tikina's hand and squeezed it gently; both women had the same look of concern in their eyes.

Nageau attempted to comfort them. "If they are indeed the fulfillment to our prophecy, then they are chosen for this and as such will be protected."

Ashack cleared his throat. "Remember, they will not be alone out there in the world. Once they return to the life they know, the Sentries will watch over them. And chances are they have already been watched over as they were growing."

The women looked at each other, nodding slowly. The Elders were quiet for a few moments more, and then Nageau clasped his hands together. "Let us adjourn. Spread the word that we will be hosting a village gathering as the sun goes down. We want everyone to attend, for what we speak of tonight affects us all. The entire community must be made aware of what is happening."

* * *

The friends were relaxing in the boys' *neyra* after a long day. The girls had dominated Aari's and Jag's sleeping bags atop the platforms, sitting upon them proudly while the two boys sat on the ground, scowling. Kody had fought for his sleeping bag, guarding it as if it were his most precious possession.

Tegan yawned. "So how was training for you guys?"

"My mentor's a complete nut," Jag muttered. "Do you know what he did? When I was trying to do a front aerial somersault on a log, he tossed this weird vine thing that wrapped around my arms as I was doing the flip, so I didn't have the balance I needed to land on my feet." He pulled his shirt up to reveal a bruise on his hip bone. "That's from hitting the log and sliding off." He pulled his shirt back down, grimacing. "That man is like a child sometimes. I was wondering why he had that roll of vine. He sure had a good laugh out of it."

"There's probably a reason why he did that," Mariah said.

"Yeah. The reason being he's completely insane." Jag sighed. "But let me tell you something. In spite of his seeming craziness, the things I've learned from Tayoka in these few days are mind-boggling. I keep discovering things that amaze me. As odd as he seems, I gotta admit I've learned to respect that man." He looked back at Mariah. "What about you? How's your training coming along?"

"To say that it's interesting would be an understatement," she replied. "Saiyu's been an amazing mentor. She's pointing out things to me that she believes I'm capable of that completely blow my mind. And here's the thing: she makes me prove that she's right. You're not going to believe what I did today."

The others stared at her. "What?"

"I can't believe I'm going to say this," she said, awed, "but I moved my meditation crystal—with my mind."

"No way," Kody sputtered.

She grinned. "Yes way. I can show you."

He scoffed. "Right. Four days into training and you're already using your mental ability? Gimme a break."

"How much you wanna bet on that, brickhead?"

"Name your price."

"Alright. If I can prove it, you have to climb up on the nearest tree and stay up there till morning. And you can't have dinner."

Kody smirked. "And if I win, you have to make me steak every day for the rest of the week. If I don't like the taste, it doesn't count."

Mariah looked around for something she could use. She saw Tegan's mug on the tabletop and pointed at it. "Keep an eye on that mug, kids, but don't you talk or I'll lose my concentration."

Amused, the others turned and stared at the cup. Moments passed, but nothing happened. "Mariah—" Aari started.

"Hush. I need to focus."

The four stared at the cup again, not really expecting anything. At first, imperceptible, there were minute vibrations, something that the friends thought they heard faintly rather than saw. As the vibrations gradually increased, the four watched with unbelieving eyes as the mug moved across the grain of the wooden tabletop, struggling against the friction, and slowly inched its way to the edge of the surface. The friends stared for a long moment until Tegan, bewildered, looked back at Mariah. "Did that actually happen?"

Mariah was holding her head in her hands, eyes shut tight. "Ugh, I've got a headache now." She rubbed her temples. "Saiyu did warn me that this would happen at the beginning. I wonder what size of a headache I'd get if I tried to move boulders."

The others laughed and Jag tackled her in a hug, Aari and Tegan joining in and exclaiming, "You did it! You actually did it!"

Kody sat quietly, hoping that if he were still, no one would notice him. Mariah turned to him and smiled. "Looks like someone is heading up the tree tonight."

"But . . ." Kody looked panicked. "But I have to eat! I can't do without food! My metabolism—"

"Too bad, buddy boy. You thought you knew it all."

Kody looked as though he might cry. The other three avoided commenting on the subject and instead stared back at the mug that stood at the edge of the table.

A woman's voice sounded outside the *neyra*. "Younglings, are you here?"

The five looked at each other and quickly scrambled out of the shelter to greet Tikina. The Elder smiled warmly at the friends. "Do you have a few moments to spare? I would like to take a walk with you and talk to you about something."

Unable to resist her pleasant and motherly ways, the five agreed and walked on either side of her. The Elder took the friends past an array of trees and bushes. The group noted a colorful bed of roses and a stretch of lavender.

"Who gardens here?" Tegan asked, impressed.

Tikina smiled. "My daughter—Huyani and Akol's mother—does. She certainly is the one with the green thumb in the family."

Kody quipped, "Judging by all the amazing colors here, I'd say she's got very colorful thumbs."

Aari groaned. "It's an expression, you idiot."

"I know *that*. Can't a guy crack a joke around here?"

Mariah turned to look up at Tikina, almost in a childlike manner. The five loved being in the presence of the Elder; there was something comforting about her. "You said that you had something you wanted to share with us?"

Tikina smiled again. "Yes. But first, I would like to inquire as to how you feel your training is coming along." The five responded almost in unison. Tikina laughed. "One at a time, younglings."

Starting with Kody, the five shared their newfound enthusiasm for their training sessions. They went on to describe how intrigued they were by the idea that the latent powers in each of them could be unleashed through training, discipline and most importantly, by fortifying the spirit. The group was in agreement that this was a lot to wrap their minds around, but they were eager to learn.

Tikina was extremely pleased. "I am very much encouraged by the zeal you have shown for the training and for your courage to explore your true potential.

"Now, I would like to share what I came to speak with you about. The other Elders and I were in a discussion this morning, and we have given this a lot of thought. We have made a determination about the five of you with regards to the prophecy. Now we believe that the time has come for the community to finally meet its special guests."

The friends, stunned for a moment, burst into flurries of "Why!" and "Do we have to?"

The Elder raised her hand and the five quieted down. "It is good for them to get acquainted with you, and for you to get acquainted with them," she told the friends gently. "You will be living here for the next little while before you head back to your families, and there are no more reasons to keep you in the shadows. You are an important part of our community, and you are destined to play a very special role. It is only fitting that you become fully immersed in the life of the village."

The five were not sure how to respond. On one hand, the Elder made perfect sense. On the other, the trepidation of being showcased to an entire community of over seven hundred people was overwhelming to say the least. They looked to each other for a cue, then to Jag. He looked pensive. Unknown to the group, he was trying to separate the facts from his emotions. Surprising himself, he looked at his friends and said, "I think we should do this."

Tikina gazed at Jag, impressed, and nodded to herself. She could see how the training was already beginning to affect the youth's decision-making, even though it had only just begun. She made a mental note to bring this up to the other Elders later.

They walked for a little longer as she briefed them on what to expect at the gathering, then instructed them to meet her behind the amphitheater in the village square. As she guided them back to their *neyra* and started back to her home, she waved at the five genially and said, "This will be an evening to remember."

The five waited until Tikina was out of sight, then Mariah spun around and poked Kody in the chest. "You got lucky this time, bozo."

Kody grinned in relief. "Saved by Tikina. Looks like I won't be spending the night up in a tree." He patted his stomach. "And I won't be missing my meal, either!"

35

The village square was essentially an open field with a tree-lined perimeter and a curved amphitheater at one end. Flanking the amphitheater on either side were two large fire pits. A gazebo was built over each pit with layered roofing to shield the naked flame from the night sky. Groves of trees were strategically planted in clusters to provide camouflage from the air. The wondrous thing about the way the groves and the attending shrubs were arranged was that, no matter where one stood, the view of the amphitheater was never obstructed.

The fire pits were already lit to compensate for the fading evening light, casting a warm glow on the faces of some of the villagers who had gathered. They chatted amongst themselves; lots of speculation was in the air as to the reason for the gathering. They didn't have to wait long to find out why they had been called upon.

The Elders stood in front of the assembly and Nageau raised his hand, calling the gathering to order. "My friends," he began, the amphitheater augmenting his voice naturally. "Let me first begin by saying that I am pleased to see your radiant faces here, and we—" he gestured to the other Elders—"are honored to address you today." He paused to scan the faces of all those who had gathered. Gazing at them, he was reminded of the precious trust laid in the hands of the Elders. The people had looked up to the council of the Elders for generations. They were not only their leaders, but they were also guides and mentors. Most importantly, they were the custodians of their culture. Always aware of this tremendous responsibility, Nageau remained humbled by the faith that the people had placed in him.

Tikina gently rested a hand on his arm and spoke. "We are gathered here for a reason. As I am sure some of you may already know, there is an illness that has befallen our village. It is unlike anything we have ever experienced and none of our age-old remedies seem capable of healing those who have been infected. We have already lost one of our brethren to this insidious disease, and have witnessed the ugly arms of this illness as it grabs ahold of the minds and bodies of our people."

A few heads in the crowd began to nod, recalling the last moments of Fiotez's life. Among those gathered were Fiotez's mate and son. Both tried to put up a brave front, but there was weariness and grief in their eyes. A few yards from them, Akol and Huyani stood with their mother and little brother. Huyani held Tibut in her arms while their mother had her hands over Akol's shoulders. The youth was enrapt as his grandparents spoke.

Tikina continued. "We want to assure you that we are doing everything we can to identify the source of this contaminant and find a cure for it. As we speak, four brave men who have volunteered to track the disease to its source are on the fourth day of their expedition. They are at the Ayen mountain range and are expected to return in the next two or three days. In the meantime, Magèo is working on finding a cure with the limited information that he has."

The community turned to look at Magèo as he stood alone, observing the gathering from under a tree with his arms folded, trying to remain inconspicuous. He saw the entire village looking at him and, with a glare, threw the hood of his robe on so only his long white beard was visible. His dislike for large crowds and the outdoors was well known. The villagers smiled and turned back to the Elders, knowing that inside that hard outer shell was a man who truly cared for others.

"In the meantime," Nageau said, "we strongly advise you to avoid consuming or coming into contact with any water outside of this valley. We have tested and determined that Esroh Lègna remains unpolluted and safe to use. However, we will be conducting regular tests of its waters and will notify you immediately if any changes occur."

"Also," Ashack said, his face stoic as usual, "hunting will not be permitted until this matter has been resolved. If you are to leave this valley at any point, prepare your own pack of sustenance."

A collection of groans rose from the crowd, mainly from the youths. Sensing the unease, Nageau decided to open the gathering to questions from the people. The Elders patiently responded to their queries. When it seemed as though everyone had gotten their answers, Nageau announced, "Now that we have put that discussion to rest, there is another matter of great importance that we must share with you. This concerns not just the future of us as a people, but it has far-reaching implications for humanity."

Hearing this, whatever remnants there were of murmurs died down and the crowd gave its complete attention to the Elders. Taking a few moments to gather his thoughts, Nageau probed, "We are all well-versed with our ancient prophecy, are we not?" He observed the crowd for a response, noticing the silent nods across the village square. "As we know, the prophecy paints for us a picture of the future. Its sanctified content, divinely inspired, guides, warns, and protects us. The prophecy, in conjunction with our sacred scriptures, is a fortress for our spiritual and physical wellbeing and has guided our thoughts and our actions for ages. One of the salient indicators given to us through this prophecy is the coming of a dark and destructive force that will befall all civilization."

The villagers began to murmur quietly again, worried looks on their faces. A few who had been sitting on the ground stood up, ears strained, trying to make sense of every word that Nageau spoke. Understanding the need for reassurance, Nageau continued. "As troublesome as that may seem, the prophecy, as you know, also tells us about the arrival of five special souls destined to vanquish this darkness. They will fulfill the signs given in the prophecy and will learn the secrets of our ways." His voice rose and his face lit with reverence. "Combined, the powers of the five will far exceed anything that we have ever known."

Saiyu stepped in. "As many of you are aware, since the last full moon, there have been amongst us five youths who were brought to our valley by the Guardians after we witnessed a flaming craft fall from the sky."

A ripple of anticipation rolled through the crowd.

Nageau exchanged glances with the other Elders and said slowly, "A lot has happened since the five younglings arrived in our village. We have observed many signs and seen convincing revelations in this brief span of time. Through lots of meditation and discussion, and having witnessed the pace at which they are able to grasp their training and realize their innate capabilities, we have come to the conclusion that these five youths were sent to us to fulfill the prophecy."

The growing murmur cascaded into a cacophony of voices as the villagers tried to grasp the meaning of this momentous announcement. Some appeared relieved and even euphoric while others looked skeptical. They all had thoughts to share, but Nageau raised his hand for silence. "Please, my friends, settle."

Someone called out from the crowd, "Do these youths know that they are the ones to fulfill the prophecy?"

"Indeed, we have had discussions with them. They are learning the importance of their role with each passing day."

Exclamations filled the air. The Elders moved to enlighten their brethren and provided further explanation and reasons. The overall atmosphere gradually evolved from skepticism, to acceptance, and finally jubilation as the Elders brought to bear their rousing insights.

As the joyful acceptance grew, Nageau signaled Saiyu to call upon the five to come and stand with them. As the group walked out from behind the amphitheater, all eyes turned to them, inspecting them closely. The five, though incredibly nervous, somehow managed to keep moving forward and positioned themselves in a row in front of the Elders. As they had learned to do in their training, they bowed to the Elders, then turned to face the crowd. They placed their hands over their hearts and dipped their heads at the villagers. The crowd broke into a roar of approval. The five blushed furiously, but straightened with smiles all around. Glancing back, they saw the beaming faces of Nageau, Tikina, Saiyu, and Tayoka. Even Ashack broke into a grin.

In the shadows at the far edge of the village square, a pair of cold, dark blue eyes narrowed. Hutar watched the proceedings stone-faced, his mind calculating. A few members of his group who were also there looked at him, trying to assess his thoughts, but his expression remained unreadable. He lowered his gaze to the ground as the five were showered with attention.

He rubbed his forehead, then looked up and jerked his chin at his comrades. Silently, he got to his feet and slunk away from the gathering. His comrades followed him. No one noticed them leaving, as they were all too caught up with the Elders and the five.

Once Hutar and his group were out of sight, they broke into a jog and headed for the stable. They slowed when they walked in so as not to alarm the horses, and Hutar's companions jostled each other for places to sit on the bales of hay.

Hutar crossed his arms. "I had not expected the Elders to announce that the five's training has begun so quickly. Nor did I expect them to be introduced as our *saviors*." He hissed the last word derisively.

"To be fair, no one called them our saviors," one of the younger boys said innocently.

Hutar snarled at him and the boy fell off the bale he was sitting on. "It was implied, you idiot."

"Sorry," the boy whimpered.

"What are we going to do?" one of the other boys asked. "Since we last met, we have not heard any plans from you."

Hutar shot the boy a sharp glare and rested against one of the horses' stalls, tilting his head back. "That was several days ago. I have a plan in place now."

The group looked at each other with growing excitement. Despite himself, Hutar smiled slightly. How he loved the feeling of being the article of awe. "Settle, all of you." He leaned forward and they in turn leaned in, eyes bright and attentive.

The words rolled off his tongue smoothly, intriguing his cohorts with his cold but charismatic ways. Delight arose from the group as he unfolded his plot. Once the scheme was laid out, he assigned each member their task.

The sun had long since set when the group exited the stable and dispersed to head off to their shelters. Hutar was the last to leave, and as he watched his group head their separate ways, he thought: *Failure is but a step toward success. The wolf attack had failed, but that was just the start. This time*—a sadistic growl emanated from deep within his throat—*I will succeed.*

36

The twin rotors of the strange aircraft whirled in unison as it descended through the thick morning mist that cloaked the mountaintop. The air beating down from its blades created a helical vortex in the cloud. Appearing to float in the air, the Osprey's descent was gradual as it approached the landing pad. With its nacelles in the vertical position, the huge plane hovered like a helicopter over the pad for several moments as the pilot made fine adjustments on his flight controls right before a perfect touchdown.

The miners who were on their break came to watch the landing. Some had their phones out to take pictures of the aircraft. Most had never seen an Osprey up close like this and were impressed. A crew was on standby as the pilot killed the aircraft's engines. Two Bobcats and a couple of forklifts stood ready to help unload the cargo.

Ajajdif observed the proceedings from behind a pair of dark Ray-Ban sunglasses. He stood with his hands in the pockets of his flat-front pants, waiting for the crew to get in place to transport the plane's cargo. The pilot of the craft stepped out of the cockpit and moved away from his plane, taking his helmet off as Ajajdif made his way over to him. "Good morning," he called out.

The young pilot looked up and smiled. "Morning." He shook hands with Ajajdif, then removed his aviators and glanced around. "You guys sure are in the middle of nowhere. It was quite a flight getting out here."

"That's for sure." Ajajdif motioned at the cargo that was being unloaded. "I really have to thank you for bringing all this. We're in dire straits right now, but this will help us get back on track."

"Hey, it's my job."

"You've got another loop to do to get what remains at Mayo, right?"

"Yeah. Once your guys are done here, I'll be off. I should be back within five hours."

"Great." Ajajdif looked down as the radio clipped to his belt crackled and the voice of the site's head of security came on.

"Sir, do you have a minute?"

Ajajdif grabbed the radio and, saying a quick goodbye to the pilot, moved off. "Yes, I do."

"I'm heading down to check on the trespassers," the man said. "What do we do with them?"

"Hold on, Elias. I'd like to meet the intruders myself. Are you heading there right now?"

"Yes sir."

"Then I'll meet you at the holding cell."

"Sure thing."

Ajajdif replaced the radio on his belt and walked away from the landing pad in the direction of the holding cell. The large processing vats were on his left, and as he glanced at them, he recalled his geologist's worries about using the leaching compound outside of the vats. He dismissed the thought. "I'm hard-pressed for time and you want me to continue using just the vats? Bah!"

He passed the equipment engineer who was heading in the opposite direction to where the cargo was being unloaded. "The equipment is here, and I want it all out of the plane in double-time!" Ajajdif barked.

"Yes sir," the engineer said. "Also, just so you know, my guys and I managed to lift the tunneling machine back onto its track."

"Excellent," Ajajdif muttered. "And not a moment too soon."

He continued past the tall engineer and walked into the tunnel. On the right was a doorless storage room. Ajajdif strode past two sets of shelves on either side of the room meant to hold spare parts for the machines and headed for a door at the very back. The door used to lead into the mining foreman's office but was now converted to a holding cell. While Ajajdif was furious about the fact that the mining site had been breached, he was also a tad curious. He'd gotten a very brief update from his head of security early in the morning, but was looking to get more details.

He knocked and the door swung open, revealing a giant of a man with a shaved head who blocked Ajajdif's view of what was behind him. Elias Hajjar, the head of the operation's security team, was a Lebanese-born ex-mercenary and a true tattoo enthusiast. His muscular arms and thick neck were inked heavily, and his eyes weren't unlike dark abysses. Standing at six feet, eight inches, Hajjar was nothing less than intimidating.

The head of security saw that it was his superior at the door and stepped aside so Ajajdif could enter. As Hajjar closed the door, Ajajdif studied the intruders for the first time. Four men sat with their hands tied behind their backs and their feet were in chains. They looked tired and badly beaten up with cuts and bruises covering most of what could be seen of their skin. As Ajajdif met the eyes of the men, he noticed varying levels of defiance in each of them. Without taking his gaze away from the intruders, he asked Hajjar, "Why are they restrained like this?"

In a voice deeper than Ajajdif's, the head of security said, "These are not your hospitable forest hillbillies, sir. Three of my men were seriously injured when they tried to capture these louts last night. They put up one hell of a fight."

Ajajdif covered his face with his hands in frustration upon hearing those words. "Continue."

"The only way we were able to subdue them was by sedating them with tranquilizers." Hajjar nodded toward the intruders. "They've got a real nasty bite to them."

Ajajdif dropped his hands to his sides and glowered at the men tied in their chairs. He slowly crouched in front of one of the intruders and searched his face. The man met his eyes and put up a fearless front, but there were small, obvious signs that he was scared. His legs were shaking slightly, although he looked at Ajajdif and Hajjar as if they were the outsiders, not the other way around.

"Where are you from?" Ajajdif asked the intruder.

The man looked at him and said nothing. "They don't understand English, sir," Hajjar said. "We tried to communicate with them through hand signals and such, but they either don't want to cooperate or they're playing dumb. They certainly aren't stupid."

Ajajdif looked at the man for a while more, then stood up. "I can't believe there are people actually living out here." He scratched his eyebrow. "Where are your injured men?"

"They're in the infirmary."

Ajajdif shook his head. "HQ won't be pleased to hear about this intrusion and loss of labor."

"Does HQ really have to know, sir?"

Ajajdif stared up at the ceiling and nodded reluctantly. "I need to find out how they'll want us to deal with the trespassers, and they are going to have to deal with the family of my tunneling machine operator. In the meantime, keep them here. I assume you know what to do if they put up a struggle."

Hajjar cracked a merciless grin. "Yes, sir."

Casting one last look at the intruders, Ajajdif walked out of the room and into the tunnel. He watched the miners scrambling around trying to repair the ore conveyor with the parts they just received, and then exited the tunnel to head back to the landing pad. A young woman was heading in the same general direction. Ajajdif recognized her as one of the Marauders' keepers. He quickly caught up to her as she neared the metal building close to the landing pad where the animals were caged and tapped her on the shoulder. She jumped in surprise but relaxed when she saw Ajajdif. "Is there anything I can help you with, sir?"

"Have the Marauders had their breakfast yet?"

"No, sir, they haven't."

"Excellent. Listen, why don't you let me feed them? You can take a short break."

She looked at him, eyes wide. "Really?"

Ajajdif nodded. The woman appeared relieved and thanked him, then trotted off to check out the Osprey whose cargo was just about unloaded. Ajajdif headed toward the building and paused at the steel door to punch a code into the security keypad. There was a buzz and he pulled the heavy door open, grunting, and slid into a six-by-six room with another entrance, this one with a thumbprint recognition system beside the door. As soon as the system evaluated Ajajdif's print, a small light on the door turned from red to a flashing green. Ajajdif shoved the door inwards and entered. It was lit dimly inside. A woman who appeared a little older than Ajajdif walked toward him with a wrist-tied flashlight.

"Credentials?" she asked, businesslike, as she shone her light and examined him. When she recognized her supervisor, she lowered her hand. "Oh! Good morning, sir."

"Good morning. I'm here to feed the Marauders."

"Oh, really?" She sounded surprised. "Well, alright. If you could just step this way . . ." She led him down a narrow metal-walled hallway and opened yet another security door at the far end. As they stepped through they were immediately greeted by monstrous snarls.

The woman looked uneasy as she showed him where the creatures' food was stored. Ajajdif noticed and she smiled at him apologetically. "No matter how many times I step through that door, I can never get used to the sound of these beasts."

"That's okay," he soothed. "They can be quite unnerving. Thanks for bringing me—I can take it from here."

"If you're sure . . ."

"I am."

The woman nodded and quickly walked back out and closed the door. Ajajdif grinned as he heard the hybrids growl again before the noises died down. Clasping his hands behind his back, he slowly marched down two rows of spacious cages—three on one side and two on the other—and caught glimpses of large shapes crouching at the far corners of their enclosures. Their dark yellow eyes scrutinized him with cold calmness as he went to grab their food. When they realized they were about to be fed, they slowly rose to their full height.

The Marauders, standing close to four feet at the shoulder and about six feet from their snouts to their cropped tails, were completely new creatures designed and created at Quest Biotech. They were the result of years of genetic manipulation and were enhanced with reconstituted DNA from some of the world's most fearsome predators. They were ferocious and unpredictable; it would have been extremely difficult—and dangerous—to train them using traditional methods. In order to have effective control, the scientists at Biotech had surgically implanted nano-transducers into the brains and nerve centers of the creatures. A handheld transmitter gave their handlers complete control over these ultimate watchdogs.

The sound of the Marauders' retractable, unsheathed claws on the titanium floor of their cages grew louder as they drew closer to the front of their barred enclosures. The cages had two-inch thick steel bars, as the hybrids had been known to bite through anything less than that.

"Hello, love," he murmured, crouching down in front of one of the cages and sticking his hand through the bars to stroke the Marauder's smooth head. He was one of only two humans the hybrids would accept any form of affection from, the other being Dr. Deol, their creator.

The Marauder blinked slowly, allowing Ajajdif to fawn over her for only a few seconds before pulling away and retreating back to the far side of her cage. He went around, greeting the other hybrids, and they all pulled back after a few seconds of contact.

It was hard to see the Marauders clearly in the low light, but the dimness allowed them to rest better due to their extremely sensitive vision. Ajajdif smiled. The Marauders were the most amazing creatures he'd ever seen and were the greatest asset to the security team. He moved from cage to cage, feeding the beasts the last of the raw chunks of meat from the grizzly bear that was killed some nights ago. Once he finished, he leaned back against the food storage door and closed his eyes, listening as the hybrids tore savagely at the meat.

37

The morning after the village gathering, the Elders stood in the convalescence shelter and watched solemnly as a blanket was pulled over a young woman's face, covering her body. Saiyu attempted to comfort the young man who was sobbing uncontrollably beside his mate's bed. "I am so sorry," she murmured to him.

"Why her?" the man moaned. "Why *her?*" He trailed off, weeping uncontrollably.

Saiyu hugged him but he pulled away, not wanting any comfort, and stumbled out of the shelter, uttering deep sounds of agony and anguish. The Elders watched him, distraught. Raw emotions that were rarely ever seen were surfacing almost everywhere they looked. The people of Dema-Ki were strong by nature, inside and out, but the epidemic they were facing was something they had never been exposed to before and it was causing many to lose their confidence and composure.

Huyani quietly walked up to the Elders. "I will take care of everything here," she said.

Nageau forced a smile and hugged his granddaughter, who hugged him back tightly. Nodding to the other Elders, he led the way outside and they slowly headed to the temple.

"Have you spoken with Magèo about the serum?" Ashack asked Nageau.

"I have. He said he is still working on it."

Ashack wasn't satisfied. "How many more of our brethren must fall ill and perish before it is ready?"

"I know you are upset, Ashack, but Magèo is working with the scarce information that is available right now. We have our men tracking the source of the contamination, and, if all is well, they will return soon. From there, hopefully Magèo will be able to do more with whatever information or affected specimen they will bring back."

The Elders reached the temple and stood there for a while, taking in the sacred structure's healing ambience. As he watched an eagle swoop overhead, Nageau frowned. "Tikina, has the courier falcon returned since last evening?"

Tikina shook her head. Nageau looked concerned but Tikina placed her hand on his cheek to calm him. "I would not worry just yet. It is not even noon; the falcon usually only comes after midday. And let us not forget that the farther they are from the valley, the longer it will take for the bird to return here. I am sure our kin are fine."

* * *

Rikèq, Keno, Breyas and Aydar watched the man who was guarding them with resentment. The villagers had lost all feeling in their chain-wrapped legs nearly an hour earlier and their arms were sore from being tied back.

"We must get out of this place," Rikèq muttered.

Aydar, irate with the current situation, snorted. "How? I have never been bound to such strong restraints. Even if we did manage to escape, we may be sedated again."

"Not if we are stealthy, my friend."

His three companions looked at him, showing a little more interest.

The guard watched them, his gun leveled, unsure what to do. How was he to tell them that they were not allowed to converse? Quickly, he slammed the butt of his riffle against Rikèq's temple, almost causing him to black out. His three friends protested, and the guard instinctively pointed his weapon at them. They became quiet but glared at the guard.

"Rikèq," Breyas murmured. "Are you alright?"

Rikèq groaned and hung his head in pain. The others, helpless, watched as their friend fought to remain conscious. Long minutes passed until Rikèq lifted his head. "As I was saying," he said, his speech a little slurred as he continued where he left off, "there is only one guard at a time in this room. Surely we can down him."

"Down him . . . and then what?" Keno asked quietly.

"Even before we can think of that," Aydar whispered, "*how* do we strike? Do you not see how we are bound to our chairs?"

"Keno, with your ability to—" Rikèq clamped his mouth shut when he saw the guard walking back over. The guard looked down at him and said something which the men did not comprehend, but it was plainly understood that if the guard was not pleased with whatever they were doing, he would not hesitate to use his weapon. The men glanced at each other and decided to remain silent for now.

* * *

The five walked out of the training grounds and quickly made their way over to Huyani's *neyra* for their lunch break. As they strolled into the living quarters, Huyani looked up from where she was working in the kitchen and smiled. "You look worn out already!" she noted.

Jag flopped down on the sofa. "You left me alone at the mercy of Elder Tayoka," he said in a mock accusatory tone.

She laughed. "You know I must come down here and prepare your sustenance drinks before you are dismissed for your afternoon meal."

"Oh, you mean our protein shakes?" Aari asked.

"You can call it whatever you please, but it is an ancient formula handed down to us by our ancestors—our name for it is rytrèni. Only the Elders and a few entrusted villagers know how to blend it. It was generated to strengthen not only your body at its cellular level but also your mind, and is specific for each of you due to the difference in your latent powers."

"That's a lot to go into a mug." Aari lowered himself onto the couch beside Jag but was surprised when a yelp sounded.

"Watch where you sit, knucklehead!" Tegan quickly pushed Aari away before he could sit on her.

"Sorry, sport," he apologized, patting her cheek. "Didn't see you there."

She 'mmfed' and burrowed into her side of the couch, allowing Aari some room to squeeze in between her and Jag. The three watched, slightly amused, as Kody trotted around the kitchen after Huyani as she prepared the friends' drinks.

"It's hard to tell if he's following yon fair maiden over there, or if he's following the smell of the ingredients she's carrying," Mariah said from where she sat on the opposite couch, leaning her head against the armrest.

The four relaxed on the couches, enjoying their break while it lasted. Mariah tilted her head so she could look at her friends. "It's a shame we don't get to see each other during training. How are you guys doing so far?"

Tegan perked up. "I'm having a blast, actually."

"Really?" Jag sounded skeptical. "Don't you just sit there and meditate or something?"

"Well, kind of, but at the same time not really. What Tikina is teaching me at this point is to focus on a basic life form and to connect with it at an elemental level."

Mariah was somewhat confused. "Oh . . . have you achieved that?"

Tegan's face lit up. "I did! And it was unbelievable. I managed to link with a grand old pine tree at the training site. I could actually feel all the minute motions inside of it, like the particles of water moving upward from the roots of the tree all the way through the trunk, into the branches and to its leaves. It felt strange, and yet it was so refreshing at the same time. I'm not going to lie, though—it was a little spooky. It's just not a sensation that we are used to as human beings."

"So technically then, you were a tree?"

"Not exactly. It was a projection of my mind into the existence of the tree."

Aari scratched his head. "Don't take this the wrong way, but I don't see how it benefits you. Seems like you're taking a couple of steps down the evolutionary ladder."

Tegan disagreed. "If you wanna get to the top, you gotta start from the bottom, right? Tikina said that right now, I'm only able to handle this level of training but if I keep exercising my mind, I can do this with more complex life forms, like birds and other animals." Her eyes shone with excitement.

Jag thought for a moment. "Say you get really good at this ability. Would you be able to one day move past animals and take this to a human-to-human level?"

Tegan sat quietly, brooding over the concept. "I don't know," she finally said.

"That would make you probably the most dangerous person alive," he grinned.

She smiled slightly, but for some reason the thought perturbed her so she pushed it aside. "Oh, hey, I forgot to tell you guys. Tikina told me a little secret." Her friends looked back to her. "Remember the lynx you and I came across when we first were here, 'Riah? Tyse?"

Mariah nodded. "Yeah."

"Well, that was actually Tikina linking with her."

Mariah didn't quite register the fact. "You mean . . . the reason it stopped and blocked our path . . . was because your mentor was the one controlling that lynx's actions?

"Bingo. Now, do you guys remember that eagle that helped us out when we were fighting the rabid wolves?"

"No way," Aari said.

"Uh huh. That was Tikina giving us a hand because she knew the others wouldn't get there to help us in time."

Jag was impressed. "That was her the whole time? I thought the animals of this forest were all just crazy."

Huyani, overhearing, looked pleased that the friends were discussing her grandmother in a good light. She turned around only to bump into Kody. "You," she said, scolding him gently. "Off with you. I must finish preparing your drinks."

Kody sulked and went to sit beside Mariah, who nudged him. "How has your day been so far?"

Kody stretched. "I'll tell you something about my mentor: There's a reason why folks here hold Elder Nageau in special esteem. He's got so much wisdom to share and he's such a practical thinker."

"Hopefully that'll rub off on you," Aari chirped.

"*Anyway*," Kody continued delightedly, "you guys know that he's got hyper-sensory abilities, right? He told me that I'd be in full possession of those abilities soon enough if I can stay focused during training."

Jag grinned. "If that's the case, it'll take you a few years."

Kody looked narked. Tegan, seeing the look on her friend's face, clobbered Jag and Aari with the couch pillow she was hugging. "Knock it off, you two. Can't you see he just wants to share without your unnecessary interruptions?"

The two mumbled apologetically. Mariah looked at Kody to continue, and he said, "Over the past couple of days—and Aari, I think you'd appreciate this—we've been working on understanding the nature of sound waves. Nageau said that before I learn it, I'll have to master stillness inside and out. I didn't know I could actually be that comfortable in silence. I mean, you guys know what I'm like. But once I got it, even though it was sort of in and out, I was able to hear every single sound of the forest around me. It was an unbelievable experience. I even heard the sound of a bird flapping its wings, but the insane thing is that the bird was *nowhere* near the vicinity."

"Where was it, then?" Tegan asked.

"Nageau heard it too, and he said it was about three hundred paces from where we were training."

"What? How could he tell?"

"He's been honing that ability for years, remember? He's able to estimate the position of a sound."

"So when you complete your training, you'll be able to do that too?" Mariah asked with wide eyes.

"Yep." Kody looked pleased. "But not just with hearing. I'll be able to do it with all the other senses, too."

The five leaned back, momentarily fantasizing about what their futures could be like with their new-found abilities. Aari rubbed the back of his head. "Were you guys told that we'd be starting the intermediate stage of the training tomorrow?"

His friends signaled yes. "Apparently the training will be intensified," Jag informed them.

Tegan looked thoughtful. "At least that means we're getting somewhere, so I guess that's a good sign."

"Nageau said that, from what the other Elders have reported, we'll be jumping from stage one to stage two in this short time because we're grasping what's being taught pretty quickly," Aari said.

Kody jerked his chin at Aari. "What about you, bud? How's your training with Ashack?"

"Eh . . . exhausting, both for the mind and the body."

"Yeah?"

"Mmhm. To begin with, we've all got our daily workout routine as part of our training, and you know that's physically exhausting. Don't get me wrong—the fact that we're getting all this strength training and also being taught the Dema-Ki defense techniques is great. Then comes the mind part, and I don't particularly enjoy it. I know there's a lot of science in this, and I love to explore reality scientifically, but this stuff is . . ." He searched for a word.

Jag tried to help. "Too far-fetched for you?"

"Yes and no. I'm a bit skeptical, y'know? But my mentor proves me wrong every step of the way. And then I learn something new, but not before it messes with my mind."

"You're working on bending light or something like that, right?" Mariah asked.

Aari nodded. "Right. It's supposed to help camouflage and make me, or any object I want, seem invisible."

"How can you do that?"

"You guys know that our vision is based on the reflection of light. We see everyday things because of light that's reflected from the objects that we're looking at. If I were to control the light particles and deflect them away into a different path, I would have made that object invisible to you. In theory, of course." He looked at his friends, searching their faces to see if they were following him. "Take this example. Imagine we're in a pitch dark cave and Tegan shines a flashlight on Kody. You guys will all be able to see Kody, but if I were to deflect the light that's bouncing off Kody and heading to your eyes, I've practically rendered him invisible to you."

The others were starting to understand. "That's amazing," Tegan remarked. "Could we get a demo?"

Aari shook his head. "Not yet. I'm just being prepped for it right now—that alone has already tired my mind and I have to get back to it after lunch. Once I get stronger though, I'll blow your minds away." He grinned.

"Speaking of lunch," Huyani called from the kitchen, "your rytrèni is ready."

The five pulled themselves off the couches and went to grab their individual mugs that rested on the countertops, then sat on the stools. As the group started on their drinks, Kody said, "I know that this is actually nourishing and is supposed to help us build up physically, but it makes me sad that this is all we get three times a day in place of actual meals."

Tegan flicked her fingers on his head. "No, dork. We still get dinner. You keep forgetting that every day."

"Oh. Two times a day, then."

Huyani pulled up a stool and sat beside the five with a smile. "I never got a chance to ask you how you felt at the village gathering last evening."

Mariah tapped her knuckles on the side of her mug. "Awkward. For me, anyway."

"It wouldn't have been too bad if it were people we knew, but we were in front of hundreds of people whom we've never met before," Tegan said as she took a sip from her drink. "Not only that, but we were being held in such high regard for something we're not entirely sure of."

Huyani looked down at the table for a moment, appearing to be deep in thought. "I can only try to imagine being in your shoes," she said slowly. "I cannot, however, pretend to fathom the importance of the role that destiny has chosen for you. The fulfillment of our prophecy is a tremendously significant event in the history of our people." Noticing the unsettled looks the five wore, she continued. "While most residents of Dema-Ki will give you their complete acceptance, there will be a few who will need time to come around to this big decision. Regardless of that, I want to assure you that you will not be alone on this journey."

The friends sat quietly for a while, reflecting on what they'd just heard. Tegan, without meaning to, glared into her drink. When Huyani noticed, she tilted her head questioningly for a few moments before slowly getting up. "Tegan," she said softly.

Tegan snapped out of her death stare competition with her mug and looked at the raven-haired girl. "Uh?"

Huyani went around and gently took Tegan by the arm. "You look as if you need some fresh air."

Though bewildered, Tegan didn't protest and allowed herself to be led out of the neyra. Outside, Huyani carefully shut the door and turned to the younger girl. "Is everything alright, Tegan?"

Tegan looked around them, nose crinkling. "Yeah."

"Are you sure?" Huyani's tone, though quiet, had an edge of firmness.

"Okay, fine," Tegan sighed. "I'm still skeptical about the training. I'd like to talk it out fully with the others, but they all seem to be kind of into it. Not that I'm not interested."

"But?"

"But… I don't know where this is going. You know, the prophecy and all."

Huyani pushed some of Tegan's hair from her face, her sisterly touch somehow comforting to Tegan. "It is natural to be concerned for one's wellbeing—"

"No, no. Not me. I don't really care for myself. It's the others. We don't have a full picture of this whole prophecy thing, but I can tell it's a big deal to shoulder and I worry about where this could lead and what the future might bring for my goofballs in there. I want them safe, that's all. So I don't understand why we're just dropping our lives and leaping into the unknown."

The older girl studied Tegan with gentle eyes. "We can never know what the future holds, yet it is up to us whether we want to rise and meet it or run back to our past. I know not how the events in the prophecy will unfold, but I do know this: The five of you were chosen for a reason. The only way you will discover your destiny is by walking the path." In an even gentler tone, she said, "A ship is safe in a harbor, but that is not what it was built for. Its destiny is to sail the oceans."

Tegan sighed inwardly but offered no further words and neither did Huyani, who rubbed Tegan's back for a while before the pair silently returned to the others inside. The four looked up at Tegan as she sat beside them, but all she did was pick up her drink and then started to down it.

Huyani gave the friends a moment before broaching a light subject. "So how does it feel to not be a village secret anymore?"

"It feels a lot freer, that's for sure," Jag answered. "At least now we don't have to move around in the shadows, and we're more aware of what's going on in the village."

Huyani nodded and let the five take a few more sips of their drinks before saying, "Another villager has passed away today from the illness."

The friends looked up, dismayed. "That's so awful . . . I'm so sorry," Mariah said. "You still haven't found a cure?"

"No, but our village scientist is working hard to find one."

"Have your dad and the other men who were sent out come back yet?"

"Not yet. The courier falcon has not returned either, and my grandfather is somewhat concerned." Huyani sighed and lowered her gaze to stare at her fingers resting on the tabletop. "I hope he is alright."

Mariah, beside her, gently squeezed the other girl's arm and the group stayed silent for a few more moments as they continued to drink. Aari set his mug down. "Tell us a little about this Ayen'et mountain that people are speaking about. I sense a little bit of nervousness when I hear people make mention of that name."

"It is folklore normally used to keep children in line," Huyani answered. "It is especially effective for encouraging them to not stay up past their bedtime."

"I'll say," a new voice agreed.

The group turned around in their chairs and saw Akol walking through the door. "I remember when my father told me that story when I was younger and refused to get to bed." A bug was circling around his head and he swatted it away. "I just came to tell you that the Elders will be expecting you at the gates soon."

The friends gulped the rest of their drinks before rising up and following Akol to the door to get their shoes on. "Thanks for lunch," Aari called as the group stepped out of the shelter.

Huyani was gathering their mugs and looked up to wave. "Good luck with your training, all of you!"

* * *

It was late in the evening as Nageau walked up to the temple to meditate before heading to his *neyra* to have dinner with his mate. He slowly strode through the temple, admiring as he always did the elegance and magnificence of it. He made his way to the far end of the temple and sat on one of the mats placed on the floor. He slowly closed his eyes, breathing deeply, and was soon oblivious to the material world.

He did not know how long he had been away when he was jolted back by a high-pitched shriek. His eyes flew open and he saw the courier falcon swooping around inside the temple before it came to rest on a pedestal near a wall. Nageau rose to his feet, relieved that the falcon had returned. He smiled as he approached the bird. "You are late," he said amiably. The falcon made a clicking sound with its beak and looked around, inspecting its surroundings. Nageau's eyes moved down to the bird's legs expectantly. His face fell. The message beads were not attached to its talons as they should have been each time the falcon returned to the Elders.

Nageau instantly knew there was something wrong. He quickly walked out of the temple and rushed to the Elders' living cluster. He knocked on each of their doors and called them outside.

Once they were all gathered, he told them what he'd just found. "We must get a search party organized and get them to leave right now," he said, pacing.

Saiyu glanced up at the sky. "It will be too dark by the time they are ready to leave, Nageau. We shall organize this now, but let them leave at first light."

Nageau reluctantly agreed. Turning to his mate, he said, "Tikina, we will need your eyes on this trip. Can you establish a mind-link with Akira?" When Tikina said she would, Nageau sighed. "I suppose all that is left to do now is pray that our four men are safe."

38

Tikina stood with the Elders at the temple with eight villagers who made up the search party. Nageau was having a quiet chat with the group, assessing their preparedness and silently checking to see if they all had their crystals. As Tikina watched, she was reminded of when the four men they had sent out days ago—one of them being her daughter's mate—stood at the temple and were being readied by the Elders the morning they left, a morning much like this one with gray clouds at first light.

She listened as Nageau briefed the six men and two women on their task. Once he had finished his part, Tikina stepped forward and looked at a young woman with natural platinum blonde hair held back by a red bandana. "I will be guiding this expedition as much as I can through Akira," she told the woman, raising a finger in the direction of the eagle that circled high above their heads.

The woman dipped her head. "That will be a great comfort, Elder Tikina. Thank you."

"Everything is set," Tikina heard Nageau murmur, almost to himself, and saw him look up at the sky. Raising his voice, he turned to the search party and said, "Dawn is upon us and it appears that the clouds are lifting. There is nothing else left to say except to bid you all an incident-free journey and a safe return with our four men."

* * *

Six logs, stripped of bark from years of use, had been placed lengthwise in a row about ten paces from each other. The first log was flat on the ground. Each of the rest was four feet higher than the one before, the highest one being twenty feet above the ground. These were the logs that many of the villagers used when training themselves in the basics of balance, though few ventured past the fourth log at twelve feet in height. For the past two days, Jag had been training on the second one, which rested on two crossbars four feet off the ground. It was the log that seemed to want to pick a fight with Jag since he'd gotten on it.

He had been doing acrobatic moves that required strength, focus, and agility since his training began. Over the past two days he'd been trying to complete a front aerial somersault on the log but hadn't been successful. Although, unlike the day before when he half wished the log would fall on him and put him out of his misery, he was determined not to lose his focus today. He was taking to heart the advice and instructions that Tayoka had been giving him throughout his training. Listening to his mentor was beginning to prove valuable as Jag felt that his focus was keener and his balance was nearing perfection. The beaming face of Tayoka and the proud smile Huyani wore testified to his improvements.

Nearing the end of his training for the day, Jag proceeded to carry out two continuous front aerials on the log, twisting around as he landed, and completed the sequence with a backflip to dismount. Tayoka and Huyani clapped, looking thrilled as they walked up to him. Tayoka patted his apprentice on the back and through Huyani, said, "I have never seen anyone learn this quickly. I am amazed."

Jag couldn't have looked more pleased by the compliment and thanked the Elder.

"That was a good session today," Huyani said, looking approvingly at Jag.

"Thanks. I guess I just wasn't really feeling it yesterday."

"To be fair, you had Elder Tayoka working to distract you."

"Sure, but I understand why he was doing it."

Tayoka tapped the pair's heads from behind and spoke. Jag looked at Huyani for a translation. "He is saying that it is time to head to the temple. Elder Nageau would like to speak with all of you about the intermediate stage of your training before you are dismissed for your midday meal."

Jag nodded. He wiped the sweat off his face with the sleeve of his t-shirt and followed his mentor and Huyani out of the training grounds to the temple. There he met his friends, who had arrived just before him. As they greeted each other, all the Elders except Nageau left. The five followed Nageau up the steps that led to the foyer of the temple, passing by the marble cauldron from which plumes of bright-colored flames streamed. The five were dazzled by the flames, just as they had been when they first saw the hypnotic glow the night they escaped from the valley.

At one corner of the grand hall were three curved benches forming a semi-circle. Behind the benches were large rocks and ornamental plants placed around two small fountains gurgling with cool, flowing water, giving the area a serene and tranquil feel. As the five sat down on the benches, Tegan observed, "This place is peaceful and calming. It's so Zen-like."

"That is an interesting expression. That would be from an ancient eastern culture, yes?" Nageau winked slyly. The five were surprised by his familiarity of the outside world. The more the five learned of the Elders' knowledge, the more astonished they were.

Standing in front of the five, Nageau continued. "First, let me begin by saying that I am pleased by what I hear from your mentors about your progress. The speed at which you are learning and beginning to display your skills astounds me. In all my years of training others, I have never witnessed anything like this. I realize that I have said this before, but you each have incredible potential. I have no doubt that the hand of fate has brought you here."

Jag listened, but his thoughts wandered off a little. *Fate? Not so sure I believe that . . .*

It took him a few moments to register that Nageau was peering at him intently, and then the Elder turned back to face the others. Almost as if he had read Jag's thoughts, he said, "And here is the funny thing about fate: I know that when some of you hear that word, it appears to mean that choice has been taken away from you, as if whatever you are or will be doing is predetermined. The truth is, there is no real conflict between fate and choice; they work hand-in-hand."

Jag's brows knitted. "How?"

"I will give you an example. Imagine a sailing boat out in the ocean with its sails unfurled, and you are guiding this craft. What do you have a choice over as far as the boat is concerned?"

The five had their answers. "The sails and the rudder."

"Good. Now, what is it that you do not have a choice over?"

"The current," Kody supplied.

"And the wind and its direction," added Tegan.

"Ah-ha: So here, the wind is like fate—it is what life throws at you, and you have no control over it. It will blow in whichever direction it wants to, but you have the *choice* to make what you can out of it by setting the sail in the direction you want your boat to take you. *That* is your destiny."

Jag sat quietly, assessing what he'd just heard. Throughout the years as he grew, he had established that there was no such thing as fate. At first he thought that Nageau was hinting his belief to be incorrect, but after some pondering, he realized that his belief wasn't incorrect, it was simply incomplete. *The wind will blow whichever direction it wants to, but I have a choice over the control of the sail. I* make *my destiny.*

Tegan's voice reached his ears. "Earth to Jag?"

He snapped back and realized that his friends were looking at him. "Oh, hi." He grinned. "Just thinking."

Nageau waved it off with a slight smile. "I am glad we had a chat about that, because it helps to set the stage for what I would like to speak with you about next.

"You are each gifted with certain talents and are here for a reason. In the coming days and weeks, your powers will strengthen and you will find yourself growing along with it. I am sure you are curious as to how your individual abilities work." The five nodded.

"The secret of the power comes from understanding that the human mind is a bridge between the physical world and the world of pure energy. The human mind is capable of channeling tremendous power from that plane to this, the physical world." He paused to let the five to digest this. "Allow me to explain this in another way. You are all familiar with the magnifying lens, yes? And I am sure at some point you must have experimented with using such a lens to focus the sun's rays onto an object. Now, imagine that the lens represents the human mind and the rays of the sun represent the world of energy, and an object upon which the rays are cast—say, a leaf—signifies the physical world. In like manner, your mind works as a lens that channels the power from the world of pure energy to this world. But it is important to remember this: For the lens to be effective, it needs to be clear of dust and impurities. Likewise, for you to reach the apex of your abilities, your mind needs to be spotless as well." Nageau saw comprehension dawning in the five's eyes.

"I think I'm beginning to see the light now—no pun intended, of course." Kody eyed Jag and Aari defensively as the two shot him unamused looks.

Tegan, her chin resting in her hand, nodded slowly. "That's starting to make sense to me, too. I've been struggling to find out how and why I'm capable of what I am doing."

"I'm just wondering, though," Mariah said. "Keeping a lens clean is easy enough. But how would I wipe 'dust' off my mind?"

"Excellent question. As you would have noticed, a fair amount of your training is spent on achieving mental clarity. It may have taken different forms, whether through meditation or a range of physical activities, or simply by just remaining still. All combined, it helps to burnish the lens that is your mind. However, that is just one half of the equation. The other half requires vigilance in your day to day thoughts and actions."

The five looked at one another as they tried to piece together what they'd heard. Aari, who seemed lost in thought, was the first to figure it out. "Personal responsibility," he summarized.

Nageau was pleasantly surprised. "Exactly right. Aligning oneself with the universal precepts found in all of humanity's cherished scriptures and traditions is the key. The more your thoughts and actions reflect these principles, the stronger your spirit becomes. The stronger your spirit becomes, the keener your mind. And the keener your mind, the greater your powers will be."

"What are the universal precepts?" Tegan asked.

"It is quite simple, actually. It is something that has guided the thoughts and actions of human beings throughout time. Principles, such as the Golden Rule of doing unto others as you would have them do unto you, or Nature's Law as revered and applied by the founding fathers of your nation. These and other similar belief systems have been society's protection against excesses. Sadly, these have lately been trampled on by the foot of apathy across the world."

Jag let out a breath. "That's a bit to take in."

"It seems that way," Nageau agreed, "but it is not a concept that will take you long to fully understand. Now, to recapture this discussion, the first thing you need to understand is that the secret to your powers lies in the keenness of your mind. To attain that keenness, you must remember that the training you are undergoing is one part of the equation. The other key part is vigilance in your thoughts and actions. With this understanding, you are now ready to progress to the second stage of your training. Before long, you will step into the third and final stage. It will be a marvelous experience."

The five, realizing the meeting was drawing to a close, looked at each other again with anticipation. As they prepared to get up, Nageau held up a hand to halt them. "You know"—he gave the friends a shrewd smile—"one of the things you will be able to do as you sharpen your minds is to communicate with each other without speaking out loud."

The five gaped at him, wondering if the Elder was toying with them. "Are you . . . are you serious?" Aari stuttered. "We'll be able to speak to each other with our thoughts?"

"In time. We shall see. The Elders and I are certainly able to when we so wish." Nageau rocked back on his heels and stretched.

He looked each of the five in the eyes, observing the different shades, and then raised his head heavenwards with a smile, awed by the workings of the universe. Just before letting them go, he said, "We will have another gathering such as this one at the end of the second stage of your training just before you commence the final phase."

The five dipped their heads at the Elder and headed to the exit of the temple. Nageau stood there as they walked away, feeling a sense of warmth and pride for them as if they were his own family. The five stopped and turned around to wave at him with smiles on their faces before strolling out.

As he watched them go, a lump grew in the Elder's throat. His knowledge of the relentless foe they would be facing in the world outside as mentioned in the prophecy was of grave concern. The memories of the decision he made over two decades ago came crashing down again. He was burdened by thoughts of what may be at the heart of the storm outside, and if the decision he made at that time had exacerbated it. The fact that he would have to inform these younglings very soon of what they were being prepared for weighed heavily on him. *There is so much to do, and so little time,* he thought as he watched the five grow smaller in the distance.

39

The mining site at six thousand feet above sea level and a good four hundred feet below the mountain's peak was teeming with activity. The crew had managed to repair most of the equipment and machinery with the delivery of spare parts two days earlier, and it looked like the weather would be clearing up for them.

In his office, Ajajdif conversed over the phone with Black and his team back in San Francisco. LeChamps was sitting on the opposite side of the table, half-listening to Ajajdif's end of the conversation as he bit the earpiece of his glasses and looked through a page of a report he was yet to upload onto his iPad. The sides of his head were lightly grayed, something he tried to hide using hair dye to conceal the fact that he had just turned forty-two.

The chief geologist for Quest Mining stepped into the office a few minutes later. Abdul, clad in a tight t-shirt that accentuated her frame and her bright red hair tied back in a long ponytail, took a seat beside LeChamps. The smell of cigarettes was strong on her person. LeChamps grimaced. Attractive as she was, he did not find the smell appealing.

Ajajdif looked up. "Nice. We're all here." He put the call on speakerphone and leaned back in his chair, eyes half-closed. "As I was saying, we've got good news and bad news over here."

Black sighed over the speaker. "How could there be bad news? We've shipped out everything you needed."

"Yes, and that's the good news. The crew is feeling very productive with the equipment now up and running properly. Within the last twelve hours, we've had a dramatic increase in our yield."

"Already? That sounds good. Do you think we can make up for lost time and put this project back on schedule at this rate?"

Ajajdif motioned to LeChamps. The mining engineer cleared his throat and introduced himself before saying, "We switched the angle of the tunneling machine last night and we struck it big. We found a new vein that's rich with deposits."

In the background on Black's end, Ajajdif, Abdul and LeChamps heard a cascade of praises. "That's great," Black said, sounding satisfied.

"It just took a little more digging around," Abdul piped.

"To answer your question, Adrian," Ajajdif said, "yes, we should be able to get back on schedule and be out of here in four weeks."

Dattalo's voice came on the speakerphone. "That's the best news we've had in a while, Vlad. Once you guys get the required amount, we're going to be the only organization in the world to have this quantity, or this mineral, for that matter."

Black cut back in. "So that's the good news. What's the bad news?"

Ajajdif rested his elbows on his table and pressed his fingertips together. "The secrecy of our operation has been breached."

There was silence on the other end until Black said acidly, "Breaches are unacceptable, Vlad. That's what your security team is for."

"Yes, I know. But these were just natives, not tourists or government authorities."

"Natives? That place is inhabited?"

"Apparently." Ajajdif took a drink from the mug of coffee that was resting on the table. "How do we deal with the intruders?"

"Quite frankly, I don't care what you do, and I don't want to know. But whatever you do, just remember that we need to maintain our cover. This operation must never go public, ever."

"Understood. I'll handle it. There is another small matter, though."

"What is it?" It was plain to hear the impatience in Black's tone.

"One of my tunneling machine operators was killed in an accident a couple days ago. His assistant was hurt too, and he's recovering in the medic camp."

Gasps were heard on the other end of the call. Black was stressed. "Died? He *died?* And you only tell me this now?"

"I have a hundred other problems to deal with, Adrian. I can't keep ringing you up for everything."

"Now we're going to have to compensate the family!"

"Just tell them it was a workplace accident."

A hard bang came over the speaker and Ajajdif presumed that Black had pounded his fist on the table. "Splendid. Wonderful. That's just great. You know I'm going to have to report this to the boss, right?"

"Yes."

"Just to forewarn you, you might be getting a call."

"So be it." Ajajdif sounded calm and collected, but fear had already begun to build up inside him and he felt its gnawing deep within his gut.

"Is there anything else to report?" Black asked.

"No. Well, actually . . . two men from my security team were injured while capturing the natives."

"You mean to say that two men, trained in combat, were injured by some primitive savages living in a forest?"

"I don't know, Adrian. You look at them and you know right off the bat that they're not exactly unintelligent. They even look different. Heck, one of them is blonde and another has green eyes. Plus, when I went through the items they were carrying, I found a few interesting things—"

"Whatever. Look, point is, they can't be allowed to ever go back, so you're going to have to deal with them."

"No problem. Oh, and thank you again for flying the parts and chemicals in. It fired up my guys into full action."

"Glad to hear it. Are we done?"

"Yes."

"Alright. We'll get in touch later." Black clicked off.

Ajajdif put down the satellite phone and pointed a finger at the door of his office. LeChamps and Abdul hesitatingly got up and left. When Ajajdif was certain he was alone, he picked up his radio and called for the head of his security team to come to his office.

"On my way, sir," Hajjar responded, his voice like thunder over the radio.

Ajajdif picked up his mug and downed the rest of his coffee, waiting for Hajjar to arrive. He didn't realize that his mind had roamed elsewhere until there was a knock on his door and Hajjar stepped in. The tattooed giant stood in front of his supervisor's desk. "Good afternoon, sir."

"And to you." Ajajdif put his mug down. "I have something for you to do. I just got off a call with the head office and I told them about the trespassers."

Hajjar listened intently as Ajajdif carried on. "They said that it doesn't matter what we do with them, just that news of the operation cannot get out."

Hajjar's lips slowly spread into a humorless smile. "They really don't care?"

"No. And they don't wish to know either." Ajajdif saw the eyes of the head of security already glazing over as he contemplated many tempting ideas as to how to get rid of the intruders. "Just bear in mind that we do not want to leave any trace."

Hajjar sneered. This, he could do. He thought for a moment, and then a quiet growl rippled in his throat. "The Marauders are hungry."

* * *

Hajjar walked out of Ajajdif's office and jogged to the security post near the tunnel. He found one of the guards who was off shift with his ear buds plugged in and nodding his head to an unheard beat. "Dave!" he boomed. The guard thrashed in surprise, nearly dropping his mp3 player. He saw Hajjar and quickly snapped to attention while removing his ear buds and putting his device aside.

Hajjar grabbed a paper cup and went to fill it from the water dispenser. "I want you to go to the holding cell and help the guard who's posted there move the intruders to the cave where we found them. I want them secured there properly."

"They don't like us getting near them, and they put up a good fight. We can't move them while they're conscious. Do we have permission to sedate them?"

"Yes." Hajjar looked out of the post's window, downing the water in his cup in one gulp.

The guard quickly moved around the room, collecting a syringe and vials of the tranquilizer. As he grabbed his gun and turned to head out of the post, the guard shot an inquiring look at Hajjar. "What are you planning to do with the intruders?"

"That's none of your business. Just move them to the cave and leave them there. I'll take care of them later."

The guard walked out of the post and into the tunnel, pausing for a moment to watch the miners at work, then turned right toward the holding cell and knocked on the door. The guard currently assigned to watch the four intruders opened it and the two talked quickly.

"Dave, I hate going down that tunnel. Can't you find someone else to do this?" the guard complained.

"Hajjar told me to take the guy who's on shift." He poked the other guard's chest. "That's you."

"Haven't you heard the talk? That tunnel can come down any time."

"Well, yeah, but this is what we get paid to do. Just hurry and get this done."

They approached the first of the bound intruders but the man squirmed, not allowing the guards to slip the needle into his arm. Frustrated, one of the guards slapped him across the cheek, leaving a bright red mark. "We're not in the mood for games! Dave, hold him still." The other guard obliged and finally they managed to inject the sedative into the captive's arm. They repeated the tactic with the other three trespassers, who also struggled against them. The guards stepped back and waited for the drug to take effect. They saw one of the intruders already beginning to nod off.

"So did you hear what Ajajdif told the miners to do?" the guard on shift asked.

"No. What?"

"They're using the leaching chemicals in the tunnel instead of just in the vats."

"So? Who cares?"

"You do know what that stuff is made of, right?"

"No."

"It's a cyanide blend, you moron! It's a dangerous poison and it's soaking into the ground— if it gets into the groundwater it could affect any and every living organism it comes in contact with."

"You tree-huggers are all alike, nothing but alarmists."

The guard on shift shook his head and sighed. Caught up in their exchange, the two did not notice a pair of eyes looking intently at them, glaring. The intruder who was listening in stayed conscious for only a moment or two longer before the drugs kicked in and he passed out.

The guards watched, indifferent, as the intruders lost consciousness one by one. Removing the chains and cables that bound the trespassers, they dragged the men's limp bodies to the cable conveyor that ran down to the cave where they'd been captured.

The guards threw the bodies in a heap into the first ore bucket they came to. "Why did they even dig this tunnel in the first place?" the guard who had been on watch duty asked.

"From what I hear, it was initially an exploratory shaft but there was hardly any mineral here, so they abandoned it and drilled that other tunnel they're working in right now. I guess they left this one to be used as an escape route for emergencies or something." He turned on the winch and watched the bucket with the intruders disappear through the underpass and out of sight. "Come on. Let's just tie them up and get out of there. Hajjar will deal with them."

The first guard sighed again and both men reluctantly stepped into the second ore bucket, which followed the first one down into the dark tunnel.

40

Rikèq came around slowly, attempting to clear the cobwebs from his mind. He tried in vain to remember what had happened. Though he strained to look around through blurred vision, he couldn't make anything out at all. Resting his head back, he closed his eyes and took a couple of breaths, then sighed.

It took a while for the grogginess to leave him and when it did, he felt released, save for a dull pain in his lower back that grew increasingly bothersome. He eased his eyes open and took a proper look around. He was surprised and puzzled to see that he was back in the cave where the men with weapons had found and subdued them. *Was I not here before? Why did they bring me back?* He took another look around the cavern. He could see the mouth of the cave and realized that the sun had just recently set.

Suddenly remembering his companions, he attempted to get up from his seated position but found himself struggling against a metal chain wrapped around his chest, pressing him back against an iron post. That post was connected to other similar posts by a rusty cable overhead on which hung large metal buckets. The line of pillars retreated into the distance until they were hidden by a bend in the tunnel.

Rikèq tried to move his hands but found that they were tied together behind him, and it then occurred to him that this was causing the pain in his lower back. *How long have I been out?* he wondered.

A moan sounded frighteningly close, startling him. He twisted his head to the side and saw Breyas bound to another face of the four-sided post. "Breyas," Rikèq breathed in thanks. "Breyas?"

The other man lifted his head, squinting. "Who is speaking?" he garbled.

"Rikèq."

"Who?"

"A friend." As Rikèq waited patiently for Breyas to regain his senses, he twisted his head to the other side and saw Aydar likewise pinned to the third face of the pillar. He was beginning to come around as well. Rikèq supposed that Keno was on the fourth side of the pillar, behind him. He called out his companions' names over and over to shake them out of their stupor.

Finally Breyas responded, his speech less indistinct. "I loathe it when those men pollute our bodies with their poison," he sighed. He looked down at the chain that was wrapped around him, the same chain that bound all four men against the post.

"Hold on . . ." Breyas sounded tentatively victorious. "My legs are not bound!"

"Mine, neither," Rikèq said. "But that does not matter much, because this chain has been wrapped multiple times around us." He struggled unsuccessfully against the bindings once more just to see if he could wiggle free.

"Breyas, Rikèq? Is that you?"

"Aydar!" the two men exclaimed. "Yes, it is us."

"Is this the cave where we were captured?"

"Yes." Rikèq tried to see around the post but couldn't. "Is Keno awake yet?"

"I am," the last of the group wheezed. "Are we alone?"

"It seems so. How is everyone feeling?"

"Just give us a few more minutes and we should be fine," Aydar said. The men rested quietly for a while, willing their bodies back to a higher level of energy; it was a form of meditative recovery that the people of Dema-Ki had been taught since they were very young, and it often proved useful.

Rikèq gazed at the chain that pressed into his chest. "We need to get out of here. I think these people have planned something and I want no part in it."

"We need to get out of these chains first, Rikèq," Breyas grunted.

Rikèq sat still, trying to think of a way to release the quartet from their bindings. "Keno."

"Yes?"

"I think I may have an idea. I will start to tug the chain my way, and when I rest, you must tug it your way. It will be painful, but unless someone else has a better idea, I cannot think of any other way."

The others said nothing. Rikèq took it as an agreement that they were going through with his plan. "Here we go," he muttered, then strained forward against the chain. He could hear violent curses as the chain forced Keno back against the post and dug deep into his chest and arms.

Rikèq continued to strain against the chain until Keno gasped, "I cannot breathe!"

Rikèq slowly leaned back. "I apologize for that, my friend—there is no other way."

Keno took a few gulps of air and tried to focus on anything but the pain. The other three waited tolerantly. Without warning, Rikèq was forced back against the post by the chain. He wheezed as the metal dug into him; it felt as if his ribs were about to break under the pressure. He held on for half a minute, eyes stinging with restrained tears from the torment, before he yelped, "Enough!"

Keno rested back against his side of the post. "Is everything okay?"

"Y-yes." Rikèq quickly caught his breath. "My turn."

They alternated back and forth for ten minutes until they both stopped, fatigued, the agony in their arms and chest nearly unbearable. As they tried to regain their strength, Breyas wriggled against the chain. "It is loosening!" he exclaimed. "I can *almost* push myself up."

Hope sparked energy into the group and Rikèq tugged against the chain again, straining until the veins in his neck bulged. Keno bit the inside of his lip until he tasted blood and used that minuscule sense of pain to focus his thoughts.

A loud creaking sounded overhead as Rikèq tugged. He tilted his head as far back as he could to look up. The post, stretching from the ground to the roof of the tunnel where log beams had been installed for support, was being shaken whenever the chain was tugged. Rikèq leaned back against the post, beginning to worry. "Keno, this next time you tug, be prepared to just force yourself out of the chain and quickly get out of the way."

"Why?"

"The post might come loose and fall over on you if you are tugging. It is already starting to—"

A deep, threatening growl echoed from up the tunnel. It sounded like no animal Rikèq had ever heard before.

"What was that?" Aydar whispered. "A wolf?"

"Wolf? I thought it was a bear." Breyas struggled against his chains urgently. "Whatever it is, it does not sound like something I would want near me."

The aggressive growls came again. At the bend in the tunnel they saw a large, human shadow accompanied by what appeared to be the shadows of massive wolves cast against the rock wall.

"Pull, Keno!" Aydar bellowed. Rikèq winced as he was again squeezed against the post as Keno strained against the chain in frenzy.

"That is enough!" Rikèq shouted when he felt the post begin to tilt in Keno's direction. Keno stopped as some small rocks started to fall from the roof of the cave. He fearfully glanced up, then at the shadows that were drawing nearer.

Using the post to support his back, Rikèq squirmed upward. "Hah!" He wiggled his feet out of the chain and, as he took a step forward, found himself on unsteady legs. He struggled to release his hands from behind his back but couldn't get them free.

Rikèq heard guttural barks and looked up. His throat went dry. Three black creatures, eyes gleaming bright yellow, were sprinting toward them, jaws snapping. "Move!" Rikèq yelled. Aydar and Breyas had already managed to free themselves and the three started off at a shaky lope.

"Wait!" Breyas stopped and looked around. "Keno!"

Rikèq and Aydar stumbled to a halt and spun around. Keno was still struggling out of the chain and the creatures were drawing closer, closing the gap until only thirty feet remained between them and the trapped human. The animal leading the attack surged forward with a burst of speed. Keno saw it and wriggled frantically, not realizing the post was tipping further every time he moved.

Rikèq, Breyas and Aydar watched in horror as the column suddenly tipped too far over. A large log beam fell, along with part of the tunnel's roof, and crushed the leading beast as it made a wild lunge at Keno. The cable attached to the post snapped and other posts along the tunnel began to sway and topple.

Keno had at last managed to free himself from the chain and turned to run, but it was too late. The post he'd been tied to came crashing down onto him. He bellowed in pain and struggled to crawl away but was quickly buried by an avalanche of falling rocks.

"*No!*" the group cried.

It took a few moments for the debris to settle and for the dust to clear. Rikèq staggered to the wreckage, followed by Breyas and Aydar. They tried desperately to push the rubble away with their feet, cursing their bound hands. The collapse had created a crude barrier that protected the men from the beasts, which were hungry for a kill.

"Keno!" Rikèq called out. "Can you hear me?" He stood still, hoping to hear his friend's voice.

"Hold on. I hear something," Aydar murmured. The group remained mute as they strained to listen.

A portion of the rubble beside Rikèq collapsed toward him and the massive, terrifying head of one of the beasts crashed through it. It gnashed its teeth, exposing three-inch fangs. The creature let out a hair-raising roar when it spotted the men and drove itself out of the rocks, followed immediately by another. The men cried out in terror and moved away from the beasts at a stumbling run.

"Get out of the cave!" Rikèq shouted.

Aydar looked back at the creatures. The two animals were fast approaching—only a scant dozen yards were between them—and the gap closed further with the creatures' every bound.

The three men raced as fast as they could toward the cave entrance, still thirty paces away. Aydar turned for another quick glimpse of the beasts. The realization that they would not make it dawned on him and he slowed down and came to a stop.

The other two turned around and yelled at him to keep running. It was then that Rikèq saw a solemn, gritty expression on Aydar's face. "Aydar . . . ?"

Aydar looked at the men with glazed eyes and said in an impassive voice, "Tell my nephew I love him." Then he turned to confront the oncoming beasts.

There was a dismayed outcry from Breyas. "What are you doing?"

As the animals drew closer to Aydar, the man yelled to his friends, "Run!"

A scream was torn from his throat as one of the creatures bit into his leg and pulled him down. The sound became a gurgling noise as the second creature leapt and clamped its jaws around Aydar's neck. Rikèq and Breyas stood in shock, unable to believe what was happening.

With silent tears, they turned and ran, rallying all their balancing skills to keep upright with their hands tied. They reached the opening of the cave and came to a halt. Staring down, their eyes beheld a steep incline that fell away from the opening. The base of the mountain lay too far below them to see in the darkness, with large trees in the way. The men faltered, not sure what to do.

Hearing a vicious snarl behind them as one of the two beasts that had attacked Aydar hurtled toward them, they threw themselves out of the cave without further thought, tumbling down the side of the mountain.

Hajjar was directing the Marauders with the controller in his hands. He climbed over the rubble under which both an intruder and one of the Marauders lay crushed. He cringed when he saw one of the animal's large paws with its claws unsheathed protruding from the debris in what must have been its final attempt to escape. Hajjar was troubled by the realization that he would have to inform Ajajdif about the loss of the animal.

Hearing the noise of frenzied feeding, he found a hybrid mangling one of the intruders and looked past them just in time to see the last two intruders launching themselves out of the cave. The second of the two Marauders that remained alive made to give chase, but Hajjar quickly used the controller to command the hybrid to return to him. He knew that if he lost another animal, Ajajdif would have his head on a stick. It was easier to say that the intruders were all killed.

The Marauder came to a reluctant stop as the nano-transducers triggered an impulse in its brain. It gazed down at the tumbling men, whining in exasperation as it kneaded the ground with its claws, then turned and stalked back toward Hajjar. The ex-mercenary bent down to pat its head but the hybrid snapped its jaws at him and he quickly pulled his hand back. He glared at the animal and pressed the remote again, sending a painful pulse up its nervous system. The Marauder howled and rolled onto its back in submission. Hajjar smiled, relishing the sense of control he possessed over such a powerful creature.

He took a proper look around the place and an explosion of expletives spewed from his mouth as he assessed the mess. He had no interest in playing the role of cleanup crew and decided he would arm-twist the mining engineer to send some of his workers in. He settled down on one of the fallen rocks and lit a cigarette, taking a drag from it as he watched the Marauders finish up their job of removing any evidence of the trespassers.

41

It was late afternoon, and nobody noticed a crouched figure in the trees as it moved around the training ground, spying on the Elders and the five as they trained.

Hutar observed the happenings below him with resentment. He had been somewhat curious about the five's progress and wanted to see for himself how far they had gotten in their training. What he witnessed made his blood boil. In less than two weeks, they had already advanced to the intermediate stage.

He was dumbfounded as he watched the five train. They were getting ever more resilient and independent, but what upset him the most was how quickly they were grasping the concepts of their individual abilities. Jag was stronger and more agile, and even Tayoka's distracting actions did not divert his concentration. Tegan was now attempting to link minds with small creatures, and her obvious eagerness for it accelerated her process. Mariah was capable of moving the smallest of objects. She still had some ways to go but it dismayed Hutar to know that she could very well soon be a proficient telekinetic. Aari, enthusiastic about light manipulation, was accelerating his learning process just as Tegan was.

He watched Mariah now as she worked. Every time he heard Saiyu praise her pupil on her progress, all he saw was red. Every once in a while his eyes went to Akol and he gripped the branch he was on, white-hot enmity spreading through him like fire. This was the nuisance that had thwarted his near-perfect plan with the diseased wolves. His nails dug into the bark as he relived that moment. He had been there, concealed high up on the rock wall, watching the five fend for themselves. He'd almost tasted victory when the friends had given up upon seeing the second pack of wolves come into the enclosure.

Hutar looked down at the base of the tree he was hidden in now. So close. He had been so close. He glanced back at Akol, then with a snarl turned and jumped to another tree, heading to Kody's training area. Here he knew he would have to be careful. With Nageau having heightened senses and Kody learning aspects of that power, he had to be extra cautious. He paused, waiting for a bird to fly by. When it did, he jumped onto a tree with a good view of the pair. It was perfectly timed so that the rush of air from both him and the bird sounded as one.

Cautiously, he looked down. It seemed like nothing much was happening. All he saw was Kody sitting on the ground with his eyes closed, and Nageau was nowhere in sight. Hutar, though, knew from experience that Kody was listening to the sounds around him. This made it hard for Hutar to gauge how advanced Kody was. He looked up and down the branch on which he was balancing and saw a tiny twig attached to his perch. Keeping his eyes on Kody, he reached toward the twig. Holding his breath, he snapped it.

Kody's eyes flew open and he stared up in the direction the sound had come from. He sat still for a moment, alert, but saw nothing. He unhurriedly faced the front again and closed his eyes in meditation.

This didn't please Hutar one bit. Kody's hearing was picking up, and so, he assumed, were the outsider's other senses.

Having assessed the five's progress, Hutar was only more determined to go through with his plan. He waited until another bird flew by before moving with it out of the training ground, a resolute mood tempering his feelings of bitterness.

* * *

Tikina walked quietly into her *neyra* and went to the kitchen to get a cup of water. The five had been dismissed for their lunch break, and she needed to check on the search teams; it was the second day of their rescue mission. After downing her drink she went to sit on the divan in the living quarter. She breathed out slowly, and then closed her eyes.

When she opened them again, she was looking through the eyes of Akira. She felt the wind beneath her wings as she glided in the sky. The view was beautiful. The sky was blue, and she could see for miles over the treetops. She tilted her wings slightly and looked down, seeing one of the search teams. She spotted the young woman with the red bandana and slowly started a circling descent.

The woman looked up when she heard the rush of wind as the golden eagle flapped her wings once. She smiled, stretching out her arm, and the bird eased down onto the leather glove she wore. She looked the eagle in the eyes and a message was shared between her and Tikina. The woman nodded and the bird launched off her arm and into the air, soaring high, and was soon out of sight.

"Where did she go?" one of the men in the team asked.

"She went to scout ahead," the woman answered. Brushing a few strands of platinum hair that had escaped her bandana away from her bright green eyes, the woman led the group of men with a stride that showed her authority. She absently spun her staff in her right hand and prayed that they would find their missing friends.

* * *

Hutar sat on a rock facing one of the lakes that was supposedly contaminated. He wasn't entirely sure if it was in fact tainted and needed to find a way to confirm it. In the pack he brought with him, he had two jars. He looked around the cove, sitting quietly without expression. Hardly anything made him smile since the death of his father, except for his uncle. Though he never told his uncle, he loved him deeply. Aydar was the only family member Hutar had left and he did not know what he would do if he lost him.

He was shaken out of his thoughts when his heightened hearing picked up the scuttle of small paws against pebbles. He froze in his place and located the source of the sound: It was directly behind the rock he was sitting on. Very slowly, Hutar brought himself up into a squat and counted to three, then did a back handspring and landed behind the rock.

A hare, frightened out of its wits by the unexpected intruder, tried to scurry away but Hutar grabbed it by the ears and lifted it up. The hare let out a bloodcurdling scream and kicked out its back legs. Hutar glared at it and was tempted to smash it against the rock to silence it, but he needed the hare alive.

His pack lay open on the rock and he removed one of the jars. He held onto the struggling, screaming hare with one hand and uncapped the jar with the other. Pushing the cap off, he grabbed the jar and strode purposefully toward the lake. There, he knelt, trapping the hare between his knees. Without touching the water, he filled up the jar. He pried the hare's mouth open and forced the water down its throat. The hare thrashed but Hutar put the empty jar down and held onto the animal, the muscles in his arms bulging from the effort. He had to wait there for almost thirty minutes, but finally he saw the foam starting to encrust the hare's mouth as the contaminant took hold of its small immune system. Hutar jumped back and went to watch the hare from the safety of his rock. The hare twisted around as if drunk and staggered away from the lake.

Hutar spent another half hour watching intently as the hare succumbed to the terrible illness. He smiled, thrilled, as he watched the creature surrender to a painful death.

42

A tall silhouette gazed out through the palm trees from where it stood by a colossal window of an enormous villa. The villa was built along a sandy cove with a gorgeous view of a rich, blue lake. Tied to the villa's dock, a single-engine float plane bobbed on the water as the breeze picked up. The figure gazed further out, watching the locals ride their sampans over the small rolling waves as the fishermen sorted out nets filled with the day's catch.

Fingering the hem of a custom-tailored batik shirt, the figure glanced at a classic rotary phone sitting atop a mahogany desk and contemplated making a call, knowing full well the huge time difference on the other side of the globe. The figure looked back out the window for a few minutes and then, reaching a decision, picked up the phone and dialed a number.

Wild knocking on Ajajdif's door rattled him from his sleep. Jumping out of bed, he quickly pulled on a t-shirt, slid into his jeans and opened the door to find his frazzled-looking assistant holding up a phone. "Sir, it's the boss."

Instantly, Ajajdif went pale. He stared at his assistant for a moment, then grabbed the phone from her and closed the door. Forcing a wide, demented smile, he put the receiver to his ear. His fingers shook as if he were cold. "Hello?"

"Vladimir. How are you doing?" a raspy, digitally-distorted voice breathed into the phone.

"Well enough," he replied uneasily. "And you?"

"It all depends on the progress up there."

"Oh, uh . . ." he stammered. "It's coming along." He switched topics as fast as he could. It was late at night and he hadn't prepared himself for the call at this hour. He needed to buy time to think. "You're not usually one to call at two in the morning. I assume that means you're in a different time zone."

"Yes, I am."

"So which part of the planet are you at now?"

"I am catching some sun on one of my favorite islands."

"Which one?"

"The one that sits on a volcanic lake in Southeast Asia."

Ajajdif was genuinely interested. "So you found a new getaway island? How do you like this one?"

"It is beautiful, and it has a significant history behind it."

"Oh?"

"It is a volcano that was presumed to have wiped out much of the human race when it erupted seventy-five thousand years ago. Rather symbolic, don't you agree?"

Ajajdif pursed his lips. "Yes, definitely. That sounds interesting. How is the weather there?"

"Wonderful. The warmth of the tropics suits me well."

"You're certainly a globetrotter," Ajajdif said with a laugh, although his nervousness gave it an unsteady pitch. "When do you plan to head back to the U.S.?"

"I should be returning in a couple of weeks . . . about the time that you'll be wrapping up your little project over there."

Ajajdif gripped the phone tightly.

"Adrian called me a few days ago and told me that he gave you a month's extension. That doesn't please me. We originally gave you four months."

"I know." His palms were getting clammy. "But the weather was horrid, and the machines weren't working properly, and—"

"Adrian told me everything. I just want to know one thing: The project will draw to a close by the end of the month, will it not?" A cold note had crept into the boss' voice.

Ajajdif swallowed. "I . . . I hope so. I mean, it should."

"That is not the answer I am looking for."

"I am pushing my crew to work around the clock and we're trying our hardest to get the mineral. We've already gotten a substantial amount, and we will try to get the remaining quantity by the deadline. I'm not making any excuses but we've run into a number of challenges here and that's the truth."

There was a moment of unsettling silence, then the voice breathed again, "Don't let me down, Vladimir."

"Of course not."

"Now... Adrian also informed me of some disturbing events that occurred over there, but he left a few gaps. Fill me in on those."

Ajajdif swore silently. Of course Black would want to deflect the heat over to him. "One of my crew members died in an accident in the tunnel."

"That is unfortunate, but there are risks in this operation."

Feeling secure with the boss' more easygoing tone, Ajajdif continued. "Four intruders trespassed into one of the tunnels. My head of security and his team managed to capture them, but not without a few casualties."

"What happened?"

"They got into a scuffle with the intruders, but they're being looked after now."

"Tell me more about these trespassers, Vladimir."

Ajajdif scratched his neck. "They were natives, apparently, but they were like no natives I've ever seen. My head of security told me that they fought with amazing strength and techniques that surprised his men before the team managed to tranquilize them. We kept them chained in a holding cell with one guard there at all times."

"Did you try to communicate with them?"

"I did, but they couldn't speak English. The security team tried to use hand signals and whatnot, but they didn't respond to that either."

"Hm." The voice on the other end paused. "Were they all young, or was there an older native with them?"

Ajajdif found the question a little strange. "No, they were all young. Why do you ask?"

A sound of throat-clearing came over the speaker. "I was just wondering if there was a leader amongst them."

Ajajdif frowned but didn't pursue further.

"Adrian told me that you were taking care of them. Have you?"

"Yes." Ajajdif knew he would have to tread carefully. Right before he'd left his office to turn in for the night, Hajjar had found him and explained to him all that had happened in the tunnel with the Marauders and the natives. "My head of security let loose the Marauders on the men."

Interest sneaked into the boss's tone. "That must have thrilled the beasts."

"Yes. All the men are dead." He had to force out the last sentence. From what Hajjar had told him, he knew that two were dead for sure. The other two had fallen down the side of the mountain. Hajjar assured him that no one could have survived that fall, especially not with their hands still tied behind their backs.

"Excellent. Less problems to deal with."

"Uh, yes. However . . . we lost one of the hybrids during that little activity."

"What? How did that happen?"

Ajajdif flinched. "Part of the tunnel they were in collapsed."

The voice on the other end was silent again.

"Are you there?" Ajajdif asked cautiously.

"It takes a lot to create these animals, Vladimir. They do not come off an assembly line."

"I understand. I'm sorry."

"Good. Is that all there is to report?"

"Yes."

"Then I will let you go back to sleep. Get some rest, Vladimir. You're going to need it."

There was a click and a tone, indicating that the boss had hung up. Ajajdif sat down on the edge of his bed and put the phone down beside him. Sighing, he held his head in his hands and thought with disdain, *Rest? Yeah, right.*

43

Jag gazed up at the third of the six logs in his training area and glanced at Elder Tayoka, who simply motioned for him to get on the beam. Jag looked back at the log. It was slightly daunting to think that he would now have to practice his abilities atop a beam that stood eight feet above the ground.

"Are you nervous?" Huyani asked, coming to stand beside him.

"Me? Nah . . ."

She smiled. "I remember when Akol first started practicing balance and some defense techniques with this log."

"How did he do?"

"He hurt himself more than a few times." She saw the alarmed look on Jag's face and quickly said, "But there is no reason for you to be truly worried. All that is needed of one is focus, determination, and practice."

Jag saw the truth in that. Having been involved in parkour for several years, he'd had his fair share of pain. But if there was ever one defining quality about Jag, it was his determination.

He scaled to the top of the log, took a few breaths to relax and waited for Tayoka's instructions. Through Huyani, Tayoka said, "We will begin with an easy move to get you used to this log. Start with a forward roll."

Jag crouched down and rolled forward on the beam, trying not to tense up. Through experience he'd learned that a rigid body would not have proper balance. He rolled all the way to the end and stopped just in time to make sure he didn't fall right off the beam.

Tayoka nodded. "Now, a backward roll."

Jag felt anxiety creeping through his body. A backward roll was the simplest of moves on flat ground, but on a log, it scared him—although he would never admit it. *Suck it up, punk*, he thought. As he did the roll, he felt something was off and realized his back hadn't been aligned well. Panicking, he tumbled backwards off the log and fell. He landed with a hard thud on his side and laid still for a few moments, stunned, the wind knocked out of him.

"Are you alright, Jag?" Huyani called worriedly from where she stood beside Tayoka.

"Just dandy," he groaned and rolled over onto his stomach before pushing himself up.

Tayoka barked a few words at Jag, and Huyani said, "He is telling you to get back up and complete the somersaults. He says you are not moving onto other feats until you've accomplished this one perfectly."

With a resigned dip of his head to acknowledge the Elder, Jag climbed back to the top of the log. He was prepared for a long, hard day ahead.

At the other end of the training ground, Kody was straining his ears, trying not to lose his focus as Nageau clapped his hands and made loud distracting noises, all the while moving in circles around him. When Nageau first gave him his task, it sounded unchallenging. All he was to do was focus on the sound of a certain cricket about a hundred feet away. He hadn't expected Nageau to create serious interruptions.

"I can't focus with all that noise," Kody grumbled.

"That is the point, my young friend!" Nageau answered and he continued to move around and be distractive. "What is the point of this ability if you are only able to use it in tranquil conditions?"

Kody tried to think of a rebuttal but couldn't and grouched instead. "Could you at least tone it down a little, please?"

"Absolutely not."

"Then I can't focus!"

"If you tell yourself that you cannot, then there is simply no way your power will grow."

Kody threw his hands up in frustration.

"Remember, Kody, for your abilities to be truly effective, you must calm yourself and not let any other emotions grab hold of you."

"I can't believe that I'm in the intermediate stage of my training and this is all I get to do."

Nageau stopped and cast Kody a puzzled look. "What do you mean?"

"Well . . ." Kody sat on the grass and poked at the dirt. "I thought there would be more to this intermediate stage than just further listening."

Nageau clasped his hands together. "I see."

"Isn't there something else we can do, and then maybe we can come back to this later?"

"I suppose we could. What would you like to do?"

Kody looked up at the sky as he thought. "I'd like to work on increasing my sense of smell."

Nageau smiled. "That is doable. Give me a few minutes while I set up an evaluation."

Kody lay down on his back and gazed up through the tall pine and fir trees. A few clouds rolled by in the sky, and he fancied one of them looked like the face of his youngest brother. He half-smiled at the thought and continued watching the cloud as it drifted away. A sudden pang of homesickness struck him and his smile disappeared. Though he couldn't say for certain, he was almost sure that he and his friends had been living with the Dema-Ki people for at least a month. The past couple of weeks had been exciting and he hadn't had much time to wonder about his family who were in the "outside world," as the villagers called it.

Well, not the whole family, he thought sadly. The Elders had never come back to him about his father. They'd never told him if his father had been found or if he was safe. They never told, and he never asked. The Elders would undoubtedly inform him if they learned any news about his father, so he didn't see a reason to keep nagging them for an answer they didn't have.

He continued gazing up at the sky, brokenhearted. *I miss you, Dad.*

"Kody?"

Kody sat up and found Nageau looking at him with concern. He quickly jumped to his feet and rubbed his eyes, then looked up at the tall Elder.

"Is something bothering you, youngling?"

He shook his head. Nageau knew it wasn't the truth, but if Kody wanted to speak his mind, then he would. The Elder led his apprentice to the center of the large clearing and gave him his instructions. "First, we must test your sense of smell, just as we tested your sense of hearing. I have placed different objects around here. Without moving, I want you to first tell me which direction the smell is coming from; and second—tell me what it is that you can smell."

For the next half hour, Kody was assessed on the keenness of his nose. It was a relatively easy task for him since his sense of smell was naturally excellent. Nageau was impressed as they wrapped up the evaluation. "Your sense of smell is astounding," the Elder told him.

Kody smiled. "Thank you. I usually use it to help me find food that's being prepared around the neighborhood during summertime. People get their grills out on their decks, so there's food everywhere." He mimed flipping a burger on a barbeque grill, then stopped and looked thoughtful. "Elder Nageau," he said.

"Yes?"

"The contaminant in the water. Does it have a scent to it? Maybe that could help locate where it comes from. Back home, we've discovered that some breeds of dogs are able to smell certain illnesses that their owners have, so I was thinking that, with a strong sense of smell, maybe we could pick up the scent?"

"Actually, I have attempted that," Nageau answered. "I must say, though, it pleases me that you thought of it as well. That is a good quality, to think of various ways to find a solution."

"You tried? So did you find a scent?"

"No. Unfortunately, it seems to be odorless."

Kody tilted his head slightly and grinned. "Can I try?"

Nageau patted his pupil on the back and chuckled. "After we finish today's training, yes."

* * *

Akira soared in the sky, drawing ever closer to the Ayen Range. With Tikina in control, the eagle scanned the ground for any signs of the four men. It had been three days since the search parties had been sent out, and their hopes of finding the men had not been met.

But when we last communicated with them, they were closer to the Ayen'et than where the search parties currently are, Tikina reasoned. She continued to look for any sign through Akira's eyes as the bird neared the base of the Ayen'et mountain. The sun was beginning to set, casting shadows across the land as it did, but the eagle had superb vision which Tikina found very useful.

Akira circled around the mountain, eyes searching, then landed on a tree to rest. Tikina allowed the eagle a respite, understanding that she had been flying almost continuously.

An unexpected noise startled Tikina. Curious, she took the bird to flight and searched around the area. The noise sounded again, quieter this time. Tikina scanned the ground with the eagle's eyes, daring to hope.

She saw a motion on the ground right at the base of the mountain, by a large boulder. She flew Akira closer to get a better look and her eyes widened in disbelief. Breyas lay on his back, his hands beneath him. His arms and face were bruised and scratched, and one of his legs extended at an awkward angle. Akira landed beside him and ran her beak over his cheek. His eyes were closed, but he groaned.

Tikina observed his injuries, her heart pounding, and quickly led Akira to fly again. They flew until Tikina spotted another form, laying facedown in the dirt not too far away from Breyas. *Rikèq*, Tikina realized with a pang. Her daughter's mate; father of Akol and Huyani. He was unconscious just as Breyas was and looked as gravely battered. *What happened to them?* Tikina wondered, troubled.

She flew Akira in circles until the sun was almost out of sight, desperately searching for Aydar and Keno. She couldn't find them. *Where are they?* She couldn't bear to think of the worst. She flew Akira around one last time, hoping to find any sign that would lead her to believe that Aydar and Keno were alive. She was unsuccessful.

Torn between feelings of relief at finding two members of the team and the urge to keep looking for the other missing ones, Tikina decided that the men she had found would need tending to quickly. *Perhaps when the search party arrives, they may have more luck finding Aydar and Keno.* She turned Akira and the eagle flapped her wings madly toward the search party, breaking the stillness around her with a shrill caw of distress as night finally fell upon the forest.

44

The two separate search parties had met just before sunset and were now sitting around a campfire as, one by one, stars appeared in the cloudless sky. Both teams had similar things to report: Neither had found the four missing men, and both had discovered more animal carcasses strewn around the forest as they traveled.

They were interrupted by a piercing caw from an invisible form. Looking around, their eyes darted back and forth. The woman in the red bandana jumped up and went to put on her leather glove, knowing that Akira was coming back with news.

The eagle's silhouette appeared as she came closer to the search party, gliding toward the woman's outstretched arm. Akira landed on the glove and cawed again, looking at the woman, her gold feathers glowing in the light of the fire. The woman half-closed her eyes and listened as Tikina shared what she had found.

"Elder Tikina has found Breyas and Rikèq, but they are unconscious and injured," she informed the members of her search party.

They shared relieved looks. "What about Aydar and Keno?" asked a member of the group.

"Elder Tikina does not know. She thinks that perhaps we might be able to find them once we reach the other two." She nodded to the eagle and the majestic bird flapped its giant wings until she was hovering above the search party. "No rest tonight, I am afraid," the woman said. "Put out that fire and we will be on our way."

* * *

"You need *another* fifty barrels of the chemicals?"

"You heard me." Ajajdif rested his feet on his desk and traced invisible lines on the ceiling of his office with a finger.

"That means I'll have to fly out one of the Ospreys again."

"Adrian, you know as well as I do that we need to do everything necessary to keep this project moving along."

"Don't use that condescending tone with me, Vlad."

"I'm just saying we need those chemicals."

"Okay, fine. We'll get them out to you. Is that all you called for?"

Ajajdif looked down from the ceiling. "Actually, no." He lowered his voice. "I happen to know that those Ospreys weren't bought just for their cargo hauling capabilities."

"Excuse me?"

"Those birds are the civilian versions meant for the commercial market, but we know full well their pedigree, no?"

Black sounded wary on the other end of the line. "Yes, it's true. Quest Defense has modified the aircraft so that we can equip it with a range of offensive and defensive capabilities. Why do you ask?"

"Well, I was just thinking . . ."

"Get to the point, Vlad!"

"With the four natives dead, I'm just worried that others might come looking for them."

"Others?"

Ajajdif sighed impatiently. "Yes, others. The others from their tribe, or whatever they call it. I detected a strong sense of cohesiveness and I'm sure they had capabilities we did not see."

"And?"

"And if others come looking for their dead friends, I'd appreciate some extra help."

"You already have the Marauders and some small arms."

"That might not be enough, Adrian. Those trespassers weren't normal. Normal people don't escape heavy chains and jump off the side of a mountain with their hands tied behind their backs. And I looked through their packs. They had weapons, and these were no cheesy sharp-ended sticks that they carved with a flint."

"You're really worried, huh?" Black said in a flat tone.

"I'm just trying to take precautions so that everything continues running smoothly. We're up to eight kilos of the mineral now. One more to go and we're back on track."

Ajajdif could almost imagine Black sitting in headquarters with his fingertips pressed together. "If you really believe that the bird is essential to getting you out of there by the deadline, then I'll see what I can do."

"Thanks." Ajajdif ended the call and walked out of his office. He passed a secure storage unit where the mineral was kept and took a quick look inside. Each kilo of the mineral was in its own sturdy container. Ajajdif opened one of the containers and looked at the fine, black, odorless powder that sparkled as light touched it. He snorted. "Three months of hard work and pain for this dust?"

As he closed the lid of the container and double-checked to make sure it was secure, he shuddered at what Quest Defense was planning to create with the mineral.

* * *

The search party had trekked tirelessly through the night. Although some of the villagers were a little bleary-eyed, no one had asked to stop for a break even though it was nearly midday. The Ayen'et loomed, casting its shadow over the search party, but they were not deterred.

The team followed Akira as the eagle flew unguided with the purpose of her flight embedded in her brain. She circled back often to see if the search party was still following her, then flew ahead. At last she lighted on a tree near Breyas and Rikèq. Both men were still unconscious.

It was only minutes later that the search party arrived at the scene. The woman in the red bandana scoped around the area and then assigned two members of the party to search for Aydar and Keno as she and the others tended to Breyas and Rikèq.

One of the villagers removed his journey pack, unfolded it into a stretcher, and set it down beside Breyas. Another member of the party did the same with his own journey pack, placing it by Rikèq's side. "Cut the ropes that bind their hands!" the woman with the red bandana ordered.

The men pulled out their knives and sliced the bindings off, then gently turned their unconscious kin onto their backs. They administered emergency treatments with the skill and precision of trained first aid responders.

When the searchers had done all that they could, they carefully lifted the unconscious men onto the stretchers and strapped them down to keep them immobilized.

The woman in the red bandana stepped back and observed the team. "Good job, everyone," she praised. "We will take a quick lunch break before returning home."

The team settled on the ground and took out their meals, hastily devouring them. The two men who had been sent to find Aydar and Keno came back, looking downcast.

The woman waved them over. "What news do you bring?"

One of the men shook his head sullenly. "We have been continuously searching but have not found them."

The woman looked distressed. "Where have you checked?"

"We hiked a little ways up the mountain but they are simply nowhere to be found," the other man answered.

She removed her bandana and sighed, running her finger through her hair. "Are you certain you have combed through the area thoroughly?"

"Yes."

The woman brought her knees up to her chest and hugged her arms around them. She closed her eyes and whispered a quick prayer, then stood up. "I will need four volunteers to remain here and continue searching for Keno and Aydar," she said, trying to keep the sadness from her voice. She turned to the others and saw that they were already done with their meals. "Let us bring our brothers back home, my friends."

As the others picked up their packs and carefully lifted the stretchers, the woman pulled her hair back and retied her bandana. She glanced up at Akira who was still perched on the tree nearby and reached out with her mind. Realizing Tikina was once again in control of the eagle, she expressed her appreciation to the Elder for leading them to the missing men.

The eagle dipped her head in response, then took flight away from the search party. The woman watched the regal creature soar, momentarily diverted by its striking magnificence as it flew away in the direction of the sun.

The woman turned back to look at the search party and inspected the stretchers again to make sure everything was secure. She gazed down at the unconscious men, eyes running over their badly bruised and scraped faces. Resting a hand on each of their foreheads, she murmured a few words of healing. She then headed to the front of the search party to lead it away from the mountain and back to the valley. She glanced over her shoulder at the four men who were staying behind to search for Keno and Aydar. As she thanked them in silence, she was disheartened at the thought that they'd only managed to find two survivors.

45

The pinecone looked astonishing. From such a close proximity, the scales appeared helix-like as they extended from the tip to the end of the cone. They were like the scales on a dragon. It was something most would have wanted to stop and inspect.

But not this creature. It had other things in mind and Tegan could do nothing but tag along for the ride. The ground squirrel scampered around the training area with frantic excitement, sniffing everything and scuttling through the grass. It froze when it swung around and nearly had its eyes poked by the antennae of a large snail that was slowly crawling over the dirt. The squirrel nosed the slimy creature curiously before turning and zigzagging away with an incredible amount of energy compacted into its small body.

Tegan's eyes fluttered open as she let go of her mind-link and placed her hands on either side of her head to steady herself. "What a rush!" she exclaimed, looking up from where she sat a few feet across from Tikina.

The Elder laughed. "Do tell."

"It was . . . wow! That thing is crazy. It has so much energy. I couldn't keep up with it so I had to let go."

"That is quite alright. It is to be expected at this point in your training. Tell me, what did you see through its eyes?"

"Everything from the dirt to the tips of the grass. All the small insects going about their business. The feel of the grass under my—uh, the squirrel's paws. And I could smell so many things, too. The clarity of it all was amazing." Tegan shook her head in incredulity. "A truly out-of-this-world experience."

Tikina lent her hand to Tegan and pulled the girl to her feet. "And imagine," she said, "this is only the beginning. At this point all you did was follow the animal around. Later, not only will you be able to link with larger creatures, you will also be able to control their movements."

Tikina had explained how mind-linking worked before they began the training. Just as all creatures shared a biological existence on Earth in the biosphere, there was a higher plane called the nova-sphere where minds and thoughts permeate. Projecting one's consciousness and seeking to connect with another mind was the basis of the meditative training that Tegan was undergoing.

Tegan was amazed at Tikina's insights. She thought of what was to come in her future and looked as if she wanted to bounce around like an excited child with a new toy, but instead opted to keep her feet planted on the ground. She couldn't help herself from grinning, though.

Tikina was pleased to see her enthusiasm. "We still have a little bit of time before your midday meal. What would you like to do?"

Tegan pointed to a gray jay that was gazing at them inquisitively from up in a tree. "I'd like to mind-link with that bird."

Tikina followed the line Tegan's finger made and smiled when she saw the bird. "That fellow takes quite naturally to us humans. Go ahead."

Facing the small bird, Tegan sat back down on the grass and closed her eyes, focusing her consciousness on finding the bird's energy field in the nova-sphere. When she found it, it was an easy task to link with it, and soon she was looking through the eyes of the bird. She could see herself sitting with her eyes closed and thought, *I really do look like I've been living in the wild.* Before she got a chance to inspect herself further, the gray jay took off, flapping its tiny wings. Tegan marveled at how the bird was able to pilot through the trees so quickly without hitting anything. Her heart skipped a beat each time the bird zoomed past a tree, avoiding collision by mere inches as it expertly navigated its way around the forest.

When the bird decided to land on a branch again, it was on a tree overlooking Aari's area of the training grounds. Curious, Tegan decided to wait and watch for a bit before breaking the link with the gray jay.

Aari was a couple of dozen feet away from the bird's perch. Ashack stood nearby, pointing to four objects that were placed in a row in front of them. Akol stood with Ashack, rapidly translating the Elder's words for Aari. The objects were pentagonal prisms that stood about five feet high, each constructed of different material. The one to the far left was transparent like glass and the one next to it appeared translucent. The third object was a solid white, and the last object, on the far right, was as reflective as a mirror.

Having described each of the objects and what was expected of Aari, Ashack and Akol huddled with the boy for a quick pep talk and stepped back when Aari nodded. The Elder and Akol went to stand behind Aari, directly under the branch the bird was on. They watched as Aari faced the transparent object. He exhaled and extended his arms in front of him at a slightly upwards angle, then pressed his palms together.

Nothing happened as they all stared at the side of the prism that was facing them. Then the top left corner of the prism began to shimmer and slowly the edges began to disappear, but only for a brief moment. Then the bottom corners of the object began to look hazy before they vanished completely. The pattern continued until the entire front face of the pentagonal prism disappeared.

Tegan saw Ashack's stone face crack into a brilliant smile. She smiled to herself as well, proud of her friend.

Feeling the bird was about to spread its wings, she steadied herself. The jay took off, fluttering over the heads of Ashack, Akol, and Aari. The trio looked up as the bird flew from their sights. Tegan laughed. Aari would be in for a surprise when she informed him that a little bird had told her exactly what he'd done today.

* * *

Standing with Relsuc under a tree, Hutar watched as the five walked over the bridge to the other side of the river and made their way to Huyani's shelter for the afternoon meal. "Is everything set for tomorrow?" he asked quietly, not taking his eyes off the group as they walked into the *neyra*.

Relsuc unsheathed his knife from his belt and held it up to look at it as the sun glinted off the blade. "Yes. All that is left to do is invite the five to join us."

"Perfect."

They turned and headed toward the stable. Hutar said nothing the entire way and Relsuc, not wanting to disturb Hutar, remained mute as well. But the silence was short-lived. As they were about to step into the stable, a torrent of shouts rose up in the valley. Hutar and Relsuc looked at each other, then turned and ran to the eastern end of the valley where a crowd of people had gathered. Hutar elbowed his way through and saw Matikè in the throng. He grabbed her arm and she turned to look at him.

"What is going on?" he asked.

She grinned. "The search party has returned."

Hutar's eyes stretched wide. *Uncle*, he thought, finally cracking a hint of a smile. He had been waiting for this moment for days. He pushed past his brethren until he reached the front of the crowd and stared, his spirits raised. Matikè and Relsuc came to stand beside him and all three saw the search party walking toward them. Hutar saw two men on stretchers but couldn't tell who they were.

"I thought four men were sent out," Matikè murmured. "Where are the other two?"

Hutar didn't say anything and watched in silence. The search party halted in front of the anxious crowd, trying to find a way through them to get the two men to the convalescence shelter. Hutar walked forward, Matikè and Relsuc following closely behind, and looked down at the two men who lay unconscious on the stretchers. Neither was his uncle. He looked up at the search party. "Where is my uncle?" he asked quietly.

The woman in the red bandana looked back at him and recognized who he was. She lowered her gaze a little and took a few moments to answer. "We could not find him, Hutar."

Hutar was unable to believe his ears. "Pardon?"

"We looked for him, we really did. But we could not find him and neither were we able to locate Keno." She looked back up at him. "I am so sorry." She reached out to give him a soothing hug but he leaned away from her. She slowly lowered her arms. "If it is any consolation, Hutar, four members of my team are still searching for them."

Behind Hutar, Matikè and Relsuc exchanged nervous looks. They saw Hutar's fists clench and unclench slowly and heard him repeat in a disbelieving tone, "Could not find him?" He turned around and strode past everyone, his heels digging into the dirt. Matikè and Relsuc followed but kept their distance to be safe. Hutar stopped when he reached the river. "My uncle . . . was sent out by the Elders . . . *to die*."

Matikè rested her hand on his forearm. "Do not say that, Hutar. You do not know that he is—"

In a flash Hutar had his hands wrapped around her neck, squeezing. His eyes were ablaze with fury. "Do not tell me that!" he spat. "You saw for yourself how badly the men who were brought back were hurt. If they could not find my uncle, what do you think happened to him?"

She tried to answer but he had an iron grip around her neck. Relsuc took a small step forward. "Hutar, let her go." Hutar ignored him. Matikè's face started to turn blue. Relsuc shouted, "Hutar, stop!"

Hutar let Matikè go and shoved her away. Relsuc caught her from behind before she fell and held her as she gasped for air. "There was no reason for that," he said, shooting the other male a glare.

Hutar disregarded his words and turned his back to them. "There is one more thing I want you to do tomorrow."

Relsuc listened with a grim face. When Hutar had finished explaining, he said nothing. Resting a hand on Matikè's back, he guided her away, leaving Hutar to himself. Hutar stared at his reflection in the water, noticing the bags under his eyes and the stubble that he would shave for tomorrow. He scratched his cheek and pursed his lips. The element he wanted to add to his scheme tomorrow was unplanned, but the return of half of the four-man team tipped the scale. It wouldn't have been nearly as bad if one of the two men found was his uncle, but that was not the case.

His uncle was the only thing in his life that had kept him reasonably sane since his father's passing seven summers before. His mother died giving birth to him, so he never got to know her. Hutar's father had raised him single-handedly and had been his rock and guide throughout his young life. Hutar had grown strongly attached to him and often refused to be anywhere but at his side.

On the day Hutar turned eleven summers, his father decided to take him out on their canoe to a pond famous for its fishing and campground. Normally, the younger boys in the village would wait in anticipation until they turned twelve, for it was only then that their fathers would take them on this ride to the pond, as was tradition. The young boys would impatiently hop around and whine to their parents after watching the older ones return with the extra swagger and the exaggerated stories of their adventures.

The pond was known among the people as "the white water pond." It wasn't because the water in the pond was white, but because on the way to the pond, the villagers had to paddle their boats through a rapid river that forked in two. One arm led to a slower-moving tributary that eventually flowed to the pond, while the other led to treacherous white waters that ended in a thundering, three-hundred foot waterfall.

Hutar had wanted to ride that river into the pond for years. He would constantly beg his father to take him out there, as he always got a thrill from being around danger. The intense sensation he got from conquering dangers left him with a strong sense of accomplishment. On Hutar's birthday, his father agreed to finally grant him that wish. He had watched his son grow and was impressed with his skill level. For someone Hutar's age, it was outstanding how he handled himself.

It was a flawless afternoon as father and son climbed into their boat. Elder Tayoka had been wandering around the area and came to greet them. "Good afternoon, Daltair," he smiled, looking down at them.

Hutar's father smiled up as he passed an oar to his son. "Good afternoon, Elder Tayoka."

"This is not a river for fishing, so I suppose you are taking Hutar to the pond?"

"Yes. My young one here has been asking for this for a long time."

"Hm. The last time I checked, this youngling here does not turn twelve for another year," Tayoka commented with a wink. Hutar looked worriedly at his father, thinking he might call off the trip, but then realized that the Elder was simply jesting when he saw the men smile.

"He is quite capable, Elder Tayoka," Hutar's father said. "I have watched him and I think he is ready for this challenge."

"Very well, then. Have fun. But be careful, my friends. Do not forget the two arms of the river. Always stay to the right when you reach the fork, because the right side is the *right* side."

"Thank you. We will."

As Hutar and his father paddled away from shore, they took in the beautiful shades of green from shrubs of junipers that wound along the riverbanks. Beyond them, the mighty pine trees and the occasional spruce filled their view.

Paddling downstream on the sapphire-blue water, Hutar asked, "This river is not *that* unsafe, is it, Father?"

"It can be to those who have never navigated it before." He smiled at Hutar. "But I have, so there is no need to worry."

Hutar grinned and helped his father row. Having paddled for a quarter of an hour, they noticed a gentle increase in the current. Hutar turned around and asked, "It feels as if we are moving faster now," he said, excited.

His father chuckled. “Yes, we are. It will keep getting faster until we reach the fork.”

They paddled on and soon noticed white crests on the water up ahead. His father pointed at the crests. “See that? That is where the river begins to fork. We will soon see a bank in the middle of the river, and that is when we begin to paddle toward the slower waters on the right.”

“Where does the left arm of the river go?”

“It turns into a magnificent waterfall. You will be hearing its rumble shortly.”

After a few strokes of his paddle, a faint sound reached Hutar’s ears and he pulled his paddle out of the water and listened. He turned around to look at his father again, blue eyes bright. “I hear it! I hear it!”

His father laughed and shouted over the water, “Start paddling on the left side!”

They entered the rapids just a few moments later and felt the ride getting rougher. They rode over the churning waters now and were paddling to switch directions. About two hundred yards ahead of them, they could see the fork in the river. The boat was gaining speed. Hutar looked around anxiously. From behind he heard his father calling over the sound of the rushing water. “Everything is fine, Hutar! This is how the river is. Just keep paddling.”

Hutar obeyed, trusting his father. Things seemed alright until the canoe picked up more speed and the ride became palpably uncomfortable. He yelled back at his father, “Why is it getting rougher? Why are we not moving toward the other bank?”

“Keep paddling, Hutar! The current is stronger than I thought!” There was terseness in his words.

The two paddled frantically, and even as the nose of the canoe started to point toward where they wanted to go, the boat itself was being forced down the rapids toward the waterfall. The current was directing their course over the water and they had no control over it. All the furious paddling wasn’t deflecting the canoe from the more treacherous arm of the river. The roar of the waterfall was now much louder.

Hutar could see that they had overshot the right arm of the river and were being dragged headlong toward the waterfall. The boat began bouncing violently over the frothing rapids. The boy was overcome by panic and began yelling back to his father for help. He saw for the first time an expression of sheer terror on his father's face.

"Hold on tight, Hutar," he called in a shaky voice just before the boat hit a submerged rock, tipping the canoe. In an instant, the rushing water filled the canoe and capsized it, throwing both its occupants into the raging river.

They were helpless as the current swept them along. Hutar's head momentarily went under the water but his father grabbed him and pulled him back up with all his might. He looked around, searching for something they could grab onto as the swift current carried them but found nothing.

They were less than fifty yards from the brink of the waterfall. Hutar, now in his father's arms, scanned around over the turbulent water. As he was about to scream for help, he saw a figure at the edge of the water. He couldn't believe his eyes. It was Tayoka.

His father must have seen him too, because with uncommon strength, he lifted his son and hurled him as far as he could toward Tayoka, shouting, "Save him!"

Hutar landed with a splash about fifteen feet from his father, gaining a precious few seconds from the edge of the waterfall. As he raised his head, disorientated, he saw the shape of a man sprinting weightlessly over the water at an astounding speed. When the shape was close to Hutar, it landed in the water and grabbed him around his waist, then swam with incredible power back toward the shore.

In a moment of clarity, Hutar realized that he had just been saved by Tayoka. But his thoughts were not for himself. He looked past the Elder and saw his father being dragged toward the brink of the waterfall and started to scream at the Elder to save him. But before the words left him, he saw his father, arm raised, mouth open in a wordless call to the heavens, plummeting over the edge.

"Father!" Hutar screamed. "*Father!*" He struggled against Tayoka as the Elder brought the wailing boy onto dry land. Tayoka reached out and hugged the child to console him but Hutar squirmed out of his grasp and fell backward, tears running down his face.

"You could have saved him!" he yelled, trying to wipe his eyes dry with the back of his hand. "You could have saved him!"

Tayoka stood there, speechless, with deep sorrow in his eyes. Hutar pushed himself to his feet and stumbled into the trees, shivering and crying. He couldn't believe it. His father was gone, with his final moments forever etched into the boy's mind.

He slumped down against a tree and wrapped his arms around himself, rocking back and forth and sobbing as tears streamed from his eyes.

The Elder had followed him and knelt down beside the boy, drawing him into his arms once more to comfort him. Hutar shut his eyes and thoughts began to flood in between his sobs. What was going to happen to him? Who was going to look after him? Who would care for him and guide him like his father did?

His uncle would eventually fill his father's shoes. His mother's brother would take him under his protective wing and continue to raise Hutar to the best of his abilities. Hutar came to love his uncle as much as he loved his father, and had begun to repair the rip in his heart as time progressed. Aydar became his minder and his tower of strength, and Hutar had believed that life had given him another guardian.

Hutar let out a short gasp as he tore himself away from his memory and found himself still crouched and staring at his reflection in the village's river. Sadness and resentment threatened to knock him off balance as thoughts of his father and uncle spun like a whirlwind in his mind.

His legs gave way. He dropped to the ground and slowly crossed his limbs. Leaning forward with his arms resting on his knees, Hutar hung his head. He was truly on his own now. No parents. No uncle.

No family.

A lone tear slid down his cheek.

46

The gates of the training grounds opened inward and the five walked out with Akol. When they learned that the search party had returned with only half of the four-man group, Huyani had quickly rushed out to tend to Rikèq and Breyas. Without her around, the friends' training had been a bit more strenuous than usual and they were glad for a break.

Jag had had a particularly difficult conversation with Tayoka before the end of his session. Akol, of course, had been there to offer his assistance with the language barrier. "Jag," he'd said. "Before we leave, there is something I would like to speak with you about, and it is something Nageau wanted me to approach you about for a while now."

Jag had looked up from where he'd been wiping sweat from his face and neck. "Yeah?"

"You have great potential, my young apprentice. Very great."

"Thank you, Elder Tayoka."

"I do not mean this with your innate abilities alone, my boy."

The phrase had rendered Jag wary. The Elder continued, resting his hands on Jag's shoulders. "You have skill sets that are natural and must be developed, and I do believe that they are progressing. However… may I ask, Jag, why is it that you tend to repress your instincts to lead?"

Jag clenched his jaw. He was torn between wanting to scream *I've had this conversation with Tegan already!* and *How can you even tell that I've been suppressing it?*

Rather than beating around the bush, he took a small step back and said gruffly, "Because we are all equals, so that doesn't give me the right to lead. And I've made a few mistakes before—an especially bad one that really hurt a good friend of mine from home."

Tayoka shook his head slightly. "Yes, we are all equal in status, but not equal in roles. It is completely understandable that you are afraid of making mistakes that prove costly to others, but letting that fear cripple you is a mistake in itself."

Jag wanted so badly to retort, to argue and prove the Elder wrong. But he couldn't. Tayoka was right—beneath his numerous layers of righteousness and denial and preservation, leading did tend to come naturally to him. The fear of hurting another whom he cared for, though, wasn't something that could be washed away overnight.

The Elder and apprentice said nothing else after that, but Jag wasn't able to shake off his mentor's words.

The Elders followed the five out, closing the gates to the training area behind them, and the group made their way past the temple and down the hill. As they reached the bottom of the slope, they saw a figure running out of the convalescence shelter toward them.

"It's Huyani," Kody said. "What's her hurry?"

As Huyani got closer she tried to slow down but couldn't and barreled into Akol, who helped stop her momentum. She was out of breath but there was excitement in her eyes. "Father is awake!"

Akol let out an elated yell and hugged her. She hugged him back and then saw the Elders over his shoulder. They looked hopeful. "Father has regained consciousness," she repeated.

"What is his condition?" Nageau asked.

Akol let go of her so she could face the Elders properly. "He is able to talk and he insists that he must speak with you as soon as possible."

Nageau looked at the Elders and they nodded at him. He turned to the five and said, "We will not meet back here to continue your training once you have had your break. I am uncertain how long this will take, therefore you will have the rest of the day off."

The five maintained their poker faces as they dipped their heads at the Elders. "Your drinks are all prepared in my *neyra*," Huyani told them as she and Akol started toward the convalescence shelter with the Elders.

The friends strode toward the bridge to cross to the other side of the valley. When they were sure they were out of earshot, they turned to each other and high-fived. "A break!" Kody exclaimed. "We can lounge around all day now."

They passed a few villagers who smiled warmly at them, and the five smiled back. "These folks are so friendly," Mariah remarked.

A group of boys around six years old jumped up and down and waved at the friends from where they were wrestling under a tree. Tegan waved back.

The five stepped onto the bridge and saw three youths stepping on from the other end. They smiled and tried to pass them but the youths blocked their path. "Good afternoon, my friends," one of them said, leaning on one of the bridge's railings.

Jag recognized the speaker. "Hey, Hutar, right?"

"Yes. And if you remember, this is Aesròn and Matikè."

"I remember you guys now," Aari said, grinning. "Man, we haven't seen any of you in a while."

Hutar chuckled. "I know, and it is a shame." He and Aesròn smiled beguilingly, their eyes briefly meeting Tegan's and Mariah's before looking away. The girls glanced at each other and did their best not to blush.

"Some of the youths are having a gathering tonight after dinner," Hutar told the group. "We would love for you to join us."

"Really?" Jag asked, surprised.

"Of course. You live here now, which makes you family. And families do things together, do they not?"

Kody watched Hutar as he listened. A twinge of unease rang inside him, but the youth was all smiles and cordial so he reasoned that it was his hyper-sensory training that was causing his anxiety.

"You guys want to go?" Jag asked his friends.

"Sure," Tegan said. "But shouldn't we let Huyani or Akol know?"

"Hold on, my gem," Aesròn said, putting an arm around her. "If you want to come, it would be best if you did not tell either of them."

Did he call me his gem? Who calls people their gem? Tegan glanced up to see him smiling charmingly again, then glanced away and asked, "Why should we not tell?"

"We know your . . . keepers . . . have their doubts about us." Aesròn raised an eyebrow. "Is that not correct?"

Tegan looked back at him. "Yeah. Are they right, though?"

Aesròn laughed. "I suppose that is a matter of opinion. Akol and Huyani are a little less, shall we say . . . flexible than most youths here. We do not know what their reasoning for telling you that we are not a good group is, but I can assure you we have never done anything that caused anyone grief. We just enjoy having fun."

Jag saw the eager but cautious looks his friends wore, then asked Hutar, "Could we think about it?"

"Definitely. If you would like to join us, just come by after your dinner. We will be at the old community center. It is a large building at the farthest side of the valley. It stands alone, so you will know which one it is when you see it."

The youths stepped aside and allowed the five to pass. As the friends walked toward Huyani's *neyra*, they heard the youths behind them speaking quietly and the roar of laughter that followed after.

* * *

The Elders were gathered in the convalescence shelter around Rikèq's bed. Akol and Huyani sat on either side of their father, each holding one of his hands. He smiled up at his son and daughter. The blood had been wiped off when he and Breyas had been found by the search team but the bruises remained, though with the herbs that had been applied, these would heal quickly. He had a fractured bone in his right arm and his upper legs had contusions to the muscles; those would take a little longer to mend.

"How are you feeling, Rikèq?" Tikina asked as she sat at the foot of his bed.

"In pain," he answered truthfully. "But as long as I know I am alive, I will gratefully take that discomfort and live with it."

"Hopefully you will not have to live with that pain for too long," said Saiyu.

"Was there something you wanted to share with the Elders, Father?" Huyani asked softly.

"Yes." Rikèq attempted to sit up but Akol and Huyani did not allow him to.

"Do not strain yourself," Akol told him, gently resting his father's head back onto the pillow.

"My children, the worriers." Rikèq smiled at his offspring. He shifted in his bed to a comfortable position before turning to the Elders to recount what had transpired. The Elders waited patiently as the rescued man took his time to recall the experience.

As Rikèq neared the end of his account, Huyani glanced out the window and saw the sun beginning to drop behind the mountains. She waited until there was a short lull in her father's narrative, then excused herself, explaining that she needed to start preparing the evening meal for the five. She kissed her father on the cheek before saying goodbye and exiting the building.

Rikèq watched her leave, then continued to speak until he was sure he had told the Elders everything they would need to know. Tikina took his hand and gave it a squeeze. "Thank you," she said, looking into his eyes with gratitude. "I can tell it was hard for you to recount all that you remember in the state you are in, but whatever you have shared is valuable. It could very well have an impact on our survival."

Nageau stepped forward. "Now all there is for you to focus on is healing." He rubbed his forehead. "We have our work cut out for us. I think we should call Magèo to the assembly *neyra* and discuss a plan. Akol, could you find him and bring him to us, please?"

Akol nodded and gingerly hugged his father, then left the center.

"Wait," Rikèq said suddenly. "Where is Breyas?"

"He is here," Saiyu answered.

"He is alive, is he not?"

"Yes, although he remains unconscious."

Rikèq sighed with relief, but the corners of his mouth curved down. "I still cannot believe Keno and Aydar are gone," he said quietly.

Tikina stroked his hair gently. "Do not occupy your mind with those thoughts. What you must do now is rest and recuperate." She carefully pulled the blanket further up his chest. "Try to get some sleep, Rikèq."

The Elders silently headed out of the building and walked up to their assembly *neyra*. They entered and left the door open so Magèo could walk in, then gathered around a wooden table. Ashack had brought out one of their many maps and spread it on the tabletop. They were discussing what they'd learned from Rikèq when Magèo entered and said gruffly, "I believe I was called upon for something?"

The Elders turned and smiled at the old man, who was wearing his bland tunic with his long beard hanging over his stomach. "Welcome, old friend," Nageau greeted, moving over so Magèo could jam in beside him and Tayoka.

Magèo peered at the map, his different-colored eyes squinting. "So. What is going on?"

Tayoka gave him a brief rundown of Rikèq's account. Magèo rubbed his beard, listening carefully. "Did Rikèq say at all what those people in the mountain are doing?"

"He mentioned that Aydar heard the people were mining for a certain ore, a rare ore. Aydar also told him that the man who is leading these miners is using a certain compound to get to the ore quicker. We are not sure if this compound is the source of the illness."

Magèo looked from Elder to Elder, slowly rubbing his fingers over the palm of his other hand. "I see . . . Do we have a map of the water tables and water sources for the area?"

Ashack reached out to grab another map and unrolled the parchment. The Elders straightened the map as Magèo ran his finger over it, following streams and rivers as he mumbled to himself. He then moved around the table to stand on the opposite side of the map and again traced a different branch of water sources. He tilted his head to his shoulder, squinting. "Hmm." He pulled out a crumpled parchment from a pocket in his tunic and compared what was written on it with the map. "Mmhm."

The Elders glanced at one another. Accustomed to his oddities, they let his brilliant mind sort out the connections. They didn't have to wait long. Magèo walked back to his original spot after quickly studying the water table at the bottom corner of the map. He looked up at the Elders and pronounced, "The mining activity atop the Ayen'et *is* the source of the poisoning of our waters!"

The Elders nodded. They had suspected so, but the old man helped to confirm their notion. "Can you say this with absolute certainty, though?" Ashack asked.

Slighted by the question, Magèo feigned a scowl. "I have made all the necessary comparisons," he rumbled, holding the crumpled notes over his head. "The elevated level of the water table inside the Ayen'et mountain is very unique. This aquifer is connected to the two major river systems in the region. All those who have been affected by this illness have been exposed to the water at one of the branches of this twin system. The compound that is being used has seeped into the underground water. It must be a poison that has reacted with the local minerals to form something even more dangerous. We need to put an immediate stop to the activities on that mountain. We do not have any other option."

47

Clouds partially shrouded the sky and drifted past the moon, hiding it from sight and plunging the valley into near darkness. The quiet gurgling of the river through the village provided a steady background din to make up for the absence of people, who had all retired for the night.

The medium-sized rectangular building on the eastern end of the valley had no windows as far as the five could tell. The logs used to build it appeared thoroughly seasoned, indicating that this was one of the older structures in the valley. With no signs of life, they couldn't tell whether it was the right building or not.

They headed for the door and Jag threw a questioning look at his friends. The others shrugged. Heaving a sigh, he reached up to knock, but before his knuckles could land on the wood, the heavy door swung open. Aesròn's unique green eyes and grinning face appeared and he ushered them in. The five, caught off guard, stumbled in as Aesròn closed the door behind them. "Welcome," he beamed.

The five looked around. Though it was older, the building was rather spacious and cozy. Overhead, large exposed log beams held up the roof. To the right of the entrance was a bar-like structure with a hot-stone grill behind it and a beverage rack against the wall. On the grill, slices of seasoned meat sizzled and an enticing aroma filled the air. In front of the five were six circular wooden tables with five chairs each. A couple of youths were sitting and watching three others playing musical instruments at the far left corner of the hall. A large, colorful rug was spread by the musicians' feet. The interior was brightly lit with a variety of oil lamps, some hanging from the overhead beams, others attached to the walls.

The two native girls in the building were wearing similar garb to that of the six boys: moose-hide shirt and pants with moccasin boots. Music filled the air and there was laughter all around. It seemed to be more like a party than a gathering.

At the opposite end of the room, two six foot tall torches stood on either side of a large wood-framed glass door. As the moon reappeared, the five could see a deck overlooking a steep drop that led to the plains beyond the valley. The friends were amazed.

Hutar came up beside Aesròn and greeted them. "You decided to come! Fantastic." He took Mariah's arm and Aesròn took Tegan's. The girls looked at each other with eyebrows raised but decided to go along. The two youths led the five to seats at the bar. Matikè was behind the counter and she smiled at the newcomers.

"What's the occasion here?" Jag asked, looking around again.

"We usually have this get-together once in a while," Aesròn answered. "It is just a gathering of friends."

"Seems like an interesting party."

Hutar and Aesròn glanced at each other with knavish grins and didn't reply to Jag's words. Hutar reached over and patted the younger teenager on the back. "How is your training going?" he asked instead.

The five took turns describing where they were in their training and how they felt about it. Aesròn nodded. "It is good to hear that you are progressing well." He leaned over the counter and received two drinks from Matikè. He took one for himself and passed the other to Hutar.

"Would you five like one of these beverages?" Hutar asked.

"What is it?" Tegan asked.

"Elýrnì—fermented drinks with a taste that dances delightfully on your tongue," he answered with a mischievous smile.

"Oh. No thanks."

The others declined as well. Hutar and Aesròn shrugged and consumed their drinks enthusiastically, then slammed their emptied mugs down on the counter at the same time with a laugh. Hutar turned to Matikè and spoke to her in their native tongue. She nodded.

"I told her to prepare some non-fermented drinks for you," Hutar explained to the five. "They should be ready in a moment."

"So this is the community hall?" Mariah asked.

"Well, it used to be. A new, bigger building was built closer to the temple, so everyone drifted toward that one. No one really bothers with this one anymore, so this is a den for the youths."

They continued with their casual chitchat until Hutar looked toward the three musicians. He stood and gestured for the five to follow him. The friends, along with Aesròn and Hutar, walked past the tables to get an up front view of the musicians.

One of the youths was playing an instrument that oddly resembled a mandolin, and another was keeping time on a hand drum. Beside them, a girl who was probably a year older than the five with her chestnut hair in a single braid, played a wind instrument like a set of Pan pipes. The music they made was cheery and upbeat, and the five felt energized listening to it. Soon toes were tapping and hands were clapping with the beat, and there were smiles and cheers across the room.

Hutar heard Matikè call from the bar. He nodded and turned to the friends. "Your drinks are ready and waiting," he smiled.

Kody was the first to take off. It didn't matter to him whether it was food or a beverage that was being served, because both were delicious when the villagers made it. He thanked Matikè as he took his drink, though he wasn't sure if she understood him. He faced the room and leaned back against the counter as his friends joined him and waited for Matikè to hand them their drinks. He gazed around and casually rotated his wrist, swirling the light-colored drink. He realized that the crowd had quieted down a little. He saw Hutar and Aesròn standing together and chatting, but as he narrowed his eyes slightly he saw that they were watching the five out of the corners of their eyes. There was an almost wicked, anticipative gleam in their stares as they saw Kody bringing his drink up to his mouth. Kody frowned slightly but thought, *Maybe they just want to see what we think of their drinks. It's probably delicious.*

As his mug passed under his nose, something made him stop with his drink halfway to his lips. He paused, trying to be absolutely certain, then put his mug down and turned just in time to see the others receiving their drinks and bringing them up for a swig.

"Stop!" he shouted. "Don't drink it!"

The entire hall stopped what they were doing; he didn't realize how loud he'd been. Aari looked at him. "What? Why?"

"Something's wrong with the drink."

"What do you mean?"

"It doesn't smell right." Kody pushed his own mug away.

Jag took a whiff from his cup. "I don't smell anything."

"Trust me, there's something wrong with it." Kody looked up as Hutar walked over.

"There is nothing wrong with the drinks, my friends," he said reassuringly.

"Yeah, I don't smell anything either." Tegan looked over at Kody. "What did you smell?"

"I picked up the scent of the poison that's contaminating the water," he answered.

"Hah!" Hutar smiled, although now Kody could see clearly that his smile was devoid of any humor. "Why would the poison be in your drink? And besides, we have heard that the contaminant is odorless."

"Nageau took me to Magèo's a few days ago as part of my training so I could take a whiff of the contaminated water. We wanted to see if I could scent it. I thought I did, but I wasn't sure. Until now." He glanced at his friends. "You guys have to trust me. That drink isn't safe."

Hutar's smile slowly fell and his eyes narrowed to slits. He motioned at Aesròn, who made his way over to the front door and bolted it shut. The other youths, including the musicians who had put down their instruments, made a loose ring around the five and Hutar. A chill filled the air. The five instinctively clustered together, forming a defensive circle. Kody was vaguely reminded that this was exactly how they had stood when facing the rabid wolves a few weeks ago.

Jag's mouth pulled into a flat line. "This isn't a party, is it?"

Hutar smirked. "You could say that it is a celebration for what is to happen."

Jag's stomach did backflips. "What do you mean?"

"You were supposed to take the drinks without a problem."

"So it really is poisoned?"

Hutar shrugged. "It does not matter now, because none of you will drink it. So we will have to deal with you ourselves."

As he spoke, the ring of youths stepped closer. Jag shepherded his friends to the door but were pushed back by two of the youths. Jag glared at them and tried to get past their blockade but was shoved away once more. He slowly walked back toward the youths, fists clenched until the veins in his arms stood out. "We're not looking for a fight," he said, his voice low.

One of the youths sneered. "What a shame." Before Jag could blink, the youth landed a hard cross-punch to his stomach. Gasping in pain, Jag doubled over, his insides churning. Kody rushed in to help but another youth thrust him away.

Jag felt the temper that he usually tried so hard to keep in check rise. "Punk," he spat. He lunged forward and tackled the youth, throwing several solid punches. Another youth came up behind Jag, his hunting knife drawn. He was about to plunge the blade into Jag's back when Tegan leapt forward and jammed her shoulder into the youth's upper body, throwing him off balance. As the other youths tried to move in to help, Mariah and Aari met each other's gazes. Mariah motioned with her eyes in the direction of the glass door that led to the deck. The two backed away slowly, then turned and made a break for the door.

Aesròn watched them from where he stood on the bar counter overlooking the scene. He crouched like a panther and made a fifteen-foot leap to one of the large tables across the room. From there, he launched himself against the wall to his left, momentarily clinging like a spider, and then bounded in front of the glass door in time to intercept Aari and Mariah. He gave them a menacing smile that chilled the two to their bones. "Going somewhere?"

At the other end of the building, it took three youths to pull the anger-ridden Jag away from their friend. They shoved him to the ground and one of the natives hooked his arm around Jag's neck, cutting off his breath. The youth who Jag had been punching sat up, wiping blood from his bottom lip and nose, then spat at Jag. Kody tried to jump in again to help but the girl who had been playing the wind instrument held him back with strength unexpected from someone her size.

"Why are you doing this?" Kody shouted to Hutar.

The building grew quiet as Hutar fixed his gaze on the other boy. It was obvious to see the abhorrence that was simmering within him as he looked at Kody. "Because," he said, "you do not belong here. There is no plausible way a ragtag group of *outsiders* are to be the ones to fulfill *our* prophecy. Handing you a right that could have only been for our people is blasphemy. It is taking away our traditions."

Jag, struggling for air, wheezed out, "It's not our fault your Elders think we're the ones."

"Hah! The Elders know nothing. They are old and flawed. Their minds are clouded with desperation for a savior, a miracle. They will take any coincidence and make use of it as much as they can. Senile, that is what they are. Senile, and therefore unreliable. A new group of Elders must come to get rid of these current incapable ones."

The five were stunned into silence by the contempt in Hutar's voice. Tegan stammered, "But they're your Elders! Everyone trusts them!"

"They follow the old ones blindly. They do not think for themselves. They do not realize that the Elders' old age is affecting their decision-making and is slowly corrupting the villagers' thoughts and poisoning our traditions. The people have two eyes, but they cannot see."

Kody was baffled. "The Elders are always thinking about what is best for the people. They're caring. They look out for you guys."

"Look out?" Hutar roared and lunged forward at Kody, delivering a right uppercut. Kody, caught by surprise, stumbled back against the wall and slid down. Hutar towered over him, nostrils flared, fists balled. "They killed off my family. I only ever knew my father and uncle. They were the only people I had in my entire life. When Tayoka could have saved my father, he refused." He paused, his eyes distant. "Of that four-man expedition the Elders sent out, my uncle did not return." He struck Kody in the stomach with his foot and the other boy rolled onto his side, shocked by the blow. "They killed the only people that ever mattered to me," he said, choked with grief and anger. "They need to be gotten rid of, just like you pests."

Jag, trying to worm his way out from the chokehold, was held down firmly by another youth who'd caught the boy's attempt to free himself. Short of breath, he managed to voice out, "What do you mean, 'be gotten rid of'?"

Hutar looked over at him, a disturbing smile slowly transforming his features. "We have poisoned the Elders' personal water supply," he responded, almost gleefully. "All they will have to do is take one drink and they will soon be choking out their last breath."

With the bombshell dropped, the five stared at Hutar in horror. Their mouths opened, but there were no words to describe their outraged thoughts.

"I have spoken enough," Hutar said. "Relsuc!"

One of the youths looked at Hutar and was addressed by his leader in their language. Relsuc grinned nastily and stepped toward Jag, unsheathing a knife from his belt. Jag started thrashing but the youth who was holding him in the chokehold was steady and didn't let him slip away. Jag glared at Relsuc. Relsuc fingered his blade, testing its edge, then sprang at Jag.

Out of nowhere, a heavy clay mug hurtled across the room and crashed into Relsuc's wrist, the force of the impact causing the mug to shatter into a thousand pieces. Relsuc screamed, dropping his knife, and clutched his wrist. His hand hung limp and he fell to his knees, sputtering curses.

Those who saw it happen were stunned into silence. At the other end of the room, Aari slowly turned to look at Mariah. She wore a cross look on her face but there was a smugness that gave away what she'd just done.

Kody, who'd been left unguarded after Hutar had kicked him, saw his opportunity and dove for Relsuc's knife. He grabbed it and rolled toward the youth holding Jag. He raised the knife as he got to his feet. "Let him go," he thundered furiously. The youth looked at Kody, distracted for a second, and Jag found his chance. He twisted out of the youth's grip and, in a fluid motion, delivered a roundhouse kick to his head. The training he had been undergoing had truly fortified his speed and strength. The impact knocked the youth back against one of the others, who held him. He hung his head, dazed and unsteady. Jag quickly retreated with a back somersault to the bar counter and crouched, hands on the edge, ready to spring into action again.

Aari, realizing everyone's attention was focused on Jag, jammed his elbow backward into Aesròn with all his might. He heard the youth gasp out heavily. Aari reached back, wrapped his arms around Aesròn's neck and flipped him over his shoulder. The youth crashed down on his back in front of Aari and Mariah. He lay there, winded.

Mariah, thinking quickly, focused on the two burning torches beside them and forced them to tip over onto Aesròn. A guttural cry was torn from the youth as the oil spilled onto his chest and the fire spread over him. He rolled around, howling in torment and fright as the fire spread to his upper body.

Seizing a chance, Mariah threw the glass door open and almost chucked Aari out onto the deck. "Go! Warn the Elders about their water!" she yelled before jumping away from the torches and Aesròn as he tried to grab her, even with his clothes on fire.

The village youths all watched Aesròn in flames, shock apparent on their faces. Matikè, who had stood rooted to the ground at what had just happened, broke out of her daze. She hurriedly grabbed a large container of drinking water and ran to Aesròn. As she dumped the water onto him, the oil and fire spread off Aesròn and onto the floor. Part of his face was blackened and his hair was mostly burnt off. His shirt was holed and smoldering.

The friends, minus Aari, gazed around at the faces of the youths. The natives' shocked expression twisted into one of pure vehemence. The youth who had exchanged blows with Jag earlier looked at Jag, who was still perched on the countertop. He bellowed and flew toward him. Jag braced himself and waited until the very last moment before rolling away. The youth was too far into his trajectory to change course and landed on the hot stone grill. He let out a cry of pain as he felt his palms and chest sizzle and his skin burn. He rolled off the grill, flailing, and landed roughly on his side.

Hutar missed that entire scene, transfixed as he was on Aesròn as Matikè tried to tend to him. Aesròn had grown to be Hutar's right-hand man. They were nearly alike; the way they thought, the way they carried themselves, the way they were usually undefeated. Seeing him downed was almost as if Hutar was seeing himself go down. The thought infuriated him. He looked past his two comrades and over at the fire that was beginning to spread to where Mariah was standing at the side of the hall.

"Witch," he hissed. He saw Tegan trying to make her way over to Mariah but a youth grabbed her hair and pulled her down to the ground. Hutar looked back at Mariah and saw her standing still, focusing. He couldn't afford another one of her tricks and tore toward her, leaping over Tegan and her captor on the floor. Tegan saw him coming and, with perfect timing, kicked up her legs from where she was pinned to the ground. Her action sent Hutar hurtling off his course as he crashed into Mariah. Mariah tried to scrabble away but Hutar managed to grab her feet and yanked her down.

Jag, who was crouched on the counter, saw Mariah in Hutar's grasp. In one bound he took off like a coiled spring and landed on Hutar, trying to wrestle him away from his friend.

While that was happening, Matikè pulled Aesròn away from the fire that was now burning toward the rug where the youths had been playing music earlier. The flames quickly jumped onto the wall and crept toward the log beams that held up the roof.

Matikè dragged Aesròn to safety beside Relsuc, who was still clutching his broken wrist near the front door. She looked around, seeing the four outsiders. She paused. There were supposed to be five. Then she realized that the glass door to the deck had been left unguarded. Barking at the other girl to follow her, she grabbed the bow and quiver that she'd stashed behind the bar and sprinted past the fire and through the open glass door to give chase to Aari.

Aari was racing like he never had before. "Gotta get to the Elders, gotta get to the Elders," he muttered, driving himself forward. *At least no one's following me.* Almost as if on cue, something whizzed past him, so close that he was sure it had nearly nicked his right ear. In a delayed reaction he stopped and ducked, then looked behind him. He could just make out two female forms running toward him. He knew he was being hunted and quickly bent double, making a run for the bridge leading to the other side of the village. The moon darted in and out of the thick clouds, casting a dim, gloomy light around him. Aari wished he was Jag, who was endowed with the power of speed, agility and strength. Though he could sense the marvelous physical training working to his benefit now, the two phantoms on his tail were relentless.

In the old community hall, Relsuc, Aesròn, and the youth who had been badly burned on the hot stone grill were sitting out the fight, much as it pained them to do so. The youth on whom Jag had landed a kick to the face had battled to remain conscious and won in the end. He was now trying to wrestle Kody to the ground. Kody was still holding Relsuc's hunting knife and was jabbing it at the villager to keep him away, saying "poke-poke-poke" with every jab and infuriating the youth.

Tegan managed to free herself from her captor after crashing a knee into his groin, causing him to limp away from her in retreat.

Jag had succeeded in pulling Hutar away from Mariah, but Hutar wouldn't let him win. With Hutar still pinned to the ground and Jag holding on to him from behind, the villager took a breath, coiling himself tight as the muscles in his arms rippled in preparation. He then pushed up with such force that he sprang vertically and left the ground with Jag still hanging on to his back. They crashed into a log beam above them, smashing Jag's back. Jag's grip on Hutar immediately loosened. Hutar landed on his feet and watched with satisfaction as Jag came crashing down to the floor and lay unmoving.

At the other side of the village, Aari was beginning to get lightheaded from running flat out as he shot past the gathering square, past the greenhouse and past the stable. He glanced over his shoulder and saw the two girls chasing after him. From their fast-paced, steady gait they didn't look anywhere near as tired as he was.

Another arrow whipped past Aari and he saw it bury itself deeply into a tree several yards ahead of him. At that point he decided it was best to duck between the trees instead of remaining on the straight path. He continued running until he saw the shapes of the *neyra* in the Elders' cluster. *Almost th—*

Something wrapped around his left ankle and he stumbled. "Oof!" He tried to shake free but saw that there were two spherical weights holding him down. *A bola!* he realized, panicking. It was the instrument that some of the people used to tangle up the legs of prey. It had only wrapped around one leg, though. As Aari got to his feet and started a limping run, one of his pursuers grabbed the back of his shirt but couldn't get a firm grip. He writhed away from her, hearing a frustrated hiss from the huntress behind him, and ran as fast as he could with the weight of the bola around his ankle. As the trees cleared he could see the Elders just walking into their *neyra*. "Wait!" he yelled, not sure if they could hear him.

The two phantoms chasing him came to a halt and looked at each other. They knew they couldn't catch Aari now without getting caught. Reaching a silent agreement, they turned and fled; not back toward the old community hall to warn their friends, but to sneak back into their shelters and pretend they were never a part of anything.

Aari saw Tikina just about to close her door and, with his legs on fire and hardly a breath left in him, charged to the door before it closed and shoved it inward. He tumbled into the shelter to see a very surprised Tikina looking at him. "Don't drink the water! Don't drink it!" he rasped before collapsing onto the floor, barely able to breathe.

Tikina dropped down beside him and called for Nageau. "Why should we not drink our water?" she asked, helping Aari sit up.

"There's poison . . . in . . . in the water," he panted, worsening the light-headedness. He tried to swallow but his mouth was too dry. ". . . In every single one of the Elders' *neyra*."

Tikina looked at her mate in alarm. Nageau looked back, then went to a secluded corner of the shelter. From there, he sent out a telepathic blast to the other Elders that stopped them immediately in their tracks. As he told his companions about the water, Tikina pressed Aari. "What is going on?"

"Old community hall . . . Hutar . . . he tried to poison our drinks." Aari could barely form coherent words. "There's a fight happening there . . . I don't know how the others are holding up . . ." He closed his eyes and collapsed back down from exhaustion.

In the community hall, Kody was keeping the youth he was tangling with at bay as he continued jabbing the knife forward. *Stalemate*, he thought. He needed to gain leverage. He chanced a quick look around and saw Mariah by herself standing against a wall, catching her breath. "Mariah!" he yelled. "Help!"

She looked up. When she saw him, she pushed herself away from the wall. Focusing on a chair that had fallen on its side, she willed it to move. The chair began to shake and the wobbling motion quickly grew. Then in the blink of an eye the chair launched itself across the room. But rather than hitting the youth, it nearly smashed into Kody. The chair shattered against the wall behind him, leaving her friend to stare at her in disbelief.

"Are you kidding me?" Kody roared. She shrugged apologetically. He stabbed the knife forward again as the youth tried to duck around to his other side. Out of the corner of his eye, he caught a motion and turned to look. Hutar was running at Mariah from behind, with a knife in his hand larger and deadlier than the one Kody was holding—and she didn't know the threat was fast approaching.

Without thinking, Kody threw his knife as hard as he could. The knife whipped straight past Mariah and buried itself in Hutar's right shoulder. Hutar stumbled back but held onto his own weapon. Mariah spun around. Realizing he had been about to stab her, she quickly moved away.

Kody had only half a moment to admire the amazing result of his throw before the youth he had been fending off seized him and threw him to the floor. He crouched over Kody, grabbed his neck, and started to choke him.

At the other end of the hall, Tegan saw Jag lying facedown, dangerously close to the spreading fire. She ran to him and knelt down, pushing his hair back to see that his eyes were closed. "Jag, come on." He didn't respond. She shook him frantically. "Jag!"

Taking matters into her own hands, she grabbed his arms and dragged him away from the fire as the flames licked closer and closer. As she pulled him, she heard a strange, cracking sound and looked up. The beam directly above them was on fire and the burning log was weakening its hold on the roof. "No," she murmured as she saw that the beam was about to give way. With a punch of adrenaline she pulled on Jag's arms, so hard that she may very well have pulled them right out of their sockets. She swung him across the floor and away from the fire just as the smoldering beam finally plummeted down where Jag had just been.

Twenty feet away, Mariah kept her eyes on her assailant. Hutar clenched his teeth and, with his left hand, pulled the knife out of his shoulder. Blood ran down his arm and dripped to the floor. Now wielding two blades, he slowly advanced toward Mariah, his breathing heavy and ragged, his face contorted in a murderous snarl.

Relsuc saw Tegan and Jag. He boomed at a youth in his own language. "Cretin! Take care of those two!" He was still cradling his limp hand as oaths flowed freely from his mouth. The youth he had given the order to approached Tegan and Jag from behind and landed a punch to Tegan's head. She fell forward, stunned for a moment, but staved off the pain and flipped onto her back, then sprang up to face the youth.

Hutar backed Mariah to the side of the bar. He held the two knives at chest level and spat, "No more of your little games, pest." Mariah looked around for something she could use to uneven the playing field to her favor, but the fire had destroyed any objects she could have used.

Hutar raised the knives over his head and brought them down. Mariah let out a bloodcurdling scream as she saw the tip of the knives aimed toward her chest.

Like a phantom appearing from thin air, a figure leapt in front of her, shoving Hutar's arms away and delivering a mighty kick to his abdomen that sent the youth sprawling back. Mariah covered her mouth and stared in disbelief. "Akol!" she cried. She leaned against the bar counter to steady herself. The burst of adrenaline left her head pounding and her entire body shaking.

There was a loud boom as the front door burst in and crashed to the floor, hinges and all. At the entrance now stood a man, straight as an arrow, with flaming red hair. And he didn't look pleased.

None of the youths had ever seen Tayoka look this intense as he surveyed the scene with indescribable fury in his storm-gray eyes. The youth who was choking Kody looked up at the Elder in fright and let go of the boy. Kody had passed out, though not before he saw Tayoka come through the entrance. He dropped unconscious with a smile on his face.

Relsuc cast his eyes downward; not in shame but in admission of defeat. He sat back against the wall and watched the fire slowly starting to move toward him. He would have rather been engulfed by the flames than face the Elders after this.

The youth who had been fighting Tegan as she stood guard by Jag had heard the boom of the door collapsing inward and turned to look. Upon seeing the Elder, he panicked and bolted toward the still-open door to the deck. His boots caught on fire as he made the headlong run but he didn't care to stop and hurtled out of the building. Tegan watched him go, utterly thankful. Seeing that the fire was drawing closer, she grabbed Jag's arms again and pulled him away.

Across from her, Akol was holding Hutar down. "You tried to kill the five and the Elders," he growled.

"Maybe I should have killed *you* first, maggot," Hutar spat. He tried to push Akol off but the other youth wouldn't allow Hutar room to maneuver away.

The fire had been spreading along the wooden beams and one directly above them creaked and groaned. Neither youth noticed; not until it started to come crashing down—all two hundred pounds of burning log—did Hutar see it. He let out a yell, eyes wide in terror as he saw the approaching beam. His terror turned into disbelief as the log came to a sudden stop, hovering in midair above Akol's head before it flipped on its side and crashed down a few feet away from the youths.

Tegan, who had seen it as well, looked at Mariah expectantly but Mariah shook her head. She hadn't acquired that level of skill yet. The girls looked around them to find an explanation. They found their answer when Saiyu strolled through the front door, wearing the same look of silent fury as Tayoka did. "Get out, all of you," she said in a fierce, icy tone.

As Hutar's comrades got to their feet and hastily exited the burning building, she added, "And I know all your faces. There is no hiding now." The youths couldn't look at her. They knew they would be severely punished for their part in attempting to murder not only the outsiders, but the Elders as well.

Mariah hurried to Kody and tried to lift him up. She managed to get him to stand by leaning him against her. Taking his arm and slinging it around her neck, she half-walked, half-dragged Kody out. Tegan tried to do the same with Jag, but Jag had bulked up with his training so she simply opted to drag him all the way out.

The two Elders in the building watched the fire with unreadable expressions. Their eyes landed upon Hutar and Akol. Akol still had Hutar pinned down but didn't look like he could hold out for much longer.

Tayoka strode toward them. Hutar saw the Elder coming. He stopped his struggling and looked away angrily. The Elder gazed down at him, embitterment written on his face. He hunkered down and looked Hutar in the eyes. "You have brought shame to your community, Hutar. Your father would have been utterly disappointed—and heartbroken." He reached for the dark blue crystal hanging around Hutar's neck and ripped it off. He then grabbed the youth by his collar and dragged him out of the burning building.

48

Taking a quick glance at the heavens as twilight finally fell upon the forest, Akira tucked her wings by her sides and dove through the clouds that hovered above the Ayen'et mountain. Vanishing for a few moments, she reappeared as she shot out from the bottom of the cloud and spread her wings, leveling off to a glide as the mining site came into view. What caught the eagle's eye was the large, roofed-over shed in the middle of the site. Curious, Akira flew lower. She didn't notice a man with auburn hair in a black coat gazing up at her as he headed to the shed, astonished at her proximity to the ground.

The sound of machines at work in the mine, though muffled due to the depth in which they operated, stood in stark contrast to the quiet, tranquil environment of the forest. The smell of fumes from the vehicles and equipment that were in use was an alien infusion to the freshness of the mountain air.

As she glided past the shed, Akira observed a few large vehicles that weren't in operation parked underneath. She did one loop of the hundred-foot outbuilding and returned to where she had started. Still gliding low, she passed a steel building on her right—the only steel structure in the area—then flew by a larger building beside it. Several men were sitting on benches and tables in an open space between that structure and another one with a large red cross on the front. They were too engaged in their conversation to take notice of the majestic bird swooping by. Passing by the building with the cross to the final one next to it that had light spilling out of glass windows, Akira peeked in and saw a few men, some in a line holding trays, others sitting down and eating meals.

Swooping to the left, she passed a large building that took up all of that side of the mining operation. Some miners were trudging into the building wearily, appearing as though they might fall asleep standing.

The eagle made another left turn and could now see a large tunnel opening on her right. She would have flown into it to take a look around if the sight of the five large, cauldron-shaped vats mounted on a raised platform hadn't caught her attention. She flapped once to gain some height and peered down into the vats. The vats were about fifteen feet in diameter and ten feet deep, holding what appeared to be crushed rocks.

As Akira flew around the vats to take a proper look, some miners walked out of the tunnel and saw her as she circled. They stopped and stared in awe, grinning. Deciding to give them something to remember, she shot up into the sky and hovered there for a moment before doing a one-eighty and rocketing back down some paces away from the men. At the last moment she opened her wings and soared by the miners with a screech, so near that the men felt the buffet of wind from her wings against their dirt-streaked faces. They stepped back, letting out calls of amazement as they watched the eagle fly around the vehicle shed and out of view.

Satisfied with her job, the eagle went around the back of the steel building into the tree line. She lighted upon a branch of a tree behind the benches and tables, observing the men who were still sitting and chatting.

In the Elders' assembly *neyra*, Nageau, Saiyu, Ashack, and Tayoka were sitting around the small fire pit, talking quietly as Tikina sat in a corner at a table with a quill in her hand and a scroll in front of her. Every once in a while her hand would move to draw as she gathered insight through the eyes of Akira as to how the mining operation on the Ayen'et mountain was laid out. With the eagle circling overhead, no one would ever fathom that she was part of a reconnaissance mission.

Still holding onto the mind-link with the eagle, Tikina looked around the area, wondering where Tyse was. The Elder had guided the lynx to the mountain earlier; she would need the animal's eyes for exploration at ground level. *Where are you, my elusive friend?* Tikina thought.

She flew Akira back behind the buildings again, trying to scout out the wandering rascal. Suddenly a head popped out of the trees right below the eagle, nose twitching as it sniffed the air, followed by a short, silverish-golden body.

There you are. Tikina landed Akira on the ground in front of the lynx, startling the larger animal. The moment both animals made eye contact, Tikina released her link with the bird and jumped into Tyse. She watched as Akira flew away from the mining site.

Tyse blinked once as Tikina readjusted herself to connect with the lynx's senses. Once she'd established a steady link with Tyse, she guided the animal toward the steel building. The lynx sniffed around, picking up an odd, unfamiliar smell. Obviously a creature had marked this as its territory, but she had no clue as to what animal.

As she sniffed around the back of the building, a disconnected, angry bray startled Tyse so horribly the animal hissed and retreated into the trees, ears pinned back. Tikina gently urged Tyse out again and steered the lynx clear away from the vicious, almost roar-like barks that came from within the steel building.

Tikina wanted to get a closer look at the vats and directed the thick-furred cat in their direction. The lynx prowled around the dark gray metallic cauldrons, keeping her belly low as she weaved in and out under the platforms. A worker walked out of the mine tunnel and saw her. He stopped and stared, unsure whether he should be amazed or worried that the cat might disrupt the refining process in the vats. In the end he decided the latter and shooed Tyse away, but wisely kept his distance from the wild animal. Tyse bounded a few steps back and watched him walk away from the tunnel before sneaking into the tunnel herself. The sound of the machines was painfully loud to her ears but Tikina held the lynx steady. Tyse skulked over the metal tracks, sniffing this and that and taking in the layout of the tunnel.

A couple of the men yelled out when they spotted her. The cat's ears twitched and she stopped to look at them. A few of the workers looked delighted at the sight of a wild creature this close, but others grabbed their shovels and chased her away. Tyse scooted off to the next tunnel beside the main one. This tunnel appeared abandoned. She only went in a little way before coming back out and turning into the doorless storage areas where the spare tools were kept. Tyse halted at the front of the door that lay at the far end of the storage area, head cocked to one side. Tikina sensed an overpowering feeling come over her as she stared up at the door through the lynx's eyes. Though she could not explain how she knew, she realized that this must have been where Rikèq, Aydar, Keno and Breyas were held captive during their imprisonment. Sadness filled her heart as she turned Tyse away and walked her out of the tunnel.

At the other side of the camp, a guard had walked into the steel building. Night was falling quickly, and it was time for the Marauders to come out.

Tikina led Tyse directly onto the path back to where she had linked with the animal. As she rounded the shed, she saw the front door of the building open and five massive, canine-like creatures step out, hackles already raised. They immediately turned to stare in her exact direction.

The lynx balked as Tikina stared at the creatures in terror. She had never seen such vicious-looking beasts, with fur as black as the night and ivory teeth so long they curved down slightly from their elongated upper jaws. As their hungry, bloodlusting eyes landed upon the lynx, they snarled and gave chase.

Tikina, thoroughly frightened, let some of Tyse's flight instincts take over as she veered the cat around. Tyse hightailed back to the entrance of the dark, abandoned tunnel and scampered in. She could hear the sounds of the beasts' panting and their snapping jaws behind her, much too close for comfort. She sped down the tunnel as fast as she could. Jumping up and over some collapsed wooden beams and rubble, she spied a large entrance at one side of the tunnel. Without giving it a second thought the lynx sprinted out of the opening and found herself stumbling down the side of the mountain. She flailed her paws until her claws hooked into the dirt, then, using the momentum she had gathered, propelled herself down the mountain, not looking back until she reached the bottom.

Once at the foot of the mountain, the cat flopped down by a tree, panting, energy spent. Using the lynx, Tikina looked up at the peak in the fading light. She could hear the faint but irritated howls of the beasts she had left behind.

This will not be as easy as I had hoped. Taking a final look at the mountain, Tikina released the link with Tyse. She withdrew back into her own mind and looked down at the parchment sitting before her on the table. The map of the mining site seemed accurate enough. Lifting the paper in one hand, she stood and walked toward the other Elders. They looked up at her, curious.

"There is much preparation to be done," she told them, showing the map.

Nageau took the parchment from her and examined it. He nodded slowly. "Then let us get started."

Tikina grabbed his arm before he could turn away, fear evident in her delicate features. "Wait." She took in a small breath. "There is something else I must tell you . . ."

49

It was midmorning and the villagers had quickly settled into the village square. They wondered what more news was to be brought to them by the Elders, who had called for this gathering in haste. The Elders watched them. Calm as they seemed, there was urgency in the air around them and their kin could feel it. The five were sitting at the very front with Akol, who would quietly translate the Elders' words for the five as they were spoken.

"My friends," Nageau said. "There are a couple of matters that we must speak off. Firstly, I presume some of you may have heard about an incident that occurred two nights ago, and some of you may have even seen the burnt-down hall at the edge of the village. I do not wish to dwell on those details right now, but yes, these were acts committed by some of our youths. It is despicable and shameful. We shall be dealing with them soon enough." He glanced down at the five, noting the bruises some of them wore. "There is something I would also like to add. That same night the building burned down, the Elders' water supply was found to have been poisoned with the contaminant which has made many of our people fall devastatingly ill."

A gasp rose from the crowd. "Was it the same hoodlums that burned the building who did this?" one man called out, outraged.

The Elders had agreed beforehand that they would not be pointing fingers at Hutar and his comrades just yet, not with bigger issues at hand. "It does not matter," Nageau answered. "The act was done. But the important thing is, none of the Elders consumed the poison—because our guests here warned us in time, thus saving our lives." He motioned to the five with a sweep of his hand.

The crowd peered over each other's heads to look at the five sitting at the front. Their faces expressed their gratitude with awed looks and smiles. The friends would have rather ducked out of view, but they sat tall and dipped their heads at the Elders. Murmurs of praise flowed through the crowd and Akol smiled as he told the friends what the community was saying about them.

"The next matter that we must speak to you about is one of utmost importance, so please listen carefully . . ."

The five sat in silence with the rest of the crowd, gleaning what the Elders were speaking about through Akol. They learned about the mining operation that sat atop the Ayen'et mountain, and discovered that the Elders had done a good deal of exploration. They had even worked on a plan throughout the night to end their quandary. Small wonder they seemed tired.

"We are not a warlike people, but our hand has been forced," Nageau said, scanning the expression of the villagers. "Now we need to stand up if we are to protect our community and our loved ones."

"We will need twenty volunteers with the right skills. We have planned for a mission that requires more stealth and less force," Tayoka told the crowd. "If you are skilled in this area, you are welcome to join us."

Far more than twenty villagers put up their hands, resolve and fierceness painted on their faces. This was *their* home; *their* people who were dying from the terminal illness spread by the miners. They would not stand for it. This trouble that was causing them to lose their kin—their family—needed to be halted and the villagers were determined to stop it any way they possibly could.

The large show of hands warmed the Elders' hearts; however, they had deemed that only twenty would join them in their plan. They handpicked the twenty villagers from those who were eager to volunteer. When they had counted the exact number needed, Ashack said, "To those who have been chosen: Meet with us at the temple once you have had your midday meals. There we will discuss the plan in further detail and get you prepared for what is to come."

* * *

Ajajdif sat with his mining engineer in his office. It was lunch time, but the chief of Quest Mining would not eat until he knew how the operation was coming along. Since speaking with the boss, he had been driving his crew harder than usual. "Progress report," he demanded brusquely, tossing and catching a stress ball that was painted blue and green, like the Earth.

LeChamps checked his tablet. "We will be back on schedule in the next two or three days if everything keeps running as smoothly as it is now. I think that we'll have the required amount needed by the end of four weeks."

"Lovely." Ajajdif squeezed the small foam orb. "Can I suppose that we'll be out of here in the next month?"

"Possibly," LeChamps smiled. "Progress has been great as of late."

"Good."

"We're going to need those leaching chemicals soon, though. We're running out of them pretty quickly."

"I spoke with HQ a couple days ago, and they said they'd send a bird in with the chemicals."

"A couple days ago? Shouldn't they have already been here, then?"

Ajajdif stood and went to pick up an eight-inch crystal sculpture of the Russian priest Rasputin from a shelf. He held it in his palm, looking at it with a pang of nostalgia. "I got an email from Adrian yesterday," he said, responding to LeChamps. "He said there was some kind of mix-up with the pilot's schedule, but the cargo should arrive sometime tomorrow morning. I want you to tell your foreman to have a crew ready when the plane comes so that they can unload the drums and other supplies."

"I'll tell him that."

Ajajdif stood up and grabbed his coat. "Have you had lunch yet?"

LeChamps shook his head. "Nope. I was planning to after this."

"Well, I'm heading to the mess hall, so let's go." Ajajdif waited for the mining engineer to step out of his office before closing the door and locking it.

* * *

Aari, Jag, Mariah, Tegan, and Kody were sitting side by side facing the river, on the opposite bank from where the gathering square was. The villagers had dispersed soon after the meeting had ended, though some lingered to talk with the Elders or express their thanks to the five for saving the Elders from the poisoned water. Some of the youths tried to worm out of them what had happened in the old community hall but Akol, who was translating, ushered them away good-naturedly.

Aari leaned back on his elbows and stared into the distance. In a faraway voice he asked, "What did you guys think of today's gathering?"

"Too many big things are happening at once," Tegan answered. "Hutar's attack, the illness, the recent loss of villagers, our training, and now this plan of the Elders to infiltrate and shut down the mining site. It's a lot to take in."

"I'd like to be part of the plan the Elders laid out, actually," Kody said from where he was lying on his back beside Tegan. His friends looked to him to continue his thought. "I mean, in a way, they're kind of like our people now. And we've been training with our powers. Maybe we could lend a hand."

"We haven't even been training for a month, Kody," Mariah said. "Even though the Elders have said that we've been progressing well, what can we do? We're just a bunch of kids."

"Just a bunch of kids with *powers*," Kody cackled.

"They're not exactly powers, remember? More like innate skills."

"It doesn't matter. Whatever it is, we have it. And I'd really like to put them to the test."

"I don't think we'll be allowed to go," Aari said. "Besides, the Elders have picked their twenty volunteers already."

"Thanks, killjoy," Kody grumbled.

"Am I really a killjoy for stating a fact, or are you just a sour-puss?"

"The second one." Mariah laughed. "I'm still kind of in shock that not everyone in this valley is as nice as we thought."

"There are always a few rotten apples in the basket," Tegan sighed. "Rotten apples that look so good on the outside."

Aari snorted. "You're such a girl." That earned him a smack on the head. "Oy!"

Jag flopped back and stared up at the cloudy sky. "I can't believe I'm saying this, but I'm itching to train again. This is the third day we haven't been able to because the Elders are so busy."

"Let's spar," Tegan said suddenly.

"What?"

"Sure we can't really progress with training our powers, but we can practice the defense techniques they've shown us."

Jag bolted up to his feet, his face beaming. "Alright. Let's go, you and me."

Tegan hooted in delight and the two moved off and began sparring. Mariah, now left between Aari and Kody, asked, "You guys up for a match?"

"Sure." Aari got up, then looked at Kody. "You coming?

"Just call me when she beats you to the ground," Kody answered, and closed his eyes for a short snooze.

* * *

Farther up the valley, the Elders took a seat on some divans in the temple as they waited for their twenty volunteers to arrive. Tayoka was absently using his foot to rock the top of a box full of gadgets that Magèo had brought to them for the mission. Without realizing it, he tipped the box too far and some of the devices toppled out. The other Elders looked over and Tayoka shot them a sheepish grin as he hastily picked up the gadgets and put them back in the box. Among the things he gathered were several fibrous coils that the people referred to as active vines. They were capable of binding an adversary's hands or legs much like a handcuff, except the coils would self-activate upon contact.

Once Tayoka had put the items back in the box, he turned back to the others. They had already decided that each Elder would lead a group of four to execute the plan up on the mountain. Nageau and his team would coordinate the attack from a vantage point up on the mountaintop. Ashack and his group would enter through the abandoned tunnel, while Saiyu and her team would approach from the east near the beasts' building. Tayoka would lead his team from the north and take position at the edge of the mountain behind what Tikina had described as the building where food was served to the miners. Finally, Tikina herself would be stationed behind the largest building—the workers' barracks—at the western edge of the site, with her group.

As they were discussing this, a thought that had been on Tikina's mind since the night before surfaced. She mulled over it for a while before stating, "I think the five should come with us."

The men turned to look at her, surprised. "Really?" Tayoka asked. "You truly wish to take them on *this* mission?"

"Yes. I have been thinking about this since we began planning the mission yesterday." She lightly scratched her cheek. "At first, I thought it was reckless, but a feeling has been nagging me. Something inside me is telling me that they must come. Everything that is happening is happening for a reason. The younglings are not here by accident. Destiny's role for them is unfolding, even as we speak."

"I agree."

The men whipped their heads around to look at Saiyu, all of them wide-eyed at the two words she'd spoken.

"The Elders who were most concerned for the five would like to speed up their endangerment?" Nageau asked, bewildered.

"That is certainly not our intent, but I sincerely believe that they have a role to play in this," Tikina said firmly.

“I do not know.” Ashack met the eyes of the women. “Their training is not yet complete. What if they cannot handle what happens at the mountain?”

“Tsk, such pessimism.” Tikina smiled, trying not to show that she, too, was anxious.

“We must have confidence in them,” said Saiyu softly. “If they can handle this with their training still in progress, imagine what they can accomplish once they *have* finished.”

The Elders looked at each other, then at Nageau. He raised his eyes and met their gazes. “Perhaps they are right,” he said, beginning to nod slowly. “Perhaps this is what we should do. If this is what the silent voice inside us prompts, then it shall be so.”

50

Nageau lay prone at the edge of a clearing at the top of the Ayen'et mountain. From that vantage point, he had a bird's eye view of the mining site four hundred feet below. The muffled sound of the machines at work in the tunnel directly below him was barely audible. It was still dark but Nageau knew the sun would rise soon.

The lack of light made it hard to see the site. Nageau pressed his forefingers against his temples and paused, waiting until his low-light vision kicked in. When he scanned the site, he was now able to see the buildings and the miners shuffling about as their shifts changed.

Focusing once more, he activated his detail vision, bringing distant objects into sharp relief. He was mildly surprised by how accurate Tikina's sketch of the site had been. He could see the big vehicle shed located at the center of the level area. To his left, along the western flank, was a large building that Tikina had identified as the miners' barracks.

Looking to his right he saw two small buildings erected away from the others. Even after a few reconnaissance missions with Akira, Tikina said that hardly anyone was seen walking in and out of those structures, save for a man with auburn-colored hair.

Nageau felt a tug on his arm and looked back. Kody was sitting cross-legged on the ground beside him. Behind them were four villagers who were also seated in readiness. Kody took a quick look down the mountain and saw the four-hundred foot drop. "Daunting," he muttered. "How much longer do we have to wait?"

Nageau nodded at the sky. "Until it brightens a little more. Tikina told us that the beasts are usually put away at first light."

"She never did say what the beasts were."

"That is because they are like no other creature she has ever seen." Nageau looked back down and scanned the site in silence for a couple of minutes. Then he stiffened. "Kody, come. I think those are the creatures."

Kody slithered closer to the Elder and stared down. "I can barely see a thing," he said, keeping his voice low.

"Remember what I taught you, youngling. This is a wonderful opportunity to use the skills you have learned."

Kody rubbed his eyes and squeezed them shut for a few moments. In the stillness, he felt a brightening in his mind's eye. When he opened his eyes again he could see what lay below them almost as clearly as if it were in daylight, except for a bluish glow in his sight. "Wow," he murmured. His gaze skimmed over the site. He saw something on the left side of the vehicle shed that frightened him even from this distance. "Found the beasts. They're like really big, really muscular dogs . . . Wait—" His vision zoomed in on one of the beasts as it turned around. "Those jaws look like they belong to a velociraptor!" He shuddered. "What are they?"

Nageau quickly shushed him. "I do not know, but Tikina has said that these creatures have incredibly keen senses. There must be a reason why they are only brought out during the night."

One of the villagers sitting behind them, a man who possessed the omnilinguistic ability, was listening to their conversation. "If you can see those beasts now, why can we not put them away for good?" He held up a crossbow and quiver with immobilizing darts attached to the tips of the arrows. The regular darts were meant to immobilize a person or animal for no longer than a few minutes, but among the other weapons and contraptions he had designed for this mission, Magèo had created these new darts that were higher in dosage. These could potentially kill if the bodies of the targets were unable to handle the increased quantity of tranquilizer delivered by the darts.

Nageau looked back down. "There is a burly man with the creatures. If we strike the beasts now, he will notice and most likely sound an alarm."

"I cannot wait to let these arrows fly," the villager said, gently shaking his quiver. "These *men* down there are destructive and are not above murdering our friends."

"We are not looking to kill these men," Nageau said sharply.

"Of course not. But I believe we have the right to give them something to remember us by."

The Elder wore a wry grin. "Oh, I think we will."

"Will we have a chance to get down to the site?" Kody asked.

"Not unless the others cannot handle it. We are their eyes up here."

"Where are the others, anyway?"

Nageau indicated to his left. "Tikina and her group will emerge from behind the miners' barracks." He pointed straight ahead. "Tayoka will emerge from behind those buildings with his team." He then pointed to his right. "And finally, Saiyu will proceed from behind that lone building."

"And Elder Ashack?"

"His group will be coming through the tunnels."

After that, not a word was spoken as everyone waited. Nageau and Kody watched the miners go about their business. Nageau was watching a couple of the workers when Kody whispered, "I think that guard is taking the animals back."

Nageau's eyes cast around until they found the large man walking behind the four creatures. The animals slunk toward the single steel building and soon they and the guard disappeared inside.

"Is it time to signal the others?" Kody asked quietly.

"No, not yet." Nageau watched the steel door like a hawk until it opened again and the burly man walked out. He made his way to the large building where the workers went to grab their meals.

Kody's eyes trailed the guard until he was out of sight. "Now?" he whispered.

The Elder exhaled and nodded. "Now."

Down in the abandoned tunnel, Ashack and his group were seated on the beams of the partially collapsed underpass. The Elder looked around, noting how accurate Rikèq's description of the place was. Without telling the others, he had searched around the rubble and debris earlier for the remains of the two men who had died there. He had found nothing except for a single torn moccasin boot.

As he looked around, Nageau's voice entered his mind. *Ashack, they have put the creatures away.*

Good. We are on our way.

Ashack motioned to the villagers, who were waiting patiently. They quickly got to their feet, grabbing their packs with the items Magèo had sent them off with, and hastened up toward the other end of the tunnel that opened to the mining site. Some of the men stuck green cube-shaped gels the size of their palms onto the sides of the tunnel where the wall appeared less sturdy. The cubes contained high-impact explosives. They had three indents on one side of the surface that were designed to function as timers. The villagers pressed the third one down, which set the cubes' delay mechanism for two hours, the longest setting available. Once the time expired, the cubes would explode, causing the tunnels to collapse. The plan was that Ashack's group would have completed their tasks and escaped before the devices timed out.

Aari jogged beside his mentor up the sloping tunnel until they could hear and feel the slight vibrations of the tunneling machine in the other tunnel. Ashack poked his head out of the opening. To his left was the miners' supply storage, just as Tikina had described it. To his right he could see the tunnel that was being mined. Retreating back into the abandoned tunnel, he silently pointed at two of the men. The men, who knew their roles, crept forward, staying in the shadows. Ashack and Aari followed. Right inside the entrance of the mining tunnel were two parked machines—Bobcats, Aari realized. The four of them crouched, hidden by the darkness of the tunnel and the cover that the machines provided.

Two workers in coveralls were across from them, shoveling ore onto a conveyor belt. They had their backs to Aari and the villagers. Ashack gently urged the two men out into the open. As the men cautiously walked toward the workers, Aari and Ashack focused their minds to bend the light around them, causing the villagers to vanish from sight.

A couple of Bobcats were rotating around as they lifted and dumped the heavy chunks of ore for the workers to scoop onto the conveyor. The workers continued with the job at hand, oblivious to their surroundings. Suddenly, they both felt something grab them around their necks from behind. They tried to twist around to face their assailants but saw nothing. The villagers, still invisible as far as anyone could tell, performed a rear chokehold on the miners. The miners dropped unconscious in their arms. The villagers hurriedly dragged their bodies to the abandoned tunnel and switched clothes with the miners. Ashack and Aari released the two from invisibility and joined them in the other tunnel.

Suddenly they heard one of the workers from the other tunnel shouting into his radio. "Joe! Grant! Where are you guys?"

Aari turned to the villagers who were hastily putting on the coveralls. "I think one of the miners inside is looking for those two," he whispered.

The men nodded. They pulled on the respirator masks and hardhats, then strolled back to the mining tunnel. The worker who had called out was a man in one of the two Bobcats. "You guys tried to sneak off for a smoke again, didn't you?" Aari heard him say accusingly. The villagers said nothing, but one of them raised his hand to put the worker at ease. They picked up the shovels the miners had been using and continued scooping ore onto the conveyor belt.

Ashack turned to the other two men from his team and nodded. They snuck out to repeat the process. Aari, with the extra confidence he'd earned when helping Ashack cover for the first two villagers, focused to bend the light away from the second pair.

One of the Bobcat drivers was returning to the conveyor belt with the machine's loading bucket full. He squinted when he saw something shimmering directly in front of his machine. He blinked quickly but saw nothing now. Shrugging, he thought, *Milroy, you've gotta quit drinking when you're this tired from work. It screws with your head, buddy.*

Suddenly he saw the shimmer again and almost let out a yell when a face appeared out of thin air in front of the Bobcat. Aari, hiding in the shadows near the entrance of the tunnel, scolded himself. Quickly regaining his focus, he bent the light around the villager again and the man disappeared once more. The worker tried to scramble out of the Bobcat, but was instead dragged out onto the ground as soon as he stepped out of his machine. The villager stuck an immobilizing dart into the man's arm, knocking him out, and quickly dragged him away to exchange garments.

The driver of the second Bobcat turned his machine around to head over to the conveyor belt and saw the other machine idling with no one in it. "Mil, you jerk," he muttered. "Where the hell did you go?" He sat back, impatiently waiting for the other driver to return so he could dump his load. As he waited, he felt the hairs on the back of his neck rise as he became aware that he wasn't alone. He turned to his left and bleated in surprise when he saw a large, tan-skinned man with a bald head and a long scar running from the side of his temple to his jaw. The next thing he knew he was pulled out of the Bobcat and slammed onto the ground. He felt something sharp stab through his coveralls and into his skin. In moments he was unconscious and the snickering villager hauled him into the other tunnel.

Saiyu and her team were crouched some ways down the eastern flank of the mountain, reviewing their plan. Mariah had become quick friends with a seventeen-year-old girl with rosy cheeks and ice-blue eyes. She and her twenty-year-old sister had volunteered to plant an incendiary device among the barrels of leaching compound that had been found stored away behind a rock wall next to the conveyor belt.

The girl held up a pyramid-shaped gel to her face. "This will not affect us when it erupts, will it?" she asked in her language.

"No," Saiyu assured her. "But you will not want to be around it when it does."

Saiyu, the Elder suddenly heard in her head. *You may proceed.*

Will do, Nageau. Thank you. Saiyu nodded at her team. Besides the two sisters, there were two men in the team, one of whom was blind in one eye and wore an eye patch.

Saiyu cautiously led them up to the mining site and they remained hidden in the tree line as a guard holding a rifle strolled by. They watched him walk into the open-faced building.

Saiyu saw their opportunity and quietly ran across the open space to the vats, the rest of the team following close behind. They crept under the platforms that held up the vats and tiptoed to the four-foot wide entrance to the left of the main tunnel. A moving belt snaked from the mining area, carrying mounds of rocks to a machine where they were crushed, and another belt carried crushed ore to the vats outside.

The team risked a peek through the opening. A worker stood only a few feet away with his back to them. Another worker stood beside the conveyor belt not too far in front of the first man, directing a cone-shaped device attached to a rotating cuff so it could swivel from side to side to prevent the rocks from piling up in one spot. Mounds of ore were piled up to seven feet in height.

The team couldn't see the actual hydraulic crusher as depicted in Tikina's sketch, but they still knew where it should be; toward the left side of the chamber, if they could only see further in. Saiyu gestured for her team to step back from the opening and looked at them. "There should be four other workers inside. We want to try to keep this as quiet as possible, but if one of them makes any loud noise, by all means silence them. If one of them attempts to escape, do what you must." She looked at each member of her team. "Is everyone ready?"

They looked both nervous and excited as they nodded. Saiyu smiled. "Then go!"

The two men on the team crawled under the conveyor belt. The first one, a freckly villager known as "The Spring"—as he was constantly jumping around with exuberant energy—immediately pounced on the closest worker and slapped a hand over his mouth.

Before the worker could react, The Spring stuck an immobilizing dart into his arm and the miner fell limp.

The man operating the cone-shaped spreader must have sensed the commotion behind him. He turned and saw his co-worker on the ground. A stranger dressed in buckskin stood over his co-worker, grinning. It was a genuine, disarming smile, as innocent as a child's. Nevertheless, the worker charged at the intruder. As he neared the trespasser, he felt a thud on his chest. He stumbled and dropped to the ground, unable to move any part of his body. The last thing he saw before blacking out was the dart that had pierced his coveralls, protruding from his chest.

Four other miners continued working behind the mounds, unaware of what had just happened, as Saiyu and the three other adults in her team stealthily climbed over the mounds and disappeared.

Mariah stayed behind with the seventeen-year-old and they peeked inside from the opening. They heard only sounds of machinery for a minute, and then a couple of deep voices shouting out in English before being silenced abruptly.

Mariah tucked her hair behind her ear and deliberated over entering the crusher area. Making a quick decision, she tugged the arm of the girl beside her. The girl looked over at her and saw Mariah crawl under the conveyor belt and into the crusher area. She followed eagerly, obviously wanting to get a glimpse of the inside too. They carefully stepped over the first worker that had been rendered unconscious, then looked around. There were battery-powered lamps hanging around the area, providing illumination so that the workers wouldn't have to constantly use the lamps on their hardhats.

Mariah heard a buzzing noise and turned her head to look for the source. It was the spreader attached to the conveyor. It was still swiveling. As she watched it, she realized that no one had moved the unconscious worker who had been manning the spreader—and the spreader was about to unload large amounts of rocks onto him. She would never reach him in time.

Thinking quickly, she stared at the spreader and tried to focus. Her breathing became panicked when she saw that the cone-shaped device was still moving. She pleaded with herself to concentrate, and slowly but steadily the spreader started to swivel away. She sighed in relief and pushed the swivel as far back as it could go, then ran to the worker who was lying in the dirt. She grabbed his hands and started to pull him away.

"Why are you so blasted heavy?" she grumbled, though she knew he couldn't hear her.

The rosy-cheeked girl watched, then quickly ran up to Mariah and grabbed one of the man's arms, and together they dragged him next to the first worker.

The girls only had to wait for a few moments more before the others returned, each carrying an immobilized worker. They placed the men next to a passageway that connected the mining tunnel to the crusher area and bound them up. The two men then picked up the workers lying at Mariah's feet and slung them over their shoulders to bind them with their co-workers.

"Good job so far, everyone," Saiyu said encouragingly. She nodded at the sisters. "Your turn. The barrels are against the wall behind the mounds."

"May I see what they do?" Mariah asked.

The Spring, who was omnilinguistic, translated and Saiyu granted her permission. Mariah quickly clambered over one of the mounds. She slipped on the way down to the other side and tumbled forward, hitting the solid rock wall with the full force of her body. She groaned and pulled away, then stumbled after the sisters, trying to regain her balance.

When she reached them, they had already planted the incendiaries into four of the chemical barrels. The barrels were painted an innocuous green in an apparent attempt to conceal the deadly poison they carried. The sisters pried open the tops of the barrels before setting the timers on the devices. They carefully placed the green pyramids point-side up into the rest of the barrels. Mariah watched the incendiaries sink to the bottom of the liquid in the barrel. Saiyu had said that once they were set, they were not designed to blow up like ordinary explosives. Rather, they would erupt in an intense flame so hot it would melt steel in an instant and would incinerate any object on which it was placed.

The younger of the two sisters pulled Mariah away from the barrels. The girls quickly scaled the mounds and made their way back over to the adults. Mariah looked at the six workers in the passageway. "They won't get hurt, right?" she asked.

The Spring shook his head. "They will be fine. The fire is intense but focused. It will not reach that far."

Saiyu took a quick look around to ensure everything was set, then led the way back outside. They crouched under the vats, eyes peeled for any sign of threats, then bolted back toward the trees. Their footsteps were quiet, but to Mariah it seemed as if they were giants pounding on the ground; she winced every time her foot landed on the earth, certain someone must have heard their collective footfalls.

They did not stop running until they were far behind the tree line. Mariah sat down on the root of a tree, panting. It was much cooler out here than among the noisy and dusty machines in the tunnel, and she was grateful for that. "So what now?" she asked the others.

"We wait," Saiyu answered. "If everything goes as planned, then we will not be needed any further."

51

The villager whom Aari had been covering for had already switched clothes with the miner he had captured. He tied the captive with an active vine which coiled around the worker's wrists instantly, binding them together. The villager then tied a cloth over the mouth of the unconscious miner.

At the far end of the mining tunnel, two groups of five miners each worked on either side of the loud tunneling machine, scooping ore into mounds behind them for the Bobcats to collect. But the machines were not returning. One of the miners working beside the tunneling machine looked back. He wiped the dust off the visor of his air-supplying respirator. Though he could barely see over the mounds, he caught sight of the Bobcats' yellow roll cages as they sat idling. He nudged the worker beside him and the worker looked up questioningly, not wanting to remove his ear plugs and ear muffs and expose his ears to the jarring sound of the tunneling machine.

The first worker pointed to the idling Bobcats and turned his hand palm-up in a questioning gesture. The other worker shrugged disinterestedly and returned to his job. The first miner contemplated asking the tunneling machine operator's assistant about the Bobcats, but decided not to bother her as she walked around the tunneling machine, constantly checking it to ensure that everything was running as it should. Casting another look at the Bobcats, the miner returned to work as well.

There was no way he would have been able to spot the six outsiders—four of whom wore coveralls identical to the miners'—as they crept deeper into the tunnel and approached the tunneling machine with their packs on their backs, making sure to stay bent so they wouldn't be spotted over the mounds of ore.

The villagers reached the mounds and remained hidden. One of them, covered by Ashack, stood and looked over the heaps of ore. "We will have clear shots at three of the miners on the left, and three on the right," he informed the others.

Aari and the men quickly wound their miniature crossbows, which were especially designed for close-quarter combat situations. They set their immobilizing darts on the weapons' grooves, then stood up and took aim over the mounds. The darts were released and each one impacted successfully, penetrating the workers' coveralls. Within seconds the six men had all dropped like flies. The group grinned at each other. They ducked back down as the other miners spun around and caught sight of their fallen comrades. The miners saw the darts protruding from their fallen comrades' clothes and scanned around, knowing that there was an imminent threat.

The villager who Aari had covered for turned to him and smiled as he pulled a respirator mask over his face. "Do not lose me this time."

Aari looked back, embarrassed. "I'll try."

Ashack motioned to the four men. They nodded. Bending their knees and bouncing a little, they leapt up and flipped, landing on the far side of the mounds with perfect form. The workers saw them but were confused. All they could see were four men in coveralls with hardhats and respirator masks. But when they spotted the bows the four were holding, they realized the threat. The miners faced the four men, shovels in hand. With the lights from the workers' hardhats now shinning directly at the villagers, Aari and Ashack cautiously peeked from behind the mounds and deflected the light. The men shimmered, and then disappeared.

One of the workers nearly dropped his shovel. "*What?*"

The last four miners and the machine operator's assistant stared at where the intruders had stood just a moment ago. "What happened?" the operator's assistant stuttered. "Where did they go?"

No answer was given. The workers only felt the stab of the darts into their arms before the numbness spread throughout their bodies and to their heads, causing them to black out.

The machine operator's assistant stood frozen, not knowing what to make of the invisible threats. She wanted to flee to safety, but didn't know where the ghosts were lurking. She needn't worry too much, because a dart pierced through her protective clothing and into her skin. A moment later, she fell limp and the invisible force that caught her gently placed her to one side of the machine.

The bald villager with the long scar looked up at the tunneling machine. He was glad he had the earplugs and earmuffs to wear; the noise was intense. He noted the operator standing on a platform at the back of the drill, oblivious to what had happened to his colleagues. As the villager watched, the operator suddenly arched and reached behind his shoulders where a dart was lodged, then collapsed in a heap on the platform, unconscious.

Someone tapped the villager's shoulder from behind. He looked over to see one of his kin beside him. Picking up that they were no longer being covered, he nodded as the other villager pointed to either side of the machine where two men equipped with back-pack sprayers and respirators were spraying the rocks and dirt in front of the tunneling machine. The workers, clad in smooth suits covering their entire bodies, had not yet noticed that the mammoth machine, though still running, was no longer moving.

The villager with the long scar nodded at the other man. He crept up behind the worker on the left side of the tunneling machine and paused behind the man, observing the worker as he nonchalantly sprayed some kind of liquid onto the tunnel walls and ground. *So this is how the contaminant gets into our waters*, the brawny villager thought. He wound up his arm and balled his right hand into a fist. "Maggot," he muttered to himself, and delivered a compact punch to the side of the worker's head, knocking him unconscious. The worker fell on his side, and the clang of the back-pack sprayer as it made contact with the ground rang across the tunnel.

"I do not think we were supposed to put them out in that manner," one of the other members of the team said, grinning.

The villager shrugged. "Okay." With a satisfied look on his face he then roughly jabbed an immobilizing dart into the worker's shoulder.

The nozzle of the back-pack sprayer was still spurting the chemical. The villager had to tinker around with the mechanism for a little before he finally managed to turn the nozzle off. "So far so good," he smiled.

Ashack and Aari climbed over the mounds of ore to help the others drag all the workers into the abandoned tunnel. They tied up and gagged the workers. Once they were done, they returned to the mining tunnel, where Ashack handed out the cube-shaped explosive gels. "Get with it," he said, gruff as always.

Up at the top of the mountain, Nageau turned to the others. "Ashack's team has secured the main tunnel. They have just begun to place the explosives."

"Excellent," one of the men said, beaming.

"Has Saiyu moved in with her team?" another man asked.

"They moved in about the same time Ashack did."

Kody was lying face down beside his mentor and peering down the mountain. He murmured, "I can see Elder Saiyu leading her team back to the trees."

Nageau frowned. "Did they plant the explosives on the cauldrons in front of the tunnel?"

"Uh . . . no."

"She must have forgotten. I will remind her." Nageau gazed down at the site and probed for Saiyu's presence. When he found it, he asked, Saiyu, have you installed the detonation gels onto the large cauldrons?

Oh no, Saiyu groaned. We missed that in our haste. I will send someone from my group back to do the task right away.

As Kody watched, he saw the shape of a girl running light-footed out from the trees toward the vats. She was carefully cradling a bag to her chest; Kody assumed that the explosives were in there. She weaved her way around the vats, carefully planting the explosives and setting the timers.

"Tayoka's turn," Nageau said to himself as he and his apprentice surveyed the ground.

Jag stared out of the tree line, eyes darting back and forth. He was looking from behind a young evergreen tree that stood behind the cluster of lunch tables, just as shown on Tikina's map. To his left would be the workshop, and to his right was what he figured to be a medical building, judging by the red cross painted on it.

As he looked up at the sky and observed Nageau's spot at the top of the mountain, he heard his name called softly. "Jag!" He turned around and saw Tayoka waving him over to join the rest of the group. He quickly headed over and stood by the Elder, who checked for the umpteenth time that everyone remembered their roles.

Who knew Tayoka was such a stickler? Jag thought, amused, as a woman rapidly translated Tayoka's words for him. While easier said than done, their plan wasn't difficult to understand. He and Tayoka were to take down the four guards on shift before the others planted the cube explosives on three targets: the beasts' steel enclosure, the workshop, and the vehicles in the vehicle shed. The Elders had made it clear that no explosives were to come in contact with the medical building or the mess hall that were constructed side by side, nor were they to rig the workers' barracks.

Jag was near to losing his patience as he waited for his mentor to dismiss the group. When the villagers at last nodded and rose to their feet, Jag straightened. "Finally," he murmured. He followed Tayoka as the Elder prowled along the tree line, looking for the guards who should have been continuously circling the site. He watched for a few minutes, but had so far only noticed one guard walking about.

Tayoka swept his hand behind him, halting his apprentice. Creating a telepathic connection, he said, *Nageau, I do not see any of the guards.*

The youngling tells me he observed one walking into the workshop building a while back and never came out. Nageau paused. *Ah, and there is another walking around the vehicle shed.*

Yes, I saw him. But what of the other two?

I believe they went into the mess hall.

Is that not where you said the head guard who controls the beasts went?

He left a while ago to retire.

So we have three guards occupied indoors, and only one is out and about. Is that correct?

Yes.

Alright. Thank you. Tayoka turned and went back to where the team waited for the Elder and Jag to take down the guards.

"Slight change of plans, my friends," Tayoka said, gathering them into a huddle again. "There is only one guard on active duty at the moment. Two have entered the dining building, and one has disappeared into the workshop."

Jag chuckled to himself. "Slackers."

"Continue as if we have already taken down the guards," Tayoka told his group. "But be mindful that they may come out at any time, so do not make a sound. Am I understood?"

The villagers dipped their heads and quickly made off. Tayoka nodded at Jag and signaled for him to follow.

The seventeen-year-old girl who was weaving around the enormous vats and planting the cube gels froze when she heard footsteps. Forcing herself not to panic, she ducked behind one of the vats and crouched down, holding her breath. Stealing a look around the large cauldron, she caught sight of a slightly pudgy guard walking around the vehicle shed from her right. As she observed him, she found the guard to be rather disinterested in his work. He walked without purpose and seemed to be in his own world. *Must be tiresome to walk the same path every day,* she thought. But if that truly was the case, then that would work more to the villagers' advantage.

She watched the guard, willing him to move faster, but he kept to his slow amble as if he were strolling leisurely in a park. Stifling a sigh, the girl hunkered down and waited for him to pass.

A young man from Tayoka's group—a tanned, light-haired lad—had volunteered to fix the explosives to the beasts' steel building. He had them all in a small bag over his shoulder and approached the building with care. Elder Tikina had made it all too clear how strong the beasts' senses were; far more so than any creature they knew.

Pausing ten feet away from the building to steady his nerves, he scratched his ear, feeling the part of the cartilage where it had been bitten off by an aggressive yearling wolf. What a memory that was. Though a piece of his ear was now missing, he remembered how he had fought the creature off boldly. *If you could handle a wolf battling you in the open, then you can surely do this with beasts in their cages without a problem*, he thought, reassuring himself.

Just as he was about to step forward, a door banged open across from where he was standing. He froze, his breath caught. With his omnilinguistic ability he could make out a groggy but irritated voice yelling out. "Am I the only one in this entire bloody place who knows when the tunneling machine has been idling for too long?"

The flustered young man instinctively dove out of sight behind the beasts' enclosure. Staying absolutely still, he prayed the beasts had not heard him; apparently they hadn't because all was quiet in the building.

More shouting ensued. Had the lad peeked around the corner of the building he would have been able to see a man wearing black pajama bottoms and an untied robe running out of his private sleeping quarters. By his tone, the villager was easily able to tell that this man was in charge of the site.

"Where's the security team on shift?" he heard the man shout.

"Here, sir!" a voice chimed in, sounding nearby. *Must be the guard from the workshop*, the lad guessed.

"Get to the tunnel and get those slugs back to work. I thought you knew it was part of your job to sniff out slackers."

"We'll get right to it, sir!"

The villager slowly got up, thankful no one had noticed him when he had been standing in between the buildings. Moreover, he was thankful that the beasts inside hadn't heard him when he'd plunged behind their fortified enclosure. He took one of the explosives out of his bag and stepped forward.

A twig he hadn't seen snapped under his foot, sounding like a gunshot to his ears. Immediately an eruption of animalistic roars and barks sounded.

What have I done?

52

Nageau heard the tumult from the beasts' enclosure and stiffened when he saw the auburn-haired man in the robe turn to face the building. "Oh no," he muttered. He watched as the man started to walk toward the steel structure.

A shape behind the building could be seen sprinting into the trees. If the robed man had remained standing at his earlier position, the escaping figure may have had a chance to go unnoticed, but the man now had a wider field of view as he approached the building and saw the fleeing villager. He immediately realized that they had a trespasser.

"Intruder!" he bellowed. "We've been breached—*again!*"

The two guards who had gone to check the tunnel spun around and stampeded back toward their supervisor.

Caution! One of us has been spotted! Nageau blasted to all the Elders.

He felt someone poking his arm repeatedly and looked at Kody beside him. "What is it?"

"That big guard who was handling the beasts . . . he's coming back out."

Hajjar stomped out of the miners' barracks, pulling a sweater over his head. As the Marauders' primary handler, he was particularly sensitive to their roars and deep barks. Even though the animals and he hardly ever got along, he needed to know if something was bothering them.

He glanced to his right toward the security post on the far side of the site. He expected to see one guard through the big glass windows but found it to be empty. Wrath erupted in him. This seemed to happen constantly with the graveyard shifts when he wasn't present.

He heard the door of the mess hall on his left burst open and looked over. Two of the guards stumbled out, fumbling with their AR-15 rifles. When they saw the head of security, they visibly wilted. Hajjar, his lip twitching as if he were about to snarl, gave them a withering glare. He stalked up to them and snatched one of the rifles. He was about to reprimand them when they heard Ajajdif's shout. "We've got an intruder! Where are the other guards, dammit?"

As Hajjar and the other two from the security team headed toward the sound of Ajajdif's voice, a series of loud booms broke out from the mining tunnel. The three halted in mid-step and looked at each other, then at the tunnel. A rumbling that rapidly grew louder suddenly materialized in the shape of the massive tunneling machine. It thundered out of the tunnel like an out-of-control locomotive and struck a glancing blow to the platform holding the huge refining vats, crushing the stand, causing three of the cauldrons to topple.

The three members of the security team barely managed to bolt clear of the machine as it rolled past them and snapped the support posts all along one side of the vehicle shed. The unsupported roof of the shed came crashing down, throwing dust and debris into the air. The massive machine continued its course and the three men watched in shock as it just missed the infirmary and then barged right through the mess hall, demolishing anything and everything in its path. Some of the miners inside the mess hall managed to jump aside in time, but others were not so lucky and were mercilessly plowed under.

One of the cooks at the back of the building heard the commotion and turned around only to face the oncoming death machine. He didn't have time to run. As the machine barreled toward him, he impulsively grabbed a handle at the front and held on as it smashed out of the building and into the trees behind.

Having crashed through several obstacles, the machine lost momentum as it neared the edge of the mining site. The cook tried to stop the engine by digging his heels into the ground but knew his actions would be fruitless.

The machine rolled halfway off the edge of the clearing and came to a stop, hanging precariously over the steep drop. The cook let out a choked cry. "T-t-thank you," he whimpered to no one.

The massive machine see-sawed and began to tip downward. The cook babbled in terror and tightened his hold on the handle. He didn't want to look down and, instead, stared up at the ninety-ton tunneling machine, eyes stretched wide. He begged for the machine to stabilize but knew his time had come as the engine's balance shifted, sending both itself and the cook plummeting to their ends.

All over the mine site, there was a moment of stunned silence as the workers tried to grasp what had occurred. Then bedlam ensued. There were yells for help and cries of pain from the workers who had been struck by the tunneling machine. Several had broken limbs, others lay crushed and unresponsive.

Workers rushed about to help friends who hadn't escaped the mess hall in time. "We need medics!" yelled one of the guards who went to inspect the damage.

Ajajdif had seen the tunneling machine ram straight through the building. Still in his pajama pants and robe, he ran toward the mess hall to help his men.

Just as he passed the workshop, a series of thundering explosions shook the site. Ajajdif instinctively ducked behind one of the two trucks in the shed, and not a moment too soon. A large piece of metal smashed into the truck, tearing away its roof. Ajajdif squirmed under the truck for cover as other large pieces of debris rained down.

He stared at one particularly large piece that landed where he had stood only a moment earlier. It appeared very familiar. He turned to look at where the vats should have been but saw instead only rubble and black ore dust scattered far and wide. He gasped. "*No!*"

As he lay prone on the ground and bemoaned at the loss of his precious mineral, a piercing screech arose from the tunnel area. The noise swiftly transformed into a roar not unlike a jet engine. A bright phosphorescence caught Ajajdif's attention. His eyes moved to the crushing operation. A blinding flash, as brilliant as the sun, illuminated the entrance beside the mining tunnel. Ajajdif realized that the ore-crushing zone where the leaching compounds were stored had come under attack. Furious, he pounded the ground violently, cursing the hell that broke loose around him. He stopped when he noticed an odd-looking object beneath a truck near where he was taking cover, and found himself staring at a glowing blue cube. Mystified, he reached out and grabbed it, then crawled out from under the truck to examine it. As he was about to push himself up, he caught sight of more cubes placed under other vehicles in the shed.

Sudden realization dawned. He jumped to his feet and hurled the cube he was holding as far away as he could and started to run to his private quarters. "Explosives!" he shouted. "The whole place is rigged!"

Hardly anyone could hear him. He careened into his private quarters and slammed the door. Grabbing a flashlight, he went down on all fours and shone it under his bed. "Ah." He put the flashlight between his teeth and reached underneath, pulling out a long, flat case. Throwing the top open, he gazed down at his prized, Russian-made Dragunov sniper rifle.

Seizing a few spare magazines from the case, he grabbed the loaded rifle and threw his window open, leveling the weapon on the windowsill. He snatched his radio from his nightstand and broadcast to the twelve guards on site. "I want everyone to steer clear of the buildings! The place is rigged with bombs. The mining tunnel has been destroyed, and the vats have been demolished. I suspect that the abandoned tunnel might have explosives too. The vehicles in the shed are rigged as well, so *stay away!* I repeat, stay *away* from the vehicle shed."

"Roger," one of the guards replied. "What do you want us to do, sir?"

"I want you to arm as many able workers as you can. We have trespassers. Shoot to kill. I don't want any escapees."

"Yes sir."

"Elias."

Hajjar's voice came over the radio. "Sir?"

"Get the Marauders out right now."

"On my way."

As Ajajdif peered out of the window, he could see the giant of a man speeding toward the Marauders' building. Just as Hajjar was about to pass the workshop, two loud explosions that left Ajajdif's ears ringing threw the big man off his feet, sending him airborne for several yards and landing him on his back, torpid and out cold. Ajajdif watched the workshop collapse, sending debris and pieces of metal and wood flying, leaving only rubble.

He picked up his radio. "Elias," he rasped, but received no reply. "Elias, answer me!" Ajajdif started to shout into the radio, demanding Hajjar get back up, but the unconscious chief of security didn't move. Ajajdif tossed his radio aside, infuriated.

Up at the top of the mountain, Nageau saw the workers crowding around the security post and the guards handing weapons out to about a dozen of them. "They are arming the workers," he said, a note of worry in his voice. Connecting his mind with the other Elders, he said, *The guards are arming some of the workers by the guards' post next to the tunnel. Engage with caution. We know that they will not hesitate to kill us if we are spotted.*

He turned to the waiting crossbowmen. "If anyone gets near the beasts' enclosure, immobilize them immediately. Keep an eye out for our people also."

Kody gazed down, watching the guards handing out guns to the workers. Worry made him sick to his stomach when he grasped that his friends were down there, about to engage in what truly was serious combat. "Stay safe, guys," he murmured.

On the western flank of the mountain, hidden from the chaos, Tikina had gotten Nageau's go-ahead to engage. She quietly informed the rest of her troop as they stood flat against the back of the miners' barracks. They could hear the miners calling to one another and picked out the sounds of gunfire.

Beside her mentor, Tegan hiccupped. "They're actually going to shoot us?"

"They did not hesitate to drug and hold our kin hostage before attempting to murder all four of them. It was lucky that Rikèq and Breyas even survived." Tikina's throat constricted. Something cold and wet touched her fingertips and she looked down. Chayton lightly nuzzled her fingers, his tail wagging. She smiled a little and stroked the wolf's soft head, gently rubbing his ears. "Stay," she whispered.

The Elder edged along the side of the building and poked her head around the corner. Miners were thronging around the security post, just as Nageau had said. One of the miners was testing the scope on his rifle and happened to raise it in her direction. He froze. Tikina inhaled sharply and pulled back out of sight just as a shot was fired. The bullet struck the corner of the building, wedging itself into the wood.

The miners knew where they were now. Tikina hurriedly ushered her group along the building so that they could sneak out the other side. What they didn't know was that two groups of three men were coming at them, one heading to where Tikina had been seen, and the other to cut off the group's escape route.

Having slipped out of the tunnel, Aari had joined the gaggle of workers that were waiting to have weapons handed over. Ashack followed close behind. The two were dressed in miners' clothing, including respirator masks that covered most of their faces. Ashack was able to convincingly pass as a worker, but Aari, who was a little shorter than the adults and less muscled, had to hope the bagginess of the coveralls would offer enough concealment. At least the boots and the hardhat fit him perfectly.

He and Ashack were covering the rest of the group, each bending the light around two natives to render them invisible as they went to lend Tikina's team a hand. The men who Aari was covering for quickly went to the side of the building where Tikina had been spotted by the worker. The miners who had already rounded the back of the building had Tikina in their crosshairs and were about to pull a trigger when two of them had their heads smashed together by an invisible force. They then felt something stab them between their shoulder blades. The third miner was lifted up and thrown violently onto the ground before having an immobilizing dart jabbed into him.

The villagers picked up the men's weapons, inspecting them curiously before walking a short way to toss the weapons off the side of the mountain. They watched, satisfied, as the guns dropped out of sight.

Aari couldn't cover for the men any longer since they were out of his view, but Ashack could still bend the light around the two villagers he was covering. Realizing everything was under control for the moment, Aari slipped his hand into one of the oversized pockets of his coveralls and pulled out a couple of darts. *Might as well take down these guys from the back.* He glanced up at the workers who were waving their arms for the guards to toss them weapons; they paid no heed to the young man hanging at the back of the group who was attired just like them. However, a guard by the destroyed mess hall—a skinhead with a shaved and tattooed scalp—was on full alert. At first he found it strange that two of the workers weren't joining the crowd of personnel demanding weapons, but when he saw one of them pull something from his pocket, his senses tingled and he knew something was wrong. Before he could react, the worker silently stabbed something into the back of one of the other miners.

As the miner collapsed, the guard immediately raised his rifle, peered through the high-power scope, and took aim at the intruder. The next thing he knew, there was a smashing force on his back and he was face-down on the ground. He groaned and struggled to raise himself up but his head was pushed back down into the dirt. The guard thrashed about for a bit and was finally able to writhe away. Rolling onto his back, he was surprised to see the face of a well-built teenager snarling down at him, amber eyes aflame.

Jag had seen the guard take aim at Aari and, without a second thought, charged out of the trees and executed a picture-perfect flying back kick, his foot landing solidly on the guard from behind.

The skinhead kicked up his leg, catching Jag in the chest and heaving the sixteen-year-old back. Kipping up to his feet, the guard scrambled to find the gun that he'd dropped. He saw it at the same time Jag did and they both dove for the weapon. The guard managed to wrestle it away, but it was a short-lived win. Jag jammed his wrist against the man's sternum and the guard fell back. He swung his arms, trying to make a wild grab for the rifle as Jag snatched it away from him.

"Hand it over!" shouted the guard as he got back to his feet.

Jag flung the weapon into the trees. "Not a chance."

The guard swore and rolled up the sleeves of his shirt. "So you want to play hardball, kid?" He glanced behind him when he heard the footsteps of two beefy miners walking up to stand on either side of him. He looked back at Jag with a smirk. "Fine by me."

Jag watched them. A sudden hesitation in his mind made him reconsider fighting, but he straightened his shoulders and planted his feet firmly on the ground to prepare himself for a brawl. He would face them no matter what, not run away like a quitter.

Just as he got ready to charge, he saw a blurred motion in his peripheral view followed by a blast of air that brushed the side of his face. He glanced to his left and saw that Tayoka had joined in. He offered Jag a tight smile, then both Elder and apprentice turned to face the three men, steely-eyed and ready to fight.

A radio attached to a wall crackled at the far end of Ajajdif's personal quarters. "Flight Zero to Q-base. Do you read me?"

The Osprey! Ajajdif dove for the radio and picked it up. "Yes, I read you, Zero."

"Great. We're approaching your mining site."

"What's your ETA?"

"Ten minutes."

"Are you armed?"

"Yes." The pilot paused, suspicious. "Why?"

"We've got intruders armed with explosives. The site's under attack. We need your help."

"Hey, buddy, look. This isn't our gig. We were just told to haul your supplies. We got no directions to engage."

"*You* listen," spat Ajajdif. "There's a reason why your plane is armed. This mining operation is crucial for the company and right now we're under attack. It is your job to protect us. Why do you think this company hired ex-mercenaries like you? You *will* comply."

Flying low over the terrain about forty miles southeast of the site, the pilot in the cockpit of the Osprey looked over at his co-pilot, tight-lipped in anger. The co-pilot shrugged. "Well, the bloke's right. We're not exactly commercial pilots."

The pilot stared out at the horizon for a moment, then snorted. "Fine." He turned to the third crew member seated behind him. "Load up the M2. Let's get it done and get out of here." He thumbed his radio and responded to Ajajdif icily. "What's our main target?"

"Every single intruder."

"Roger. Zero out."

Ajajdif crawled back to his window and looked down his sniper's rifle. "Soon," he muttered. "These fools won't know what hit them."

53

The group of three miners planning to cut off the intruders rounded the far side of the barracks, behind which Tikina and her team were positioned. The workers did not know that their colleagues had been taken out of action and they were now on their own. The man leading the group halted. Very slowly, he stepped forward and stretched out his arms to point the barrel of his gun around the corner of the building.

A piercing screech from above caused the man and his coworkers to wince. The sound emanated once more, sounding dangerously close. As the leading member of the group cast a glance skywards, he saw the silhouette of a massive eagle swoop down. One of the bird's talons tore the worker's left cheek as the other set of talons ripped the rifle from his hands. The worker let out a clamorous cry and gripped his face and neck as crimson soaked his skin and clothes.

As the eagle flew over the building to toss the weapon off the edge of the mining site, Tegan gazed up at it, then at her mentor. Tikina stood facing away for a few moments, unblinking. She then broke her link with the eagle and faced her team. "That is one weapon less that we will have to worry about." She paused, listening to the moans of agony that could be heard just around the corner of the building. "And by the sounds of it, we probably have one less opponent to deal with as well."

The two miners that remained glanced at each other. Like most of the others, they were untrained in armed combat and did not know how to continue on with one of their number hurt. Both workers stooped down to lend their friend a hand.

With that window of distraction, Tikina shouted from behind the building, "Go!" The entire team leapt out to tackle the workers, but these were powerfully built men with attitudes to match. They managed to throw several hefty punches that caught the villagers square in their jaws or stomachs. With greater agility and speed, the group eventually managed to wrestle the two uninjured workers to the ground. Tikina and Tegan hastily moved around the workers, sticking darts into their thick necks. The workers quickly ceased to move and the natives pushed themselves to their feet, sighing. One of the villagers wiped blood from his broken nose.

The woman with the red bandana who had volunteered for this task had a gash on the side of her head from where one of the workers had struck her with the muzzle of his rifle. She pulled her bandana off and pressed the cloth against the wound. Tikina checked the villagers worriedly, but they waved her off, assuring her that they were able to continue.

Tegan looked up at her mentor. "Were we lucky, or was that skill?"

Tikina managed a short laugh. "Both. Now come. This has only just begun."

At the window of his private quarters, Ajajdif was gazing through his scope. "Come on," he silently urged. "Step into my sights, you pathetic delinquents, and I'll send you on a joyride to hell."

He crouched, patiently waiting for a target. Without warning, a reverberating bang sounded and one of the four Bobcats in the shed exploded, sending parts and glass flying in every direction. Ajajdif seethed as he watched the vehicle's destruction.

Just as the dust was clearing to reveal what remained of the Bobcat, an excavator exploded. The hydraulic cylinder connected to the bucket was wrenched off and flew through the vehicle shed. It hurtled toward Ajajdif's accommodation. The man dropped down, covering his head. The cylinder smashed through his living quarters and embedded itself in the back wall.

Ajajdif, his fingers digging into his head, looked up. There was a big gaping hole at the top left corner of the front wall where the cylinder had entered the building.

Inching himself to his feet, Ajajdif thought the explosions were over, until four more booms, erupting one after the other, shook the entire site. He dropped back down and huddled under the window. The initial fright that had taken a hold of him was gone, replaced by a thirst, a need for revenge on whoever was responsible for this.

It took several seconds for the echoes of the explosions to subside. Ajajdif slowly returned to his weapon at the window. Looking out, all that was left of the shed was rubble and a million shards of glass and metal. One of the two trucks, dented and covered in ash, was still standing only because Ajajdif had found the explosive under it and had thrown it far away.

As he continued to look out the window, it finally occurred to him that he was now able to see the entire mining site with the shed now out of the way. He could see his workers and guards grappling with the intruders, but he noticed some of his men had collapsed for no apparent reason. *There must be snipers around here*, Ajajdif figured. *But two can play that game . . .*

He looked through his scope and aimed in the direction of one of his workers engaging hand-to-hand with an intruder. Taking a breath to steady himself, Ajajdif squeezed the trigger. The native dropped onto the dirt with a bullet embedded in his head. The worker, realizing he'd gotten help from somewhere, leered down at the intruder and kicked the body aside.

Ajajdif looked around for another target. He focused on a woman with a red bandana who was darting around two men, attempting to jab something into their necks and arms. As he watched, he admired her determination and found her form and grace alluring. He sighed. *What a shame that such a lovely woman must go.* He pulled the trigger.

Nageau's heart jumped into his throat for a moment before melting into a pool of sorrow as he watched the woman in the red bandana crumple to the ground. She was the second villager to be felled by a shot fired from a weapon somewhere. Nageau scanned around but saw no one with a gun who had aimed in her direction. As he cast an eye over the site for a likely culprit, he saw another member of the village collapse, lifeless.

The Elder bit the inside of his lip. While his crossbowmen next to him were rapidly firing away at the workers, an unseen marksman was methodically taking out the villagers. The Elder knew the shooter had to be stopped before more of his people were killed.

"Kody." His apprentice looked at him, all ears. "There is someone taking down our people, but he or she does not seem to be any worker in our sight. My guess is that the person is hidden away, perhaps in the trees or in one of the buildings. I want you to attempt to locate the shooter."

"Got it." Kody's gaze raked over the entire site, meticulously scanning every inch of the place. He started from the miners' barracks on the left and continued right. It was hard to not be distracted by the action that was happening below him. The still bodies of the three villagers were particularly disturbing to look at, yet he found himself going back to them every once in a while. *No, concentrate, Kody. Concentrate.* But the roaring of the caged beasts clashed with the sounds of gunshots and yells and sporadic screams from the conflict, making it hard to focus.

Forcing every sound out of his ears, the teenager's emerald eyes skimmed over the ground. He zoomed his vision in and out but could not find anything. With a shake of his head, he sat up. "Don't see anything."

Then his eyes picked up a momentary bright spark on the far right side of the site that could have only come from a gun. "Huh. Someone's not using a suppressor . . ." He quickly lowered himself down again to get a better look. He blinked, zooming in on two joint buildings standing on their own not too far from the helipad. He zoomed in further and spotted the muzzle of a rifle sticking out a window. "Bingo," he breathed. He sat back up and hurriedly tapped his mentor's arm. "Found it."

Nageau focused on the direction Kody was pointing and found the muzzle as well. "Wonderful—Saiyu is behind that building, in the trees. I will notify her."

There is someone in the building by your designated area, Saiyu. He has taken out three of our friends and nearly shot down a fourth. I want you to stop him.

Understood. I am on my way.

Nageau took a breath and rested a hand on his pupil's shoulder. "Good job, youngling."

Amidst the battle, the lad with the torn ear snuck back out of the trees. There was no activity this side of the mining site, with the exception of the gruesome uproar coming from within the beasts' building that stood ten yards from him. He glanced down at the sack he was holding. Through the folds of cloth he could see the blue color of the explosive charges. He took one out and looked at it, determined to plant the cubes on the building and get rid of the beasts as he had originally intended to do. When he ran away earlier, he'd felt spineless for leaving the job incomplete. Now he was going to redeem himself and aid his brethren. He trooped toward the steel structure confidently, ignoring the braying inside.

What he didn't know was that he was in the sights of an armed worker who had gone around behind the infirmary. The worker quietly moved toward the villager as the lad knelt at the back of the building and fiddled with the blue cube.

The worker aimed his weapon before calling out, "Psst, Injun!"

The lad jumped. He saw the threat lurking to his right, with the barrel of a gun pointing straight at him. His face transformed into a look of pure terror. He quickly tried to scramble back to the trees. The worker, an experienced marksman, waited calmly until the lad was perfectly aligned in his sights before firing a few rounds. The young man flopped onto his back on the ground, trembling for a few moments before going still.

The worker lowered his weapon and walked toward the intruder who lay splayed before him, eyes glassy. "Boom, you're dead," he chuckled. He picked up the cube the lad had dropped. The explosive wasn't armed but the worker didn't know it and did not want to take chances. He put the cube back inside the villager's sack, then flung the bag into the trees before strolling away.

Hajjar groaned as he came around. Opening his eyes, he stared up at the brightening sky. He tried to recall what was happening but his senses were coming back to him slowly. It wasn't too long before his ears began to work again and he picked out a smorgasbord of sounds, predominantly shouts from the guards and workers. Then it all came rushing back.

As he pushed some rubble off himself, he heard his name being called. He looked around, a frown creasing his brow, until his eyes landed on his radio that was by his hand. He picked it up. "Somebody called for me?" he asked, sounding hoarse.

Ajajdif's voice came on. "Yeah, me. You okay?"

Hajjar stiffly pushed himself up to his feet. "Yeah."

"Good. Get the Marauders out. Keep your eyes peeled for the intruders, though."

"Yes, sir." The head of security dusted himself off and pulled out a 9mm Glock from his holster. Holding the weapon in one hand, he warily made his way over to the Marauders' building.

One of the crossbowmen up at the top of the mountain spotted the giant man as he hurried to the beasts' enclosure. The villager quickly turned his crossbow toward the man and let loose an arrow.

The arrow missed Hajjar by an inch as he was punching a code into the security keypad. He saw the arrow bounce off the steel building and land by his left foot. He whipped around to look behind him, both hands gripping his sidearm, but no one was there. His eyes narrowed in suspicion. He reached behind him, pulling open the heavy door with one hand. As he turned around and stepped in, another arrow whistled just over his shaved head and hit the second door in front of him. He slammed the first door shut and turned to look down at the arrow. He picked it up and eyed it. "Arrows against guns?" he scoffed. "They really think they can outdo us with these?" He shook his head as he pressed his thumb against the thumbprint recognition scanner. As he walked inside, he boomed to the terrified handler behind the steel counter, "Get my controller. I'm setting the Marauders loose."

54

Ajajdif scanned the site from his window, striving for clear shots at the intruders as they tangled with the workers not too far from the security post. Unfortunately, the intruders seemed to have guessed that there was someone eyeing them from across the site and danced around his employees. The workers always ended up being the ones in his sights instead. Piqued, Ajajdif changed direction of his aim. He swung the muzzle of his weapon around to see where the other intruders were. A group of them stood not too far from the destroyed mess hall and were firing arrows from their bows.

A tall brunette with light brown skin seemed to be the center of that group. She appeared mature but was lithe and elegant in her movements, making it impossible to guess her age from afar. Ajajdif watched her carefully as she called out to the others. Her actions were leading him to the notion that she was the group's commander. Gunning her down could weaken the link in the intruders' attack plan and give his workers a slight boost—or so he hoped. A young girl, perhaps fifteen or sixteen by her looks, hung back around the woman while the others actively sought out the workers and engaged them in skirmishes.

Ajajdif inhaled and could hear the pounding of his heart in his ears as he held his breath. He aligned the crosshairs to the woman's head. Just as he was about to fire his weapon, the excavator's cylinder that had embedded itself into the wall behind him came crashing down. Startled, he squeezed the trigger but his aim was off. The bullet struck the woman in the chest, just a couple of inches above her heart. She buckled from the impact and stumbled back into the arms of the teenager, who looked utterly shell-shocked. Ajajdif knew the hit would be critical enough to put the leader out of action. He watched as the girl gently lowered the woman to the ground. He deliberated taking her out as well, but decided to leave the girl alone. He needed to save his ammunition for the real threats.

Tegan knelt beside her mentor, unable to tear her eyes away from the blood on Tikina's chest. The Elder's breathing was rapid and shallow. Her skin was quickly becoming clammy and moist. Tegan whimpered as her mentor's head started to loll and her eyelids began to droop. She placed her hand on the wound, trying to stem the flow of blood, but kept pulling her hands back each time the Elder hissed in pain. Even though she had taken the basic first aid course in school, she wasn't prepared for anything like this. The simple training she'd gotten was rendered non-existent as dread set in her mind. *What do I do, what do I do, what do I do?*

Tikina's eyes suddenly opened wide and she grabbed her apprentice's hand, holding it with an iron grip that stunned the teenager. "Tegan," she murmured. Her pupil leaned in closer. "You must take over for me. Use Chayton and Akira, youngling. Use them."

"What about you?" Tegan croaked.

"You must leave me be."

"No! You can't ask me to do that, not when you can't even move!"

"You must, Tegan!"

Tegan shook her head angrily. "No. I'm not leaving. I'll find a way to help you."

"Do not do this, youngling. I . . ." Tikina's voice ebbed as she faded into unconsciousness.

Losing her nerve, Tegan looked around for anyone to help her but the other members of the team had spread out when Tikina had ordered them to. She looked down at the Elder and desperately tried to remember everything she had learned, but her mind continued to draw a blank. She harangued herself as she sat by her mentor's side, again pressing her hands against the wound in an attempt to halt the blood flow.

The door of the Marauders' building swung outward and the four creatures stalked out, their unsheathed claws digging into the soil. They paused, drawing themselves up to their full height. They took a long sniff to identify the direction of the intruders. With raucous growls they lunged forward across the wrecked vehicle shed in search of the trespassers.

Hajjar slowly followed out after them, watching the animals as if they were the single most wonderful entities to have ever been created. Without realizing it, he tightened his hold on the remote, relishing the power in his hands. The feeling of dominance over such destructive beasts never grew old with him.

His eyes followed the beasts as they began to terrorize the intruders. The intruders intuitively scrambled away whenever the Marauders drew close, but Hajjar knew they would not last. The hybrids were designed to kill.

Tayoka and Jag had just about finished up with the three men they were facing. The last man, not yet tied, was face-down on the ground. As Jag stomped down on his arm and stuck a dart into him, the sounds of the beasts on the other side of the site became more distinct. Puzzled, Jag looked over at Tayoka. The Elder looked back at him. They both turned when they noticed shadows streaking across the site, moving so fast they almost appeared blurred. The two watched, speechless, as one shadow jumped onto the back of a villager who was firing arrows from his bow, sending him tumbling down. The man let out an ear-splitting, inhuman sound that was quickly cut off as the beast shoved him down, clawing and tearing into him.

Jag and Tayoka could barely look at the grizzly sight. Neither had ever witnessed a creature attacking violently for the exclusive need to satiate its instinct to kill. To Jag, it seemed as if the creatures were enjoying the massacre. He backed away from the scene and glanced at where he expected Tayoka to have been standing;

instead he found the Elder sprinting toward a giant man by the beasts' building. He yelled out to Tayoka and started to run after him, but the Elder turned around and held a hand up, instructing Jag to stay put. Jag's eyes followed his mentor as Tayoka headed toward his target again.

It was only a matter of a few seconds for Tayoka to reach the big man. The Elder was moving swiftly, too fast for his opponent to move out of the way as Tayoka leapt and landed a scissor-kick to the man's neck. Twisting his body, the Elder forced the man down.

The giant was stunned by the surprise attack. He shoved Tayoka away and got back up. Tayoka rose up as well, glaring at the other man. The man had to bend his head to look down at the Elder and was more than surprised to see that his aggressor was at least twenty years older than him. Taking a couple of steps back, he tucked away a black device and whipped out his pistol, pointing it at the Elder. Like greased lightning, Tayoka struck the gun out of his hand and kicked it aside. The giant watched the weapon slide away, then looked back at the Elder and advanced malevolently toward the older man.

From their concealed position behind the building that Nageau had pointed out, Saiyu, Mariah and the man with the eye patch were preparing for an assault on the sniper. The man crawled on his stomach from behind the building, and unknown to the sniper at the window, positioned himself right next to him.

Saiyu and Mariah were on the opposite side of the building. Staying low, Saiyu peeked around the corner of the building and spotted the barrel of the sniper's rifle. She signaled to Mariah to stay close to her as they readied themselves to barge through the door and take down the man behind the gun. They stopped cold when they heard a crackling sound. Then Mariah heard a radio communication that seemed oddly close. Realizing that there was a conversation happening indoors, she strained her ears to listen and heard the tail-end of the radio exchange.

". . . ETA in two minutes, and we're comin' in hot. Flight Zero out."

She heard a mumble, probably from the sniper, but it was almost inaudible. As she crouched beside Saiyu, she thought through what she'd overheard. *Coming in hot? That's military jargon, isn't it?* She froze at the notion and immediately scanned the sky, half-expecting to see an aircraft. *Nah . . . this is a mining activity, not a military excursion. It's gotta be something else.*

The barks and roars of the beasts had stabbed fear into Aari. He stuck close to his mentor, but even Ashack seemed to have gotten flustered as they caught sight of two massive, black-furred beasts stalking two villagers. Coordinating their moves, they trapped the men.

The villagers knew right away that flight was not an option. They took their defensive positions and covered each other. The men put up a brave fight in what was to be their last stand, for within moments the beasts dragged them down and tore them apart.

Aari nearly bit through his tongue as he saw it all unfold before his eyes. Ashack stood protectively in front of him and a distraught bellow rose from the Elder, shattering his stoic demeanor. Aari winced, feeling the raw anguish from his mentor. The speed of the attack had taken even Ashack by surprise, leaving him helpless as he was unable to use his light-bending skills to save the men.

A lamenting cry shook Aari from the shock of what he had just witnessed. He craned his neck to look behind him and saw Tegan kneeling on the ground beside the limp body of Tikina. Seeking to get Ashack's attention, Aari grabbed his arm and turned him toward Tegan and Tikina. He looked at his mentor, searching for direction, and from his peripheral vision noticed the large shadowed figures of the beasts turning toward the fallen Elder and her pupil. The creatures tilted their heads up, taking a whiff and picking up a scent. They seemed to know that there was an injured quarry.

Both Ashack and Aari recognized their intentions. The Elder met Aari's eyes briefly, his intent clear. With a nod of understanding, Aari broke into a mad sprint. "Tegan!" he screamed.

That jolted Tegan to look up at him. She seemed confused by his panic, but then her eyes drifted to the ominous silhouettes charging behind him. The frightening scene froze her in her place.

Aari grabbed her, and without slowing his stride, hauled her along at full speed toward what was left of the mess hall. Tegan was in a near panic. "Tikina! We can't leave her!"

"Ashack's got her covered!" he yelled back. "Just *run!*"

Tegan glanced back and couldn't find her mentor, but saw the beasts stall, yards away from where Tikina should have been, looking confused. Then one of them looked up directly at the fleeing pair and gave chase. Tegan goggled. She tore away from her friend's grip and raced past a surprised Aari. "Hurry!" she screeched.

Jumping over rubble, they careened past the dining section with the beast no more than fifty feet behind them. Aari could hear the creature's growl, sounding closer than it actually was. The two vaulted onto the food serving counter and leapt onto the half-demolished wall behind it that separated the dining area from the kitchen. They jumped down onto the kitchen floor and looked around for somewhere to hide. Aari happened to glance up and saw a trap door in the ceiling, the kind used by maintenance crews to service the exhaust fans. He clambered onto the stove counter and reached for the trap door. It was locked. He looked around frantically and found a fire extinguisher attached to a pillar next to him. Grabbing it, he smashed the trap door open. He leapt and pulled himself through the ceiling, puffing out a breath.

He looked down for Tegan and found her staring up at him in dismay. "You could have told me about your plan!"

"Plan? What plan? I just found a hole in the ceiling!"

The sound of the beast scrabbling over the broken wall doubled the friends' anxiety. Aari reached his hand down for her. "Come on! I'll pull you up!"

Tegan jumped onto the counter and reached up to grab his hand. He managed to grab hold of her fingers but she slipped and fell onto the floor. Just as she sat back up she saw the enormous paws of the beast reach over the wall. Its razor-sharp claws raked into the drywall, gouging the plaster like a hot knife through butter. She shuddered and looked up at Aari, realizing she was out of time.

Ashack stood with his feet planted firmly on the ground, focusing all his attention to bend the light around Tikina. The beast that had stayed behind while its comrade went after Tegan and Aari sniffed around where the fallen Elder had been. It was confounded. It could clearly scent Tikina, but she was not where the beast's nose told it she should be.

Abandoning the puzzling search, the beast slowly turned around to look at Ashack. The Elder's back went rigid. He needed to cover for Tikina but that required a line of sight between them. He backed up little by little, all the while keeping Tikina's position in his sight. The beast bared its gore-soaked fangs at him and quickened its pace until it was racing toward him.

Ashack, rooted to the ground, did not know what to do. As he watched the terrifying beast make a bound at him, something black and furry rocketed out of nowhere and smashed into the beast, throwing the animal off its course. The Elder exhaled the shaky breath he had been holding.

Chayton stood in front of Ashack, fur bristling and fangs exposed as he fanatically shielded the Elder from the beast. The wolf was nowhere near the size of the muscle-bound opponent but was prepared to fight as if it were his own life that he was defending. The beast, outweighing Chayton, jumped and drove the wolf to the ground, hooking its three-inch claws into his chest. Chayton let out an agonized howl and shoved his paws against the beast as his adversary gazed downward. Clawing away, Chayton pushed himself up, his limbs shaking from the shock of the deep wounds. He looked back at the beast, ears straight and forward, the fur on his spine bristling. The beast slowly licked its black lips and began to circle around with the wolf.

Ashack, careful to not attract any attention to himself, edged toward Tikina. When he drew close enough to her, he ceased bending the light and she became visible again. He crouched beside her, taking stock of the bullet wound, then gently lifted his friend. The door to the barracks was just twenty feet away and he reached it without incident. The door was unlocked and he pushed it open. The workers were all outside battling the villagers so the building was vacant. There were cubicles after cubicles of bunk beds past a common washroom. Ashack carried Tikina toward the far corner of the building away from the door and set her down on one of the lower bunks. Pulling a leather pouch from his belt, he tended to her as best he could.

Outside, Chayton had managed to scratch both sides of the beast's face and nicked its ear, but the beast was hardly bothered by the lesions. It lunged and grabbed the scruff of the wolf's neck and shook its head vigorously, ripping several clumps of fur out. Chayton snarled and pounced onto the beast's back, biting and piercing its flesh. The creature twisted around and the wolf fell backward. Seizing its chance, the beast reared up and came down on Chayton with its full weight, crushing the ribs of the smaller animal. The wolf struggled to breathe but was rapidly weakening. He tried to push the beast away but all he could manage to do was feebly cycle his front paws above him.

The beast peered down at the wolf, cropped tail up in dominance. It rose on its hind legs once more, letting out a triumphant bray, before crashing down again and digging its jaws into Chayton's neck. His vertebrae crushed, the valiant animal went limp instantly.

Kody witnessed everything from the top of the mountain. No amount of training could have prepared him for this scene and he was revolted by the brutal slaying. This was flat-out murder. Chayton was dead, being ripped apart like all the beasts' other victims.

Sickened by the carnage around the demonic animals, Kody turned away with a cold shiver running down his spine. He looked toward the mess hall he'd seen Tegan and Aari run into with one of the creatures following. He itched to run into the destroyed building after his friends to make sure they were alright, but there was no way he could get down to the site both safely and quickly.

Beside him, Nageau was calling on his crossbowmen to aim their fire at the beasts. Both he and Kody watched as the arrows with the more powerful immobilizing compound struck the animals, two arrows each to the three beasts that were in open view. They expected the animals to drop like a basket of rocks from the doubled dosage but instead the beasts halted, reached for the arrows protruding from their bodies, and yanked them out with their teeth before continuing to oppress the villagers.

The crossbowmen let fly several more arrows, all hitting their targets precisely, but again the beasts simply wrenched the projectiles off. "This is not working!" one of the men shouted.

"I will warn the others!" Nageau shouted back. "Do not let your arrows go to waste! Fire at the workers!"

As the bowmen signaled their understanding, Nageau sent a telepathic blast to the Elders. *The beasts are impervious to the darts! Inform the others!*

Within moments, he could hear the message being relayed through the chaos at the site as the villagers shouted the warning to one another. He gazed down worriedly, then turned toward the miners' barracks where his mate was and he probed for Ashack's mind. *Do you have her?*

Yes.

Is she alright?

She . . . she is unconscious, but I have administered to her wound. Unfortunately I am unable to extract the projectile on my own.

Nageau rested his fingers against his forehead, eyes closed, praying for his mate. After a moment of silence he said, *Please inform me if she gets better or worse.*

I will.

Nageau opened his eyes and scowled down at the beasts. Kody followed his gaze and said, "There has to be some way to kill them. They're able to withstand the darts, but a direct strike to their chest or heart might take them down."

"That is probable, but it will be quite a task to get close enough to do that."

"Then what else can we do?"

Nageau didn't answer as he stared down at the beasts, trying to find a solution that would minimize injury and death. Without intending to, he watched as one of the creatures broke away from the others and tore toward the two joint buildings where the sniper was located . . . and where Saiyu and Mariah were positioned.

The one-eyed villager in Saiyu's group peeked around the edge of the building, staying out of the sniper's line of sight, and made eye contact with the Elder. As they nodded to each other, he picked up a galloping sound. He looked to his left and upon seeing the oncoming threat instantly nocked an arrow to his bow and faced the beast. He let the projectile fly and rapidly nocked another, firing several shots on target but the creature was not deterred at all as it drew closer and closer.

With one last look at the Elder, the man dropped his bow and quiver, unsheathed his glistening ten-inch knife from his belt and charged at the beast, letting out a manic war cry. The villager threw himself at the animal as the beast lunged at him and wrapped its massive paws around his head. The man let out a yell of pain but plunged his knife into the beast's side. The beast let out a rippling growl and thrust the villager to the ground, teeth and claws tearing away.

Saiyu hastily blocked the sight from Mariah. She reached behind her to shake her pupil's arm and pointed to the door of the building. With every sense heightened from the adrenaline rushing through her body, Mariah followed the Elder toward the door. Saiyu quietly tried to turn the knob but it was locked. Taking a step back, she aimed her foot just under the doorknob and kicked with all her might. The door cracked and flew off its hinges. Rushing into the office to catch the sniper by surprise, they stopped cold when they saw a man standing with his weapon pointed at them. He was shorter than the Elder but had a mesomorphic body. His wavy hair was tousled, and he had a prominent jaw line. His square face was set in a menacing expression as he stared the woman and the girl down with his hazel eyes. In a deep baritone, he said, "What, you thought you could just sneak up on me?"

55

Aari looked down at Tegan through the broken trap door in the ceiling as she stared at the beast clawing its way over the wall. "Tegan," he hissed. "Tegan!" She sprang to her feet and looked up, terror in her eyes. "Don't move! I'll cover you."

She said nothing in return, keeping her eyes on the looming threat. Aari took a few breaths to slow the pounding of his heart and then focused. His friend shimmered, disappearing just as the beast pulled itself over the wall and landed in the kitchen.

Tegan watched, stiff with fear, as the creature prowled around. Its claws sounded like nails on a chalkboard as they dug into the broken concrete. Its dark yellow eyes were slits under a heavily creased brow and its elongated jaws were parted, revealing two rows of teeth that looked capable of slicing flesh like scissors cutting paper.

Struggling not to break down, Tegan clenched her shaking hands into fists and stood still. The beast raised its head to sniff the air. It could smell the girl but could not see her. It whined in frustration and stepped closer to Tegan, puzzled. She found it difficult to stand her ground with the beast's head nearly at her height and its snout mere inches from her. She held her breath and tried to stop herself from breaking into a run.

She heard Aari frantically yelling at the animal to divert its attention. The beast whipped its head up, muzzle wrinkling as it growled when it spotted the boy's head poking through the ceiling.

Aari found the animal's gaze intimidating but his focus didn't waver. Relinquishing its search for Tegan, the beast stalked past her and leapt up onto the counter behind her. The beast looked up once more and Aari could have sworn it was giving him a baneful, murderous smile. Fear seeped through his body, chilling him. *Worse than Slenderman*, he concluded. *Way worse.*

He watched as the creature bunched its muscles and leapt toward him. Aari let out a gasp. The beast scratched the ceiling beside him but wasn't able to make it through the trap door and fell. It was back on its paws in a split second and growled at Aari challengingly before hopping onto the counter again.

Aari knew the beast wouldn't give up until it got a kill. "Tegan, I can't keep this up," he called out, his voice trembling. "This freak's going to eat my face if I don't pull back. You need to hide somewhere—*quickly!*"

Still shielded from view, she hurried toward a stainless steel storage cabinet on the other side of the kitchen. She eased the cabinet's door open and a mountain of canned food crashed to the ground around her. The racket caused both Tegan and Aari to cringe.

The creature twisted around, taking in the opened door and spilled cans, its head tilted to one side. For a minute neither the humans nor the beast made a move. Then the animal sniffed the air once more and scented Tegan. It lost interest in Aari and crept along the counter toward the cabinet. As it prepared to jump down from the counter, the cabinet door slammed shut.

Provoked by the noise, the beast lunged at the cabinet and brought it crashing to the floor. The seven-foot tall steel container lay flat on the ground with Tegan trapped inside, screaming. Hearing her, the animal went into overdrive. It jumped onto the cabinet and assaulted it savagely, looking for a way to get in. It scraped its claws over the material, leaving deep gouges in the metal.

Tegan could hear the grating and shouted for help. Aari wracked his brain for a solution and, though he knew he wasn't fully trained, wanted to attempt something. He eyed the cabinet.

The long steel box pulsated for a few seconds before it vanished—leaving Tegan completely visible.

Tegan, on her stomach, could see the floor practically under her nose and the whole kitchen around her, yet when she reached out, her hand hit an invisible barrier. Realizing she was still in the cabinet, she muttered, "This is so weird."

Above her, the beast was going berserk trying to reach its prey. It didn't understand. It could see the girl clearly, but every time it tried to pounce or bite her, it hit an invisible obstruction. It seemed to be standing on thin air even though it could feel a solid object under its paw pads. Enraged, it hopped up and down along the cabinet, ravenous for a kill.

Tegan could hear the beast above her and turned her head to look over her shoulder. She saw the creature staring down at her with its lips curled threateningly, drooling. She shrieked. "What are you *doing*, Aari?!"

"I'm sorry," he yelled. "I tried, but I can't cover both inanimate and animate objects at the same time. Would you like me to let go?"

"Yes please!"

As soon as the cabinet reappeared, the beast went into a frenzy and started ramming the cabinet violently with its head. Inside, Tegan let loose a barrage of screams, begging for divine intervention. The beast tried to bite through the cabinet but its teeth slid off the smooth surface. Confused, it jumped off the cabinet and searched for an angle to chomp down. It found a corner and crunched it with its jaws.

Tegan heard the noise and turned her head to look. Two curved fangs had pierced through the corner of the cabinet. They quickly disappeared, leaving behind two holes. Light from the kitchen shone through them.

Knowing that Tegan would be close to panic, Aari quickly took stock of their options and called out to her. "Tegan, I want you to listen carefully. I think I figured a way out, but I need you to calm down. Focus, alright? You need to make a mind-link for support. We can't do this on our own."

Her muffled voice shouted back. "That'll be tough! Who do I link with?"

"Whoever is the closest that you can sense."

Hearing Aari's voice, the beast left the cabinet and jumped back onto the counter. Aari groaned. "The thing's coming for me again. I'll keep it distracted. Link now!"

As the beast moved along the counter, it met Aari's gaze, making the boy quiver from its intimidating expression. Aari silently pleaded for assistance as the animal slithered closer. It lowered itself, pausing, then lunged up at Aari. He pulled back just in time. Just before the beast's large head shot through the trap door, a shadow flitted across Aari's sight. Both the boy and the beast heard a screech echo in the kitchen.

The creature dropped to the ground and looked around suspiciously. It heard the powerful flap of wings and growled in pain as the talons of an enormous golden eagle sank into its muzzle and ripped upward, tearing the flesh, barely missing the beast's eyes. Reacting instinctively, it leapt at the bird as she took off through a large opening in the damaged roof.

Shaking off the pain from its fresh wounds, the animal faced Aari once more. Before it could climb onto the counter again, the stealthy bird of prey reappeared and struck the beast on its face one more time. Instead of fleeing through the roof again, the eagle glided low, taunting the beast as it flew through the dining area and out through the demolished main entrance. The ploy worked. The beast left its quarries in the kitchen and took off after the eagle.

Aari sat back, pulling his head to his knees and sighing with relief. Once he'd caught his breath, he peeked down to make sure the beast was truly gone before lowering his legs through the ceiling and jumping down. He ran to the toppled cabinet and struggled with it for a bit before turning it onto its side. He pulled open the door and Tegan crawled out. He crouched beside her and slowly helped her up, hugging her tight.

She pulled back after a few moments and wiped her cheeks dry. "We're still alive?" she asked, half-whispering, half-laughing.

Aari laughed as well, letting out his pent-up fear. "Yes, we are."

"You did good back there."

"Yeah. You too." He stopped to listen to the sounds of gunfire and shouting. He glanced at Tegan and she nodded. They climbed over the broken wall and cautiously made their way out of the building.

Standing in the shadow of the big man, Tayoka irked his beefy opponent simply with his mischievous appearance. The head of security detested the Elder's brazen look and sought to wipe it off his face. He threw a straight punch, but Tayoka was ready and he bent over backwards until his back was parallel with the ground. The giant took in the older man's elasticity with disbelief.

As Tayoka unbent himself, the big man threw several rapid left-and-right blows. The Elder dodged them with ease as well, swiftly swinging from side to side. The head of security stepped back, face as dark as a thunderstorm, then performed a spinning back kick. Tayoka bent back once again but this time into a bridge position. As the giant's leg swung past, swaying his body around, Tayoka tucked his legs toward his chest. Using his arms like loaded springs, he kicked out and caught the bigger man in the back, sending him tumbling a few feet away. The giant lumbered back up and turned to look at Tayoka. The Elder could see the look of sheer incredulity on the man's face.

The giant then looked past Tayoka at the pistol several yards behind the Elder. Tayoka sensed his intent and steadied himself. The giant charged at the Elder as if the other man was a matador and he was the bull. Tayoka didn't blink as the big man came closer. Balancing his stance, the Elder waited until his rival was close enough before stooping low. As the other man's legs connected with Tayoka's shoulder, the Elder quickly straightened, and using the bigger man's momentum, flipped him far over his shoulder.

The giant crash-landed beside his pistol, looking up at the sky and groaning as pain shot up his back. He slowly sat up. When he saw the Elder approaching him, he snatched the gun and rose to his feet, pointing the weapon at Tayoka. Tayoka froze, eyes trained on the barrel. The big man fired a round. The Elder dropped down as the bullet shot over his head, then to the giant's surprise, sprinted toward him. Another two rounds were fired but Tayoka deftly sidestepped those bullets, never once breaking his stride.

Eyes wide, the big man began to back up, unable to comprehend how any human being could dodge what should have been direct hits. He continued to shoot, flabbergasted but unyielding.

At the speed he was moving, the world seemed to have slowed down for Tayoka. He could see the bigger man firing his weapon. The projectiles that were rocketing toward him appeared to travel at a fraction of their actual velocity and he easily avoided them. Upon reaching his opponent he grabbed the man's neck and, leveraging the momentum he had built, lifted and hurled the titan off the ground. The head of security was airborne, flipping in midflight and crashing through the window of the medical building. There was a moment of stillness. Tayoka watched, wondering if the big man would come charging at him again. He cautiously walked toward the building and, as he approached, he could see part of the other man's limp body on the floor. Noting that his foe was out cold, he pulled an active vine from his belt to tie him up.

A movement from the corner of his eye caught his attention and he halted. He looked up and saw a large, jagged piece of glass precariously attached to the top of the windowpane. It was beginning to come loose from the frame. Tayoka tried to reach the man to pull him to safety but was too late and the glass plummeted toward the giant.

The Elder turned away, swinging the rope in his hand. Suspecting that there would be no need for the active vine any longer, he left the scene.

Nageau and his team were steadily picking off the workers; most were down for the count while a few others were still tromping around, brandishing weapons they took from their immobilized comrades. The Elder rubbed his forehead. The villagers were in a position to win—if only the beasts could be taken out of the picture. Nageau watched in pain as two of the animals tore a woman apart. Sitting next to him, Kody looked away, unable to bear the sight. Although the team shot a few arrows at them, the creatures did not fall, nor were they weakened.

Kody clucked his tongue and turned to his mentor. Just as he was about to ask if the beasts would ever be brought down, the sound of an aircraft in the distance reached his ears. Sharing questioning looks with Nageau, he tilted his head toward the direction of the sound. Understandably, the others didn't seem to notice anything and continued loading their crossbows.

Nageau tilted his head as well. He asked Kody, "Tell me where you think the sound is coming from." Kody concentrated, and then pointed to his right, toward the east. Nageau nodded. "Good."

"It sounds like a plane," Kody said, shielding his eyes from the rising sun.

The sound steadily grew louder and less than a minute later a large aircraft rose into view, turning from the east to approach the mining site. It hovered a hundred feet below the team's vantage point and about three hundred feet above the landing pad. Kody gasped at the aircraft as it appeared to magically hang in midair, his dread growing.

The co-pilot in the cockpit took in the devastation below. "What the—it looks like a war zone down there!" he exclaimed.

"You got that right." The pilot was equally surprised by the scene. "I guess the guy really wasn't exaggerating when he said his operation was in trouble."

"There's only one reason anyone would want to hire people with our kind of record." The co-pilot inspected the site. "I wonder how this started."

"It doesn't matter how it started, we're going to finish it." The pilot turned around and yelled for the third crewmember to get into position. The man nodded and gripped the .50 caliber M2 machine gun attached to the loading ramp as the ramp was lowered. The pilot turned the Osprey around to give the gunner a view of the site. The gunner was clearly intrigued by the fray below.

"You see 'em?" the pilot asked.

"Swing around a little more to gimme a better angle!"

"Roger that. Turning around."

The gunner looked around, picking out potential targets as the pilot unwittingly flew the plane closer to where Nageau's team was situated and hovered at that spot. He settled for mowing down three natives who were grappling with a couple of workers just outside the entrance to the mine tunnel.

Up at the top of the mountain, one of Nageau's men dropped his crossbow in shock as he watched the three villagers being gunned down. "Brother!" he screamed as the second man was obliterated by the massive rounds from the weapon. "*Brother!*"

Kody quailed at the uncontrollable torment in the man's voice. He brought his knees up to his chest and wrapped his arms around them, rocking back and forth. *I want to get out of here, I want to get out of here, I want to get out of here.*

Had he looked behind him, he would have noticed rage distorting the villager's face. Something had snapped in him as he watched his brother's final moments. The man retreated as far back as he could, and with a burst of power sprinted with incredible speed toward the edge of the peak and leapt off before anyone could stop him. Soaring through the air with the velocity he'd gained, he closed in on the plane and landed on the large horizontal stabilizer before falling onto the ramp. Whipping out his hunting knife, he charged at the gunner like a madman.

The gunner turned his weapon and instinctively fired at the man. He watched him collapse and roll down the ramp out of the plane. The gunner released his grip on the trigger. He was speechless. How anyone could have gotten onto the plane was beyond him. He scanned around the site and shook his head in disbelief.

The pilot called back to the gunner. "Hey, bozo! Keep that thing going! They're all running for cover!"

As the gunner placed his hands on the machine gun again, he could hear a series of clink-clanking sounds. He frowned. What on earth was going on? Then an arrow whizzed past him, nearly embedding itself into his shoulder.

"I can't believe it!" the co-pilot exclaimed. "Tenacious bunch, aren't they?"

"Tenacious bunch of lunatics, you mean," shouted the gunner when a couple of arrows whipped past him and clanked inside the aircraft. When a third nearly struck him, he yelled, "I'm in their line of fire! I need some cover!"

No sooner were the words out of his mouth than an arrow was shot clear through his neck. The gunner fell over, writhing. The co-pilot looked back, wondering why the firing had stopped again, then saw the gunner. "*Ay dios mio,*" he seethed. He quickly unbuckled himself and left his seat. "Ron's down! I'm gonna go check on him!"

"Get on the gun!" the pilot shouted. "I'll reduce our altitude to give you better firing solution."

"Copy that!" his counterpart answered as he checked on the gunner. Realizing it was too late to save him, the co-pilot took up his post at the machine gun with resolve to avenge his fallen colleague.

56

Jag tied up the last of the three men he and Tayoka had fought with. Too heavy for him to carry, he laid the man down and rolled him to the side of the miners' barracks with the others. He stepped back to observe his work when he heard a clicking sound and felt something press against the back of his head. "Don't try anything funny," a voice said.

As Jag slowly raised his hands, he said, "Please don't shoot. I'm just a kid."

"You sure don't fight like any kid I know. Who are you people?"

Jag said nothing. Then, in the blink of an eye, he whirled around and socked his aggressor's wrist. The pistol fell from the man's grip as he let out a cry and clutched his hand. Jag stooped down, picked up the gun and pointed it at the man. He backed off to a safe distance, keeping his eyes on the worker. He was surprised to see that it was a lanky young man, probably only twenty years old, with a dyed high-and-tight haircut and a sunken face.

While Jag took stock of the man's scrawny build, the worker stared down his nose at Jag and sneered. Looking with bloodshot eyes, he started to walk toward Jag.

"Don't move!" Jag shouted, keeping the weapon aimed at the worker. He was tempted to pull the trigger and end it right there. He tried to convince himself that this was no different from when he'd shot the deranged wolves with the flare gun. But something deep inside him held him back and he eased his finger from the trigger. "Hit the ground," he snapped.

The worker continued to advance. Jag fired at the ground right in front of the man's feet. The man stopped and jumped back. "Hit the ground," Jag repeated, glaring.

Seeing the steely look in the teenager's eyes, the man complied and slowly knelt. Jag approached the man, gun in one hand, and removed the last immobilizing dart he had from his pocket. Keeping the pistol pointed at the worker's head, he plunged the dart into the man's back. The man went limp and collapsed face-down on the dirt. Jag tossed the gun aside and pulled out an active vine from his belt. He slapped it on the workers hands and watched as the vine curled around and locked itself on his wrists.

Jag took a deep breath. He remembered the words of wisdom from the Elders regarding the responsibility that came with power, and was thankful that he'd gotten through the encounter without losing his humanity.

His thoughts were broken by the resumption of airborne gunfire. Jag dove for cover behind the miners' barracks and looked from around the corner. He could see the huge rotors of the aircraft in a vertical position as the plane hovered like a helicopter. A spray of bullets hailed down from the open ramp at the back of the plane. *What are they shooting at?* Jag thought as he lowered his gaze to the ground. He halted when he saw Tayoka sprinting amidst the rubble toward him, ducking and weaving to avoid the projectiles. Jag yelled and waved his arms, urging his mentor to hurry to safety next to him.

As the Elder closed in on Jag's location, gouts of earth erupted behind him as bullets struck the ground. With unbelieving eyes Jag watched as Tayoka lurched forward, stumbling for a few paces before landing on the dirt. Jag shoved his knuckles into his mouth to keep from crying out as he watched. He forced himself to hold his position until the ramp-end of the plane swung away, then sprinted out of cover toward the Elder.

Aari and Tegan, who were crouched just inside the mess hall, had also caught sight of the Elder's fall. They heard Jag's scream and saw him run toward his mentor. Tegan yanked at Aari's arm and the two raced after their friend. As they reached Tayoka, with

Jag kneeling beside him, they could see the blood soaking the Elder's tunic from the injury in his back. Jag placed two fingers on his mentor's neck and felt a very faint pulse. He slammed his fist against the ground, knowing Tayoka was hardly hanging on.

"Is he still alive?" Tegan murmured.

"Barely."

Aari looked up at the Osprey. "We need to get him out of here. The plane's going to turn back soon."

"Take care of him," Jag said, an edge to his voice as he stood up.

Tegan caught a look in his eyes and knew something was brewing in his mind. "What are you—"

"Just get him to safety," he cut her off, turning to look at the plane. Without another word, he started to sprint in the direction of the aircraft. He heard his friends shouting his name but his mind was set and he was not turning back.

Inside the sniper's office, Saiyu and Mariah faced the muzzle of the weapon with astonishment. They hadn't expected to be intercepted so quickly. Saiyu instinctively shoved Mariah to a corner of the room. Forced to choose a target, the sniper pointed his weapon at the Elder while keeping a close watch on the girl.

Mariah watched the man as he spat at Saiyu. "Filthy savages," he snarled. "You've destroyed everything and killed my men."

Gathering courage to respond, Mariah said, "Your workers are mostly just immobilized."

The man turned to look at her, perplexed that she spoke in English, then snapped his attention back to Saiyu. "Doesn't matter. You've destroyed *months* of my hard work." He looked at the Elder with unadulterated fury in his eyes. Just as his finger moved to squeeze the trigger, he caught a movement to his right and turned in time to see the crystal sculpture of Rasputin hurtling through the air toward him. It smashed into his face, breaking his nose on impact and shattering. He fell back, hitting his head on the desk behind him. The desk toppled over, its drawers sliding out and sending papers flying.

Saiyu turned to look at Mariah in surprise as the girl joined her mentor. She gave her apprentice a tight squeeze for her quick thinking, then removed an active vine from her sash and moved forward to tie the gunman up.

As she approached him, the sniper shook his head and grabbed a revolver that had fallen out of the desk. With blood dripping down his face, he pointed the weapon at the Elder for a second before turning it on Mariah and pulling the trigger.

Mariah heard the bang and squeezed her eyes shut. She thought her life was over as she covered her head in a feeble attempt to protect herself. Two heartbeats later, she realized she was still standing. Lowering her arms and opening her eyes, she saw a scene that appeared frozen in time.

No more than six inches from her face, the bullet hung in midair. The gunman stared and rubbed his eyes in disbelief. Mariah watched as the bullet dropped to the ground, then looked at her mentor. Saiyu gave her a short nod before turning to the man, fierce anger scrawled across her face as she brought the full force of her power to bear. Mariah had never seen the Elder in such a rage before.

The sniper raised his hand to fire another round but found himself being lifted from the ground and smashed into the ceiling. Mariah winced as she watched him drop back to the floor in a daze before being picked up and smashed into the ceiling once more. Upon being released for the second time by Saiyu, the man plunged to the floor, screaming all the way down. For the finale, he was lifted off the floor at such a tremendous force that he crashed through the ceiling, leaving him stuck with his head and shoulders exposed through the roof. He shouted obscenities at the top of his lungs, unable to understand the force that had buffeted him into humiliation.

Mariah gawked at her mentor as Saiyu sent a message to Nageau, informing him of the sniper's position. The Elder glanced at Mariah and smiled. Together they stared up, grinning at the wriggling legs of the man before he went limp as one of Nageau's men shot him with a dart.

Sprinting at an inhuman speed, Jag's blurred figure tore across the mining site toward the plane as it swung back around. Leaping onto the roof of the steel building that housed the beasts and using it as a springboard, he bounded off and propelled straight toward the open ramp of the plane. Traversing a distance of about a hundred and twenty feet within seconds, he smashed headlong into the man at the gun and sent him tumbling backwards toward the cockpit. The co-pilot sat up, stunned by the hit, and struggled to get to his feet. Looking toward the ramp, he saw a figure charging at him. He managed to yell a warning to the pilot before receiving a whirling kick to his helmet that floored him.

Jag, knowing he had no darts left, tried to knock the man unconscious. The pilot glanced back, and seeing that his colleague was under attack, tilted the plane violently. Jag was thrown off balance and smashed into a bulkhead. Seizing his opportunity, the co-pilot whipped out his pistol to shoot Jag but lost his footing and fell toward the boy as the plane leveled off.

Still holding on to the gun, he had barely picked himself up from the floor when Jag dove onto him, tackling him back down. They rolled toward the ramp. They were two yards from the edge when the co-pilot gained the upper hand and stopped the rolling. He sat over Jag and hit the teenager across the head with his weapon. The sharp pain stunned Jag briefly but he would not give in. He used both hands to grab the arm that was wielding the gun and held on.

The co-pilot turned his wrist and slowly started to point the pistol toward Jag. He was a breath away from pulling the trigger when Jag twisted his wrist. Three shots fired in rapid succession into the cockpit. The man looked back angrily and swung his other arm, punching the boy on his ear. Jag gathered his strength and kicked the man over his head and out the ramp. Realizing what he'd done, he quickly flipped over and tried to grab the co-pilot, but the man was already out of reach. Jag looked away, unable to bear the sight, then picked himself up and headed toward the cockpit.

Kody, who'd witnessed Jag's amazing leap into the plane, was dumbfounded into silence for the first time in his life. "You, my friend," he muttered under his breath, "are a remarkable nutjob."

Aari and Tegan were tending to Tayoka behind the barracks, one on either side of the Elder. Tegan sat back in frustration. "We can't handle this on our own. We need the Elders."

"Would you like to step into a shower of bullets and go look for them?" Aari asked exasperatedly.

"Then what do you suggest doing?" she snapped back. "He needs help."

Aari rubbed his forehead. "I know, I know," he groaned. "I—"

He halted in midsentence, eyes bulging out. Tegan looked at him and then slowly traced his line of sight toward the end of the building. Her nails dug into the dirt. "You have got to be kidding," she whispered.

One of the beasts was staring at them from forty feet away, head down, back arched. Seeing it had lost the element of surprise, it burst into a sprint, covering ten feet with each stride. Aari and Tegan tried to back away but were frozen with horror as the animal covered the distance and was moments away from bounding onto them. As it made its final leap, all paws in the air, a colossal shadow flew across the beast's trajectory and bulldozed the creature into the building, demolishing a large part of the wall.

A loud, thunderous roar vibrated the air. Aari and Tegan covered their ears as they stared, agape, at the humongous shape of a muscle-bound creature. Rearing up, the black-furred bear stood at three-quarters of the height of the two-story building. It was the largest animal they had ever seen. It turned to look at them with a curious gleam in its dark eyes, and for some inexplicable reason the two felt their fear wash away.

Picking itself up, the beast charged back out of the damaged building but wasn't quick enough to surprise the bear. In spite of its massive size the bear turned swiftly and smashed an enormous paw into the side of the creature, sending the beast hurtling through the tree line. Undaunted, the beast rebounded and raced back to attack the bear. It leapt, maw wide open, instinctively going for its adversary's throat. Its massive jaws clamped around the bear's scruff and its momentum pushed the bigger animal down. The bear countered by rolling over the creature, crushing it against the ground.

Getting back up, the furious bear stood over the beast and swiped one enormous paw over the animal's face. The beast's head snapped back and a gurgling howl escaped it. The bear leaned down, peering at its foe, then swung its other paw with incredible force. There was a sickening crack as the animal's head twisted around at an odd angle and the beast went still.

Having witnessed the astounding battle, Tegan and Aari leaned closer to each other, shaking. The bear turned to look at them again and the two gazed back with gratitude. Dipping its massive head, the bear turned away from them.

Poking Aari's arm, Tegan started to whisper in awe "That must be a Guar—" when another roar reverberated from across the site. The bear raised its head, alert, then broke into a run and rounded the building toward the center of the mining site.

Nageau's group looked on in astonishment as a Guardian faced three beasts by the rubble of the vehicle shed. Two of the animals clambered onto the silver bear's back and another fixed its jaws around its adversary's throat. The weight of all three pulled the immense creature to the ground.

As Nageau watched, Ashack's voice came into his head. *She is awake, Nageau.*

Nageau immediately linked with his mate. Tikina!

Hello, beloved. He could almost hear the smile in her tired thought.

How are you feeling? How bad is the wound?

It hurts, but Ashack has done the best he could with all that he has.

We will get you properly cared for soon, I promise. He paused when he heard the bear roar as the beasts assaulted it viciously. *You managed to summon the Guardians? How?*

It was not easy. If only I had more energy. She paused to sigh. I only managed to call on two, though.

From around the side of the barracks, the black Guardian loped toward the first, ripping one of the beasts from its companion's back and flinging it into the only vehicle that remained standing at the vehicle shed. The beast crashed into the truck and smashed the windshield into a million pieces before sliding off the hood and falling onto the ground in a daze.

Nageau followed the Guardians' movements, exultant. *Thank you, Tikina.*

Let us pray the Guardians will be the saving grace we need.

Nageau gently said goodbye to her and linked back to Ashack. Though he found it difficult to ask Ashack to leave his mate, he knew Tayoka was in dire need of assistance. *Ashack, Tayoka is down. You must help him.*

Tayoka? What happened?

He was shot. I do not know his condition but he did not appear responsive.

I will take care of it. But . . . Nageau? I have not yet had a chance to contact Saiyu. Is she alright?

She is just fine, my friend. She and her apprentice have managed to remove a threat.

Thank goodness. There was a pause. *Where is Tayoka?*

Behind the building you are in. Tegan and Aari have moved him there.

Understood. Ashack cut off the link.

Kody looked up from watching the large bears battle the beasts. "Are those the Guardians?" he asked quietly, wide-eyed.

Nageau managed a smile. "Yes."

"One of them looks like it's having trouble. Should we help?"

Shaking his head, Nageau responded, "It is best not to interfere." He turned to his team. "Take every single one of the remaining miners out, and let the Guardians take care of the beasts."

The men nodded and readied their weapons once more.

Kody looked back down to watch the bears fight. "I sure wouldn't want to get tangled with that," he said, shivering.

The pilot of the Osprey was struggling with the flight controls as Jag closed in on him. A plume of smoke trailed toward the roof of the cockpit from the control panel. Jag took a quick look at the scenario. He only had time to deduce that the shots fired into the cockpit earlier had caused the damage before the pilot turned around to see him. He glared at Jag and then pitched the nose of the plane up violently. The aircraft tipped skyward almost instantaneously. Jag was thrown backwards and tumbled all the way to the ramp. He tried to reach for something to hold on to but his flailing arms couldn't find anything to grab and he slid off the back of the plane.

At the very last moment his fingers caught a groove at the end of the ramp and he held on, gasping. As he steadied himself, he looked down and regretted it instantly. The site lay about two hundred feet below his hanging feet with the plane hovering erratically at an awkward angle. Huffing, Jag used all his strength to haul himself back onto the ramp, managing to get only one foot over.

The pilot was having difficulty leveling the plane after the pitch. Smoke had filled the cockpit. Coughing, the pilot tried to wave the smoke away and noticed a fire had broken out in the control panel. The plane was losing altitude. With a sinking feeling he continued to fight the controls but the plane was not responding. "Come on!" he barked. "Raise your big butt off this bloody mountain!"

Atop the mountain, Kody noticed the plane was wobbling from side to side. He watched the nacelles of the aircraft tilt forward as the pilot executed a desperate attempt to gain forward momentum. The Osprey was losing altitude and Kody watched powerlessly as it slowly drifted past the landing pad.

His attention was jarred back to the mining site by two distinctive roars. The black-furred Guardian that had rushed from behind the miners' barracks tore the second beast away from its comrade's throat. It smashed the creature against the ground a few times. The beast kicked out, sinking its claws into the bigger animal's muzzle. The Guardian shook its head to throw the creature off but couldn't. Using its full strength, the beast pulled up with its front paws digging into the bear's muzzle and leapt over the Guardian's head onto its back, then bit into the base of the bear's neck. The Guardian grunted, twisting around and bucking, but its assailant would not give. It pierced and tore through the bear's thick fur until the Guardian gave a furious shake of its massive body and the beast skidded off.

In a fraction of a second the bear had the beast pinned. The Guardian reared up and glared at its foe. Before the creature could escape, the bear crashed down with its full weight, crushing the beast's skull under its humongous paws. The Guardian cautiously lifted its paws off the beast and stared at the animal's pulverized head before swiping the carcass aside.

The silver-furred Guardian had gotten onto its feet and attempted to shove away the beast that clung onto it. Tearing away at the silver bear's face with its claws, the beast grazed the Guardian over its eye. Momentarily blinded, the Guardian took a couple of steps backward, bellowing. The beast found its chance and rushed for the bear's throat. The Guardian reared and tried to tear the animal away. Its comrade, fresh from its victory, charged over and ripped the beast away from the silver Guardian. The Marauder held on with its teeth for as long as it could before relenting.

Falling onto the dirt, the beast whimpered and scurried away. The bears were instantly on its tail, carrying their massive weight at an astounding speed. They split around the beast with a pincer maneuver, effectively trapping the animal. Realizing it was cornered, the animal threw everything it had left into the fight and lunged at the black-furred Guardian. The bear dipped its head and rammed the beast toward the silver Guardian, who picked the beast up by its scruff and banged it against the ground twice before severing the creature's neck in its bone-crushing jaws.

A roar sounded some distance from the Guardians. The bears turned to face the last surviving beast, the one that the first Guardian had thrown against the truck earlier. The silver Guardian roared back, drowning out the other creature's call of warning, and both bears slowly started toward the beast.

Nageau, Kody and the rest of the team watched the spectacular encounter in silent awe. To Kody, it felt as though he was watching two titanic forces clash in the battle of the century.

As the Guardians made their way toward the beast, Kody's eyes inadvertently drifted back toward the Osprey in its unsteady flight. He sat rigid, watching with growing dread as the plane drifted toward the tree tops. He could see Jag hanging precariously over the ramp, trying to clamber back into the aircraft. "Jag!" he yelled, even though he knew his friend would not be able to hear him over the din.

The others on the mountain top turned toward the Osprey and murmured nervously to one another. Wide-eyed, they watched as the shadow cast by the plane drifted toward the edge of the mine site.

Tegan and Aari had left Tayoka in Ashack's hands. Peeking from behind the barracks, they gaped at the huge plane, its rotors now tilted mostly forward as it chomped through the tops of the trees in its path. Pieces of the rotor blades and chunks of trees whirled away and were spat onto the ground and the surrounding landscape. They could see a form dangling from the edge of the aircraft's ramp and cried in dismay when they recognized the figure.

The pair exchanged horrified looks, then stared upward again when they heard the sound of the aircraft's engines increase. They watched as the Osprey attempted to lift itself over the treetops. The plane vibrated violently when a large piece of a rotor broke loose and struck a fuel tank, setting off a fiery blast. The noise resounded across the mountain and the engine began to sputter. The aircraft tilted over, losing altitude rapidly, then tumbled over the edge of the mine site. A thunderous explosion rocked the ground and a towering cloud of black smoke mushroomed from the side of the mountain.

Tegan and Aari sprinted around the building, heading toward where the plane had gone down with only one thought in mind—to find their friend. As they ran past the rubble of the shed to their right, a couple of earth-shaking roars halted them in their tracks. They turned to see two Guardians making their way over to the last beast that stood over the debris. As they watched, the beast slowly twisted its head back to look over its shoulder at the friends, its fangs bared. It stood still for a moment, then, with a twitch of its cropped tail, leapt away from the oncoming Guardians and sped after Aari and Tegan. Within moments the beast was in striking distance.

Knowing he couldn't outrun the creature, Aari frantically searched for something to protect himself with. Spotting a torn metal door on the ground, he hurriedly picked it up and held it as a shield. In his haste—and not realizing just how heavy the door was—he swayed backward, off balance. The beast took advantage of this and lunged on top of Aari, knocking the boy to the ground. Aari let out a cry of pain but held onto the door, which was the only thing protecting his body from the animal's deathly jaws.

The beast struggled to sink its teeth into the flat metal. Frustrated, it grabbed the edge of the door in its maw and peeled the corner back until it revealed its prey's face. Aari stared up at the frightful creature in horror as its eyes bore into him, ready for a kill. Unable to do anything, he watched, terrified, as the beast flung the deformed door aside. With its victim now fully exposed, it moved in to finish the job.

As Aari shut his eyes and covered his face instinctively, he heard the beast let out a surprised yelp. Opening his eyes, he was shocked to see a long steel pipe piercing the creature's side. Tegan stood a few feet away, shaking. She let go of her end of the six-foot spear she had plunged into the beast and fell to her knees beside Aari.

Distracted by the momentary pain, the animal moved back and yanked the blood-stained pipe out of its side with its jaws, then dropped it to the ground. Furious, it turned back to the friends with a snarl and sprang at them. They were within its reach when a large form leapt over the beast and knocked the creature aside. The silver Guardian reared to stand protectively in front of the friends. It growled and eyed the beast threateningly. Quickly backing away, the beast turned to flee but found itself face-to-face with the black-furred Guardian. It cowered, snapping its teeth and swinging its head from one side to the other as the bears closed the gap.

Still shaking, Tegan and Aari managed to get to their feet and darted away from the titans. Aari glanced back when he heard a blood-curdling howl and, against the rising sun, saw the silhouette of the beast in the jaws of both the Guardians. The last thing he heard was a booming roar from the victorious bears as they reared to their full heights of fifteen feet, the remains of the beast strewn across the dirt.

Having brought down Ajajdif from the ceiling and tied him up, Saiyu and Mariah headed towards the exit. Just as she was about to step out, Mariah noticed something shiny peeking out from under a broken shelf on the floor. She knelt down and picked it up, studying it for a few moments before slipping the curious object into her pocket; she decided she'd bring it up with Saiyu later.

As Elder and apprentice poked their heads out of the door, their eyes stretched in shock at the sight that met them. Mariah saw Aari and Tegan running into the trees and followed after them. "Where are you going?" she called out.

"Jag!" they shouted, ignoring her question. "Jag!"

Mariah dashed after her friends, Saiyu close behind. Weaving through the debris and the blackened vegetation, they reached the edge of the mining site and peered down the side of the mountain. A few hundred feet below them, the charred fuselage of the aircraft was lodged between several trees. Fire and smoke were scattered all around the crash site. With worried looks the four strained to find Jag. They began to despair as there was no sign of movement. Tegan and Mariah clutched Aari's arms. Saiyu stood close behind the friends, a look of deep sadness on her face.

Tegan slowly knelt down to look closer at the wreckage. She stared for a long while, silent, and a couple of tears slid down her cheeks. Mariah joined her as she too began to cry quietly. Aari stood with his arms crossed, his jaw working and his eyes red as he bitterly fought back tears. No one spoke, but all were quietly grieving.

A figure crawled up from the mountainside some yards away, puffing. Pulling itself up, the tall form stumbled shakily over to Aari and draped an arm over his shoulder, looking down at the plane with the others. "Never want to go through *that* again," the figure said in an exhausted, husky voice.

Aari froze for a moment, then slowly turned to look to his right. A smoldering, ragged Jag stood next to him with a lopsided grin. "*Jag!*" Aari bellowed. "You . . . you . . ." He gave the other boy a hard thump on the arm before wrapping him in a bear hug. "You crazy sonofagun! What were you thinking?"

The girls jumped up, staring at Jag, stunned. With ecstatic cries they tackled Jag into a group hug. Saiyu covered her mouth with a hand and looked at Jag with relief.

A round of cheers burst from the top of the mountain when Nageau and his team spotted Jag, so loud that it could be heard all the way down at the mining site. Jag squinted up at the top and waved, though he could barely see them, then turned back to the others with a smile.

Saiyu stepped off to the side as Nageau linked with her. *This conflict is over. We have halted their destructive activities. I will join you shortly.* With a twinge of sadness, he continued, *Let us gather our people, both the survivors and those who have sacrificed, and bring them back home.*

57

Sitting on top of several large boulders by the rock wall at the end of the valley, the five stared out at the village as it lay in the midday sun. They could see the emerald river flowing through the valley and young children waddling by the edges, squealing happily and splashing water at one another while their parents stood back and chatted. Several villagers walked in and out of the temple to the friends' right, often pausing to greet each other with warmth. The entire atmosphere exuded a sense of calm and contentment.

The five were fond of Dema-Ki. It had become their home and the people had become their friends. Since returning from the Ayen'et mountain, the residents had invited them for gatherings and meals, most of which the friends politely declined so they could rest and recuperate.

Jag rubbed his head, feeling the shorter haircut he now sported since having some of his hair singed off. Thanks to Huyani and Saiyu's medicinal skills and healing powers, most of his injuries had been taken care of and he was well on his way to full recovery. The others had not been as badly injured as he and were faring well.

He lowered his eyes from the village and turned to his friends as they continued to gaze out silently. It had been a life-changing summer for the five. Since the plane crash and their subsequent treatment and training in the valley, they had each grown in body, mind and spirit. The skills they'd learned, although powerful, had taught them the importance of keeping their feet firmly on the ground. It was an uncommon path that the five were treading and they were doing it with strength and courage that surprised all of them. Though their experiences and contribution during the siege at the mountain had strengthened their faith in the prophecy, they were still attempting to come to terms with the roles bestowed on them by the ancient scripture.

All five had learned much through their training, giving them more confidence in themselves. Through the extraordinary sustenance provided during their rigorous drills, the friends witnessed noticeable changes in their physiques: The boys were bigger and fitter and the girls were more athletic. And it felt good.

"I can't believe it's been a week since we were on the mountain," Jag said, breaking the quiet. Since returning, the group hardly spoke of the experience; it was almost as if they shied away from the subject.

Tegan, sharing the boulder with Jag and Mariah, nodded. "Never in my life did I think I'd be a part of something like that." She sighed. "And never in my life did I ever think I'd see such mayhem and destruction."

"Me neither," Kody murmured.

Jag glanced at where his friend sat on a smaller boulder. "You probably saw way more than we did up there, didn't you, bud?"

Kody pressed his palms to his cheeks and rubbed. "Probably," he said bitterly. "It was brutal. I lost count of how many people we lost that day."

"At least their sacrifice wasn't in vain," Tegan said.

Kody snorted. "In my opinion, there is no such thing as a victory if even one person has to die."

"Well . . . sometimes lives are lost in order for good to prevail. It's been like that throughout history. Sitting on our hands and doing nothing can't be an option if we have the ability to make a difference."

Mariah looked over Jag's head to smile at Tegan. "Well said."

Jag outlined a cut on his arm that was nearly healed, then let out a scoff. The others looked at him, puzzled. "Off topic," he apologized, "but I was remembering the look on that guy's face when the Elders gave him a shot to restore his consciousness."

"You mean the sniper Saiyu and I took down?" Mariah grinned.

"Yeah, him."

"It's interesting that the Elders were compassionate enough to leave a radio tied to that man so he could call for help," she observed.

Aari jumped down from the boulder he was sitting on and went to pluck some dandelions before returning to sit. He held one up and blew the seeds off. The friends watched as the seeds rode on the gentle breeze toward the village.

"I saw Tayoka walking with a cane this morning," Tegan said, smiling at Jag. "He's getting better every day."

Jag smiled back. "I know. If we had these folks with their healing powers in the outside world, imagine how they could help." He nudged her. "How's your mentor?"

"She's healing."

"She and Tayoka got really lucky."

"I know." Tegan watched the children playing by the water. "Didn't Nageau say Magèo estimated that the contamination in the water outside of the valley would wash away in the next six months or so?"

"I wonder how he came to that conclusion," Kody mused.

"It's like wondering how the scientists back home figure things out," Mariah answered with a shrug. "You won't know exactly unless you're one of them. And Magèo is practically the scientist of this village."

"The scientist and the old coot," Jag quipped.

"You're awful."

"And you're trying not to laugh."

". . . Whatever." She watched as Aari let another batch of dandelion seeds blow away. "You guys remember that silver coin I picked up from the sniper's office while we were clearing the mining site, the one with the weird symbol on it?" she asked. The others nodded. "When I showed it to Saiyu and she looked at it, she had a strange look on her face, almost as if she recognized it or something."

"Do you still have it?" Tegan probed.

"No. She asked if she could take it to show the other Elders."

Jag rubbed his chin. "Hm . . . that's interesting. There's gotta be some significance to it."

"That's what I figured, but it raises more questions."

"You know what I have questions about? What those beasts were." Kody shuddered. "They can't be natural."

"I doubt they were," Aari said. "At the site's medical building, there was this huge guy lying dead in the rubble. He had a device strapped on him and it looked like a remote control with a screen on it. On the back there was an engraving that said 'Marauder Control Unit'. I think that's what the creatures were called."

"You're saying those animals were actually controlled by a remote?"

"They might have been."

"But that would make them some kind of machine, wouldn't it? When the Guardians tore those suckers up there were no metal parts. They were all flesh and bone like any other living creature."

"Well, it's just a thought."

The five winced inwardly at the idea and brushed the prospect aside. Collectively taking a breath and exhaling, they leaned back. They watched the villagers go about their day for a while until they saw Huyani strolling up to them with a basket in her hand and Akol next to her. As they arrived, Huyani greeted them with a wide smile. "Here are the heroes again!" she said teasingly, although the awe that radiated from her was unmistakable.

"The tales of your bravery are spreading like wildfire, my friends," Akol told them. "You have achieved so much, so quickly. We are all astounded."

The friends glanced away, faces flushed from the kind words. "Thanks," Aari mumbled. "But we know there's much to learn and more training ahead of us."

"You sure were missed up there, though," Mariah said, looking at Akol. "It would have been great to have you by our side."

Akol beamed. "I would have done anything to stand with you against those intruders. However, the Elders had another plan for me—I was instructed to watch over the village in their absence."

"They definitely picked the right person for the job, then." Jag smiled, respect evident in his eyes.

Akol dipped his head. "Thank you, Jag."

"The entire village has an elevated faith in the Elders for recognizing the five of you as the ones promised by the prophecy," Huyani told the friends.

There was a moment of silence. Tegan seized on it to change the subject. "So what's happened to Hutar?" she asked. "No one has said anything since . . . that night."

"The Elders found more than one crystal in his possession and confiscated those," Akol answered. "As you know, each individual in this community is presented with one crystal, and that is the one they will carry with them all their lives."

"Then how did he get the rest?" Mariah asked.

"It is assumed that they were stolen from the temple. No one has ever done that before."

"So they've taken away the crystals. What will happen to him, though?" Aari pressed.

"They have decided to send him to an edification program that should aid in centering and restoring his spirit."

Kody was puzzled. "Wouldn't it be safer to just lock him up in a reformatory or something?"

Akol shook his head. "Putting Hutar away will not address the root of the problem. One of the foundations of the belief system in our community is the proper centering of each individual's spirit."

"So . . . he'll be allowed to run loose?"

"Not quite. He will spend five moon cycles in a special *neyra* where the Elders will take turns working with him to improve his ways. For half a day every day during that time, he will be active in rigorous community service. He will tend to the crops in the greenhouse, help build new *neyra*, assist wherever he can in the stable, and he will be rebuilding the old community hall."

The five were both intrigued and content with the answer. "Why would you want to rebuild the old community hall, though?" Tegan asked. "Don't you already have a new one?"

"It will not be a community hall, as such," Huyani said, finally breaking into one of her charismatic smiles. "It will become a youth center."

Tegan raised an eyebrow and grinned. "Nice."

Jag, who had been only listening all along, joined the conversation. "If he improves, what will happen to him then?"

Akol pointed over the river to a large building below the temple. "He will be teaching the young ones at the school."

"What?!" The friends stared at him in disbelief.

"I don't understand," Aari said. "Why would you do that, putting him in a roomful of kids?"

"And he doesn't seem like the educating type, if you know what I mean." Kody shuddered.

"Teaching is an essential part of learning," replied Huyani. "Learning is just like breathing in, and teaching is like breathing out. It is necessary for our progression. What the students are taught inside the school are virtues, sciences, our relationship with nature, understanding our bodies and minds, and harnessing our innate skills."

"How does teaching that help Hutar learn?"

"If you wish to lead others, you must learn to lead yourself first, no? Through teaching he will learn patience and gain maturity among other valuable assets. Once he has successfully completed his rehabilitation, then perhaps one day he will regain the sole crystal he had been given and be a responsible member of this community."

"What if this doesn't work and he doesn't change?" asked Mariah softly.

The siblings went quiet for a few moments, then Huyani said, "That is not a thought we wish to entertain. Positive projections are what Hutar requires to regain stability in himself. The alternative is unthinkable."

Not wanting to explore the subject further, the friends nodded, hoping that the corrective program would help Hutar in becoming the better man he could be. The seven of them slipped into silence again, then Huyani held up the basket she was holding. “We know you are supposed to be meeting with the Elders soon, so we brought your midday meal here. You may eat and then head to the temple.”

The five laughed and slid off the boulders. “Thanks, Huyani,” Jag said, taking the basket from her. Kody snuck up behind him and snatched the basket before frolicking off.

“Hey!” Jag exclaimed.

“You snooze, you lose.” Kody sat down on the grass, opened the basket, and dug in. “I’m gonna miss your cooking when we leave, Huyani. This is delicious.”

The others rolled their eyes and shared their mirth with Huyani and Akol before joining Kody for a satisfying meal.

58

The vibrant plumes of colorful flames from the cauldron cast a warm glow in the foyer. Down the hallway that led further into the temple, murmuring voices could be heard mingling with the soothing gurgle from two small fountains. The Elders were assembled on the benches where the friends had sat during their first discussion with Nageau about their training a few weeks before. Five polished, wooden chairs were set up to complete the semi-circle the benches formed. The Elders spoke softly so as not to disturb the other villagers who were in the temple.

It was only a few minutes later when the friends walked in to join them. They dipped their heads to the Elders, who each in turn embraced them, and took seats on the chairs to face their mentors.

Tikina asked, "Are you younglings doing well?"

"We are." Tegan titled her head at the Elder. "What about you and Elder Tayoka?"

"We are feeling better, thank you. The physical wounds heal much faster." There was a twinge of sadness in her words.

Tegan ventured softly. "How many people did we lose?"

"Each soul whom we lost was one too many."

Seeing the solemn looks on the friends' faces, Tayoka began to speak and Nageau translated. "But they gave their lives not in vain. With their bravery and courage we managed to put a stop to the destructive forces that were wreaking harm to our land."

Tikina looked back at the five. "In the meantime, you younglings have a far-reaching road to travel and immense responsibilities on your shoulders. You have shown tremendous courage and selflessness, and you have brought the people much hope." With a radiant countenance, she added to the firm nods of the other Elders, "The promise of the prophecy unfolds through you. You are indeed the shield that protects. You are indeed the saplings of Aegis, growing, advancing, rising."

The friends had no clue how to react to such a statement of faith. Kody scratched the back of his neck. "Sooo . . . when do we resume our training?"

Nageau let out a hearty laugh. "You five never cease to amaze me. You would like to get right back into training, would you not?"

"We decided we've had a long enough break," Aari told him with a small grin. "And we know we've got more to learn."

Jag looked up. "By the way, do we know what happened with the workers after we left the mountain?"

"I did a quick sweep of the mountain with Akira," Tikina answered. "I am relieved to say that the workers have all been evacuated and they took their machines with them."

Jag seemed reassured. "Good."

"Chayton will be sorely missed," Nageau said wistfully. "The children have adored him since the moment he wandered into our village as a youngling."

Tikina sighed. "He was truly one of a kind."

After a moment of silence, Tegan spoke up again. "We found it thoughtful that you left the radio for the man who headed the mining operation. I'll admit that if it were me, I may not have done that."

"If we had left them there helpless, they may have perished," Nageau told her. "That was not our aim."

"I have a question," Mariah said. "There was a coin that I found in the sniper's office, which I handed to Elder Saiyu . . ."

"Ah, yes." Nageau nodded at Saiyu and the Elder pulled the coin out from the fold of her tunic. She passed the coin to Nageau and the Elder held it up for the five to see. An intricate symbol was etched onto the surface. The friends leaned closer to get a better look.

"What is it?" Kody asked.

Nageau responded. "It is part of an ancient symbol belonging to our people."

The five exchanged confused looks. "How is that possible?" Jag asked. "I thought this civilization was concealed from the world."

Nageau handed the coin over to Mariah so she could take a look at it and pass it around to the others. "I shall get to that in a moment, Jag. Let me begin by enlightening you on what this symbol means. This symbol is a part of a pair that represents duality in all of existence."

He motioned to Ashack. The black-haired Elder raised his hands to show a glowing crystal ball. Inside the violet sphere were two symbols on opposite sides. They looked like the last letter of the modern-day alphabet with a horizontal line cutting through them; one appeared bright, while the other was dark.

Aari, who now had the coin, held it up next to the sphere and the five could see that the symbol on the coin was the same as one of the symbols inside.

"What exactly is meant by the duality in existence?" Aari asked, his eyes glued to the symbols in the crystal ball.

"We believe that the entire universe exists in harmonious balance. There are many terms that various civilizations have used in history to express this." With a knowing sparkle in his eyes, Nageau said, "You probably have heard about the philosophy of yin and yang."

Tegan squinted at the Elder. "How do you know about that?"

Nageau just smiled and continued. "Matter and anti-matter in your recent scientific discoveries is another example, as is the cycle of composition and decomposition that we see around us. The pairing of male and female within this biosphere we call Earth is yet another illustration. Even the religious concept of Heaven and Hell is based on this duality, which in a recent revelation is referred to as the twin pillars of reward and punishment upon which justice rests. Likewise, these two symbols you see in the sphere signify something important." He paused to meet the friends' anticipative gazes. "Creation and destruction."

Ashack placed the sphere on an altar behind one of the benches. Mariah took the coin back from Aari and pointed at it. "So which one does this symbol represent?"

Nageau ran his hand through his wispy white hair and his blue eyes were sullen. In a quiet voice he said, "Destruction."

There was silence as five young minds tried to grasp the impact of what was just said. Aari shook his head. "What does this all mean?" he asked.

Jag frowned. "And how did this get into the hands of an outsider?"

Before responding to their questions, Tikina said, "It appears that your being here is predestined. The events that have unfolded in such a short time since your arrival have only served to assure us of the validity of the prophecy. Your finding of the coin is, to us, a sign that you need to be made aware of certain truths which we intend to share."

The five waited expectantly. She continued. "While our existence here as a community has remained—and must remain—a secret as directed in our scriptures, we have, in anticipation of what our prophecy has forewarned us, taken certain unconventional measures. Over the last two generations or so, we have placed a league of what we call Sentries within your civilization."

The five were perplexed. "I beg your pardon?" Aari said.

"Allow me to shed some light on this. We have people out there living amongst you," Nageau said, "and in their own ways they are aiding humanity to face the dark clouds that are gathering."

"What dark clouds?" Mariah asked.

"Civilizations can only move forward based on universal principles such as truth, justice, honor, and love," Nageau said. "Is it possible for any society to function effectively based on the opposites, such as deceit, injustice, dishonor, and hate?"

The friends frowned, heads shaking. The Elder continued. "Since the turn of the last century, humanity has been marching forth at a relentless speed toward a questionable destination. In the last few decades, we have seen this momentum accelerate. Mankind has passed a fork in its journey, and has unfortunately taken a path of self-centeredness fed by greed and corruption. Having strayed from the great traditions that have been its guide for ages, it now finds itself in a gathering storm. This has happened many times in history with the rise and fall of civilizations, but this time, by the sheer immensity of what is about to happen due to its global nature, this is far different from anything humanity has ever experienced.

"The clouds that gather feed off these weaknesses, but at the center of this storm is a catalyst far more destructive than anyone can fathom. This entity aims to accelerate humanity's journey down this road of self-destruction. Although this force of darkness gathers, there is still light left in many good souls that illuminate the world. It is this light that our Sentries across the planet seek to nourish, sustain and protect."

Tegan pinched her cheeks as she tried to comprehend the Elder's meaning. "What is this catalyst? And why does it want to speed up our demise?"

"Those are valid questions and you will have many more as you ponder on this further. What we have revealed to you suffices for now. As you complete your training, we will gradually enlighten you with all the knowledge you must have to fulfill your role in the prophecy."

Jag took the coin from Mariah and held it up. "That still doesn't explain how this symbol got out."

The Elders shifted and glanced away momentarily before Nageau said, "That is something we are waiting to affirm. We shall hopefully have knowledge of that soon."

"What about the Sentries?" Kody asked. "Who are they? Will we get to meet them?"

Tikina, her green eyes spirited, smiled. "It is most likely that you have already run into at least one of them in the course of your young lives. They may have been a school teacher, a firefighter, the owner of a corner store, or even someone you pass by on your daily errands."

The friends' minds raced through images of people they'd known all their lives to figure a possible match. Noticing the silence, Tayoka playfully remarked, "Look at all those furrowed brows! Easy, younglings. I am sure you will figure them out in time. In the meantime, we must discuss the completion of your training."

"One moon cycle? That's about four weeks!" Mariah said in a bittersweet tone. "Is that all the time we have left here?" She looked at her friends; they'd all grown close to the people and had become attached to Dema-Ki.

"When you leave after your training, you will go back to your homes and live your normal lives," Nageau said. The Elders gazed affectionately at their apprentices.

"It will not be a goodbye that lasts forever," Saiyu assured them through Tikina. "We will remain connected."

"How?"

"You will know in time," Tikina said. She then turned to Kody with a smile. "Youngling, I have some wonderful news. You will be pleased to know that your father is alive."

Taken by surprise, Kody blurted, "What . . . how . . . Where is he?"

"We do not currently know for certain where he is, but we do know that he made his way to a small town at the edge of the forest."

"Will I be able to see him?"

"Chances are he would have been taken back to your hometown. That is all we know for now."

The boy was euphoric. He looked as if he was ready to bounce around the temple, but contented himself with just swinging his legs back and forth with a huge grin on his face.

Nageau looked at his apprentice warmly. He then stood up, beckoning to the five, and walked past the friends. The other Elders followed, as did their apprentices. Nageau led the way to an altar on which stood a gold-plated, five-sided pyramid. Nageau fiddled with the latch and one of the pyramids' faces opened. Reaching in, the Elder removed a black velvet sachet and pulled his hand back out. Tayoka, knowing what was coming, smiled and gently directed the fives' hands up with his cane, palms open.

From within the sachet, Nageau placed a crystal in each of their hands. The crystals were all different in color and shape. The five gazed at the objects, transfixed. "When you have completed your training, these will be yours," Tikina told them. "These are not ordinary crystals, younglings. These ones will help to strengthen your spirit and galvanize your minds."

The friends stared at the crystals with hungry fixation for a few more moments before Nageau gently took them and placed them back into the sachet to tuck away into the altar. He latched the pyramid up and the Elders guided the friends out of the temple. Bidding the friends goodbye, the other Elders headed to their *neyra*, leaving Nageau to walk with the five along the winding path by the river.

The sun was beginning to set and a conflagration of pink, orange and yellow welcomed them. A couple of young children ran past them, then quickly backtracked to bow to the Elder and glance at the five with admiration before scampering off. Nageau and the friends grinned and continued walking until a girl about ten years old shyly came up to the friends. She bowed, then reached up to tuck a primrose wildflower into Mariah and Tegan's hair. The two smiled, and using some words they'd learned, quietly thanked the girl in the villagers' language. The friends had been showered with tokens of appreciation like this since their return from the Ayen'et and were deeply touched by the sincerity of the villagers.

The five found the gentle burble of the water relaxing as they crossed one of the bridges over Esroh Lègna. The knowledge imparted by the Elders during the meeting occupied their thoughts and the soothing sounds of the river calmed their minds.

As they neared the friends' *neyra*, Nageau came to a stop. The five turned to look at him. They knew the Elder well enough to know that there was something on his mind. They gathered around him and he looked each one of them in the eyes. "There is something I wish to say to you," he began. "It is something that we have spoken about before, but its importance cannot be stressed enough. You have all learned and grown so much with your training in such a short span of time. Though your powers will continue to strengthen, you must always remember that these abilities are channeled through you to bring light to the world.

The battle between the bearers of light and the forces of darkness is intensifying, and your roles will always be to hold up and diffuse this light. I promise you, though, you will not be alone. And remember, it is essential that you always, *always* do the right thing as prompted by your spirit—though doing the right thing may not always be the easiest."

The five stood in silence, allowing the words of wisdom from the beloved Elder to sink in. Mariah stepped forward and gave Nageau a hug. Tegan joined her. Nageau saw the boys standing off and waved them in with a warm laugh.

At the end of the group hug, Nageau smiled affectionately at the five, then turned and began walking away. The friends watched him stroll toward the setting sun at the end of the valley. High above the Elder, they saw a golden eagle swoop across the sun and disappear past the mountain ridge.

EPILOGUE

It was a cool August evening in Central Park. Families were out and about. Couples were strolling and teenagers rode on their bikes, calling out to one another. Right across from the Delacorte amphitheater, famous for its Shakespeare in the Park performances, a lone figure clad in a long black coat with a golden hood sat on a bench, holding a golf ball-sized violet sphere, and watched a flock of ducks in the sky coming in to land on a pond. Several children trotted toward the edge of the water to feed the birds that paddled toward them eagerly.

The figure watched them for a little while before glancing at a gold Rolex watch. It was nearly eight-thirty, which meant that Adrian Black would have just gotten off work on the west coast and be heading home. Drawing out a cell phone, the figure punched in a number and counted the rings.

From the basement parking lot at the head office of Phoenix Corporation, Black's brand new Lexus merged with the rush hour traffic. Just before turning onto a freeway, his Bluetooth ringer beeped and he glanced at the caller ID on his dashboard screen. His heart skipped a beat. In his haste to find an opportunity to pull over, he nearly slammed into a passing minivan. The driver of the vehicle honked and glared at him. Cursing, Black found a break in the traffic and pulled over to the side before hitting the answer button on his steering wheel. "Hello?"

"Adrian." The boss's voice filled the car through its eight-speaker sound system. "How are you doing?"

Black flinched. "I'm good, thank you. You're back in the States?"

"I arrived in New York this morning, and I got your email."

"Oh. I, uh, sent it about five days ago."

"Yes . . . I didn't feel like responding to that report, considering how unreliable you've become."

That verbal slap on the face shot fear through Black. He stammered, "I . . . I want to assure you that we've cleaned up the mess and left no trace. Vlad and his men have been evacuated. They managed to salvage eight kilos of the ore."

There was a silence, then the voice probed with an edge in its tone. "What was the amount that was needed, Adrian? What did I ask for?"

"T-twelve kilos."

"Mmhm. Now what good is eight kilos to me? You know what it takes to fire up the plans we have made with Quest Defense. They have all their ducks in a row and you can't even deliver a handful of *dust* to me?"

Black rested his forehead against the steering wheel. "I'm sorry. I trusted that Vlad was up to the task. Had I known of his incompetence, I would have taken other measures."

"Listen, you imbecile," the boss hissed. "Vlad may be the head of Quest Mining, but you're the head of the corporation. He reports to *you*."

Black remained quiet; there was no response he could give to allay the situation. The boss pressed on. "You should have foreseen that and put alternate plans in place." The voice paused. "Just like I've done."

Black lurched back. "What do you mean?"

"I've put in place an alternate team to drill for the same ore in Siberia."

"But I was told that site up in the Northwest Territories was the only place that contained the fenixium."

"You were told what you needed to know. I expected you to stay focused on the operation in Canada and do whatever was required to meet your objectives, but you have failed me. I've learned to never put all my eggs in one basket and I've been proven right. The Russian site will produce more than enough ore to complete the required amount within four weeks."

"I'm relieved to hear that." Black reached for his water bottle to moisten his dry mouth. "So the plan continues as scheduled, then?"

"Would I have it any other way." It was more of a statement than a question. "Do you understand what is at stake here, Adrian? Do you not see why I have raised this corporation and its subsidiaries? Have you lost sight of the objectives of the Arcane Ventures? You and Vlad are, for now, the only ones with considerable knowledge of my intent. If you need to be schooled again, then perhaps I should reconsider your value in the future of this corporation. There is no room for error or complacency as we prepare to unleash an incursion that will alter the destiny of our planet.."

"Let me prove my worth to you again," Black pleaded. "I assure you that I will not fail you anymore."

Back in Central Park, the figure gazed up at the sky as the wind picked up and caught sight of dark clouds gathering on the horizon. Standing up, the founder of Phoenix Corporation pulled on the gold-colored hood. "You better keep your word then, Adrian. There is a fierce storm brewing that no power on Earth can stop. And when it passes, I will be there to sow the seeds for a new harvest."

List of Characters

The Five:
Aari Barnes
Jag Sanchez
Kody Tyler
Mariah Ashton
Tegan Ryder

The Elders:
Ashack [Ay-SHAK]
Nageau [Nah-GO]
Saiyu [SAY-yoo]
Tayoka [Tah-YO-ka]
Tikina [Tee-KEE-nah]

The Villagers:
Aesròn [Ay-zuh-RON]
Akol [AY-cole]
Aydar [AY-darr]
Breyas [Bray-YAZ]
Diyo [DEE-yo]
Fiotez [FEE-oh-taz]
Hutar [HYOO-tar]
Huyani [HOO-ya-nee]
Keno [Kay-NO]
Magèo [Ma-JAY-oh]
Matikè [Ma-tee-KAY]
Mitska [Mitt-SCA]
Mokun [Mo-KOON]
Pèrzun [Pair-ZOON]
Relsuc [Rail-SOOK]
Rikèq [REE-cake]
Tibut [TEE-boot]

Dema-Ki Animals:
Akira [Ah-KEE-rah], a golden eagle.
Chayton [SHAY-tun], a wolf
Tyse [TYCE] (rhymes with rice), a lynx

Phoenix Corporation
Adrian Black — CEO, Phoenix Corporation
Dr. Albert Bertram — CSO, Phoenix Corporation
Arianna Abdul — Chief Geologist, Quest Mining
Elias Hajjar — Head of Security, Quest Mining
Francis LeChamps — Chief Mining Engineer, Quest Mining
Jerry Li — CFO, Phoenix Corporation
Dr. John Tabrizi — Chief Executive, Quest Chemicals
Luigi Dattalo — Chief Executive, Quest Defense
Vladimir Ajajdif — Chief Executive, Quest Mining
The Boss — Owner, Phoenix Corporation and all subsidiaries

We hope you have enjoyed this novel, the first of many Aegis adventures!

We would like you to know that by purchasing this book you are supporting a great cause. A portion of sales from this book goes to Aegis League, a non-profit that helps young people living in places and conditions that deny them the opportunity to explore their potential. Aegis League works with like-minded organizations to provide life-skills training and micro-loans to fund small businesses for disadvantaged youths and encourage them to give back to their community.

For more information and on how you can participate please visit:

www.aegisleague.org

Acknowledgments

Aegis Rising went from being a simple manuscript to an intricate novel in the span of four years. I must say, writing this book has been quite an adventure in itself. The unforgettable field trips, excursions and countless hours of exploring the landscape of the internet in researching this novel have enriched my experience as a writer.

This book would not have seen the light of day if not for the incredible support and encouragement that I received throughout this journey. There are several wonderful people whom I would like to take this time to express my gratitude to. First and foremost my amazing parents: My mother for her patience, her love, and her edifying counsel; my father for his countless hours of reviewing the manuscript, designing the cover and illustrations and being a great sounding board for my ideas, as well as persevering through my sometimes willful ways; my editor Gordon Williams for his expert advice, thoughtful methods and being a great coach; my grandparents for their amazing and infectious enthusiasm; Jennifer and Dan for being there from the beginning and for their enduring support; my family for their love and zeal; my advance readers for their helpful feedback and to my teachers for their encouragement. Finally a special thank you, to you the reader, for picking up this novel—I look forward to continuing this exciting journey with you.

It really has been an experience that I am not bound to forget anytime soon, and the great thing is, we are just getting started!

S.S.Segran,
October 2013

About the Author

S.S.Segran spent a good chunk of her childhood exploring the enchanted forest of a million tales in the mystical land of books. In her early teens, she began crafting intriguing new worlds and conjuring up characters who came alive with the flick of her wand . . . err . . . pen. Charmed by the magical response to her debut novel from readers around the world, she has embarked on a quest to take her cherished fans on a thrilling journey deeper into the Aegis universe. Even as she delves into her creative endeavors, the author intends to continue her work of supporting youths in developing countries in realizing their potential through her non-profit organization AegisLeague.org.

When not devouring a book or writing one, S.S.Segran can be found standing behind the cauldron of life, stirring a potion made up of chores, parkour, drawing, horseback riding, and—having enjoyed jumping out of a perfectly fine airplane at fifteen thousand feet—perhaps skydiving..

AEGIS LEAGUE

Bestselling Teen & Young Adult Apocalyptic Action-adventure Thrillers

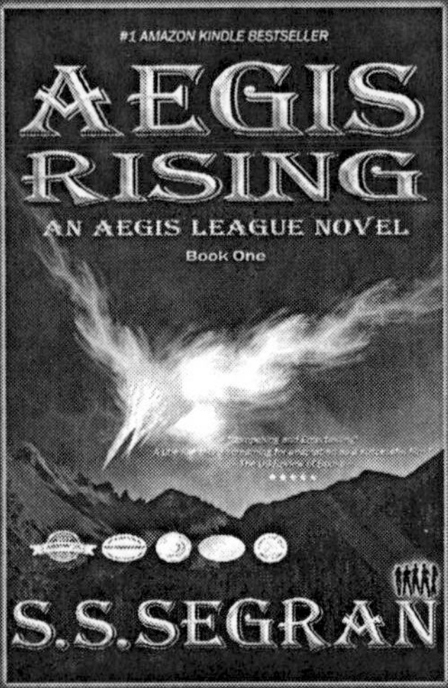

AVAILABLE NOW

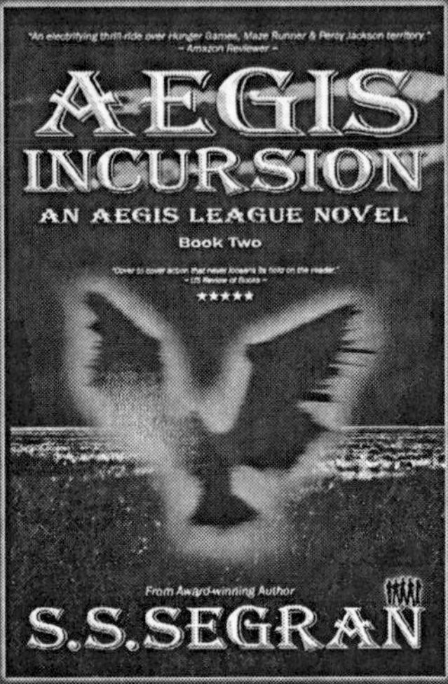

AVAILABLE NOW

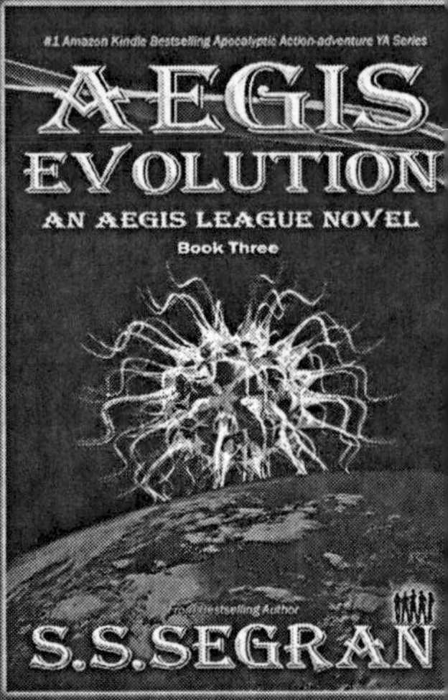

AVAILABLE SUMMER 2016

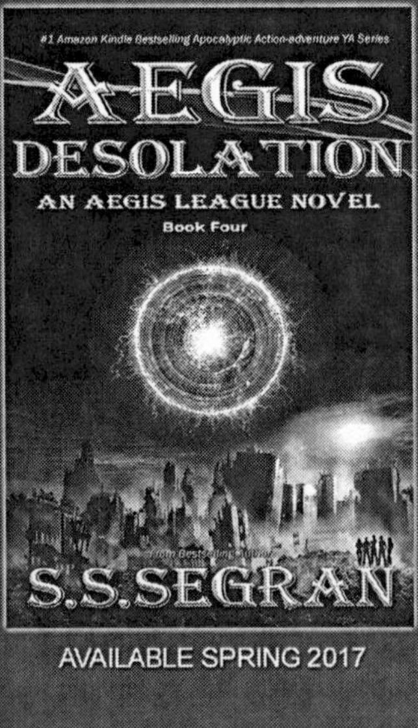

AVAILABLE SPRING 2017

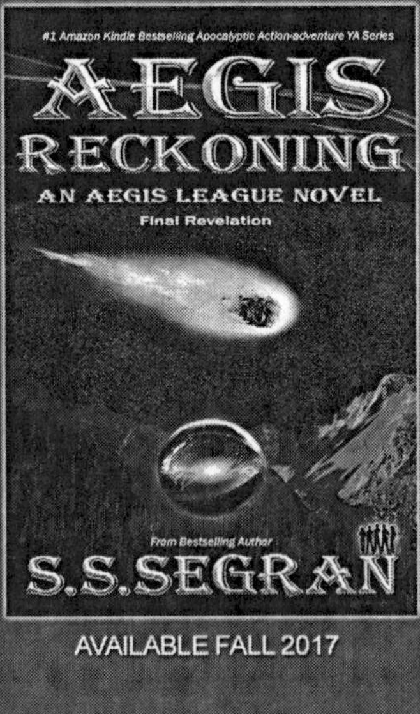

AVAILABLE FALL 2017

If you would like to be notified of new releases, please sign up for Aegis Insider updates at **WWW.AEGISNOVEL.COM**

"An electrifying thrill-ride over Hunger Games, Maze Runner and Percy Jackson territory." ~ Amazon Reviewer ~

"Astonishingly Imaginative and thoughtful..."
~ Samuel F. Pickering - Professor Emeritus of English, University of Connecticut and Inspiration for the film Dead Poets Socie

CPSIA information can be obtained at www.ICGtesting.com
Printed in the USA
LVOW10*1532260815

451112LV00003BA/11/P

9 780991 081301